BE NO MORE

BE NO MORE

G.K.TAYLOR

BE NO MORE

iUniverse books may be ordered through booksellers or by contacting:

iUniverse
1663 Liberty Drive
Bloomington, IN 47403
www.iuniverse.com
844-349-9409

ISBN: 978-1-6632-1645-8 (sc)
ISBN: 978-1-6632-1646-5 (e)

Print information available on the last page.

iUniverse rev. date: 01/29/2021

"Death is Nature's remedy for all things..."
Charles Dickens.....'A Tale of Two Cities

"Time is, time was, but time shall be no more..."
James Joyce...Portrait of an Artist as a Young Man

I would not have been able to write this, my first novel, without the loving support of my family.

Thank you

CHAPTER ONE

Click...Click...Click...Click...

This metronome dogged his heels as he pulled his suitcase from the baggage carousel over the tiled floor of Bonojara International. A clumsy handler, at one of the four airports involved in this last-minute flight, had rearranged a wheel to cause the clicks. He passed under the sign '*Bienvenido a / Welcome to REPUBLICA REAL*' to stand in line at Customs. After a short shuffling wait he slid his passport for inspection. A cursory glance compared his face to his photo before the passport was scanned. It was quickly returned as there was no security objection triggered by his name: Rushton Lewis Sterne. He now looked overhead to find, then to follow, the arrows to *'Parada de Taxis.'*

The Terminal had a roof but was otherwise open and the late afternoon's Caribbean heat and humidity came inside to meet him. Most of those on his flight from Miami, now commingled with a charter from Chicago, headed to *"Buses/Camions" which* would take them to the northwest, an hour's drive away, to the new resorts on the coast. His destination was to the northeast coast, to Porto del Norte, his next-to-last stop before reaching the Hospice on Isla Cresciente.

There were two cabs at the curb. The first had a decal *'AIR CONDI'* on the rear window and out the driver's window stuck a tattooed arm and a stream of cigarette smoke. Rush went to the window and asked, "Porto del Norte?" He received a nod and an almost silent "Si" as the driver turned on the ignition but simply sat there, obviously not offering to help, only flicking his cigarette butt out onto the sidewalk. Rush opened the rear door and slid his suitcase across the seat, then settled himself in behind the driver. He tried to find the seatbelt but only found one strap that would not extend fully across his waist; he would just have to trust the driver.

He sat back as the cab accelerated over the smooth pavement of the airport roadway illuminated by bright lights now needed as dusk closed in. There was still enough light for Rush to see the devastation that Hurricane Zena had done the week before. He had seen the newscasts videos as this season-late storm scythed across this section of the Caribbean and had wondered then if his friend's island had been affected. At the end of the airport road the cab turned right onto an older rougher road, with no lights overhead, as it sped off into the fast closing night that only gave glimpses of storm debris piled beside the road. They passed flickering lights and Rush heard dogs barking in reaction to their passing. He had his window wide open; if the cab had functioning air conditioning the driver was not bothering to use it. After about a half hour or more there were more lights and then Rush guessed that this was Porto del Norte as the taxi began to slow down. He leaned forward and instructed: "Casa Gaviota". There was no acknowledgement but after a few minutes the taxi braked to a quick stop outside a small hotel signed as Casa Gaviota. Again the driver offered no help so Rush pulled his suitcase out the door and asked the driver "Cuesta?" The response was a hand with four extended fingers. Rush only had dollars so he pulled out two twenties, handing it over to the driver who took it, then drove quickly away, leaving Rush to wonder how much he might have overpaid.

The cobblestone walk to the hotel might have defeated even the sturdiest set of luggage wheels so he had to pick up his bag and carry it into the lobby. It was small and dominated with a large desk with mail slots on the wall behind it. There was an archway just past the desk from which he could hear the sound of dishes and could smell the aroma of food, obviously the dining area. Then an elderly couple came from there into the lobby, a silver-haired woman helping a frail-looking man, grimly holding onto a wheeled walker. They both looked well into their eighties. The woman, with pale but still sparkling blue eyes, gave Rush a quick smile, then guided her partner past the desk towards the side hallway. Suddenly this tandem lurched forward, stumbling, with the walker getting ahead of them. Rush was close and quick enough to grab the bar of the walker and support the man's elbow to steady him. His wife, with a look of relief, gave him another smile and, in English, thanked him, "Oh, thank you. These tile floors are sometimes too much for us to handle."

"Can I help you? To your room?" offered Rush.

"No it's just down the hall. It's all quite level. I'll get Jimmy settled as he's very tired from our flights. It was such a long day for him."

"Good...then sleep well."

"Oh I don't have time to sleep right now. I'll be back for dessert and a nightcap." She turned away then back to face him again. "If you haven't had dinner yet I suggest the chicken, not the beef...it comes in those doughy shells...with rice, beans and some other things...whatever they call them down here." There was another smile, "Perhaps I'll see you later." Away they went, slowly navigating down the hall.

There was a flash of a face passing the entrance to the dining room uttering a "Momento Senor." Rush took out his passport and credit card in preparation for check-in. The face was now back, sliding behind the desk, with a professional welcoming smile, "Senor...Welcome to Casa Gaviota. I am Manuel, here at your service." His English was accented but practised. He glanced at Rush's passport and then his smile widened, "Si,Senor Sterne...you were expected...the special guest of Doctor Daveed." He returned the passport but didn't even look at the credit card. "Innecesario Senor...not needed." Then he raised his eyebrows "You need dinner?"

"Yes, but do I have time to shower first?"

"Si Senor." Then Manuel turned to pick out a key, "Numero Nuevo." He pointed to the stairs. "Come back for dinner, no hurry."

Rush's second floor room wasn't modern but it was clean and tidy enough. The dresser was large and would have sold well at any antique store back home. The bathroom had an old sink and toilet but it was clean and the bathtub had obviously been removed and replaced with a modern shower. The water was hot and helped rinse the travel from his body and as well as refresh his mind. He hung up the clothes that he had worn since early that morning and decided on short sleeves and summer khakis, presentable enough, he thought, for dinner at Casa Gaviota.

On entering the dining room Rush saw only a couple of occupants glance in his direction. A quick count showed two women at one table, six men equally sharing three more. The only buzz of conversation was from two of the men, facing each other, gesticulating with one hand, the other busy on their plates. The remaining occupants were silent so it was easy to hear, but not to understand, their rapid Spanish. Rush wondered if his entrance had quietened the others but they stayed silent even after he had taken a seat at the only remaining table. Suddenly Manuel bustled out of a side door. He appeared to be both the front desk clerk and the waiter; Rush wondered if he wasn't also the cook. After delivering dishes to two of the silent men, he turned towards Rush "Cerveza, senor?"

Rush nodded and a beaded bottle was soon in front of him along with a small blackboard with four dinner choices chalked on. There was a line drawn through the fish dinner so, when Manuel returned, he ordered the chicken quesadilla and then re-surveyed the room. The two Spanish speaking diners were as animated as ever, but were now sipping coffee. The rest stayed abnormally quiet as if each was totally preoccupied in their own thoughts. Rush now had his meal and a second beer placed in front of him. Just as he was finishing it the silver-haired lady came in and, with another quick smile, gave Manuel her order for dessert and a cup of tea, presumably her choice of a night cap. Then looking at Rush, she asked if she could join him. He was quickly out of his chair to assist her into the seat opposite.

"Thank you again for your help."

"I hardly helped. Is your husband fine?" asked Rush.

"Oh yes. Jimmy was so tired and I gave him a little extra pill that had him asleep within minutes. It's been such a long day. Two long flights but tomorrow's flight will be much shorter."

This made it probable that she and her husband had the same destination as did Rush. He wondered if it was her husband that needed the services of the Hospice. He didn't ask but simply extended his hand across the table. "I'm Rush, Rushton Sterne."

"I'm--we're the Sandersons--from Minnesota. I'm Irene, my husband is James but has been called Jimmy since he was young. It's so nice to meet you. What brings you to..." She tried but failed to remember its name, "... to here?" Just then Manuel was back with her order. He asked Rush if he wanted anything more. "Just coffee, por favor."

Rush was still unsure of the real reason why David had summoned him, asking for his help, so he simply answered her question as "Business." This seemed to satisfy Irene Sanderson as she quickly went on, "Tomorrow we will be going to see our son, Jimmy Junior. We haven't seen him in…

in...quite a long time." Then she was silent, her mind far off, as if looking back in time. Rush now assumed that their son was a patient at the Hospice on Isla Cresciente and tomorrow they would reunite with him, at least for a short while, depending on his condition. She now refocused on Rush, "Do you have children?"

"Er...no." It was the second time Rush had lied to that question today although, in reality, it was close to the truth. Irene didn't challenge the hesitation. "Well, now it's a choice but in our generation it wasn't. We didn't question what our purpose was, here on Earth, and in this life. We knew it was, if we could, to have children. Jimmy and I were married for years before we had our only son." Rush thought back to his own parents with a similar story. Irene sat back and then started to rise, "Well yes, it is time to go to bed. Will I see you in the morning?"

"I would hope so. Buenas noches Senora, sleep well."

She beamed back at him, "...and to you Senor Rush".

Manuel now returned with his coffee and cleared the table. It was strong and flavorful, much better than any he'd been served by the airlines. The room began to empty, first the men then one of the women, the one who had sat facing him. She had a morose face that, every time he had noticed her, had never lightened. She left solemnly, as if in a funeral procession. This only left Rush and the woman whose back had been to him. She arose, fished in her purse, and left money on the table. She glanced at him with what might have been a slight nod but, if it was, he had no chance to respond before she was past him, into the hall. He finished his coffee thinking that whoever she was, she certainly was attractive. However, he doubted whether he might ever see her again so it would be simply a case of ships passing in the night. This was, for Rush, often the case. He had become accustomed to it.

Irene heard Jimmy's snores as soon as she entered the room. She had slept with him for sixty-one years and another night wouldn't be a problem for her. He looked so peaceful, as peaceful as she felt since their decision had been made. It was the right decision, guaranteeing them that neither would ever live alone and, with no doubt in her mind or in her faith, they would soon be reunited with Jimmy Jr.

As she slipped on her nightgown she wondered about the others at dinner and particularly that nice young man. Rush, that was his name, who she had just met. He'd only said he was here on business. She doubted that he had the same destination as she and Jimmy had. He was young and looked in good physical health, although you could never know, could you, about anyone's mind or body.

CHAPTER TWO

The shutters were folded back, the window half open, allowing the morning sun to fill his room along with the fragrance of the garden outside. Although Rush didn't really need another shower he took a quick one, not knowing what the facilities might be on the island. As he dressed he wondered again what the problem was on Isla Creciente and what he could do to help David to solve it.

It was less than two days ago that he received this phone message from his friend: "David here...our phone doesn't work too well and I'm hoping this message is clear enough at your end...look...I...we...would like your help if you are able to get down here...right quick...for a few days...maybe a week at the most...I will understand if your job won't allow it...it may be best that you email me...that's the safest way of communication...try me at drdavid@caribtalk.com...let me know if you are free to come...I'll give you more details...I think you can help and at least it'll be a week of sunshine... at no cost to you...let me know ASAP. . .all the best ."

Getting free for a week was no problem for Rush as he was still under paid suspension, a fact that had grated, angered and frustrated him for the last ten days. Seeing David again and possibly assisting his friend, a friendship that went back over twenty years, would be a welcome distraction. He considered whether he needed to let his Superintendent know of his absence but thought not, they had put no strings on their decision, only that he was off duty until further notice. He did need to let Lou know so he picked up the phone.

"Hi Maria. . .is Lou there?" Lou's wife thought he was down in his workshop and went to call him upstairs.

"Hey Rush...what's up?"

Rush didn't give Lou much in the way of detail only that he had an opportunity for a week's free vacation in the Caribbean. He said that he would try to stay in touch by email in case there were any further developments in finding Birdie. It was her accusation, before she disappeared, that was the reason he'd been suspended. He asked Lou to take care of the Department and said he hoped to be back behind his desk as soon as this mess was cleared up.

Lou hesitated a moment, "Er…Rush…I should tell you that we will have a new addition to the squad tomorrow." He waited for Rush to comment but the other end of the line was quiet so Lou continued, "I think it's HQ moving to that gender equity thing...you know…what the papers are going on about."

"So it'll be a PW?"

"Yeah...coming over from Juvenile Crime...apparently an up and comer. Don't worry though we've moved in a new desk. She won't take over your desk. It's still here waiting for you."

After hanging up Rush wondered if this meant his suspension would be a long one and that he might not be returning to his desk. Perhaps it was best that he get away and not stay here to worry about his future with the Force.

He then replied to David by email::

> *David: Sure I can make it ...give me some details as to exactly where you are. I only have a vague idea of your location at some hospice on an island in the Caribbean. What's the best way of getting there? You can also give me a few more details as to why you think I might be able to help…...Rush*

There was a reply within the hour.

> *Rush: I'm on Isla Cresiente about thirty miles off the north coast. Best you get a flight to Miami then over to Bonojara International here on Real Republica. Then take a cab to the town of Porto del Norte. There is a hotel there, Casa Gaviota, and I'll book you in there once I know when you'll arrive. There are two arranged flights a week to the island. Try to be down here for ten a.m. on Tuesday. Let me know…David*

Rush clicked on his laptop checking for the fastest way of getting down to Real Republica. He quickly booked a route firstly to LaGuardia, then to Miami and then over to Bonojara. It would leave at 6:30 tomorrow morning. He then realized that he had not said anything to his father. He was quickly up the stairs to the main level where his father, a widower of four years, seemed content to live alone, although with his bachelor son only down a flight of stairs in his lower level compact apartment. His father was reading the evening paper with a coffee mug gripped in one hand. He certainly had no problem with Rush going away for a few days. He had always dismissed his son's concern for his welfare as unnecessary. He was glad that they had heard from David as over the last few years, since David's return from Africa, there had been limited contact. Russell said he'd be fine and there would be no problem in that he was self-sufficient, which Rush knew was clearly the truth.

Packing was quick but finding his passport took longer. He thought about when he had last needed it. He checked his carry-on bag to find it in the side pocket. So he set his alarm for four-thirty in the morning. He would drive to long term airport parking, bus to the terminal, then onto this island, for whatever was there and whatever he was needed for.

The next morning had security lines shuffling slowly with a mixture of young families, couples, singles, mostly male, presumably on business. He ended up sitting beside a young couple, excited to be reviewing what they would do in New York City, obviously a first time for both. He was tempted to interrupt to give his advice as to what was not to be missed but stopped short. It had been a few years since he'd been to New York for only the second time. Twenty-two years before that was the trip that he and David took together, when he had met David's mother. Rush felt this couple would no doubt find their own way and create their own memories.

On landing at LaGuardia he had more sitting before shuffling through security and then another wait before boarding his Miami flight. He slid into the window seat until a troubled looking young woman, with a boy about five or six plus a baby in her arms, settled into the two seats beside him. The boy was excited, asking his mother a list of questions: "Are we going to fly over Disney World? Can we see it? Are Grandma and Grandpa going to meet us at the airport? When is Daddy coming?" His mother answered the first questions calmly but was evasive on the last. Rush glanced over to see her tear up, take a deep sigh and look away towards the aisle.

The boy now had earphones on and became totally engrossed with the cartoons on the seat back screen ahead of him. His younger sibling was quiet and content to keep snuggled against mother. Soon they were airborne and Rush tried to concentrate on the *Economist* magazine he'd bought at LaGuardia but his mind jumped back and forth from the known mess he'd left behind to whatever lay ahead. They were somewhere over the coast of the Carolinas when the boy took off his earphones and, with an anxious face, said "Mommy I need to go." She unbuckled herself, straightened up and looked around for a flight attendant's assistance. They were busy with drinks and snacks down the aisle. Rush could see that she was trying to figure out the dynamics of getting all three of them into a small washroom without waking her sleeping child. Rush quickly offered, "Here I'll hold your child--a girl ?" He had guessed correctly. "She's Suzanne" the mother said but with a look of apprehension on her face as she considered whether she should leave her child with a stranger. She then realized the comparative safety of leaving Suzanne with this pleasant man in the window seat. She muttered thanks, handed over her bundle to Rush, unbuckled her son and was off down the aisle. Rush took the baby into his arms with his mind going back years ago when he had held his son and looking at her sleeping face he guessed she'd be about the same age as when he had last held Stefan.

When they came back the boy quickly settled into the middle seat, put on his headphones and was back engrossed in cartoons again. The mother stretched to pick up her child but Rush, enjoying the feel of the child said, "I'm OK. She's OK." He'd seen the tired look on her face, "Why don't you have a little rest?" She smiled with appreciation and then settled her head back and closed her eyes.

Rush wasn't sure if she actually slept but about twenty minutes later she opened her eyes and reached over her son to retrieve her daughter murmuring her appreciation for his help and adding, "You look as if you've done this before." He shook his head, avoiding a spoken lie, avoiding any further reminders of when he had last held his son. "Well thank you, you're very kind and I certainly needed a little rest." As her eyes left his face he still saw, as she lowered her head, tears forming. "I'm sorry, I'm a bit emotional right now," she explained. Again Rush could only nod. The closeness of seats in the row, added to the unspoken fear of flying, tended to bond strangers into momentary friends, even becoming confidants. She continued, "We're going to my parents, they live just outside Miami. My husband…their father won't be joining us as....as he's probably being laid right now."

It was hard to tell if her words were born from bitterness or hurt. Rush thought from both, offering at first a sympathetic encouraging look, as his mind cynically scored another victim of matrimonial misery. Thinking he should at least say something, however lame, he offered, "Well you've taken the first step. Keep going." She smiled, hugged her child and remained silent for the rest of the trip.

Rush tried to return to the article he'd been reading but he kept on thinking ahead to David and his request for help. He then thought back over the years of their friendship as to whether David had ever asked him for help before. His friend was largely self-sufficient even when they first met at the University Residence. Rush had been told he would be sharing a room with a Robert Prentice, also in his first year, in room 213, however a sudden appendectomy operation had delayed his entry to University by four days. On arrival Rush was advised that he had been re-assigned to room 222 with a pre-med student: David A.M. Newton. He had lugged his two heavy cases up the stairs and knocked. There was a muffled "Come in."

A very tanned David Newton was stretched out, nearly meeting both ends of his bed. He was on his back, one hand propping up his head, and he continued to read as Rush advanced slowly to the middle of the room. Finally the book was lowered and the head and eyes focused on Rush, "You are?"

"Well I've been assigned here, to this room…" David waved off any further explanation. "Good. Unpack. I have to finish this, then we'll talk."

Rush took the empty dresser, sorted out his clothes, found some room in the already crowded closet rack to hang up his one suit, two sports coats and three pairs of pants. Underneath he squeezed in his luggage, initialled 'R.L.S', beside one stamped 'D.A.M.N.' All the while the lanky man on the bed continued to read. Finally Rush moved over to the other bed and waited until the book was thrown aside.

"Hello... I'm David. Tell me about yourself."

Rush not entirely sure if this was an interview and whether he would be accepted as a roommate but slowly gave his name then quietly explained where he was from and what was ahead of him.

"Law. You want law... why?" asked David. Not waiting for an answer he continued, "All right I'm not entirely sure why I want to to be a physician... so let's just leave it at that."

Rush, with a step up in confidence, chose to ask why he had been reassigned to this room, to spend this year with David.

"Yes. A good point. I'm in Pre-Meds and, whatever his name was, my ex-roomie, he was in his third year of Far Eastern studies. I have no objections to that field but, just think of it, wouldn't it be better to go to the Far East to study?" He paused, "Furthermore it became clear, from the onset, that we were not compatible..." He stopped, carefully searching for the right words, "...you see we had...a dispute over values." Rush left the comment without asking for clarification but a moment later David provided just that, "You see he had so many values and I have so few."

So began their friendship. Alike in some ways, very dissimilar in others, particularly in their extremes. Within the month Rush saw the immense range of David's character, capabilities as well as his weaknesses. He was bright, more than bright, having an easy path to absorbing, evaluating, relating and remembering his course materials but also demonstrated a keen interest and knowledge in other matters, such as politics and music, classical and contemporary. As well he was athletic. A strong tennis player having learned this from an early age on year-round courts in his native Trinidad and then polished at a boarding school in England. He was also very good around women. They were quickly in love with this tall, very handsome, man and he took full advantage in the few weeks of each new relationship. It turned out that the disparity of values with the first roommate had to do with his high regard for morals, purity, and virginity. David didn't share these. Rush wasn't a prude but within that first month, when Rush came back from lectures, it was to find David enmeshed on his bed with clearly female flesh. Rush backed out muttering apologies. Later he and David settled on a simple plan. David pulled, from the flap of his luggage, a '*Please Do Not Disturb*' sign from the Clivebourne Hotel, London. This would, on the exterior door knob, signal that the room was in private usage.

David's romances had, perhaps from the start, only a half-life for him but this timing was not necessarily shared by the lady in question. One morning he advised, really warned Rush, that he was trying to, as gently as possible, extricate himself from the lovely Leanna.

"Leanna?"

"Yes,...you remember, last week when you interrupted us." Rush had never seen her face, only the pulsations of her naked hips.

"Well…she's being persistent…not yet getting the message...so...if she calls...or comes around…tell her I'm out...away somewhere...invent something."

The next day she did come around, banging hard on their door, "David...open the door...I need to see you…we need to talk!" Rush was alone, deep into the French Revolution. In reaction to her sudden rapping he had scraped his chair, clearly audible in the hallway. He couldn't hide this, so he opened the door to Leanna who was stretching to see beyond him and asking, "Where's David...where is he?"

She stormed into the room, eyes searching, as if David was hidden somewhere. Satisfied he wasn't, she issued a firm, "I'll wait". They sat there, in silence, on the two separate beds until she spoke, slowly at first, then with increased volume and velocity, the words poured out vilifying David, his treatment of her, and on and on until she stopped, her anger expended. Then came the tears and racking sobs. Not sure what else to do, Rush grabbed a handful of tissues and went to sit beside her. She buried her face into his shoulder. He felt her tears on his neck, then her lips, as her arms were now around him, pulling him down onto the bed. The sobs continued as she pulled at his track pants, pulled up her skirt, and before Rush could even comprehend it, she was on top of him, on her path to either solace or revenge. Rush's masculine response was immediate but not lasting. Leanna suddenly disengaged, staring at him as if she'd never seen him before. Then she was up, re-arranging her clothes, wiping her face on her sleeve and, just before she slammed the door, turned to him, "Tell David to screw himself! You too. You're…pathetic !"

Feeling like a used dish rag, Rush could only conclude he still had no idea as to the workings of a woman. This was reinforced later in his first year when, on a first date and after a few beers, he managed to entice another freshman to his room, carefully slipping the card on the outer doorknob. She was as inexperienced as he was and they fumbled their way each to a confusing climax, followed by mutual embarrassment. She left hurriedly and, whenever he'd see her later on campus, she always looked away.

His reminiscences were interrupted by the lurch of the plane as the wheels were lowered and they began their descent, soon to land in Miami. He remained in his seat as the now single mother, towing one child and toting the other, filed down the aisle heading towards the comfort of her parents.

His seat companion on the last leg to Real Republica ignored Rush throughout the flight, only speaking to the attendant to order one, two, three then a fourth vodka. He fell asleep before they landed and was still snoring when Rush exited, down the steps, out onto the tarmac of Bonojara International, now only a half day from David's island.

CHAPTER THREE

Rush wasn't the first to breakfast but automatically took the same table as he had the night before. He looked to see a few others, also in their same positions. There were three tables still empty but then the Spanish-speaking twosome, with briefcases in hand, sat to resume their animated conversation. Manuel was now in the room pouring, without asking, coffee into their cups then over to Rush, filling his. Then the first woman from the evening before, the serious-looking one, quietly slipped into her chair but it was only a few more minutes later that the younger, clearly her more attractive table-mate from dinner, smilingly arrived to take the chair opposite. The other woman looked up, giving only a faint response. The Sandersons were missing and Rush hoped that they, particularly Jimmy, were well. Just then Jimmy, now more confidently in charge of his walker, entered with Irene, her eyes scanning the room, positioned carefully at his side. She smiled at every table with a special one for Rush.

Manuel was very busy with breakfast. There was no menu, all received the same egg, pepper, onion and doughy mixture, with fresh juice and much more coffee. The room was now back to the same seating plan as the night before, all quiet except the two businessmen and Irene Sanderson. Rush saw another male twosome, sharing the same table as at dinner, but remaining just as silent, seemingly wrapped up in their own worlds, devoid of any need, or want, for communication. At another table were another two men, also quiet, but one man seemed involved, with his face towards the half open window, peering out, interested in something in the garden.

Winston Cushing was trying to identify the flash of colour of a flitting bird just outside the dining room. It looked like a small parrot. He thought Ginnie would have probably known its name, she was good at that, either back in Vermont or here in the Caribbean. They had, avoiding Florida and many of their friends there, two week holidays on the various islands of the Caribbean for many winters. Last night while attempting to sleep he counted the islands that they'd enjoyed, he reached fourteen. They liked going to different places testing the different foods, scenery, meeting new, if temporary, friends. Their last trip was just over a year ago. Ginnie was already weak, although the last series of treatments had helped a little. The two weeks in Grenada raised his hopes that the chemotherapy was really working and not a wasted effort. Four months later she was gone. At first in a dull daze, he'd managed but each passing week only served to intensify his loss, his inner pain. Dr. Smithson had given him a prescription for relief but he did not feel any improvement. Friends were trying to help but their attention to him had lessened over the months, which suited him and his isolation. His sons were both miles away, both out on the West coast. They called regularly but the conversations became forced and stilted, each side trying to stretch out the minutes of conversation.

The rains of autumn enforced his despair and his inability to accept and adapt to the loss of Ginnie. Each sunrise brought the same day of darkness. He began to think of the ultimate relief, becoming more and more convinced it was a better alternative to living his current life. It was merely an existence; a poor substitute for life. Death had been playing a game with him and he was merely a pawn. First it had been his two brothers. They and two close friends, who had also stood beside him at the altar as he waited for his bride, Virginia Chester, to be escorted down the aisle towards him, now all were gone. Death had erased them from the Wedding Portrait. Death seemed intent to strip him too, though with slow torture. He decided to fight back, not ever to win, but to succumb on his own terms.

Beginning to consider methods, he first looked at the beams overhead in his garage. However, he had never liked to leave a mess and, whatever method he chose, quick or slow, would involve someone finding him, probably decaying, and then his sons would be faced with the details of the funeral, burial, and all the paperwork over his death, even though he wasn't leaving that much of an estate. He had researched, with increasing interest, accounts of others seeking alternative ways to end their suffering. Most travelled to European countries where laws and practices were in place. Then he heard of a facility offering a seemingly painless solution but not one entangled with any medical pre-conditions, only requiring competent consent. The cost was fairly high but he noticed, with his New England sense of practicality, it was all inclusive, including the cremation.

He compared this cost with the cost of a natural death and felt it worked out to about equal and was certainly faster.

He found a new purpose and he was able to shift from his melancholy as he planned all the details and confirmed the legalities necessary for this pre-planned exit. He had to arrange selling his small home without any local realtor being aware of it. He had also involved an out-of-town lawyer to ensure that everything was in order once he left Vermont. When everything was in place, he contacted the doctor on this island and satisfied their checklist of requirements, and then arranged for the money to be sent to an account in the Cayman Islands.

Writing a letter to later be sent to his sons, explaining his choice took a few rewrites. Although he anticipated their immediate 'Whys' he could foresee that they would both come to recognize the sensibility of his decision. He knew his younger son could certainly use half of the inheritance as it would help with paying off his too-high mortgage, necessitated by his wife's status-seeking demands. When he had finished he sat back and smiled for the first time in months over all the arrangements he'd made. He now had to sort out clothing for either the garbage or for charities. He would only need a small suitcase to reach that Island. Now here he was, sitting peacefully, with a sense of accomplishment, having dotted all the i's and crossed all the t's that he could foresee, looking out onto the garden, watching the birds.

Rush had returned to his room, repacked and, again with no change or local currency, left another twenty dollar bill on the large dresser. At the front desk, Manuel confirmed there were no charges for his stay, all having been taken care of by 'Doctor Daveed'. Rush pulled out another twenty for Manuel, receiving an enthusiastic "Gracias". He asked if there'd be any help, particularly for the Sandersons, in getting them and their luggage down to the dock. Manuel confirmed that this was taken care of. A taxi, a larger van, was bringing a patient from the airport directly to the dock then would come back to the Inn to pick up the Sandersons and anyone else who needed assistance down the streets to the jetty. Rush extended his hand over the desk to shake hands and thank Manuel for all of his attention. He picked up his suitcase and was out the door and then was onto the cobblestones. He could see that the streets were clear but there were trees that had been decapitated by the Hurricane and piles of branches and fronds still to be picked up. The winding street had an incline. He could smell a salty tang so he could sense the sea before he saw it, the shoreline, the docks and the moored boats. No pleasure craft here, all working boats. The sun, even this early, was strong. He wore sunglasses but had left his hat packed in his case. Even though he had a short sleeve shirt on, he still had a mild sweat as he came down to the portside. Then he saw the plane, already moored at the longest jetty. Immediately he identified it as a Twin Otter. He suddenly was flooded by the memory of putting, with the overuse of glue, this model together. It had been a Christmas gift that occupied him for weeks when he was only ten or eleven. He wondered how old this particular plane was, nearly forty years he guessed, as he wasn't aware they ever resumed assembling them. He also, at first, wondered why such a large seaplane was necessary for such a short hop to the island. The double doors of the plane were open and two husky youths, presumably local, were loading supplies up the ramp on board. A man, in a not overly clean white shirt, wearing a crumpled captain's hat, was checking off items on the sheets of his clipboard.

Rush now looked behind him to see the progression of other guests from Casa Gaviota. Pulling or toting their cases down the street to the dock, were four men and the two women. Then a van, a taxi sign on its roof, pulled up beside the dock, the side doors slid open, a ramp was put down and carefully a wheelchair with an inert man securely strapped ramped down to the road A very tired looking woman slid out the doors to stand with him, a handkerchief mopping his forehead. The wheelchair was battery operated and the man's fingers must be managing the controls as it bumped its way onto the dock, towards the plane. Rush now appreciated the need for the Twin Otter's size, given the supplies needed, wheelchairs and, he presumed, the occasional bed carrying a patient to the Hospice. The taxi van left but within minutes it was back, delivering the Sandersons and their luggage. Rush went to the cab helping Jimmy out his door and steadying his hands onto his walker. Irene was soon to Jimmy's side ushering him down towards the plane. Rush picked up their suitcases and followed.

Cartons and crates seemed to be now inside the plane so the presumed pilot then flipped over a sheet on his clipboard, turned to the assembled passengers, gave a brief hello, confirming he was their pilot then asked each for identification. He began to read out names. Rush, with his usual practice, tried filing their names into his memory. The wheelchaired man was Lyman Aldredge, his wife Lisa. As the four other men answered to their names Rush realized these were the first words he heard from their mouths. He didn't catch the surname of a Lorraine but the attractive younger woman was a Marielle Lebow, a French name, a French bearing, that self-assurance, that class that he remembered from his few days in Paris, now ten years back, following David's marriage in England. Whether she was eighteen or eighty, all Parisiennes had captivated Rush then and that feeling still lingered on today.

After the pilot double checked his list of names with their passports, he began to direct them up the ramp into the plane. He sent the two women, Marielle and Lorraine in first, to sit behind the cockpit. Afterwards came all the men, then the Sandersons, with assistance up the ramp supplied by one of the young muscular local men. Finally, again with the same assistance, the wheelchair was navigated up the ramp bringing the Aldredges on board. Just before the ramp was pulled away there was shouting from the dock, in Spanish. A swarthy middle-aged man, puffing, almost gasping for air, was now inside the cabin rapidly explaining, in more Spanish, to the pilot his need to be on his way to the island. Whatever was said seemed to satisfy the pilot so he directed this man to the empty seat beside Rush. The man then deposited, almost on Rush's foot, a large canvas tool bag that clunked as it hit the floor.The pilot, satisfied the Aldredge's wheelchair was secured to the floor clasps, locked the doubled doors, striding forward, checking that the seatbelts were in use, then to his seat in front of the controls.

The starboard engine then coughed to life and gained rpms, along with a roar and fumes that quickly invaded the cabin, startling some of the passengers. Rush had never flown in a Twin Otter but he had flown before in float planes and knew what to expect as he waited for the port engine to start up, adding more noise and fumes. He then felt the pontoons start to plow ahead, the waves slapping back in a brief battle, and after much more noise, the float plane struggled airborne. Now it battled gravity but slowly, ponderously, won out to rise into the blue sky.

Lisa Aldredge had almost bitten through her lower lip as they cleared the waters of the bay and lumbered skyward. All this had ignited her fear of flying. Latent fear, now roiled with the seesaw emotions that had ruled the last three years of her life, was intensified by this trip to this strange island. It was clearly Lyman's decision, one she could fully understand, given his prognosis, one they knew all about except the timing. Lyman would now dictate that timing and Lisa, with admiration for his courage and respect for his choice, was also saddled with the guilt for thinking about the relief that his death would give her. Three years ago she had spent weeks stalling, waiting for a good time when she could sit down, then summon the courage to tell him that their marriage was over for her. She would tell a half-truth, that she only needed out, needed space, couldn't deal with his increasingly confrontational attitude. At the same time Lyman was having those problems at the office and some embarrassing lapses in his work. He'd been forgetting things, important matters. His partners were not happy. He was losing squash games to those he normally handled easily. Finally he saw doctors, began the tests. It took only two months for the final diagnosis to be made. There was no way that Lisa could leave him now, now that he needed, if not love, her care. Todd hopefully would wait. Lisa had explained to Todd, in their secretive escapes together, that she couldn't leave Lyman at this crucial stage of his life. Lyman had scanned all the latest research to begin special therapies, searching for keys to reverse the creeping shrinkage of his muscles and functions. She had to give him support, not to pull the rug from under him. She owed him that much from her marriage vows and she made that decision, risking losing Todd, to stay beside Lyman, more of a caregiver than a wife. She would fulfill that vow of twenty years ago: 'til death do us part'.

Over time, Lyman accepted the reality of his disease, and he turned his research to assisted-death, looking first to Europe, but then heard of Isla Cresciente. He quickly made all the necessary arrangements, advising Lisa, with his failing voice, but never asking for her opinion. She wondered if Lyman's decision was only based on relieving their mutual suffering or was he granting her a faster future with Todd. She'd never know.

CHAPTER FOUR

It seemed only minutes between the pilot finding a level altitude before the engines eased and the plane began a slow banking swing downward. Rush could now see the island, well named, looking like a croissant, thin at the points, thicker in the middle. The pilot adeptly smoothed out of the turn descending lower towards the bay of the island. Rush had a glimpse of a building in the middle of the island, facing the bay, solar panels and wind turbines facing south, back to Real Republica. Then the pontoons began to clip the waves, then catching, to splash heavily into the water. The engines were cut back as the plane settled into the aquamarine surface of the bay. A permanent dock extended from the beach and soon the Twin Otter was secured to it. The doors were opened, the ramp put in place, and then a tall bronzed figure was up the ramp into the plane unfastening the wheelchair from the flooring and then wheeling Lyman Aldredge onto the pier. Rush only caught a flash of acknowledgement from David as he did this. Rush remained in his seat until everyone else had disembarked. As he then came down the ramp he saw the procession was already heading down the pier led by a golf cart putt-putting with the Sandersons onboard. He could see David and a white clad female accompanying the Aldredges as the wheelchair motored to the end of the jetty. A young muscular man was loading luggage onto a handcart. Rush picked up his own luggage and soon caught up to the rear of the group. The path was now sloping upward towards, then beside, the fortress-like wall that was the base on which the Hospice was placed.

Once to the top he saw this main building, the Hospice, was surprisingly small, especially since it was placed in the middle of a large rectangle cemented surface topping the solid concrete base. The area in front of the Hospice was tiled but the remainder, around the sides, was the flaking upper deck of the structure. Rush saw two iguanas at the far edge, seemingly surveying the newcomers. He pushed Jimmy, now off the golf cart and sitting in a wheelchair, to the open windowed doors, a wide entry to the building. There the lady in white, presumably a nurse, was in efficient charge and, with a European accent, was welcoming the group. The Sandersons and Aldredges formed one side, then the group of four men in the middle, with Marielle and Lorraine on the other flank. The nurse had a clipboard and after calling out names was giving, in response to each, a room number. Rush stood back looking for David as the group slowly moved further inside, to a large interior room, then were directed through open double doors down a hallway. Rush had moved forward, intending to push Jimmy's wheelchair, but the nurse took the handles so Rush could only stand back to watch the group disappear down the hallway.

Rush went back outside, to the edge of the parapet, and looked over a railing between him and the pathway. He saw the beach edging an atoll-like bay. He now saw David escorting the dark skinned man, the late arrival on the plane, toting his bag, heading away to the left, toward a small plain looking bungalow. Beyond this, at the water's edge, was a smaller building and beyond that, almost at the far western tip of the island, was another small square building with a large smokestack, leaning at an unhealthy angle. At first Rush thought it was his own eyesight but then realized that this stack, as well as the building, was slightly swaying as if not fixed on land but tied to the shore line, floating gently on the waves. To his right, to the east, the inviting beach stretching out, sheltered by the far arm of the island. Near the dock he saw a small table, with a few chairs, a private alcove set back, as if this was a resort. On the crest of the island the windmills were furious in capturing power and, flanking them, glistening in the sunshine, the solar-panels were quietly doing the same.

Now looking back to view the Hospice, Rush again was surprised at its size. There couldn't be that many rooms as he counted the windows facing out to the bay. It then dawned on him that it didn't look as he had expected, not at all like an active medical facility. It seemed to be designed as a large one-storey villa, a holiday retreat, not a hospice.

Marielle Lebow had started her day immediately awake, her mind reviewing her plans, her options, wondering if she could expect cooperation or would there be barriers placed in her way. The assignment she was handling needed confirmation whether a Death Certificate was legitimate, strong enough to be accepted in a Court of Law. All that centered on the ethics and competence of the physician who signed his name on the document, Dr. David A.M.Newton. She had researched both this island and Newton. There was more background on the doctor than the island as he seemed to have been a successful surgeon after post-graduate studies in England. He was in his early thirties when he joined, as a senior surgeon, St.Jerome's Hospital in London. There was then a marriage, no indication of children, and then his leave to join Medecins Sans Frontieres in the Horn of Africa. That lasted a few years, then there was an appointment to Real Republica's main hospital, located in the capital, Santo Vincenza. Her search on this island emphasized that it was a hospice, only adding a notation that late stage assisted-dying, along with crematorium facilities, were available. She guessed that its specialization may be known better by word of mouth, physician to physician, than by any overt advertising.

When she had arrived at Casa Gaviota in the late afternoon of the day before, Manuel the waiter-clerk had placed her at dinner with a very morose middle aged woman. All Marielle received from her was her first name: Lorraine. It was not until the next morning that the pilot's list had given her surname: Flanders. Since conversation with her, both at dinner and at breakfast this morning, seemed futile, Marielle had, without being too obvious, reviewed the others, trying to assess who'd be on the flight with her to the island. She'd ruled out the Spanish speaking twosome but, in addition to Lorraine and the elderly couple, that left five men. The two men near the window spoke in English, although briefly. The other two men, seated together had never appeared to make eye contact and totally ignored each other, as if under some type of silent protest. Then there was the man, about forty she'd guess, who came in for dinner alone but was joined later by the white haired lady. She noted his eyes had searched the room, like she had, analyzing everyone else. Their scans, a couple of times, caught each other's gaze, without lingering to see who would avert their eyes first. She disqualified him from her initial list of who'd be on the flight with her to Isla Creciente.

She was on this flight under false pretences, and at considerable cost to her employer, Antioch Life Insurance North America. She anticipated her true motives would be uncovered soon after her arrival. She would not be joining the others for a self-chosen fate. Marielle intended to return home, fully intact, not in an urn. On the jetty, waiting to be checked off the pilot's list, she had been surprised to see the single man there, answering to the name of what she heard as 'Storn'. His reason for being there was unknown, not as obvious as the man strapped to his wheelchair accompanied by his grim faced wife.

Lorraine Flanders finally looked up and around the room she'd been assigned to. It was full of mid-day sunshine and for the first time in days enjoyed what she saw. This would suit her fine for the day or two before she would take the final step, the one that would suppress her memories of Stephanie, the rejection then the void, the bottomless gloom that had been left to rule her life.

Rick Fornacchia thought back in segments, the events of yesterday and this morning on his arrival to the island. He didn't worry about the missing pieces. He had come, after years of increasing frustration, to adapt to these lapses. The doctors had been helpful explaining the transition process, not clearly, but enough to understand the progression of his deterioration. As much as his short-term memory left him, he still remembered, clear enough, the smell of the locker room, being fitted into his uniform. Then out on the field, the hours of training, the coaching, the chalkboard diagrams of the plays, and then on weekends, first at High School, then College, finally in the Pros, getting out on the field to all the cheering from the stands, the yelling from the bench, and then into the crunching contact on the field. His name was on the back of his uniform for all in the stadium and thousands more on television to see. His mind might wander and leave lapses on most of his day-to-day necessities but his mind was clear about this decision. The diagnosis they had given him made him confront the inevitable. He was fixed on taking the next step to bypass any further progressive stages of dementia. He'd always been proud of his body, his strength, his stamina and while he had some semblance of these traits left, he would use them. Rick never had slid off his opponents blocks if he could meet them head on, helmet to helmet, so when he'd made his decision, then was accepted by the doctor down here, he sorted out his affairs. With only one sister left as family it wasn't difficult. She was out in Montana, living with a cowboy type; they only exchanged Christmas cards. His only thoughts of his two ex-wives were their great bodies and their divorce lawyers. His one regret was that, with cremation, he wouldn't be able to donate his brain for research to add to the statistics on football injuries. In preparation for Isla Cresciente he'd flown to Miami, taking an expensive room overlooking the beach. He spent his money on good food, good bourbon, and for two nights hired two girls to satisfy his body. His mind might be going but his groin was still functional.

Rush had wandered back inside, to the main room with tables set to one side, nearest the doors to the corridor, and on the other half of the room, an array of leather covered chairs and lounges, with two coffee tables and, in the corner, a television set. He took one of the chairs and waited. Fifteen minutes later the doors opened and David came in. As Rush rose to meet him David was already there, hand extended to grab and pull his friend up into a welcoming hug. "Damn glad you're here. Have a good trip? Did Manuel take good care of you?" Rush nodded as now David's arm was around his shoulder walking him to the wide window overlooking the bay. "Great looking place, isn't it? Let's get you settled in first. You'll have to bunk with me for one night, then you can have a room of your own." He was then off towards, then opening, the doors to the corridor still talking as they started down the hallway. "Sorry things are still a bit of a mess after the storm but it's getting sorted out, slower than I'd like." Rush noted all but one of the doors were closed but one, where he glimpsed the woman with the French name, with her head turned, looking out her window. At the end of the hall David turned to the left, down a hall only about ten feet in length, to open a door. "Here we are. You can take the bed. I'll take the pull-out. It's only for a night."

Rush scanned the compact quarters. At the far end was a bed and a set of drawers that were separated by a partition from the sparse living room with only a coffee machine, a toaster on a shelf, a small refrigerator, a full bookcase and two chairs bracketing a couch. A large window showed the south edge of the island, rocky with no discernable beach. David opened the refrigerator reaching in, "Sorry there's no beer, we don't allow alcohol on the island--unfortunately." He offered a can to Rush, clicking open his own, "It's only soda...but cold. Here's to you for coming...short notice and all." He took short gulps as he spoke, "We really need your help, your expertise. You're the expert in missing persons up north. We have another for you, right down here."

He set his drink down on the counter then turned towards the door, "Sorry, we'll sit down later after supper and I'll load you with my...with our problem. Hope you don't mind operating out of your suitcase for one night. We will have a spare room tomorrow. It's occupied right now. If you're hungry there'll be snacks out in the dining room but dinner will be at six. Now I've got to check on some more problems, storm problems, see clients, but I'll be back soon. I'm sure you have some questions."

Rush sipped the too sweet soda and, sitting down, now alone, wondered once again why he was here. What could his 'expertise' offer? Another 'missing person'? Here on an island this small? And what about this island? A hospice? Where were the needed nurses and doctors? He'd only seen one of each. Why was the building so small? Why was there no hospital equipment to be seen? The only person in need of a real Hospice was the man in the wheelchair. Everyone looked physically healthy, at least on the outside. Yes, he would have a few questions to ask.

CHAPTER FIVE

The afternoon dragged by too slowly for Rush as he had paced about David's small apartment looking out over the Caribbean watching the occasional flight of birds, heading south towards the Republica, seeking a better landing than on Isla. Rush glanced at the large full bookcase, shelves filled with books as well as CD's, with a few stacks of books on the floor, mostly paperbacks. Having nothing else to do, he finally began to scan titles of the varied library: a lot of junk, a few classics, with mostly 20th century authors plus a few history books. He saw one of Catton's trilogy on the Civil War, *The Coming Fury*. He reached for it, settled in the most comfortable chair, and was able to escape his present problems on the island and those back at home as he walked with Lincoln towards the Civil War. When he finally put the book down to look out, the still bright sun was far to the West; he realized he was hungry, it was close to six. David was obviously still busy so he went out the door then down the hall to the dining area in the main room.

Two women, in similar uniforms with matching aprons, were bringing in various dishes setting them on the side table next to a grouping of a half dozen tables. Then one of the women picked up a small bell and, at the open interior doorway, gently rang it, echoing down the hallway: the invitation to dinner. Rush's fellow passengers from the plane slowly responded, filing in, looking at the tables, wondering where they should sit. The Sandersons, his wife making sure Jimmy could manage his walker, took a table near the window. Rush decided that he would ask if he could sit with them. Irene, with her usual smile, welcomed him.

"Mr. Sterne wasn't that a pleasant flight and the view... wasn't it spectacular as we circled the island. It's really like a resort isn't it?"

Rush could only give affirming nods as responses to her continuing cascade of compliments of the island: the comfortable room, the nice doctor, the pleasant nurse.

"Jimmy and I are so pleased with all of this. I hope that whatever your business is..." she was reminding him of it of his evasive comment of the previous evening, "... that it will go well." She paused, "We may not see you much more after tomorrow, that's when we'll be going to meet Jimmy Jr." She finished with a note of proud certainty. Jimmy Sr. wheezed as he added a simple affirmation, "That's right...we're ready."

Irene then lowered her voice, as if others might be listening, adding, "We made a pledge at our wedding to love until death do us part…well …" Her voice became even more confidential, "We have kept that promise but death will not part us. We've always done things together as partners and we will…" she giggled "...not let death separate us. Oh no we won't." She ended with a triumphant smirk of satisfaction. "Now I wonder if we should serve ourselves or…"

Since a few others were up to the side tables choosing their dinners, Irene took two plates and made her choices for both she and her husband and brought them back to the table. Rush then followed, standing behind two of the quiet men. The larger outweighed the other by about 50 pounds plus six inches in height. He had a dark complexion and a full head of darker hair with matching deep set eyes. The much smaller man was shifting his weight from foot to foot without much success in finding comfort. He clearly looked apprehensive but remained silent. They then took a table all to themselves to continue their disconnected solitude.

The food was simple, mostly cold, but with one hot entree, a tangy fish based soup. Rush finished his bowl quickly realizing how hungry he'd been. There was only water and soft drinks and, as David had indicated earlier, no alcohol. Rush was tempted to go for a second helping of the soup but seeing the dessert tray he opted for a pastry and coffee. He returned to sit with the Sandersons and then as he digested his dinner he digested what he had heard and what he'd already seen. The realization suddenly hit him as he sat there, finally dawning on him just what kind of facility this was. It wasn't a hospice. It was all about physician-assisted suicide. Clearly it was his very good friend Dr. David Newton who was the assistant! As he sipped his coffee he wondered just how dumb he'd been, not to have seen this earlier. If they had been giving out medals of stupidity he would be first in line for the gold!

Rush now looked around him. Beyond the Sandersons to all of the others in the room. Was he the only one intending to fly back home and remain intact? He tried not to show it but he was feeling both angry at, and deceived by, David. Again taking in the room he saw each person was attentive to the plate in front of them, with only an occasional comment, rarely responded to. The only noticeable exception was, once again, the French-named lady, who was alert, eyes scanning around her, maintaining a bearing of confident class. The effort of all the rest, even Irene now, was to avoid each other, and perhaps even themselves as they finished their meals.

David then strode into the room smiling and nodding at all those seated. He took a chair at the Aldredges' table, seemingly assuring them with another confident smile. Rush noted that all eyes followed David as he then quickly rose, chose some food from the side table, then resumed his seat with Lisa and Lyman. There had been almost no conversation before he arrived but now there was a deathly silence that Rush wanted to shatter. He wanted to yell out, "Do any of you know what you're doing?" He remained quiet, realizing that if they came this far they must know what they were doing.

As a pall of silence continued to hang over the room, the tables slowly cleared. First Irene assisted her husband, then Lisa followed Lyman as he motored through the doorway back down the hall towards their rooms. Only one man, the heavily muscled one with a brush cut, didn't move back down the hall. He went outside to the patio, pulling out a pack of cigarettes as he did.

David came over to Rush, "What a day! What a week!" He waved at the plates and the remaining food. "Leave this to the staff...let's get out of here."

Back in his apartment David went immediately to the refrigerator reaching for two cans apologizing again for the alcohol ban, "It's my rule... for my own good...you know me...don't you?" Rush did. From those first months together at university Rush had come to know David's extremes, alcohol included. "Well I still drink, often too much, but not here. We take a four day break each month-end. I have a deal with Jose's resorts, just along the coast. I'll look at any health problems the part-time staff have in return for free room, meals, booze and...let's just say...female companionship." Then he turned back to Rush his finger pointing directly at his face, "Now...why you're here. You saw me with Antonio, the guy on the plane...he's Vuk's temporary replacement, may be permanent...who knows, we'll need somebody...he's helping get the island back in workable order, after the storm. It was the hurricane, or something, that took Vuk, my right hand and the guy who kept us functioning, into thin air. He's the missing person...why we asked you down here...to find him...or at the least...to find out what happened to him."

Rush had intended, at first, to ask about the island, this so-called Hospice, but his attention had now been refocused. He waited for David to continue, "I've only got half an hour before I interview the Sandersons. I've already done Lyman Aldredge. Naturally he was accepted. Nearly all do but I still follow the same necessary procedure." He paused, leaving this vague, again to focus directly on Rush, "You have figured out what we do down here, haven't you?"

Rush nodded, not admitting it took him too long to figure it out, then answering, "Yeah, it's a drive-through suicide shop, isn't it?"

David shook his head. "Rush, don't be too judgemental. We do serve a purpose here, but let's leave that for the moment. We can debate it later."

Glancing occasionally at his wristwatch, David now began to give a summary of the week before, the oncoming storm, the need to evacuate, the return, then not finding Vuk.

With a final glance at the time, David was out the door, leaving Rush to lean back and contemplate what he had just been told. The interviewing techniques he first learned in Police College involved tapes and notes, now he had had neither so he reviewed, from memory, what David had, too quickly, told him.

Vuk, Rush hadn't been given any other name, had already been on the island when David first arrived. He handled almost all the internal functions and machinery needed to have Isla run successfully. David and Heidi handled the 'clientele'. Evalina, Carmena and Estella took care of the kitchen, cooking and housekeeping, Gustavo and a student helper, currently Jorge, previously Edo, took care of the crematorium. Vuk was responsible for all other aspects of the operation including connecting with the other staff when they had any problems they couldn't solve.

The Caribbean had the normal annual invasion of tropical storms. The only questions were how many they would have, what their intensity would be, and which of the islands they'd hit. In the two years that David had been on the island they'd only had one previous storm come their way and that fortunately caused little damage. The original forecast for this unexpected tropical storm, named Zena, was that it would pass safely by Isla only expecting heavier rains than usual. The forecasters were wrong. When Zena's path changed and headed for the northern coast of Real Republica, David was advised to evacuate the island. The timing was only a day before they would normally vacate for their month-end four day break. They only had time to secure the island as best they could in anticipation, and to leave a day earlier than normal. The Twin Otter that they would normally use for transportation was in for an engine overhaul and they would have to rely on a smaller Cessna that could only squeeze in four passengers plus some cargo, so that two trips would be necessary. There were heavy winds and sleeting rain when the first trip left with the female staff plus Gustavo. All that remained of the paying clientele of that week were five urns. David explained that Vuk had never left the island previously on these scheduled month-ends. David could only guess why he wanted to remain safe in the security of the island. However, he urged Vuk, busy tying down what was most susceptible to the storm, to pack a bag to come with David and Edo on the second flight. At one point David thought Vuk agreed but when the Cessna landed, with the storm increasing, visibility worsening, only Edo and David were there to meet it. David had said that they waited as long as they could, peering through the rain, to see if Vuk was coming to the plane. David said they had no choice, the pilot was worried, yelling that they would have to take off immediately. They managed to safely get back to Porto del Norte.

David cut a day off his normal hedonistic stay at the resort to return to Porto once the storm passed northward. He explained to Rush that Edo was only on a three month placement at Isla. This was normal as Gustavo supervised the cremation functions but it wasn't an up-to-date system. It didn't have any powered mechanized crusher to grind the bones down to size. A young strong muscular man was needed for this. The three month placements were advertised at all the funeral colleges in the Caribbean as well as Florida. David explained that Jose had some percentage of ownership in many of these facilities.

Rush had finally been able to interrupt David to ask, "Who is this Jose?" David waived his hands wide. "Jose Carlos Fuentes owns this island. He owns, it seems to me, a large chunk of the Republica, as well as other islands, plus properties in Florida and Mexico. You've probably never heard of him. He keeps a low profile but he's very rich and very powerful and, for down here, surprisingly honest."

David had then gone on to finish his comments about the young Edo whose island stay, shortened by one day due to the storm, was to end. His replacement, Jorge, was not expected for a few days so David had asked Edo not to return immediately to his college near Miami but stay at the Casa, in Porto, and, once the weather cleared, return to the island for a few days. David anticipated that there'd be damage and Edo could help Vuk with the clean-up.

David and Edo flew back in the Cessna to find damage, but less than David had expected. David had also anticipated that Vuk would be on the dock to greet them. He wasn't. David explained that, at first, they expected Vuk to appear at any minute. Then David was worried that he'd been injured by the storm. There was no significant damage to any of the buildings. The main Hospice (David still used that term) was solid and other than some loose shutters, unscathed. The other buildings had damages but all were repairable. Some solar panels had disappeared into the Caribbean and three wind turbine towers weren't functioning. They checked about the island but Vuk could not be found. Later that day the Cessna brought in the rest of the staff. Another search was organized. The women checked all the buildings, except the crematorium as they never went anywhere close to it. The men checked all of Isla, from each tip and on both shores. Again no Vuk.

David contacted Jose Fuentes asking what to do. Should he notify the Republica Police, file a report? Jose told him to wait; he would get back to David. When he did it was to hold off, to continue searching, though David knew that would be futile. Jose had many friends in the capital city and the government. This had allowed Jose to set up this facility on Isla, in a country still with deep Catholic roots. Taking one's own life was a sin. Your body would not be buried in consecrated ground. That choice made your body, and your soul, an outcast; your family was disgraced.

Jose had come to own the island when it had defaulted to him. It had been collateral for a loan that hadn't been repaid. At that stage the Island had not been inhabited since its usage by Americans and British in World War II. Jose's wife, Catalina, had just been diagnosed with cancer and Jose's first optimistic plans were to build a villa for his wife as a quiet refuge to assist her as she recovered. Her last few months were extremely painful, in differing ways, for both of them. She was suffering from her illness; Jose suffering with his inability to help her, despite all his money. There was no assisted-dying service available in Real Republica and even if there had been, Catalina's religious beliefs would have prevented her from even considering that option. Jose's own beliefs were shattered by the silence of his God to his many prayers so, following her death, with the exterior shell of the villa completed, Jose decided that he would finalize its construction, in her memory, for those whose religious convictions, if any, would allow them a more speedy and less painful end. It's purpose had to be disguised from the official regulations and moral standards of the Republica. It was registered as a clinic and, being offshore, and with Jose's connections, the state maintained a blind eye allowing Isla to function, almost as an independent country. Vuk's disappearance would be a problem if the authorities were called in. Jose and David discussed their options. Jose wondered if an impartial third party investigation might be enough to show that Vuk's disappearance had been investigated, should that become necessary. David immediately thought of Rushton Sterne, both a good friend as well as head of a Missing Persons Unit of a reputable Police Department. Jose had agreed; David had contacted Rush.

Now Rush was sitting, reviewing all of David's hurried comments, wondering what he could really do at this late stage. Well he'd better get started. He pulled out his notepad from his luggage and began listing all the questions that came to his mind. There were many.

CHAPTER SIX

The door opened and in one fluid motion David was stretched out on the couch, filling it. "We are not getting older...are we Rush? I like to say I'm only forty, but coming next, if I'm honest, it'll be forty-five..." There could be both disgust and denial in this forecast, "...anyway where did we leave off…?"

Rush let the question sit for half a minute, "It was about Vuk...but first...I need to know more about this place. It's not what I expected. I need to know more, exactly what you do here."

David now sat up, serious and ready to explain, perhaps defend both Isla and himself.

"All right. I've already told you about Jose getting the island as a payment for a debt. Before that the island was empty, only used by fishermen if they were caught too far offshore in a storm. Around nineteen forty-two the Americans and the British built a concrete fortress here. It served two purposes. It allowed them to listen in on U-boat traffic and it was also used as a beacon for Allied planes. This was part of the southern route for aircraft being shuttled over to North Africa and then later onto England or Egypt. The route went over the Caribbean to the tip of Brazil then across the Atlantic. It was longer than the northern route over Iceland but apparently safer. That's why we still have the solid concrete foundation. It protected the equipment and the personnel as they were afraid that a U-boat might surface close in and use a deck gun directly on the island. Originally Republica was neutral partly due to the continuing influence of Franco's government in Spain even though the Republica was officially independent. They quietly allowed the Allies use of this tiny island and now, with Jose's help, they still leave the island, and us, alone. That has made it easier for us to set up this facility. We don't broadcast our services here but we're well enough known elsewhere so we are never short of applicants. They firstly have to submit a notarized statement of why they're choosing assisted-dying. I review all of these submissions. If they pass that first stage, we send them papers to sign, again all to be notarized, to prove that their decision is both rational and voluntary. Then we ask for money, quite a lot, but the upkeep of the island is expensive. I don't see the final balance sheet. That's done by Jose's accountants but it's probably, at best, a break-even proposition."

He paused, as if deciding which way to go next, "Well you know that after my marriage break-up, and that mess I got myself into, well it was time to leave London. A change of scene, a challenge. . .so to Medecins and Africa. Drought, civil war, disease, warlords, political corruption. . .well it kept us busy, really too busy. For relief I started, truthfully re-started, to drink. Most did but I overdid it. I lasted nearly three years but I then became a liability. I came home to Trinidad to recharge myself. Then there was another spot of bother so it was best I move on. There was a surgical opening here in the Republica, at Santo Vincenza. I knew a bit of Spanish, I applied and was accepted. It was there that I met Jose Fuentes. He had donated a lot of money for a new Oncology wing. Then I got into another... you know...another bother with a lady already married...to a very jealous husband. I needed to leave...sounds like you've heard this before, doesn't it?" David was not apologizing, only explaining as he went on.

"Jose had told me about Isla Cresciente before but then as I was to take off back to Trinidad, he told me there'd been an opening, a need for a new medical director to replace Dr. Ernesto. He and Heidi, that's my current nurse, my assistant, had started when the hospice opened. They had a regular little lover's nest here but Jose told me Ernesto's wife, back in Santo Vincenza, demanded he should return to the family fold. Clearly Jose was in need of someone to continue the operations here. At first I said no, then after a night sleeping on it, I reconsidered. I knew death, only too well, particularly after Africa. Jose was needing somebody. I liked Jose, I didn't disagree with the concept so I said I'll try it for a couple of months and, as you can see, I'm still here."

"Enjoying it? The power to play God?" Rush was taking a hard line.

"God? I don't make the choice but I do make sure that their choice is thought out and they are fully committed to it. After all it's their final decision in life. I'll admit that my ...our standards are flexible. We don't need a diagnosis of a terminal illness, although we do get many of those. I need to be convinced that they see this as their only option. I've sent some back on the plane, suggesting they go back home to try life, not death. I don't know the percentage of those I reject who then take their own lives, probably some, while others may manage to find a reason to keep going. I have had two that I had rejected come back again. One I accepted, the other I provided with another return flight."

David stood up and went to the window. Clouds were filtering out the glow of a half-moon into the room. "Rush, do you object to all this? On moral grounds? You've always had morals and you may now have religious objections...fine...if that's your belief...but that belief should govern your own life, or those you are responsible for, not the lives of strangers." He hesitated. "Perhaps you believe in the concept of the sanctity of life? All life? Never to step on an ant, slap a mosquito, never set a mousetrap? Or just human life? If so, when society allowed you, as a Police officer, a gun to carry did you promise never to use it?" He stopped, inviting an answer.

Rush, gathering his thoughts, then responded, "Well, I've never believed in capital punishment and I guess, if I had no real semblance of a meaningful life left, like Aldredge, I would consider it...but what about the Sandersons...what about all the others on the flight? They all look like you and I, with lots, or at least a few more years, left in them."

"Listen Rush. I always interview them once they arrive. I only approve and schedule their visit to the clinic if I'm totally satisfied. Take your planeload, you and Antonio excepted. I have each client's submission, but I always go deeper, face to face, before giving my approval. If I'm in doubt then they have to go back."

"What about this group? Who have you approved?"

"I've only seen Aldredge and the Sandersons. Lyman is obviously qualified, perhaps should have been here months ago. The Sandersons... well...they are firmly, totally convinced they'll see their son so I won't deny them that hope. I'm guessing Jimmy Jr. died of AIDS. They didn't say so but the year of his death, in San Francisco, suggests it. I saw you talking to the Sandersons. Would you deny them?"

Rush didn't say anything but, remembering Irene, doubted he could deny her any wish. He shifted the topic, "What about the rest?" His mind suddenly focused on Lebow, Marielle Lebow. David seemed to read his thoughts. "The lady with the French name? Yeah, she looks too good, too young. She's out of place here, isn't she? Her submission was vague but she did include her photograph, which was unusual. I'll admit I was intrigued. I can always send her back can't I? She'd be back on the same flight as you...unless it's just her ashes. Anyway she's not scheduled for tomorrow. First it's Aldredge, then the Sandersons. Irene insists that they go together, simultaneously. That's a bit tricky in the clinic but we can fit them in, side by side. The crematorium can't fit two at once but, by that time…" He stopped to run his hand through his hair. "...Rush, I'm a bit tired. It's been a busy day and I have to prepare for tomorrow, early. I need some sleep. You take the bed, I'll take the pull out."

"No. You take the bed. I'm not tired. I'll go out to the lounge, read a bit. I'll be fine."

Getting up, David gave Rush an appreciative slap on his shoulder then picked up Catton's book and headed out the door, down the hallway to the lounge. Opening the door he saw Marielle Lebow, rising to her feet, dropping a magazine down on her chair. She gave only a curt nod of acknowledgement then, as he took only steps into the room, she was by him, out and back down the hallway. As he settled into the seat she had just vacated, still warm from her body, he thought that this would be the closest they'd ever get. He opened his book and tried to concentrate on Washington, over one hundred and fifty years ago. He only lasted about an hour then he returned to David's apartment, a light left on for him by his friend, now sound asleep. The pullout bed had also been prepared for him and he was soon in it.

CHAPTER SEVEN

He slept fitfully at first, then deeper, lost in unremembered dreams, waking to see slants of sunlight on the wall, then seeing David, now dressed, quietly leave the bathroom and slide to the door open it then leave. He didn't bother to check his watch. He lay back, half asleep, half awake. Here, he was on an island almost isolated, held by threads to the rest of civilization, containing just over a handful of permanent residents, one so far unaccounted for. As he became fully awake he reviewed what he needed to know: how the island operated, all of its staff, their functions, their interactions, and whether there was a logical explanation as to why one was missing.

He decided it was time to get started by surveying what he could of the entire island. Quickly dressing into shorts and he spread suntan lotion on his exposed face, arms and legs. He went through the hallway, still quiet, passing closed doors, into the main area. He could see this was set up for breakfast and he heard culinary sounds from the kitchen but no one else was present. Then he was outside onto the patio. It was fully exposed to the early-morning eastern sun, immediately bathing his body in light and warmth. Looking up to the left, to the West, he saw a wisp of smoke start from the stack of the building at the Western tip of the island. The stack was now fully straight but slightly swinging in concert with the building and the barge that it floated on. Then he saw David just going into the larger building. Even at this distance it looked antiseptic. This had to be the Clinic. Lyman Aldredge would probably be in there, if still alive, sedated, almost dead. He wondered if his wife was with him or whether she'd already said her goodbyes.

He then walked over to the right edge of the patio. There, just to the east, was the jetty where the Twin Otter had docked. Just inland was the top of a large tank set inside a fenced perimeter. He could hear the hum, presumably from generators within. There was somebody inside the fence and then he saw Antonio, at work early, checking the diesels. Further to the southeast he could see the rise to the spine of the island and hear the whine of the wind turbines providing accompaniment to the mechanical chorus of the generators below. Over his shoulder to the rear side of the building, above the roof, were sloping panels which he guessed were part of a system to catch rainwater. Although quickly warming, the air was still fresh and reasonably free of humidity, the kind of weather that was friendly, inviting, enticing, compelling. It seemed at odds with the purpose of the island. As he stood there, soaking in the sunshine, he was momentarily lulled by its embrace. He then shrugged this away, with reluctance, to turn, walk back, then re-enter the hospice.

Inside the staff were setting out breakfast. There were cereals, lots of fruit and some type of pancakes. He poured a small glass of juice, a freshly made roll as well as a cup of coffee and sat down at the same table that he'd occupied with the Sandersons the night before. Soon the full complement of yesterday's newcomers, except the Aldredges, were choosing breakfast and returning to sit at their usual tables. Rush was at the side table, eyeing the pancakes, pouring more coffee when he realized that Irene was beside him, pouring out two small glasses of orange juice. With a quick smile she leaned close to him, "The doctor said no breakfast, but juice would be fine. I'll take these back to our room. Jimmy's waiting, we need to be together. Goodbye ...again…" She strode, erect, and proud towards the hallway as David entered, sidestepping to let Irene pass. Rush heard her say, "We'll be ready."

David, hurriedly slapped some food on a plate, filled his cup with coffee, and pulled his chair beside Rush, "Sorry but I'll be busy for a couple of hours. We can talk again before lunch. Can you find something to do until then?"

"Yes, I want to explore the island. Any snakes, scorpions here?"

"No, but if you are going out there to cover all of the island you'll stir up something, better use lots of repellent and... look behind my door...on the hook, there's a walking stick, probably a century or two old, a family antique from Scotland. You can use it to defend yourself from iguanas... or whatever."

Back in David's room Rush sprayed himself with repellent then, looking down at his shorts, thought of the scrub ahead in his search. He had packed a pair of walking pants and changed into them. Checking

David's dresser he found a pair of longer socks. He decided not to take any chances out there. He returned back into the lounge. Only Marielle remained, sipping coffee. This time it was his turn to only give a cursory nod, then he was outside.

He started to go west, along the south side, at the corner of the battlement left from a war seventy years ago. The spine of the island was lower here than to the east, but with more vegetation. Now, out of sight, he stuck his pant legs inside his socks and used the stick with, he thought, authority on the bushes ahead of him. He soon reached the western tip of the island, only encountering a few scuttling land crabs but with no evidence of any human activity or the real reason for his search, any potential grave. He was now just beyond the smoke-stacked crematorium, standing on a rock, waves licking his shoes, at the furthest extremity of the Isla's western finger. He was tempted to call out, to ask "Vuk,where are you?" If the sea knew, it was keeping it a secret.

Working his way back, skirting the side of the crematorium, he saw a small dock, parallel to the shore. Moored to it was a sturdy boat, a good eighteen feet long, with a 40 hp outboard attached. He checked the boat's interior but it gave him no clues as to Vuk. As he followed the shoreline towards the clinic, he suddenly stopped, retreated back against the foliage, seeing a courtage of Heidi, in her nursing outfit, leading Jimmy, with Irene a step behind, both in white shroud-like gowns, heading into the clinic. He felt he was invading their last moments and stayed still until they were inside.

Heidi Furman had prepared the clinic for the arrival of the Sandersons. They had previous experience of couples choosing to be hand-in-hand, to take this last step together. However, it took a little more preparation than normal. She was up to it. She'd always wanted to be a surgical nurse and had never wavered in this pursuit. She had been top of her nursing class and was easily accepted at the hospital, convenient to her family home at the edge of Dresden. By thirty she was a senior nurse in surgery working with the best surgeons, helping with both the up-and-comers and assisting the older doctors, some who should have already been retired, needing her discreet assistance.

She continued to live at home. Her mother had been forty when she was the first and only Furman child conceived. Her father was a bus driver who was crushed, on a foggy morning, in the terminal by a half-drunk trainee driver. Heidi was twenty-two then but continued to live with her mother in their small house. She had only a few dates as a student as her devotion was to her profession. She didn't try to beautify herself; a pleasant, intelligent but plain woman, not trying for male attraction. The Hospital surgery was her life until five years ago while trying to cover up Dr. Mastrich's surgical error, she became the scapegoat for the death of a young mother. Dr. Mastrich's standing after nearly fifty years in the hospital was protected by the hierarchy. No formal investigation took place; there was no official admission of negligence. The Hospital handling was subtle but the message was clear to all the surgical staff. Heidi was moved to be only an assistant in the Recovery Room. Heidi could not accept this treatment and made it known that she would take action. The Hospital responded by offering Heidi a termination allowance and a positive reference letter in return for her silence. Her mother, a lifelong smoker, had always had a cough but it had worsened. Heidi had pushed her to see a doctor and, almost coincidental to her problems at the Hospital, came the diagnosis of lung cancer. Heidi didn't seek any new employment. She remained at home caring for her mother for the year it took her to die. Heidi had often thought, during the last few months, of alleviating her mother's suffering by terminating it. She had the medical knowledge but simply couldn't apply it to hasten the inevitable. She remained a dutiful loving daughter for her mother right to those last, fortunately morphined, weeks.

She was then a thirty-three years old, technically an adult orphan, a little lost about what to do with her life. She had never travelled far but now, free of any attachments or responsibilities, she began searching travel brochures and within two months after the funeral had a rough plan to travel, to see a world that so far had been limited to a radius of two hundred kilometers from Dresden. In preparation she expanded on her school taught English. She could read it well but was haltingly limited in fluency. She bought instructional tapes and tuned into the BBC channel to practise. The small house, with a lovely garden, sold easily and she was on her way eastwood to Greece, then onward to Turkey, India, Thailand and Indonesia. Fortunately she was well inland when the tsunami roared ashore but quickly went to assist. After two months of hospital volunteering, receiving only a cot and meals as compensation, she continued on her way.

She didn't really like Australia, too much of an active lifestyle for her, and then decided to go on to Panama, then up to Costa Rica. She again felt the tug of her love of nursing. She had no current accreditation, knew only a few words of Spanish, but was accepted at a local hospice on the outskirts of San Jose. There she met Dr. Ernesto Manuel who was on a volunteer placement. He was close to fifty, a bit short, a bit overweight but Heidi quickly saw how dedicated he was to his profession, to his patients, helping to ease and comfort their dying. They came to respect each other's talents and concerns and their lives began to gravitate together both inside then, with time, outside the hospice. She learned he was from Real Republica and had a wife and adult son there. While neither she nor Ernesto would have be seen as particularly attractive to the opposite sex their bonding didn't need, at least at first, the sensual. It was only when he announced that he would be returning to Real Republica that their relationship, much to the surprise of both, propelled them, tumbling into her bed.

He promised that he would find work for her in Santo Vincenza to continue their new found passion. Within weeks he was back to her advising a new Hospice was being set up on an island off the north coast. He would be the medical director and they could continue their work and their affections there. It was only when she arrived on Isla Cresciente that she learned of its true function. She had no second thoughts. She accepted it as just another way to help patients, albeit different than what she'd done before. She and Ernesto would be together most of the time as he only had to return to his family for a few days at the end of each month. There he slept in a separate bedroom from his wife. On Isla he and Heidi had separate rooms, but only for appearances.

For Heidi this was an idyllic existence, their work, their privacy complete but then it suddenly changed. Ernesto's son had drowned, caught in an undertow. Heidi thought he'd soon be back but Ernesto's distraught wife, needing to show her friends, her society a family united in grief had demanded Ernesto stay by her side, to put on brave faces through the extended period of mourning. The Isla had to shut down temporarily, turning applicants away. Jose Fuentes wondered if it shouldn't stay closed but then David Newton, who had become well-established both medically and socially, in a few short months in the capitol, was caught in a web of his own making. He was about to return to Trinidad when Jose proposed that he consider Isla.

Heidi had been jolted by Ernesto's letter trying to explain that his duty was to endure the family facade of sorrowful unity and remain in the City. After many readings of his letter she finally burned it. When Senor Fuentes advised that the Hospice would continue she decided to stay, to work with the new director. Heidi came to enjoy working with Dr. David. He was so very different from Ernesto but just as qualified. Ernesto kept writing to her, finally advising he would be able to get free to meet her, at the Casa in Porto del Norte, for a few days at most month ends.

She enjoyed working with Dr. David. She observed he had the same skills as Dr. Ernesto but a very different personality. Ernesto was solid, predictably so. Dr. David could light up an already sunny room, bring smiles to those who were waiting to die. Occasionally there were days when he did not want nor need any company. She said nothing more than necessary on those days, fulfilling her assistant's role, echoing the same silence of Dr. David.

Even though it was a short distance to the clinic, the sun still had time to burn into the exposed shoulders of Jimmy and Irene, only partly covered by the white light shifts they wore. Heidi, as a caring nurse should, carefully guided them down the path from the main lodge. Irene would have wanted to hold Jimmy's hand with each step but she could only extend her hand to touch his shoulder. Then they reached the door and Nurse Furmer turned to give them a sincere welcoming smile and soon they were all inside.

Rush hoped he would be unobserved as he walked back eastward past the Hospice. His pant legs were tucked into the long Argyle socks he'd taken from David's dresser. He was unsure of what to do with the thick knobby walking cane, also from David. Should he tuck it under his arm, or sling it over his shoulder? He laughed at himself, thinking he only needed a pith helmet to complete the picture. The base of the foundation gave him some cover from anyone who might be looking out. He now set out to search the remaining larger portion of the island still looking for anything out of place. He would be surprised to find an immediate answer to Vuk's disappearance and, as much as he was hoping to find some clue, he realistically only expected to confirm the earlier fruitless searches. The eastern half of the island was more open with small shrubs, only a few trees, none very tall. He guessed that any tall tree, with a limited root base, would fall victim to the predictable Caribbean windstorms. Still it was hot work. He realized he should have brought water with him but he kept to his organized grid like survey. Finally he was at the eastern tip, miles of clear sea and sky before him. He kept to the shoreline of the bay as he headed back, shirt and pants sodden with sweat, towards the broader beach nearer the jetty. Then he saw David heading towards him barefoot in the sand.

"Any luck?" asked David. Rush shook his head in answer.

David examined his friend, "You look like you just crossed the Sahara. How about a dip in the bay?"

Rush had to peel his wet clothes off so that David was already ahead of him, white buttocks contrasting with his brown body, as he splashed out beyond the shallow shore. He was already immersed into blue green deeper water when Rush finally caught up to him, diving under, tasting salt. David's natural athleticism, on land or on sea, soon outpaced Rush as he stroked further into the bay. Rush didn't try to compete but stayed treading water, buoyed, both in body and mind, by the refreshing warmth of the sea.

Marielle had just left Lisa Aldredge, now officially a grieving widow. They had sat together at a table near the window with Marielle, at first, wondering what sincere words she could use to console somebody that she didn't even know. There were minutes of silence as if Lisa appreciated just the presence of Marielle. Finally Lisa began, with only a few hesitations, to unload her conflicting grief and guilt. Perhaps it was easier to pour out her feelings to a stranger, to someone she'd never see again. She related the start of her affair with Todd, her plans to leave Lyman until his failing memory and functions were diagnosed. With his bleak future and his need to have someone care for him, Lisa made her decision to stay with him. She also confided to Marielle there were many times she'd started to pack a suitcase, to run away with Todd. She admitted to being emotionally torn between genuine sorrow that was clashing with the sudden relief now that she had a future with Todd. As Marielle heard of Lisa's conflict she thought back to her own break up with Luis, not by death, but by her slow realization that their relationship was atrophying, until she was able to recognize its sad finality. Was that ending so different from Lyman and Lisa? At least Lisa had Todd to go to.

"Thanks for listening to me. It's really helped. I think I'll go back and rest a bit." Lisa then looked with concern. "Oh my God! I've never asked about you...why are you here?"

"I'm fine. I'll be back on the plane with you. We'll both be leaving together." Marielle reassured her.

Marielle wasn't about to go back to her room. In just a day her room had become a cell, the island a prison. Once she had the information needed she would be tempted to swim back to the Republica rather than wait for the next flight. She went out onto the patio. Seeing the telling smoke from the western tip she walked to face out over the eastern part of the bay. There, in the water she saw thrashing of what she thought, for a second, was a school of fish. Then she saw the heads of the doctor and his buddy. She hadn't yet figured out what this Rush character was doing on Isla but clearly he was here as a guest of Dr. David Newton.

Then the two heads became bodies as they splashed, like school boys, through the shallows to shore. Marielle had recently needed glasses for reading but there was nothing wrong with her far-sighted acuity. Newman, the taller figure, bronzed except for his white abdomen, had his penis flopping from side to side as he ran full frontal to the beach. His friend, very much whiter all over, was just behind him, his penis just a pale dot nestled in a dark patch, like a single egg in a nest. Well, she thought, all men aren't created equal, are they? She also thought, aside from the pleasure of the show of male nudity, how refreshing it was to see life, even boyish exuberance, on this morbid island.

CHAPTER EIGHT

Rush's clothes were still clammy as he pulled them on. Striding beside David he asked about the Sandersons.

"Fine...they were just fine...perfect...hands together...music by Dvorak's '*Going Home*' ...it went well. They'll soon be blended together in one urn. They'll be with you on the flight back, on their way back to Minnesota." David paused for reflection, "I don't believe in any sort of afterlife, but they did, and I won't deny them their hopes on finding their son. If they did it would make my involvement...well...more satisfying."

They were now heading up the path to the Hospice. "David, I need more information. I'd like a list of all the personnel that were here before the storm. I also need to see Vuk's room and what he left there."

"Come on. We both need showers, you first. I'll list the staff for you. Then you have lunch. I've got another interview and then another procedure this afternoon". David chose ambiguous words for his work inside the clinic. "You can check Vuk's room later. Nothing has been changed, moved a bit, but all still there."

"When do you have lunch?" Rush asked.

"I eat when I can. I know where the kitchen is."

The shower cleared salt, sweat and grains of sand from Rush. As he dried David jumped into the stall but was soon out, dressing quickly, then out the door, pointing to a notepad on the desk as he left.

Rush sat at the desk to review the list:

David Newton...Medical Director
Heidi Furmer...Clinical Assistant
Evelina Bautista...Head Housekeeper
Carmenia Solitara...Asst Housekeeper/Cook
Estella Sanchez ...Asst Housekeeper/Cook
Vuk Losavik...Mtce Supervisor

Gustavo Estevan...Crematorium Supervisor
Edo Vantar...Student /Assistant
Franco Clemente...Pilot

Any professional analytical assessor, particularly a Detective Sergeant, would sit back evaluating what he knew, what he didn't, and how to resolve the difference. So far Rush had little concrete to work with. However, he wasn't in a sprawling city, with thousands milling among themselves. He was on an island with less than a dozen permanent inhabitants, isolated with limited means of entry or egress to the rest of the world. One person was unaccounted for. Could he have left unobserved, alone? Would he have needed help? A collaborator? Why wouldn't he have just left openly, leaving no mystery, no reason for David to call for his help.

Then Rush, for the first time in days, had his mind switch back home, focusing on Robin Partridge, not surprisingly known as 'Birdie'. It was Birdie who was the cause of his suspension. It was her accusation that he beat her up so badly, blows to her face, that she couldn't even talk when she first arrived in emergency, just hours after Rush, alone, had interviewed her in her small rented room. Birdie was only one of the contacts that his unit was checking with while trying to locate Lucy Marie Fairweather. Lucy's file had been opened a few weeks earlier in Missing Persons. They had three other new cases on that day but the others were resolved fairly quickly leaving Fairweather in their 'Unsolved File' along with too many other young women. Some of these had now aged over the years, buried in the data banks. The older they became, the deeper they sank into 'Unsolved', the less likely to ever be found, dead or alive.

It was not unusual for an adult, living alone, not to be missed for a few days. Lucy Marie didn't live alone but shared a small apartment with a flight attendant, Marylou Parsons. Marylou had been on a flight to Jamaica and had managed a two-day layover in the sun before returning home. She admitted that she and Lucy were not the closest of friends. They shared a two bedroom rental in an older complex but they kept their private lives separate. It was more a matter of economics than anything else. Marylou was away for nearly half of each month and she later told the police that Lucy was agreeable to pay two-thirds of the rent for the additional privacy. Marylou had arrived back late on a Monday night, slipped exhausted into her bed, slept late the next day. In the afternoon, thinking about dinner, she had phoned the Clinic where Lucy worked to ask her if they would share a meal that night. The Clinic was run by two doctors, brothers, both still single, both past sixty-five. Finally the phone was answered by one of the brothers. No, Lucy wasn't there and there was no one to handle the desk, the patients and to answer the phone. No, they hadn't heard from her at all. Clearly he was not happy with the situation. Could she please find Lucy and get her back at her desk, tomorrow at the latest.

Marylou had then checked Lucy's bedroom. The bed was made, everything fairly neat. Her closet held most of her clothes and an empty suitcase. Marylou then went out to the parking area. Lucy's prized small pick-up was missing from the parking lot. Marylou was scheduled for a flight Wednesday afternoon but felt she just couldn't leave without being satisfied Lucy was fine. She really didn't know much about her roommate's private life. She wondered if there had been an accident; maybe Lucy was in a hospital. She wasn't sure which hospital to call then decided to call the police asking for the Accident Bureau. They said they would check all the hospitals and get back to her. Finally she went to bed.

The phone rang just before eight, waking her up. No, there was no record of Lucy at any of the local hospitals. Marylou hung up unsure what she should do next. At nine she called the Clinic again. Whichever doctor brother answered her call advised very brusquely that Lucy was again absent, they had been forced to hire a temp and Lucy should not expect to have a job if and when she returned. Finally at noon, as Marylou was getting herself ready for a five o'clock flight she called the police again and was directed to the Missing Persons Unit. She filed a report.

A data bank file was now opened: LUCY MARIE FAIRWEATHER.

***

Lunch was quieter than breakfast, not due to anything unsaid, but simply due to the empty chairs. Marielle still sat with the ever silent Lorraine. The two sets of men were facing each other at their respective tables. Lisa Aldredge had presumably stayed in her room; Rush sat alone, without the Sandersons as company. This did give him more time to, once again, consider those at the other tables. The two men, Rush recalled at the jetty were identified as Nick Sternos and Dan Lemone, who had never, in the brief time Rush had been near them, spoken a single word to each other. If eyes could have had daggers the smaller man would have already mutilated Nick. Sternos remained unmoved by anything around him, his only attention, when focused on his smaller companion, appeared as if he was a silent watchdog.

Rush could not stop his eyes from scanning, as quickly and unobtrusive as possible, to the table of the two women. Fortunately, his angle on Marielle allowed him her profile and he was able to glance away when her head rotated in his direction. Even so he was caught, for a mini-second, a few times. At the other table the elderly man and the bulky brush-cut one at least showed some animation, but only in short spurts of conversation. Finally they began, one by one, luncheon finished, to push back their chairs to leave the dining area. The brush-cut man went out to the patio pulling a pack of cigarettes out as he did. Rush then realized that only Marielle and he remained seated. She stood and turned to him.

"I think you and I should talk," she said and then walked to the lounge area, seated herself at one of the single chairs and coolly looked over at Rush, who was still glued to his chair.

He suddenly felt he'd been summoned into the Principal's Office for some misdemeanor. Slowly he walked over to take a chair, a safe five feet away from her.

"You're Rush...?" Marielle asked. Rush tried a smile, as he filled in the blank, "It's Sterne, with an extra 'e', S-t-e-r-n-e."

Marielle took a second for her mind to register the connection. "Sterne? As in Tristram Shandy?" He tried a stronger smile this time. "Yes but, to my knowledge, no family connection."

"Your buddy, the doctor god down here--Newton--is he related to Isaac?"

Rush only heard sarcasm, no humour, in her comment before answering "I don't think so. If I remember correctly Sir Isaac created his famous Laws but no children, never married." Remembering David's mother and her consuming desire for prestige, he thought she might have wanted that family connection but Marielle interrupted the thought. She was now back to being serious.

"I'm guessing that you are not here for the...process? Good. Since I've noticed you tracking me, and since I'm not acting as if I'm readying for my own funeral, you have probably formed the same impression of me."

Rush was about to say he was pleased to hear this but thought it better, once again, to simply nod in agreement.

"So I guess we're the odd couple." She paused briefly, "So who tells who first?" She then answered her own question."Okay I'll go first. I'll be seeing the doctor, later this afternoon or tomorrow morning. I'll tell him why I'm here, not for the injections, but for what he'll tell me about the death, the apparent death of a man, three months ago. We need to know how legitimate his death certificate is, the exact time of his death, any independent confirmation--facts that will stand up in a court of law."

"We?" enquired Rush.

"Oh yes...my employer...The Antioch Life Assurance of North America...You've heard of them?"

Rush responded immediately, "Well, I pass its Head Office almost every day, on my way to work, depending on what the traffic is like." This momentarily quieted Marielle with the realization they lived in the same city, but then it was her turn to question him. "Where's work?"

Unsure if he should admit to being a police officer Rush decided on the truth. He didn't want to have this start with Marielle flounder on a lie, even a small one. "Police Headquarters."

"Well, we have something common anyway. I'm a senior investigator with Antioch and I'm down here to get some straight answers. Can I trust your friend's answers?"

"I've known him for years…his answers are usually brutally honest." Rush replied at the same time that his mind rejected the designation 'senior' applying to this young looking woman who sat, still hostile, across from him.

"Are you here on Police business?"

"No, just for a few days in the sun. To see an old friend."

"A vacation? On this...Devil's Island?" She hesitated then returned her focus to David Newton. "Well you can tell your old friend, if you see him before I do, that I'll be expecting his full co-operation. If he doesn't then I…Antioch...will press some buttons down here to force him."

Rush held back from offering 'Good Luck' to this threat. David could dig his heels in and Jose Fuentes, according to David, had many influential friends in Republica's Capital. Wanting to continue the conversation, his first with this intriguing woman, he switched the subject, "So tell me, if it's allowed, what you're looking for?" Marielle knew that her motives would soon become clear to Rush and she began to explain the legalities of 'Luciani vs Antioch', her position as Antioch's investigator, and why there were blanks that needed filling.

"We investigators always have suspicious minds..." Rush had to silently agree as she went on, "...but this whole case stunk right from the policy application to the Death Certificate. We wonder if Luciani really died. This could easily be a scam and he's back somewhere in Italy waiting for his share of half a million dollars. We need to know who can confirm there was an actual death, who saw the body. Was there any post mortem? Are there any signs of long-standing health conditions that were never mentioned in his application for Life Insurance where he signed that he'd had regular check-ups and was in good health, confirmed by a doctor, but guess where that doctor was? Back in his family's home town in the middle of the hills of Cambria. We would have a tougher time to subpoena that doctor than we would your friend from here. We can serve them but we can't compel them to fly back to testify in a civil court."

"You think there was something material not disclosed in his application?" Rush asked.

"The beneficiaries are his two business partners. They run an importing business, tiles and ceramics, from Italy. Luciani was the buyer who was in Italy on a regular basis. That's why his family doctor, who signed the medical, was back in Italy. Our underwriter, who approved the policy, should have insisted that Luciani see one of our Medical Examiners. We goofed."

"What makes you suspect something?"

"Well I did some checking. I identified the Group Insurer for the company. I was able to get a list of prescriptions he used..." She wasn't going to admit that this information should have been confidential, "...and they suggested an ongoing heart condition. My checks with his neighbours showed that for someone, not yet fifty, he had trouble walking up the front steps to his condo. If he did want to commit suicide, he had to wait until the Contestable Death Period had expired. Do you know what that is?"

Rush remembered this from his second year course on Insurance

Law. "Isn't that a clause that says suicide is not a Life Insurer's defense to a payout if it takes place after two years?"

"Yes, the Death Certificate is conveniently dated fifty-three weeks after the policy started. That's why I need to not only confirm an actual death but confirm the exact date."

To break the sudden silence and to continue having her stay, Rush asked, "How's Mrs. Aldredge doing?"

"I guess one could say that she's doing as well as can be expected, given the circumstances."

"It doesn't make things any easier even if you have time to prepare, does it?"

Marielle thought back to her conversation with Lisa and her confession about loving Todd coupled with genuine grief over Lyman. She considered whether she should share this confidence with this stranger who now sat beside her. She compromised. "All marriages have their secrets and Lisa and Lyman had theirs. Now that he's dead she'll never know what he knew and that is going to haunt her for a bit." She paused, wondering if she'd said too much but then added. "Sorry to be enigmatic but she told me, in confidence, about those last years together. She's one tough lady and will be able to handle all of it. I think, once she gets home, goes through a few months of widowhood, she'll find herself clear to start a new life."

"Is that the advice you gave her? Perhaps, as a sideline to being an investigator, you're a marriage counsellor"

"Perhaps I am." She gave him a questioning look. "Are you in need of advice?"

Rush surprised himself with his frank response. "Not currently. You're years too late."

She dove right in, suddenly interested in this serious looking man. "Divorced?"

He gave a shrug, "Sort of. There was no official marriage."

"How long ago?"

Rush normally wouldn't expose himself like this, especially to a stranger, but he felt a surprising level of comfort with her, despite her initial coldness. "Quite a few, now just over twenty."

"Children?" asked Marielle.

"One, a son."

"How's that relationship?"

"None. It's non-existent. I haven't seen him for twenty years." He looked out the window as if counting the darkening clouds. "He'd be a young man now."

"I'm sorry. That can't be easy." Rush looked back to Marielle. Her face showed her sympathy was genuine.

"How about you?"

"Oh, like you, never officially married but enough years to legally qualify. No children though."

"Any regrets?"

"About the relationship? No, it had its good times but it wasn't strong enough to survive. It had passed its expiry date." She then reconsidered the question. "Or did you mean children? If you did the answer is no. My mother raised me on her own for the first few years. She married and had another child but the marriage didn't last and she became a single mother again, this time with two children." Marielle didn't add that, after her mother's death, she herself took on the single parent role, caring for her half-sister, a role that seemed continuous, despite the fact that Sylvie was now well into her twenties. Minutes passed and then Marielle stood up. She had suddenly felt that she'd exposed too much. She'd earlier seen this stranger naked but now she had been uncovering herself in front of him. She reacted by returning to her original stern stance, "I still don't really know why you're down here but I know why I am. If you see your doctor friend tell him I'm ready to see him and he'd better be ready to see me." She left, with purposeful strides, out of the room.

Rush felt the coldness left in her wake and hoped it was only due to her attitude about the island and David's part in it. He had to agree with her about the island. It was draped in strange gloom despite all the sunshine. He still wasn't sure if he had accepted that Isla's services really served a legitimate place in humanity's conduct of itself. He only hoped that David's patients had fully explored every other option before coming here.

Lorraine Flanders, still enveloped in the fog of her own making, had been in her room reviewing, then confirming her decision to be here when there was a quiet knock on the door. It was the nurse. With her slight accent the nurse explained, "The doctor will see you after dinner. You know he'll have to sit down and carefully go over your election to make sure it's your decision and that you have no doubts. You know you can change your mind, we've had clients who've done that before. You understand your options don't you?"

Lorraine answered calmly but with conviction," Yes, I'm completely sure."

"Do you want dinner here in your room tonight?"

"Yes, perhaps that would be best."

Heidi slowly headed towards the door, half expecting the next question.

"Do you know when... when I'll be scheduled?"

"That's up to you and the doctor. I can tell you that tomorrow morning is available if you choose it."

Lorraine only managed a soft, "Thank You", before Heidi left.

Yes, Lorraine thought, tomorrow morning would be fine.

She went back to the small table by the window and for the umpteenth time reviewed her letter wondering if she should give it a final revision. She would have to ensure that it was sent back on the next plane and then sent by express mail to Stephanie's address .

My Dearest Stephanie:

I write this letter, my very last letter, out of love for you. I admit that four months ago when you decided to leave me I was full of hurt, mortally wounded, and vengeful. I wanted all sorts of awful retribution against you as well as against Emily, your choice as my replacement.

The hurt is still there. It's too deep to ever recover but as I now think back over the ten years, two months and three days (yes I'll never forget the exact moment when we met, when I saw you look at me, first with only interest, and then later with passion) of our life together, I have too many very wonderful memories, the only happiness I ever really knew, so I cannot leave this life with feelings of anger and hate for you.

So I can only wish you every happiness with Emily but I must give you advice. Love Emily as you loved me but promise never to leave her, never to cause her the same heartbreak as I still feel now only a few hours before the beating of my heart will stop forever. Lori

CHAPTER NINE

Rush returned to the apartment but David was not there. He took out the list of who was on the island before Vuk was last seen. He reviewed his few notes of David's comments then set up his tablet and plotted a timeline for each of the staff. He had discounted the slight possibility that any of the island's clients of that week had, before ending their own life, in some way ended Vuk's. It didn't take Rush long and, in the end, no revelations jumped out at him. He got up to pace, only a few steps each way in this small room, to come back to his first conclusion. If Vuk, with whatever secret means or intent, had successfully left the island, then he had little to offer David or Jose. As much as he would want to offer such a solution for Vuk's disappearance from Isla, he knew he couldn't confirm that possibility. The other possibility he could deal with was that Vuk had never left the island voluntarily. If that was the case he was dead, either out to sea or buried somewhere secret on the island. The first could be Vuk's or the storm's choice, the second not.

He decided to go to the kitchen to interview the staff there. One woman jumped up from a large table centered in the kitchen almost upsetting her cup of coffee. She seemed to be in charge as the two other women, working at a side counter, obviously deferred to her to answer Rush's questions. David had clearly advised them of his friend's need to meet with them. Evalina, the Head Housekeeper, had a reasonable ability in English. She confirmed she had been employed at the island since it first opened, over three years ago. She said Vuk and Gustavo were also original employees but claimed that other than meeting them in the kitchen, where the staff ate separately from the clients in the dining area, they had little other contact. She could not add anything in background knowledge about Vuk but she did, after Rush revisited the point, admit that he was strange, secretive and very private, never giving any hint of his past before landing on Isla. She acknowledged she, with Estella, helped clean the men's rooms once a week, but she never examined anything, even if it was lying about. She could speak limited English but had little ability to read it. She had seen some books in Vuk's room but they were not in Spanish or English but in a strange, unknown language. Interviewing Carmenia and Estella was more difficult, both with very limited English, Rush with even less Spanish. They kept turning to Evalina for help. He then learned that Estella had left the island four days before the storm as her daughter was in labour and David allowed her to fly back to Porto del Norte. In the end Rush heard nothing that offered any clue about Vuk's actions on the evening before or the morning of the sudden evacuation. Neither Evalina or Carmenia could recall if he came in for dinner that last night. They'd been told that they would be flown out in the morning as soon as a plane was available. They were all busy trying to tie down anything that might be affected by the rain or wind. They had only left sandwiches on the table for supper. No breakfast had been prepared. Getting safely to the mainland was the only priority.

As Rush thanked them and left the kitchen, Carmenia wondered if she should have told this friend of 'el medico' that she had seen Vuk that morning before she flew away to escape the storm. She had hesitated for a number of reasons. She was always deferential to everyone else on the island, partly out of shyness and partly to avoid saying anything that might endanger her job. She was always fearful of the island but was more frightened of losing her position and having to return to live, full-time, with her lazy husband. Whatever money he picked up from part-time work was quickly converted to alcohol and, just as quickly, consumed. With this job she had her own money and, other than a few days at each month-end, could avoid her husband's drunken invasions of her body. She hadn't realized the real purpose of the island until a week after her arrival, on her first flight ever, praying all the way. She was happy to work in the kitchen, help with the cleaning and bed-making and avoid as much as she could even looking at 'la caldera' at the tip of the island. If she did happen to see it she would always cross herself. That morning of the storm, in all the confusion, the increasing winds, the crashing waves hitting the beach, she had only a quick glimpse of Edo, who she liked, and Vuk, who she didn't, out on the small veranda of the cottage where the male staff lived. So she said nothing to Senor Sterne; it was safer to keep your head down, your thoughts to yourself.

Rush was back in David's small apartment. He'd been told that a separate room would be available today. He guessed, if it had twin beds, it would have been the Sandersons. He began to organize his things then David barreled in, nearly knocking Rush over. He went to the fridge, took out a can. "Dammit I need a drink...a real one." He flopped into a chair, "Jesus ...Rush...you've got to help me. Jesus, I try. I do try to do the right thing even when the choices are not easy. Now all the choices are wrong." He looked, with anguish, at Rush. "You've got to help me choose."

David, voice rising,explained his dilemma. "You know the two men... never said anything to each other or to us. All I knew in advance was that Dan, he's the smaller one, was down here with his cousin Nick, the big guy, for support as Dan had a terminal illness and wanted our services. You know I always have an interview before any approval."

He stopped to take a deep breath, to settle his temper, before continuing. "When I sat down with Dan, Nick had wanted to be included but, unless it's a married couple, I don't allow it. Nick didn't look happy but stayed outside. Anyway Dan was evasive when I pushed to know his medical history and diagnosis. You saw him, small, slim, but healthy enough looking. I began to question him closely as to whether he was making the right decision. He kept saying he was. I needed to be sure that I agreed. When I began to suggest I wouldn't approve he finally opened up with the truth."

David was now up, his long legs pacing to the window, then back to Rush as he continued, "He pleaded with me. He said it was totally voluntary. He said it was either his life or his son's life. One of them would die. It was Dan's choice. My mouth may have been open as he explained the situation. It's really unbelievable what is happening to Dan and how I, Jose, all of us, are being played for fools!"

He then flopped back into his chair. "Dan is from Newark. A piece, a small player in the Mob...admits he's been with them for years...claims he's broken the law more than once, did two years time...and now was into collections...cash...often lots of cash. Then the temptation hit him. He had a bag, from a scam, that was heavy with lots of money. He took off with it. Flew to L.A....tried to hide out…afraid to spend too much money, afraid to go out. His New Jersey pals sent Nick out to search. Nick found him. Dan told me he didn't expect to leave California alive but they brought him back to Newark. Most of the money was recovered but the Mob had a problem. Dan had to pay the price. It would be a message to all of their other 'associates'. The problem was how they'd do it as the both State Police and the FBI were already investigating them, really pressuring them. Somehow the top guy had heard about us and figured we were a perfect way to commit 'legal' murder. He is letting us...me...do it for them. If Dan didn't cooperate, if he managed to take off, then his son would replace him and they promised their method wouldn't be as fast or painless. His son would pay the price. Rush...you have a son...what would you do?"

Rush's first thought was that there was no 'have', only that he'd once had a son.

"Would you save him? If you had a choice?"

Rush couldn't form the words at first but then they came out: "Yes, I would."

"Well ...I guess we'll be...what would you call it? Accessories to a crime, one that we'll commit tomorrow morning. Maybe we should commit another...get rid of Nick too. You know what he wants? To be there. Confirm Dan is dead. Probably take photos. He's the one that should go."

David was now explaining that he'd give Dan his answer either tonight or tomorrow morning but Rush was thinking about his answer, not whether Dan should live or die here on Isla, but why he had instinctively said he would sacrifice himself for his son, a son that couldn't even walk, couldn't talk when he'd last held him. He didn't second guess his initial reaction; his only thoughts were on whether his son was alive, where he was living, and if Stefan knew that Rush was his father. Then he picked up the thread of David's voice. "...I can still change my mind...but. . .I'll see that NFL guy now...if he's agreeable...then we can go ahead with him before dinner." He took his mind away from his schedule to remember Rush's needs. "Oh yeah, you wanted to go through Vuk's stuff didn't you. Go ahead...it's the bedroom on the left. I told Antonio...he's using the bed...not to mess with anything else in there." Then with his usual acceleration, David was out of his chair, out of the room, leaving Rush to wonder if his schedule took precedence over the reality of what he was doing, out there in his clinic.

The heat greeted Rush as he set out to continue with his investigation. It was only a short walk to the bungalow that housed the male staff with the exception of David. It was hot inside as he entered the front room but at least he was out of the sun's direct rays. The front room had four chairs around a square table next to a sink and counter with a few appliances. There was a small two-seater couch and two other chairs facing a coffee table with a small TV set on a VCR. It was a spartan setting that few females would have tolerated but must have satisfied Gustavo and Vuk. He wondered how the much younger men, still students, managed even for just a three month placement.

There were three separate bedrooms plus a small bathroom with a sink, toilet and a shower. He glanced into the two bedrooms on the right. Again strictly functional, no extras. Then he opened the door to the room on the left. The bed had been made and a small suitcase was on it. That would be Antonio's, Vuk's temporary replacement. There was a small bedside table with a lamp and a radio. A window, with flowery curtains, filled the rest of the outside wall. There was a closet, decent size, no door, and beside it a four drawer dresser with a small mirror on top.

Rush started at the bedside. In the smaller top drawer he found an assortment: reading glasses, lip-gloss, a half empty large tube of suntan lotion, a note pad with no script, a few pens, a bottle of aspirins, and a pair of scissors.The lower had two pairs of clean work socks, a stack of Spanish magazines and about a half dozen books. He flipped through the magazines. Not porn but more photos than text with an emphasis on breasts and butts. Only one book was in English, an out of date visitors guide to the Republica. The other books were all in a language that Rush could only guess was Eastern European. They were textbook type. There were a few photos of men, most in military uniform. Portions of the text were underlined as if these were important to Vuk. The pages were well thumbed. Rush assumed that they were political in nature. From one of the books a passport slid to the floor. Rush saw it was a European Union issue. Inside was a photo of a stern gloomy man perhaps in his forties, it was hard to tell, but Vuk's birth date confirmed he was, if alive, now fifty and born in Ludlodki,Yugoslavia. Rush had never heard of Ludlodki. He knew little about the Balkans as a whole and now that Yugoslavia had fractured itself into independent, but still warring, countries Ludlodki could be in any one of them. He checked the pages of the passport. Vuk seemed to have visited a number of countries before entering the Republica. That date was hard to read but seemed to indicate it was just over three years ago.

Prior to that Vuk didn't appear to have stayed in any place for any length of time. Rush sensed he was on the move prior his arrival here. He then saw that the passport had expired over a year ago. Rush wondered if Vuk had ever applied for an extension. If he hadn't, that could that mean he'd never contemplated leaving, felt secure enough, here on Isla.

Rush then went to the top drawer of the dresser which was organized. Personal toiletries, shaving supplies, toothpaste, shampoo to one side, more socks in the middle. The remaining third contained a fanny pack, envelope of photos, a wallet, a watch with a second hand that didn't move, and a small box with various currency, mostly in coins. He did find confirmation of Vuk opening a Bank Account with the Primer Banco de Republica but it only had the opening balance of a thousand pesos. That was dated over two years back and had no other entries. David had already told him the staff were paid by deposit to Primer Banco.There was no need for cash on Isla.

The lower drawers contained only clothing. most suitable for the climate of the island, but some heavier work clothes. Rush checked the labels. The summer clothes were in Spanish but others showed European sizing. Finally, the closet held a few shirts and a winter type jacket on hangers. On the floor was a large wooden oblong box. On opening it he saw it was a well organized toolbox. Rush saw a pair of pliers and he slipped them into his own pocket thinking he could repair the wheel on his own suitcase. A well used suitcase was lying flat on the floor. Rush took it to the bed and opened it but was disappointed to find it empty, nothing in the side pockets. The exterior only had some small isobar airline stickers. He managed to peel off three of them, reasonably intact, and, out of habit, stuck them to a page of a notebook he had brought with him.

Then, again from habit, he double checked the room but it had nothing further to reveal to him. It suggested that if Vuk somehow left the island voluntarily, by means unknown, he took nothing with him. Rush didn't label this thought as a conclusion. He tried never to jump to one, but a conclusion that kept pushing for his attention was that Vuk had not planned to leave the island, storm or no storm.

As Rush was about to leave, his hand on the door, he caught sight out the window of Heidi the nurse, and just behind her, Rick. He obviously agreed to be moved up on David's schedule. Rush had never spoken directly with Rick but did know he was an ex-professional football player.

His build identified him as a lineman. Rush thought it incongruous to see him draped, as were the Sandersons, in a white gown. He waited until the two were inside the clinic before he opened the door and headed back to the main Hospice building.

Rick followed Heidi inside the clinic. He looked to confirm Heidi was inserting the cassette he'd chosen to be played. He quickly glanced around. Everything was neat and clinically organized. It reminded him of the trainers' rooms under the stadiums, except his memory of their odours there didn't fill his nostrils here. Heidi had suggested, when she came to get him in his room, that perhaps he'd like a mild sedative to help him relax. He declined. Unlike many of his teammates, he had avoided drugs unless the pain of his numerous injuries became too intense. He hadn't minded at all when Dr. Newton came to him asking him if he'd mind going to the clinic this afternoon, not tomorrow afternoon. Rick didn't mind at all. In his first few years, as well as the last two in the Pros, he'd sat on the bench, hoping the coach would turn, call his name, and tell him to go out onto the field. He always, as he sat there, prepared himself for that call, making sure he was ready. Today was no different. He was now ready for the doctor's arrival and then to drift away, listening to Frank Sinatra singing his favorite: 'My Way'.

Rush had waited to make certain he wouldn't interfere with workings of the clinic but then he saw Gustavo, on the pathway, was heading past the clinic towards him. He waited, thinking this might be an opportunity to interview him, but Gustavo didn't stop, only glanced his way, as he continued around the back of the main building. Rush followed to the south side, to a small patio holding a barbeque, to see him open a rear door to the kitchen. Rush decided to try Gustavo now. Rush found him already seated at the table, Carmella pouring coffee for him. Rush slid into the seat opposite. Carmella reached for and filled another cup and, although Rush didn't need more coffee, he thanked her.

"Gustavo, you know that Dr. Newton has asked me to help find out what has happened to Vuk?"

There was only a mouthful of coffee muffling Gustavo's response. Rush recalled that David had told him not to expect a lot from the reclusive crematorium attendant but he pushed on, hoping his English would be understood. Gustavo knew a little more English than he'd ever admit.

Silence was his first line of defense. If that didn't work, he'd plead that he didn't understand the question. This would give him more time to half-answer, on his own terms. So he listened to the questions of this man, this friend of 'el doctor', and carefully framed limited answers. It wasn't that he was hiding anything. He kept his nose out of the daily functioning of the island, keeping his attention on the crematorium. He was, by practice and by necessity, a loner and despite living beside two other men, remained apart. Vuk had not been a problem as he was as much a hermit as he was. The young strong men that came for their short stays soon, within days, learned that the two older men they shared the living quarters with were off in their own private worlds. These younger men usually gravitated to sit, bother, and amuse the female staff in the kitchen. Soon Gustavo's English questioner finished. He had told the truth. He'd seen Vuk, as he did every day, from time to time, but on the day of the storm warning, their need to leave the next morning, his attention was on the crematorium and the barge that held it, moored to the shoreline. He was only vaguely aware of why it was only attached to the island; it was something to do with having it registered as a ship, in Panama, so as to avoid falling under the regulations of the Republica. Whatever the legalistic reasons, to Gustavo it was just a crematorium, out of date but, with his care, still functional. He told his young assistant to make sure that the barge was double-roped securely to land. In anticipation of the storm and rough waters, the aluminum boat was pulled, with Edo's help, well up on shore, as safe as they could make it. He'd gone, after a quick supper in the kitchen, back to his room, and had fallen asleep. The next morning he went, with his suitcase, to the kitchen for a leftover sandwich, then boarded the plane with the women, leaving the island. No he hadn't seen Vuk that morning at all, but assumed Vuk was busy on the island preparing it against the increasing wind and rain.

Gustavo, despite the Spanish name, was an Estonian, raised in a small village, a two hour bus ride from Tallinn. He left school as soon as his sixteenth birthday passed. He never enjoyed or did particularly well in either academics or friendships. He took odd jobs then at eighteen, left home, moved to Leningrad, marvelling at its palaces, but struggling to sustain a bed and food for himself. He quickly returned to Estonia in 1991, when it separated from the dissolving USSR. It was good to be young, part of the emerging new country, but jobs were still scarce and after final goodbyes to his family, he was off to Germany, finding temporary jobs, and a temporary by-the-hour female to lose his virginity. He struggled with the language but slowly learned enough to get by. One day, practising reading German, he saw an employment advertisement from a funeral home. Soon he was an apprentice and somehow the subdued slow pace was to his liking, dealing mostly with the dead and less with the grieving was strangely comforting. Of course he wasn't licensed to handle any of the deceased but then his employers amalgamated with another company. They handled cremations. Gustavo, now not needing any accreditations, was assisting in that process, receiving on the job training.

All went well for a few years. Gustavo and a shy cosmetician were slowly working towards a relationship when he, inexplicably even to himself, allowed normal desire for living flesh to cross the line with death. It was repellent and he was ashamed but a few months later, with a young female cadaver awaiting his attention, he succumbed again. This time he was seen, immediately exposed by the cosmetician, quickly dismissed. Leaving Germany, he moved on to Spain. The weather suited him and he found a position, assisting at a crematorium on the outskirts of Madrid. Now he began to learn bits of Spanish and settled into a quiet existence, allowing himself, once a month, the services of a 'prostituto'. Then, a few months into his now comfortable position, a vacationer from Germany recognized him. They had worked together. His secret could be exposed. Looking to move anywhere, he saw an ad for a position in Republica Real. Within a month he was settled, secure, feeling safe on Isla Cresciente. He kept to himself, did his job, managed to train the young students. The scattering of ashes and release of blood taken from the newly dead involved using the boat moored next to the barge. With the boat Gustavo found his one relief to the tedium of his life on the island, fishing. With time and practise, he became more adept and soon he was the supplier of fresh catch to the kitchen. Sometimes Dr. Newton would go out with him. They would anchor off the shoals that had formed a few hundred metres out from the western point. They rarely spoke, unless it was concerning their immediate needs, and after an hour or two, would motor back, in silence. Once they had gutted and cleaned the catch, Gustavo would take it to the kitchen to enjoy the compliments of the ladies and, at dinner, enjoy the meal they would prepare.

As he left the kitchen the questions posed by the Doctor's friend still floated through his mind.The disappearance of Vuk was firstly, to his mind, connected in some way to the storm, but now, thinking it over, he wondered if Vuk's past life, like his own, held the reasons why he had sought refuge here. Vuk had never left the island. At least Gustavo took advantage of the month-end break to get away to seek, at a price, physical attention to his needs but Vuk stayed rooted to Isla. Only, at each month's end before Gustavo flew back to Porto, Vuk gave him an envelope to post. He'd looked at the address but it was to a place he'd never heard of. There had to be an explanation of how he'd disappeared. Maybe it was the storm, maybe it was something else. Whatever it was, it really was none of his business, not his problem to solve. He hadn't mentioned the one thing to the Doctor's friend that had puzzled him when he first arrived back after the storm. It stayed a puzzle to keep to himself deciding not to mention that the furnace seemed warm even though he had last fired it four days before. Maybe Edo had fired it up to test it, who knew? It wasn't Gustavo's place to solve the reason.

CHAPTER TEN

From experience the kitchen staff knew the math as there was less food and fewer plates set out for supper. When Rush arrived Dan and Nick, as stoney as ever, were seated but with only Nick enjoying his dinner. Rush was glad to see that Lisa now had Marielle as company and hoped that this signalled a step forward for her. Rush took his meal to a separate table but then the grey haired, always pleasant looking man came in, and after filling his plate, came over and, with raised eyebrows, silently enquired whether he could join Rush.

"Please do." Rush extended his hand. "I'm Rushton Sterne."

"Hi. I'm Winston Cushing." He settled into his chair. "I bet Rushton is a family name...right?...mine too... but no relation to Churchill." They were quiet for a few minutes as they ate. Dan and Nick then rose, in unison, and left. Rush noted that Dan had left his plate more than half full.

"Did you ever get to meet Rick? He left this afternoon." Winston made it sound as if Rick had just caught a train. "Do you remember him? In the NFL?...No?...well I did. A tough customer. Of course you had to be... just to survive. Did you ever play football? No? I did but only in Junior High. I never got much bigger so never made the senior team. I always kept an interest though, both College and Pros." He stopped to take further forkfuls of his food. Turning directly to Rush he went on. " You don't really seem like a...like a customer down here."

"No, just visiting. Dr. Newton is an old friend of mine."

"Good. Good thing. I'm glad he's here, doing what he does. Mind you it's not for everyone but..." He stopped. "Sorry I'm babbling on. Am I bothering you?"

"No, not at all," replied Rush.

"Well it'll be my last day..." He turned to look out the window at the sun's slanting rays."...and it has been another nice day. I've been fortunate. I've had a lot of good ones, but not too many lately, since most of my friends and my wife have passed." He paused. "Are you married? No? Well,

I was lucky but never thought of trying it again. Even if I could have found someone and really cared about her, even half as much as I did for Ginnie, I couldn't go through another death again, burying a wife. Tomorrow will be easier than that."

Winston then was up then bringing back coffee and a piece of cake to the table pointing his fork directly at Rush. "Now you're young enough and I hope you have lots of life ahead of you but when you pass eighty and your mind still works and if you are alone, there aren't many reasons to simply add more years to the total. Also, just think about what is being saved, all the hospitalization, the prescriptions, all those expenses that somehow get passed on to the younger taxpayers. Now I'm not looking for a medal...or anything...perhaps I'm only trying to make a bit of sense...so you'll understand what I'm doing."

Rush now realized that Winston was waiting for some response. "I'm not here to judge you, or anyone else I flew in with. It's an individual's right to make that choice and you sound as if it's been thought out and, for you..." Rush's voice trailed off as Winston, looking down at his hands, suddenly put his left hand up, as a stop sign, towards Rush.

"Look. I forgot one thing. My wedding band." He rotated it about his finger, "I guess it became such a part of me that I totally forgot about it. I've taken care of everything else but my ring." Winston was now considering what to do, then he decided. "I've asked my ashes be sent back, scattered or interred, I don't really care which, on Ginnie's grave." He was giving it further thought. "Can I be sure that my ring would be mixed in with my ashes? It's probably not worth that much but it is a part of me. Maybe I should just leave it on and it will be melted down to really..." He gave Rush a smile, "...then it really would be part of me, wouldn't it?" They both knew that nothing further needed to be said. Winston stood up, nodded twice as a thank you to Rush, then left the room. Watching him leave Rush thought of the similarities between Winston and Russell, his father. It wasn't only the age factor or that they were widowers, each still grieving. It was the practical matter-of-fact approach to life and, in Winston's case, to death. Rush knew that his father was managing better than this man from Vermont but wondered if Russell's brave face was really for his son's benefit. Perhaps, when he returned home he should pay much more attention to his father, sit down, discuss what his father needed, what he foresaw needing, in the years ahead.

Then he saw Lisa and Marielle rise from their table and, as they left the room, Marielle's arm around Lisa's shoulder.

Rush spent the next hour back on David's couch, reviewing Isla, its current staff, its passing clientele, the mystery of Vuk, and, dominant in his mind, David and his role here. Then, David was in the room, striding to flop, as he often did, in a chair.

"Marielle Lebow! Did you ever talk to her? I just did. I knew something was wrong right from when I received her application. I should have thrown it out but then there was her photo. Damn it, she is a classy looking woman. You've seen her. What do you think?"

Rush had formed that same opinion from the first time he'd seen her but let David continue as his voice now turned aggressive. "She barges in. Right off the bat, questioning my honesty, my integrity, all about a patient that I had a hard time remembering. I felt I was on trial, on the stand, and she's the inquisitor. She even threatened that I might be dragged into court. She acted as if she wanted my balls for breakfast!"

Then David was up, still fuming, but with each stride, back and forth within the small confines of the room, he slowly relaxed. Now with notes of both vindication and satisfaction, he continued. "When I took over from Dr. Ernesto I felt he'd left Isla exposed to questions that might be asked about the Certificates of Death and their accuracy. So I began to take samples, a few snips of hair, a clipping of a nail, filing them away just in case any identification issues might come our way. I also took a photo of the body with a digital clock visible showing the time. I realized that I could be accused of fixing the time but then it would be up to someone to prove it was wrong. Up to now I never needed these precautions but when I told this ...this Portia...she finally shut up. I told her that if she, or the Company that had sent her, wanted to pay for the DNA analysis, I would send on the samples. The only other question she asked was where we sent the Certificates to, here in the Republica. I told her. She then asked how she could get a flight to Santo Vincenza. I can only guess she wants to check whether we registered the death of this...whoever he was...officially. I told her I could book her a seat out of Bonojara. By the way..." He changed course "... Jose wants to see you. Will your investigation be finished by tomorrow night, to fly out on Friday?"

"Yes. I would think so but why would this Jose want to see me?"

"Rush. Think. He's paying your way here and back. Knowing Jose I assume he wants to know what you've decided."

David didn't ask Rush to answer that question. Rush still wasn't entirely sure he could answer it himself. "Will he have more information on Vuk? On Edo? You've told me little about them."

"Rush I really can't tell you much about either. Vuk was already here when I arrived. He was efficient, looked after the functioning of Isla, even in the Clinic when we had any issues. He kept to himself, but that's a common trait here. You don't come here to enjoy the scenery. There are usually other reasons."

"What about Edo?" asked Rush.

"As I told you, the crematorium operation requires assistance for Gustavo plus the muscles to crush down the ashes. It's a three month placement for students.They get free room and board; no fee for the semester but they earn a credit. I grant you it's boring but has its advantages."

"What about their backgrounds, Vuk and Edo? I'm guessing they are both from the Balkans. What do you know about them?"

"Rush, you've seen me in these few days. I don't have much free time. I'm involved with the patients. I don't talk much to the staff except Heidi and the kitchen staff. It's a small island but, perhaps that's the reason, we don't socialize, we keep our distance, we keep our privacy." He stopped then resumed, "Jose, or his accountant, handle the personnel. When you see him you can ask him all about them."

"Good, I'll see Jose to ask him."

"Fine. I'll book you on to Santo Vincenza, but I'll leave it to you as to when you want to leave there to get you back up north. I'd think It'll be easiest through Miami. See what's available and remember to track all your expenses to get down here and back. You'll be reimbursed."

"Edo's college is in Miami isn't it?"

"Sounds right but I can't even tell you its name. Jose will fill you in on what he has on Edo." David checked his watch. "Off again. Need to meet two more tonight, to prepare for tomorrow." At the door he turned back to Rush. "Oh, we need to get you settled in a room of your own. We'll do that after I get back."

"No. I'm fine here, on the pull out.. No need for me to move." David only shrugged his shoulders as an answer before leaving. Rush then wondered why he'd said that. Indeed he felt comfortable here in David's small unit but he then had to admit, just to himself, that he didn't want to take over a room, use the bed of those who had not needed it for the next night. He wasn't, he thought, superstitious but still he preferred to stay right here.

Sitting down, he considered how to fill the time before David returned. He picked up the history book, tried to pick up where he'd left off, but his concentration wasn't back into the Civil War. Instead it firstly floated, then fixed back to the files on his desk back home. Lucy Marie Fairweather was not the only outstanding Missing Person but it was that investigation that had led, by just a normal follow-up step, to his interview with Birdie Partridge. When he'd left her small room she'd been as healthy as when he found her, not that she looked that healthy to start with. She was a patient at the Clinic where Lucy worked. When he questioned one of the two doctor brothers who ran the Clinic they really could not give any input on Lucy's life outside their doors. When asked about friends she'd made within the Clinic they could only say she seemed friendly with everyone. Rush had pressed further and one of the look-alike brothers recalled Robin Partridge. He had often seen Lucy and Robin chat in the waiting room but assumed that was more to do with sharing their native heritage as their age differential was significant. Rush obtained Robin's address. Normally, for any interview, particularly with a female, he'd be partnered but Lou had taken the afternoon off to see his dentist and Rush went alone.

It was a three story rooming house. The exterior gave its age as over a half century ago. The front entry confirmed that redecoration was not a priority, perhaps not even a consideration. There was a row of rusted mailboxes, a few broken, only half with names, one of which read 'R Partridge #306'. The stairwell would not have passed current Building Codes and the strong disinfectant smell showed that at least someone was trying to fight back, but with limited success.

After increasingly harder unanswered knocks on the door Rush was about to turn away but then the door was opened, held by a chain to only a few inches, and a cautious eye, half hidden by hair, peered out to look at him.

"Whaadayawhant?"

It took a few minutes before Rush convinced her to open the door but only after sliding in his identification, wondering for a few seconds whether it would be returned. It was after he repeatedly mentioned Lucy Marie that the safety chain came off and he was inside. The interior, a bed sitting room, a tiny kitchenette, had well used furniture but was, to Rush's surprise, neat and reasonably clean. There was a closed door, he presumed to a bathroom. Robin settled herself in one of the two aging armchairs and waited.

The interview started slowly with Rush asking simple questions often receiving a shrug in response. She mumbled, occasionally with a slight slurring of her words so that Rush suspected she might be a user, perhaps alcohol, although he didn't detect any odour or see any bottles. With further questions gradually she admitted to being a patient at the Clinic and yes she had got to know Lucy Marie, not close, just someone to talk to, as she waited to see one of the doctors or wait for her pills to be renewed.

"Robin," He paused wondering if he should be that familiar.

"It's Birdie. Everyone calls me Birdie."

"O.K. Birdie...When was the last time you saw Lucy Marie?"

It took a minute but Birdie did seem to be concentrating. "A week... no..more...maybe two...maybe three. A while ago."

"Did you chat then? Did she seem to be ready to leave her job there? What did she say that day?"

Birdie remembered that they only spoke for a few minutes and that Lucy Marie was "as nice as ever". She said she'd never seen her outside the Clinic, wasn't sure exactly where she lived, didn't know if she had a boyfriend or knew of any particular friends. When Rush asked about her shared heritage with Lucy she said that they came from different tribes. Lucy was mostly Cree, Birdie was from "out west". It was clear though that the two had formed a sort of friendship, even if it didn't extend beyond the Clinic.

Also clear was that Birdie was upset at her young friend's disappearance and was genuinely worried about her. Then she just sat there, head down. Rush rose from the chair, thanking her for her time. He took out his business card and laid it on the table in front of her asking her to call him if she thought of anything more that could help find Lucy Marie.

As he reached the door, Birdie, in a quiet voice, apologized, saying she hadn't helped Lucy much, should have done more.

"In what way?" asked Rush.

"I shouda told her to be careful."

"Careful? Of what?'

Of the bad guys."

"Bad guys? Who's the bad guy?"

Birdie didn't reply so Rush asked her again.

Her reply was evasive. "There's always a bad guy."

"His name?"

"Different names...Boss...maybe Lucky...something like that..." Her voice was now little more than whisper and Rush wasn't sure if he'd fully heard her.

Rush tried but if Birdie knew anything else she wasn't voicing it. She wouldn't repeat the name. As he left he pointed to his card on the table reminding her to call if she wanted to really help find Lucy Marie.

Back at the unit he met Lou coming in at the same time. Rush saw his face, flushed a bit, and asked him, "How was the dentist?"

"Dentist?...Oh yeah…well nothing too serious. How did you do?"

Rush related his visit with Birdie and her last few whispered words. "Know of any of our 'street friends' called Boss or Lucky?"

"There's probably dozens but I'll check with the Drug Squad. They're up to date on who's who at street level."

"Good. Also ask them about Robin Partridge--she goes by as 'Birdie'. I think she's using something but I have to guess she's a small player, maybe below the radar."

Rush's mind now shifted back to the present, to why he was here on Isla, searching for Vuk, but the events of a few weeks back, Birdie's accusation, was the reason he had the time free to answer David's call for assistance. If it wasn't for Birdie he'd be sitting at his desk back at Headquarters. He had been sitting there, reviewing two new 'Missings', called in that morning, the morning after seeing Birdie. That's when he was called to report immediately to the Superintendent's Office. Lois Anderson was seated and motioned to Rush to take the other chair, opposite Superintendent Wiley. He smiled a 'Good Morning' to both but neither responded with enthusiasm. He had worked with Lois before, when they both were assigned to the thankless Internal Affairs unit, disliked by all the force, and now she was in charge of it.

She started, "Rush we need to talk, to review your activities of yesterday afternoon."

She leaned forward to switch on a recorder, not asking any permission to do so.

Rush realized that the only active duty he'd done yesterday afternoon was to interview Birdie so that had to be the problem. Somehow he anticipated the worst. He was right. After hearing his version of the interview Supt. Wiley had picked up a document and read out an incident report filed by officers called to City Hospital early the previous evening. A woman had arrived by cab at Emergency, suffering trauma to her upper body and face, so severe that she was unable to talk. When the officers tried to question her as to what had happened she could only pull out a card and point to the name. It was Rush's card.

Rush knew that the Force had recently installed a 'Zero Tolerance Policy', strongly enforced, especially if it involved minorities or women. Birdie qualified under both criteria. When he was dismissed he was told to go home and that he'd be called after a further review of the matter. He received the call early in the afternoon. He was being suspended, with pay, until further notice. His first call was to Lou who had already heard the rumours. Rush confirmed them.

"If I hadn't booked off…" Lou hesitated, "you know...to see the doctor…" Rush remembered that it was to see a dentist but didn't contradict Lou who continued, "... If I'd been with you then this crap wouldn't be thrown at you."

Rush had to agree but it was his fault to interview Birdie alone, to expose himself. He brought Lou back to the reason he had called. "Lou, someone beat her after I left. I saw her to enquire about Lucy Fairweather. There has got to be a connection. Keep after it. Check out Birdie. Check all the 'Bosses' and 'Lucky's' that are out there. Keep me advised. You know where I'll be. At home."

Now he wasn't at home. Here he was, sitting, albeit comfortable, on a sunny island surrounded by miles of the Caribbean, watching the sun, in its final blaze, settle down into the western waves.

David strode into the room, did his customary flop to drape his body over his chair, and said with a smile, "Thank God. No more surprises, plots, lies...all is back to normal. Winston and Lorraine are ready for tomorrow." He then asked, "Did you ever meet Winston? Good. What would you think appropriate to play, in the Clinic, as he's drifting off?"

"You mean dying, don't you?"

"Rush...Rush...You still have problems accepting what we do here, don't you?"

"Yes, to some degree, but why are you asking me? Didn't he have a choice of his own?"

"No. Not at all. I suggest, when I give approval for clients to come here, that they bring their preference of the music that they'd like to be played as they drift...alright ...as they are still conscious. Lorraine had brought hers. K.D. Lang singing ' Hallelujah". Good choice but Winston said he hadn't really thought about it. I told him we have lots of CDs left here. He asked me to choose so I'm now asking you to choose for him. Check the lower cupboard..." He pointed to it, "...take a look." Rush was quickly aware that he hadn't mentioned Dan but assumed he was also scheduled for tomorrow, possibly first then Winston or Lorraine next. It would be a busy day for David as well as Gustavo and his helper at the crematorium.

With this though Rush was reluctant to look over the collection of music. It seemed as if this entangled him, made him an accomplice to the process that would end Winston's life tomorrow morning. Still, as he remembered with affection the similarities of Winston to his father, he opened the cupboard, grabbed the box full of CDs, then went back to spread some on the table. "Quite a variety, isn't there?"

"Yes, a wide range but, thank God, no rap music yet. I've heard both Presley and Pavarotti...Miles Davis and Willie Nelson...but please don't choose 'Going Home'. It's played too often." He then remembered. "Sorry... you like Dvorak, don't you?"

"I like him a lot. One of the few composers with a sense of humanity, not all doom and gloom. Remember though that Dvorak didn't write the lyrics to 'Going Home', just the score." He kept looking at the selections left by those that had wanted them as their dirge. "Well, you don't have

'Moonlight in Vermont'. So how about Copland's 'Simple Gifts'? Not quite Vermont but close enough."

David reached over to take the CD. "What about you Rush? What would you choose? That is, if you were in Winston's place. Okay, I know you wouldn't choose his route but what…?

Rush cut him off with his own question, "What about you? What would you choose?"

David hardly hesitated and afterward Rush wondered if David had imagined himself on the Clinic's table, not standing beside it. "I'd pick Sibelius. His Fifth...but only if it could be timed I'd lose it on that final chord. I'd rather go out with a bang than a whimper." He rose quickly, almost jumping out of his chair, looking at his watch. "Looks like we may have missed dinner. Let's see if there's anything left." He then led Rush out the door, down the hall.

There was dinner left and some even left over after David and Rush had filled their plates. There was clear evidence that the remaining guests had eaten then left the dining area. Rush did a quick count of those remaining. Tomorrow night there'd be less. Rush wanted to have David recount, in more detail, the events of that morning of the storm, as well as ask more questions about Vuk and Edo but thought it best to wait until they were back in David's apartment. Instead their conversation wandered back in time, remembering Rush's two visits to Trinidad, the first while they were still in University and the second when Rush, learning of the death of David's mother, had taken a quick flight down to attend her funeral. Then they each reviewed the remembrance of their mothers; clearly, but with unspoken words, with Rush having much more loving thoughts of his than did David. Rush remembered the Newtons as kind and thoughtful, but lacking any real warmth, especially to their only child. In particular, Mrs. Newton seemed more comfortable with friends, even strangers, than with her own husband and son. Rush remembered her preening pride at being the mother of the groom at David's wedding to Victoria Longhurst. Victoria's family wasn't quite up to rank with British nobility, but they weren't far off, besides which there were two or three actual titled guests in attendance, friends of the bride. Rush vividly remembered one of them and his brief adventure following the wedding.

They took coffee back to the apartment and then their conversation, comfortable to both with no mention of the island, covered the range of their recollections, none of them serious, of some of the ridiculous, bumptious characters that had entered their lives, some in common, most from their separate experiences. Rush told David about some of the characters and situations he encountered during his time with the Force. In turn, David recalled stories of doctors, nurses, patients, sticking to the comedic, not the tragic aspects he encountered in hospitals, even when he was with Medecins. Neither ventured to talk about their brief attempts at living with a woman although David did ask if Rush had anyone 'serious' in his life. Rush quickly answered that there wasn't anyone even "casual'. It seemed best for both, more comfortable, to reminisce about strangers, not family, not people close to them. Although Rush still needed to question David about Vuk and Edo, as well as that last morning, he decided to wait until tomorrow.

"Tomorrow." David made it not an option."We're going fishing...in the afternoon...after I finish up at the Clinic. You remember we went out, on your first trip to Trinidad." Rush did remember bouncing about on the waves until he almost vomited over the side of the boat. David must have remembered the same. "Don't worry. It'll be a lot calmer here. There's a shoal not far out. We can anchor there. Spend an hour. I can almost guarantee we'll catch dinner."

Their conversation then dwindled down, enough that David pushed himself up and headed to the bathroom. "I'm going to shower, then hit the pillow. You stay up, the light won't bother me. I've learned to sleep wherever, whenever."

Rush grabbed his book. "No, I'll head to the lounge. Read a bit more."

The lounge was empty. He had half-hoped that Marielle might be there although he wasn't sure what he could have done to have her stay, to sit, to simply talk to him, and he to her. He wasn't uncomfortable around women but, after Ana, preferred to keep any connection platonic. He realized this was a defensive position as it protected him both from being hurt again and, lacking confidence, being found a disappointment to a woman's wants. So whenever he initially met someone who attracted him, someone who he might want to explore a continued relationship with, he would back away. Life was simpler this way. So he directed his thoughts away from Marielle by opening his book to read on about Lincoln and the carnage of the Civil War for an hour. When he returned to David's room, as quiet as he could to open the door, it was to hear David's heavy breathing, only a few decibels short of snoring. He undressed, slid into the narrow bed and concentrated on the beauty of the island, not its darker secret.

CHAPTER ELEVEN

Rush slipped slowly from sleep to see David unfolding himself from his bed and, clearly trying not to disturb Rush, grab his clinical gown, use the bathroom, then was out on his way down the hallway. Rush had stayed still, neither needing or wanting to interfere with David's start to his day. Then he was up, very much awake, firstly into the bathroom.

The small mirror over the sink reflected back a questioning face. His own eyes queried the other set, flat but focused, with the same question they sent to him. Neither supplied the answer as to what he was accomplishing here. If he solved the mystery of Vuk would it mean much? It didn't seem, based on his search of Vuk's belongings, that Vuk had a family awaiting an answer. David and Jose seemed only to want a response that would satisfy the authorities of the Republica, if indeed they'd even ask for one. David didn't miss Vuk as a person, only as a valuable cog in keeping Isla functional. Still, with his ingrained sense of duty, as well as his friendship for David, Rush would do what he could to pursue the question.

He took a quick shower and back to the mirror, shaving, his eyes played out the ongoing contest with those opposite. He now widened this conversation with the mirror beyond asking why he was here and was he really needed. More questions began to rebound back at him. Exactly who was he? Where was he heading to? He always had self-doubts, especially after Ana had left him, taking both her and Stefan out of his life. After a few difficult years he'd managed to accept this as a fixed reality. He had stayed, a dutiful son, enjoying the love of his parents, only a few steps from them, down the stairs. At work, on the Force, this fact gave rumour that, if he wasn't actually gay, then he was probably asexual. This was enforced by a number of comments. First, he had rebuffed the efforts of a young assistant in Personnel who had tried, on two separate occasions, to involve him in her life, possibly her bed, and passed this fact around to all her friends and acquaintances from where, like a virus, it spread. Among the male staff it was noted that he didn't bowl, play hockey in the winter, or softball in the summer. Possibly worse was that he didn't even own golf clubs and admitted to enjoying badminton. His career path with the Police had not been routine either. After less than a year on a beat attached to a Precinct, he'd been moved to help the Prosecution Office at Criminal Court, then after a few more years another move sent him to Internal Affairs. Any officer summoned by I/A considered it almost equal to the Spanish Inquisition. Even if your conduct had been cleared, there was a stain and a resentment that all your buddies shared. It really wasn't until he settled in at Missing Persons, particularly with Lou and the assistants, Grace and Theresa, that he felt a sense of belonging.

After brushing his teeth, combing his hair he turned away from the mirror, his questions unanswered but with a sense of relief to be away from the introspection of his own image. Soon he was dressed, ready for the day and out down the hall a few steps then turning towards the dining area passing the closed door where he knew Marielle was staying.

Marielle was facing the small, much too small, mirror in her own room. It was a room that she had compared to a cell, part of this prison, like Devil's Island, away from civilization. Tomorrow morning she'd be flying away, back to the small portside town, then a cab to the Bonojara Airport, and another short flight to the Capital. There she hoped to uncover, at the Department of Statistics, some further light on the documentation supplied by Dr. Newton from Isla. Then, she'd be back to her office to give Antioch Life a report, but not before she scheduled a stay-over for a day on Miami Beach. Other than book a hotel she'd not made any definite plans. Maybe a bit of shopping, but mainly lounging by the pool as she had crammed a bikini into a corner of her suitcase. Who knows she might meet someone, at least to be invited to dinner. She'd never liked eating alone, unless she was in her own apartment. At hotels she would order room service rather than sit as a single in a restaurant. She was used to sleeping alone, but it was not a nun's vow, not a hard and fast rule of abstinence. Her thoughts drifted back to the brief affair with her Lecturer of English Literature, that was over a year ago and there was very little sleeping involved. Now, back before the mirror, she finished brushing her hair and then left, probably to find Lisa again and share the breakfast table with her.

Breakfast was again set out on the side table. Rush was the first to it and, as he took his seat, he considered the absentees. He assumed that

Nick would be down at the Clinic ensuring that Dan was paying his price to the Mob. Lorraine and Winston, if they were interested in breakfast at all, may have chosen to be served in their rooms, awaiting their summons. These thoughts had him only poke at his plate with diminished appetite as Lisa entered, looking beyond Rush, to half-fill her plate before taking a seat with her back to Rush. He did finish his coffee but not his food and started to leave his table just as Marielle entered, smiling only at Lisa.

Rush slid open the door to the wide patio, already bathed in morning sunshine. His sandals slapped against the concrete, barely disturbing the three iguanas sunning on the far wall. He was then down the steps, purposely turning his back on the Clinic, going down the path past the jetty, to jump down onto the sand. After a few steps his sandals were off and he started to jog, his toes grinding into the sand to propel him to the eastern edge of the beach. He wasn't really winded but already sweat was beading over his body. His return back was more leisurely and, feeling somewhat childish, he ran, skipping, splashing through the shallow shore, to reach the jetty. As he did he looked up to the Hospice. He saw, with relief, no one had observed him. The other day when he and David ran back to the beach to collect their clothes following their dip in the bay he had glimpsed a shadow up on the patio.

He wasn't sure if the two women may be lingering over breakfast so he skirted around the far side of the Hospice, around the back, to enter by the kitchen door. The kitchen staff gave him friendy 'Holas' as he poured himself a second cup of coffee to take back to David's room. There he reviewed the few traces he had taken of Vuk from his room. He had no connection to the Internet here; he'd have to wait until he could find that access to research further.

Edo had left no traces. Rush only had the vague comments of David and the even less informative recollections of the staff. He really needed to ask more questions of David. He wasn't that enthusiastic about the planned fishing outing but this would provide the chance to try to fill in some of the blanks. Purposefully, he was first to the dining area, waiting for lunch to be brought to the side table. Although breakfast had only been a few hours before, he was hungry, ate quickly and managed to finish before anyone else arrived. He realized he was not only avoiding the remaining guests but the empty chairs of those not remaining. He left, again via the patio, back to the beach, barefoot in the sand, for another walk eastward and, despite the heat, wanting the beach to be much longer, to prolong his need to turn back, to return to the Hospice. As he neared the jetty he turned around then slowly retraced his footprints back to the far end. Returning again, more sweat beading on his body, he then was past the jetty and back inside for a quick shower, then to sit, try to read, to wait for David's return.

He may have dozed for a few minutes as he was startled when David, already shedding his surgical whites, walked into the room, "Ready Rush? Slap some sunscreen on, repellent too. You'll need a hat. I've got the rest that we'll need. Let's go". Rush was reminded of his days as a Boy Scout. Don't question. Follow. He did.

The boat was now moored to the main jetty, well away from its normal place next to the crematorium. As Rush followed David down the path he guessed that the boat had been moved purposefully as the smoking stack on the furthest building was evidence that 'el fornano' was operational. As he clambered into the boat, Rush saw fishing gear, three coolers and, hopefully not needed, two life-vests. He hoped his stomach wouldn't need an empty bucket out there. It was relatively calm as David motored the boat out of the bay but, even beyond the eastern tip, the waves, although bigger, didn't appear threatening. Now, with the small island behind them, their far horizon was only sky and sea, and they were just an insignificant dot on the water. David then cut the motor down and Rush saw they were heading to a patch of short slapping waves. This was the shoal. David expertly maneuvered the boat to the lee side calling out instructions, "Grab the anchor. Just in front of you. Throw it out as far as you can."

Rush's first try was successful as the anchor grabbed and David shut down the outboard. He was clambering past Rush to pull the line tighter so that the boat was prow first into the breeze just a short distance from the shoal that Rush could now see was only slightly below the froth of the waves. David opened one small cooler, "Here's the bait. You cast out behind, to the right, let the lead sink for a few seconds, then slowly reel it back to the boat. I'll take the port side."

Rush really didn't care if he caught any fish. He was content, lulled by the gentle rocking of the boat, the salty air, the colour of the sea complementing the horizon. David then pulled up a wriggling fish, fighting for its life. He unhooked it, threw it back : "Grow bigger!" Rush wasn't keeping track of time. They spoke only when necessary, all relatable to the fishing. David was having more success probably due the range of his casts but Rush had a few bites and landed three, only to toss one back. David had four keepers, all larger than Rush's, and then he reeled his rod tight and took a plank from under the seat and, with practised surgical precision, gutted and filleted them, sliding them into a sturdy plastic bag, then emptying the entrails of their catch out away from the shoal. "The crabs and fish will race to see who gets the most."

David opened the second cooler, tossing Rush a cool can. "Again apologies. It should be beer."

Rush then began to ask David for more detail on Vuk and Edo but the answers were not much different than Rush had heard before. David explained that his focus was on the Clinic and its clients. He never had sat down with either to enquire about their lives. David had become distinctly aware, shortly after he arrived on Isla that Vuk, Gustavo too, were islands unto themselves, not sharing anything of their past, or plans for their future. The only real difference between the two was that Gustavo would fly back to Porto at month end. What he did for those four days was unknown to David but he suspected that they might share a common pursuit, except David didn't pay for his women. He did remember once talking to Edo about his studies at his school and about his future plans. David remembered Edo saying he doubted that he'd get his green card to work in the States and so he would probably have to look for something back in Europe.

"Did he like dealing with the dead, with their bodies?"

"Rush, I don't know, This island simply has a function to provide a service for those committed, fully committed, when assisted-dying is the only answer. The end product are cadavers. That's the end product of all lives isn't it?"

"Yes, but some don't accelerate the process."

"You still don't approve of what we...what I... do down here do you?"

"David I don't disapprove of assisting those who are at Stage Four, terminal, or whatever medical diagnostics apply, when they are at the stage that suffering becomes a cruel torture."

"But you disapprove of those without a doctor's stamp on their forehead?'

Rush looked out towards the reach of the sea before answering, "Yes, I suppose so."

"Rush, down here I'm the doctor with the stamp. I really do review each case. I've told you that I do refuse some. I send them back to whatever lives they've left behind. You have to believe me that I do ask them to prove to me that this is the only answer."

"But you do realize, and I'm being the policeman here, that legally, in many jurisdictions you could be charged with homicide."

"Look, I have no guilt. I only assist. The procedure, once inside the clinic, is to explain the buttons that start the procedure. Everyone is responsible to trigger their own exit. Even Lyman Aldredge was able to press the button to the first of the two injections.The second, once they are comatose, is an automatic slow flow of the drug that, usually within ten minutes, halts their heart, then their brain. I wait to confirm death and, after the photo, take DNA samples, enter the necessary data into my computer. Later I generate two Death Certificates. Since the Republica doesn't legally, or morally, recognize "el suicidio" I need to list it, in Spanish, as a sudden stoppage of the heart. That satisfies officialdom down here. The English version is simply self-induced death."

Rush still felt some aversion to the workings of Isla Cresciente but he had begun to waiver. He wasn't condemning but was still short of condoning it. David's reasoning was having some effect but Rush wondered if his friendship was more of a factor.

Whether David took Rush's silence as acquiescence to his defence of Isla wasn't evident. He simply turned to the outboard motor but, before starting it, he turned back to Rush, "See that other container. I'll go further out. When I get upwind I'll wave and point to which side you can open in it and, as gently as you can, say a final good-bye to Dan... remember Dan...from Newark? When I asked him where he would want his ashes sent he simply pointed to the window and said 'Out there'. I then asked about his son, the son whose life he was saving by giving his own to satisfy the Mob. He then told me that they had little contact, and hadn't spoken in years. His son didn't approve of his lifestyle. Dan then said that he couldn't have a life if he knew that if keeping his would condemn his son, a son he hardly knew. Now I wonder if his son will ever know of his father's choice." With that, the engine coughed alive and churned ahead, now with Rush fulfilling the role of Charon, scattering behind the boat's wake the ashes of a stranger.

The sub-tropical sun was sliding westward, still strong enough to illuminate the south side of the Hospice where David had lit the gas barbeque. The kitchen staff had their instructions for two separate dinner meals. The usual for the dining area, now down to Nick, alone at his table, and as far away from him as possible, Marielle and Lisa. Gustavo, Antonio and Jorge had eaten earlier. Now in the kitchen, the women encouraged by David, were preparing a send-off dinner for his friend, leaving tomorrow morning. There would be spicy side dishes, learned from their mothers' teachings, that would complement the fish that David was about to grill outside. David was insistent that all three women should sit with him and Rush, share together around the table. When David brought the sizzling fillets to the table they were soon passing around bowls that the women had prepared. Rush only regretted the absence of some sturdy wine that would not only enhance the food but help moderate the spices. David kept the women happy with his compliments for their efforts. They responded shyly, in Spanish to him, but only cast quick glances at Rush to see if he was enjoying the special dishes they had prepared. His mouth did, he could only hope that his stomach would later agree.

Finally, back in David's room, they both leaned back, at first seemingly content to avoid any mention of what had brought Rush to Isla. They spoke of their widowed fathers. David's was in Trinidad in the family's musty, dark, now too large heritage home, assisted by the long-caring Alma. Russell Sterne was only upstairs from Rush, still very active, serving clients in semi-retirement. Both appeared, at least outwardly in good health, good enough not to worry either son, each assuming, perhaps blithely, that this condition would remain constant.

David then reviewed Rush's coming day. It was all arranged. There would be the taxi from Porto to Bonojara, the short flight to the Capital. There a driver would be waiting who would take him to see Jose Fuentes. David assured Rush that this wouldn't be an inquisition. Jose simply wanted to meet him, discuss a few matters then Rush would be taken to the hotel to enjoy the evening there. Jose, or at least one of his companies, owned the hotel and David advised Rush that he'd be an honoured guest there, "Just enjoy the evening. It's on Jose's tab."

The darkness of the Caribbean night conflicted with the clock. On any evening both men, if they were back in the real world, would have many reasons to stay awake but here, on Isla, after they took turns in the washroom, neither reading or wanting any further conversation, it was into their respective beds. With the room totally black soon Rush heard David's breathing signalling sleep. His mind flitted back over these last few days to the strangers he'd met, most in the last days of their lives. He again thought of his conversation with David about their fathers. He felt his relationship with Russell was warmer than David had with his father. Then, as if for the first time in his life, he considered Russell's relationship to his father, a grandfather Rush had never known. He did the math to reflect that there had been only a few years to establish any firm bond before his grandfather volunteered, then was off on a troopship, his one way trip to Europe. As he drifted asleep Rush was thankful that no wars had required Russell's involvement and, so far, his as well.

CHAPTER TWELVE

Although David had no Clinic duties that morning he was at his desk, reviewing files and checking his computer in anticipation of a new set of clients scheduled to arrive on the Twin Otter in mid-morning. The female staff had bundled the used laundry and the non-degradable refuse to be taken back, along with five passengers, to Porto del Norte.

Rush assumed that Marielle and Lisa, along with Nick from Newark, had already had their breakfast in the dining area. He had waited then followed David into the kitchen to share the table with Heidi, Gustavo, Jorge, Antonio and David. What little conversation was in Spanish but Rush didn't mind the exclusion. His mind was on his meeting, later that day with Jose Fuentes, half wondering if he'd be told what the conclusion of his unofficial investigation should be.

Back in his apartment David apologized, "I'll have to say good-bye here, I'll be too busy down at the jetty with the new arrivals. They'll be a bit confused, they always are, in need of a bit of shepherding." He now wrapped his arms around Rush, "I do appreciate you coming down here. I won't ask what your conclusions will be, maybe you have to see Edo first, but it's always great to see you. You'll have to book another visit but not here. Let's meet at one of Jose's resorts when I take my month end break. There are always interesting and available women there in need of... let's call it companionship." He then gave a stiff slap to Rush's shoulder. "By the way, I've booked you and that Marielle woman into the same hotel tonight. Be warned or be prepared, your choice."

David was then out through the door. Rush made sure he'd collected all his belongings and packed them in his suitcase. He then remembered the wonky wheel, found the tool he'd taken from Vuk's belongings, and tried to straighten it, to at least reduce the clicking noise. There were still more airports left before he arrived home with plenty of time to do more damage. He anticipated having to throw out and buy new luggage before his next trip. Then he saw Catton's book. Perhaps he should leave it here but instead slipped it into a side pocket of his case. He could read it tonight in Jose Fuentes' hotel. He'd be sure to be alone.

Toting his case out onto the patio into a morning that was giving a final gift of sunshine for his last day on Isla. Light blue skies streaked with films of thin clouds meant there would be perfect conditions for the flight back to Porto. He decided to go down to the jetty to see the bags and luggage, including four urns, all ready and waiting for the arrival of the plane, with Nick was at the end of the pier, puffs from his cigarette drifting away with the breeze. Under the partial shade of a small tree, at the table set back from the beach, sat Lisa and Marielle. Rush carried his bag to place it beside the other luggage and, like the others, waited. It was not long before he heard the low drone of the plane and then it was an increasingly larger dot that banked to head straight at them, spraying the bay as it landed to chug noisily to the dock. The energetic Jorge had emerged from the path to sprint past Rush to dockside reaching for the wing tip as the pilot cut the engines. Soon the plane was secured, the doors opened and the ramp was down just as David and Heidi, she in her nurse's uniform, arrived on time to greet the arrivals.

Rush had stepped back, closer to the women seated under the tree. None of them wanted to interfere, even to be noticed by this new group who, once down the ramp onto the dock, craned their heads about, to take in the island, their first glimpse of their last earthly stop. David and Heidi expertly took charge and soon they had organized this handful according to their ambulatory abilities, with the chugging golf cart, Gustavo driving, carrying two elderly men up towards the Hospice. The rest followed on foot looking up and ahead, not seeming to notice those nearby who were waiting to leave the island. Once the incoming baggage and supplies were set aside, awaiting the return of the golf cart, Jorge and the pilot, seemingly still in the crumpled shirt and hat he had worn days before, were loading the outgoing cargo to the back of the plane. Included was Lyman's motorized wheelchair. Then the outgoing passengers filed into the interior. Rush hadn't seen Antonio but then, with a shout preceding his arrival, he was into the plane, throwing his tool bag to clank on the floor, this time clear of Rush's feet. The pilot locked the doors and, as he passed his passengers going to the cockpit, he muttered, "Seat Belts", but didn't bother to confirm they were in use. Then the coughing engines commanded their attention but both smoothed out promising they were airworthy enough to climb, then level out only for minutes before the descent to splash safely down, taking them into Porto del Norte's dock.

There a muscular young man had settled the ramp once the doors were opened. Nick had grabbed his bag and was out first. As Rush left the plane he saw, at the end of the dock, two taxis that had been pre-ordered by David to take the four of them that needed further flights from Bonojara International. The larger one would be needed to haul Lyman's wheelchair as David had already told him that Lisa was having it shipped back to be donated to her local hospital. It was parked just ahead of a smaller taxi. Rush had presumed, with distaste, that he'd have to share this cab with Nick, leaving Lisa, Marielle, their luggage and the wheelchair to take the larger vehicle. However, as Rush grabbed his own case and walked down the dock he saw Nick had the first cab's door open and was pulling notes from his wallet, waving them at the driver. The money worked its usual wand as Nick threw his bag inside and then was closing the passenger door as the taxi roared away.

This left the smaller car, a hatchback, and, with effort, the wheelchair was wedged inside once the rear seats were folded down.The rear overhead door wouldn't shut tight and it was roped closed. There remained only enough room for Lisa, in the front seat and her luggage behind, squeezed in beside the wheelchair. After hugs with Marielle, and a few tears exchanged, she was off. Marielle had used her fluent Spanish to ask the driver if he would have another cab sent to Porto. His face suggested he wasn't sure so he pointed up the hill. After the cab sped away Marielle began walking up the hill, pulling her case, Rush followed gripping his luggage as Marielle, her head half turned back toward Rush, explained that she'd been told to see Manuel at Casa Gaviota to make arrangements for the trip to the airport, hopefully well in time to catch their flight onto the capital. Manuel, smiling at their arrival, was eager to assist but, after a few phone calls, admitted that all of the airport cabs had been used by the tourists going to the resorts and they would have to wait until Nick or Lisa's cab was able to drive back to pick them up.

Marielle checked her watch calculating whether they would be too late and miss their flight. At that point a young man came to the desk asking Manuel to sign something attached to his clipboard. Then there was a flurry of rapid Spanish before Manuel turned to explain this was the delivery driver who'd delivered the Inn's beer supply and he was heading back via the airport and would be glad to convey them there. Marielle looked dubious but there was little choice. She looked a little happier when she saw the truck looked modern and the interior of the cab appeared clean.

After thanking the still smiling Manuel, Rush looked inquiringly at Marielle asking her where she preferred to sit. She chose the outside, nearer the door leaving Rush to sit between her and the driver. As they began to bounce their way over the broken road to the airport Rush was very much aware of the driver's body odour on his left and Marielle pleasant perfume to his right. Whether their young driver felt that this was an emergency requiring the skill and speed of an ambulance driver or whether this was his normal practice wasn't known but they rapidly covered the miles to Bonojara.

Fortunately there was little traffic either way which allowed him to steer the truck clear of as many potholes as he could. His resulting flying elbows had Rush, no middle seat belt for use, to repeatedly lean over onto Marielle's side. She appeared to tolerate the intrusions as she didn't complain nor dig her elbow into his side as a warning. On the other hand Rush quite enjoyed that part of the trip realizing it was their first physical contact; they hadn't even shaken hands before this.

Safely arriving at the entrance to Bonojara the driver was out, retrieving their luggage from among the cases of beer in the refrigerated truck box, placing them down on the sidewalk. Rush, still with no other change or currency, gave him twenty dollars that obviously pleased him. A security guard was yelling at him. Rush couldn't translate but the meaning was clear: 'Get that truck out of here!' Marielle was already paces ahead of him so he didn't try to accompany her to confirm their tickets, arranged by David from Isla. Rush was not entirely surprised to find that his flight had been prepaid. He lost track of Marielle as he checked in his luggage, then through a very casual security inspection, then a quick trip to the washroom before boarding the turbo-prop for their quick flight to Santo Vincenzo

Rush navigated his way down the aisle of passengers most trying to fit their bulky carry-ons into the small overhead bins. When he found the outside seat of 18B Marielle, in 18A, was giving him a look that said "you again!" Rush's quick smile was meant to be an apology before he looked straight ahead at the seatback They settled in, as if strangers,clipping their belts and waiting for the cabin crew to check them. As the plane taxied it was Marielle who broke the ice between them.

"Your friend, the doctor arranged my ticket. I should have guessed he'd be up to something. Were you in on this arrangement that we sit side by side? Perhaps he was also having Nick take the first cab. Arrange for Manuel to have that truck ride together? Can I also guess that he's booked us into the same hotel? Perhaps the same room?" There was no hint of humour in her list of accusations.

Rush didn't answer her but leaned out to signal an attendant. She was already buckling herself in, preparing for take off. After they were up and the seat belt sign was off she remembered his summons.

"Senor." She either knew or sensed he was not Spanish speaking, "How can I assist?"

"Would there be another seat I could move to?" Marielle's hand was quickly on his arm. "Really that's not necessary...unless it's me."

"No, it's not you, not at all."

She, in Spanish, thanked the attendant who moved away. She had released her grip on Rush and, turning to face him said, "Sorry. It's just that...that...that damned island, and your friend, got to me. I'm still carrying it with me, even as I'm leaving it. I guess I'm blaming you...I apologize, it's not your fault." A smile accompanied the apology, with Rush looking at her face, into her eyes, trying to analyze why he enjoyed the view. She wasn't alluringly beautiful but was much more than pretty. Somehow the combination of eyes, mouth, cheeks, the blending of them together into her face which, to Rush, still held his first reaction, that he might have seen her before, perhaps in Paris.

"You are a Police Officer so you might know. Is there a death penalty here, in the Republica?"

For the first time in their brief relationship Rush sensed perhaps she was not being serious, not protectively aloof, but he could only give her a shrug, "I don't know. Who do you have in mind?" He now second guessed his first reaction. Was she really thinking about David? She wasn't.

"That Nick guy. I knew he was a creep from that first time I saw him, before we even got to the island."

"You are too kind. He was much more than a creep…" Her eyes asked him why. "Sorry, I can't give you details. If I did then you might not hesitate to plead justifiable homicide. Also I might be an accomplice to the crime."

Well, thought Rush, at least they had something in common, even if it was only an imaginary murder.

"You've not told me the real reason you were at the island. Can I ask why you're going on to Santo Vincenzo?'

Rush saw no harm in telling her. "Jose Fuentes owns the island. Created it as a …" He looked directly at her, "...will you accept the term Hospice?" She neither accepted nor rejected it so he continued to explain as accurately and concisely as he could what David had told him of Cresciente's purpose and the involvement of Jose Fuentes. "So I'm on my way to see him, at his invitation." Now Rush paused purposefully to steer away from the real reason for his trip.

"Can I ask you why you are also going to Santo Vincenzo?" It was now Rush's turn.

She remembered what she disclosed to him only two days ago. "You know I was down here to investigate a reported death on the island. Well your good friend…" There was still a snub to using his name, "...he partially satisfied some of my doubts but not completely. I still need to check the official records of the Republica to make sure that what Newton told me is officially documented down here, not what Antioch Life has been supplied with so far."

"If I remember, your company issued a policy to insure a life and are being pressed to pay the insurance, but you had doubts he even died on Isla? Is that still a question?"

"Less and less." There was reluctance in her concession.

"So your defense might be that he died a suicide, within the two year contestable period?"

Marielle looked out the window, in resignation. "If Newton's records stand up...that might not be defensible either."

"But you told me that his application for the policy didn't disclose any pre-existing medical conditions but your investigations uncovered that he had been taking medication for high blood pressure, didn't you?" Rush asked.

"Yes, but we also discovered, and we suspect, he and his partners, the beneficiaries, already knew he had cancer, and that also wasn't disclosed."

"But you can't prove he knew this before applying?"

"What we suspect, we can't prove. His trips back and forth to Italy meant he was being seen by a doctor there whose records we can't legally access."

"So, the high blood pressure medication is the only defense?"

Marielle, flying high above Real Republica, now wondered if she wasn't back in a meeting room at Antioch Life, with their Defense Counsel reviewing their legal position.

"Maybe so. He was dying of cancer and decided to take his own life, who knows... perhaps pressured by his business partners...but if the official cause of death is either cancer or suicide, then we may have to pay out half a million."

Rush remembered what David had mentioned about Death Certificates. The English version acknowledged correctly, death by volition, but the Spanish version, filed with the Bureau in Republica's Capital, wouldn't be acceptable if classified as 'suicidio'.

He passed on this thought to Marielle. "Make sure you get an official copy of the registered cause of death. You might find that helpful."

Then the plane was being readied for descent to the airport at Santo Vincenzo and the blinking seatbelt sign seemed a message to close off their conversation. Even after landing their silence persisted as they filed down the steps to the ground. As Marielle strode ahead of him, Rush wondered if he should have told her that David had booked them at the same hotel, Castello Ciela Grande, another of Fuentes properties, but certainly to separate rooms. No, Rush thought, that would be just another grievance for Rush to handle. He didn't see her as he pulled his luggage, now with only slight repetitive clicks to echo him, as he came out of the Terminal. He saw his name on a sign and an eager young driver, in shirt and tie under a jacket, was soon opening a rear door to a large Mercedes at the curb. Soon Rush was whisked away, with the driver's exuberance matching his skill, as he wove through busy traffic, applying the horn at anyone who dared attempt to challenge him.

The traffic then became spaced until there was none as the Mercedes was now climbing a curved road, then slowed to turn towards a large set of gates. The driver had opened his window, extended his arm to wave and, in response, the gates slowly opened. Just inside, a beefy custodian, in a crisp white uniform, greeted the driver and gave a wave to direct them, crunching gravel underneath the tires, a distance further ahead to stop at the base of a wide flight of steps leading to an even wider 'pasarela' that skirted the main building's front facade. There was sufficient space for the Mercedes but, on either side was a collection of other large high priced cars, clearly showing that Fuentes had other guests already here. The driver, on opening Rush's door, pointed up the stairs to the massive set of front doors. Rush did as expected and, within two steps of the doors, one side opened with planned anticipation, he was bowed inside and a smiling uniformed attendant was leading Rush over an expanse of polished tile, some twenty feet below the well corniced ceiling of the large front entry. Then Rush was ushered into a wide room made smaller and more comfortable by the grouping of plush settees and chairs centered in the middle of the room. Rush took a seat and waited.

"Senor Sterne. Buenos Dias. So sorry to keep you waiting."

As they exchanged the usual polite opening conventions Rush was doing a quick study of Jose Fuentes. His English had the cadence of Spanish, with only a slight accent, but otherwise perfect. He was slim, with a receding hairline, but would be considered handsome, even by much younger women. He wore a tuxedo comfortably as if it was his normal attire.Then an attractive maid appeared with a large tray, from which she distributed a selections of olives, nuts, fruits along with a selection of small bottles of liquor, wine, ice and three bottles of beer before quietly leaving the room. Jose spread his hands gesturing for Rush to help himself so he took a beer with a local label and spooned some cashews into a small dish. As Jose poured himself a glass of mineral water he apologized that his schedule this evening prevented him from inviting Rush to dine with him but, with a look of resignation, advised that the combination of business and politics must often take precedence over pleasure and he would soon, as he now glanced at his watch, have to leave Rush.

"Our good friend David thinks very highly of you and we appreciate you finding the time to come down to us to assist us with this...this problem. If you had found our missing man I would have already heard so I can now only ask if you have come to any conclusions to explain his disappearance."

Rush slowed his reply to swallow a mouthful of beer, "Sorry that I can't yet solve the mystery. The missing component to my investigation is the young trainee Edo. David tells me you have a file on him. I need to see him, to interview him. I assume he's back at school, in Miami."

"We don't have a great deal of information on him but I asked my accountant's office to copy the file and send it to your hotel room. It should be there by now. I'll also make sure the director of Edo's school will expect you and give you his full co-operation. When do you expect to be there?"

"I'll go tomorrow morning." Rush replied. He finished his beer and felt he should leave now to allow Jose to return to his more important guests. "Once I get back home I will complete a full report and...should I send it both to you and David?"

"Gracias si. Here's my card." Jose was now up and escorted Rush out into the hallway apologizing that he could not be more hospitable, here in his home. "My driver will take you to the hotel. Please use all of its facilities; you are our guest there. Be sure to dine there. There's a fine chef and an ample wine cellar. Don't hesitate to order the best. Perhaps you will find someone to dine with you. It's always better with a companion."

As he settled into the rear seat of the waiting Mercedes Rush wondered about Jose, a widower, and whether his closing comment was because he too often had to dine alone. He also noted that there was no outward show of concern for Vuk as a person, only as a problem that could, if no satisfactory answer was provided, cause complications for Isla to threaten its privacy as well as Jose's. Rush now, if he hadn't fully admitted it before, realized he had been called to provide an acceptable report, enough to satisfy the local authorities, should they ever raise questions. In other words, Jose expected him to explain the disappearance as an act of nature, due to the storm, or alternatively, that Vuk took his own life, and somehow, in the process cast his body into the sea, committing it to the deep. Either way Isla Cresciente would be protected.

The driver carried his case to the front desk of a very expensive looking Hotel before giving a slight bow then he was gone before Rush could offer a tip. Rush waited until the counter cleared of those ahead of him. He slid over his passport and credit card and immediately the clerk's disinterest was replaced by an effusive beaming smile and a welcome to the Castillo. His fingers snapped, the credit card returned as not needed, and suddenly a porter had his bag as well as the card to his room. Rush, realizing that he needed to exchange his dwindling supply of twenties into smaller denominations, took out his wallet to exchange some twenties into fives. As the porter opened the door to his room he unfolded one in preparation.

CHAPTER THIRTEEN

What he wasn't prepared for was the size of his room. You couldn't call it just a room; even being called a suite might have been slightly insulting. After he was left alone, he crossed the spacious sitting room to the sliding doors leading to a large balcony with views south over the city then to the sea. A bar was already set with much the same array of snacks and drinks that he had seen before at the home of Jose Fuentes. The tiled washroom could have bathed a small harem and the bedroom, over bedded with two Queens, again had a walkout to the balcony. He took out his cell phone, that he had yet to use on this trip, and snapped images of each room. He would need to show these to both his father and Lou as a mere verbal description would not have done justice.

The porter had picked up a manila envelope and placed it on a large executive desk. This would be from one of Jose's assistants with additional information on Edo. Opening it he found a copy of Edo's hand written application to the Academy in Miami, dated over a year ago. Rush scanned it. It showed that Edo would now be twenty-three, born in an undecipherable village or town in Yugoslavia. In Rush's recollection this was in the last few years of Yugoslavia while still an entity, before splintering. The Visa Application, to be a student for a three-month course under the tutoring of Dr. D. Newton on Isla Cresciente, gave no new information.

The only conclusion that Rush came to was that both Vuk and Edo, despite their age difference in years, came roughly from the same corner of the world, a corner of historical and ongoing conflict, if technically just short of actual war. This was a thread, a connection, that offered the best line of future inquiry.

He now realized he had not been in touch with anyone back home. A quick call to his father found he was fine, only wondering why Rush would be even concerned as to how he was doing. The conversation was brief but served its purpose. Next was a call to Lou, now at home. He was envious of Rush's tropical locale and described the sleet and snow blowing outside.

"Anything on Birdie?"

"No, still missing. I think the brass is now not sure what to do. I've heard that she never did directly accuse you at the hospital. As she couldn't talk, she only waved your card about and nodded when asked if it had been you. That won't stick and they know it."

Rush knew that this accusation, even unproven, left a lot of presumed guilt stuck to him, that would be waiting for him when he returned. Lou told him the unit was managing, somehow, to survive without him and their new addition seemed competent.

After the disconnect, Rush's mind switched back to his own problems and away from those of David and Jose. He snapped open a beer pouring it into a tall crystal glass, walked out to the balcony, the lights of the city glimmering below and further out the glistening of the rising moon on the waves. Well, Jose had told him to enjoy tonight and he might as well take advantage of the invitation.

First would be a shave and shower. As he stripped the walls of multiple mirrors in the opulent bathroom seemed to shrink his body down, in every proportion, within this expanse, to insignificance. This was not new for Rush. Since puberty he had never strode around in any change room, or bedroom, with masculine self-confidence. He concentrated on his face and, after shaving, almost swam inside a shower with adjustable heads and with enough room, Rush thought, for a 'menage a trois', or even more.

Drying off with a rug sized towel he saw the phone on the wall and thought about tomorrow's morning trip to Miami then to home in the early evening. He asked the front desk to connect him with the airline and soon had confirmation of his flights. Taking Jose's blanket invitation to use all the benefits of the Hotel, his next call was to request a pick up of clothing, that he would need by early morning, for cleaning. This took all of Rush's limited Spanish to be understood but he had less trouble when next connected to the dining room.

"Si, Senor…a table for...si, Señor,..para?...si, para uno...Que hora?... si, Senor, seven-thirty...a tie?...no Senor, not necessary…a jacket?...si, recomendado...no es un problema...tenemos...we supply...tu talla?…talla?...

tu size?...si forty...cuarenta...si Senor your jacket and your table await you at seven-thirty…Buenas Tardes."

Dressing in his last clean also most presentable clothes he turned on the television to quickly find both American and British channels. He flipped between the two to catch up on international news finding, fortunately, that no major wars, recessions, floods, earthquakes, political upheavals had occurred over the last few days that he'd been out of touch. However, there were lots of minor, still serious,political issues that the newscasts, particularly the American, were trumpeting up in importance. The door buzzed and it was the pick up of his laundry. With still over a half hour before dinner he, with a sudden whim, thinking it could do no harm to try, picked up the phone and asked to be connected to Senorita Lebow's room. He was nervous as it rang but a message, first in Spanish, then in English, asked that the caller leave a message.

"Hello, Marielle. It's Rush here...Rush Sterne...look…" he stumbled, as if still a teen-ager. "I've been fortunate, courtesy of Jose Fuentes, to have an expense paid...a carte blanche....in their main dining room. If you are hungry and desperate for company I have a reservation for seven-thirty. If you have other plans then I guess, since I'm leaving here early tomorrow, I'll say my goodbye now…Adios."

Precisely at seven-thirty the maitre'd had a linen jacket, a pastel that even matched his shirt, ready for him. His table was obviously a choice location, at the edge of open windows overlooking the city and sea beyond. A large heavy leather covered wine list and a similar tome like menu were presented. The wine selection was broad, international and well above Rush's normal budget, but he decided to take advantage of Jose's generosity. When his waiter came to take his order he chose a half bottle of a Premier Chablis and then taking further advantage of Jose's offer, a half of a Third Growth Bordeaux. The waiter asked if he'd be dining alone. Rush looked at his watch and raised just one finger so the waiter began to remove the setting opposite him but then, looking past Rush, began to reset it just in time to stand back to allow the maitre'd to pull back the empty chair. "Senorita."

Rush tried to get up, not smoothly, as Marielle, after a smiling "Gracias", slipped gracefully into her chair. Rush quickly grinned, in hopes that, if his mouth had been open, this might cover his surprise. If his face had flushed he couldn't do anything about that. Fortunately Marielle seemed perfectly at ease.

"I thank you, and I suppose Jose as well. I don't like eating alone when I'm away and I needed a reason to dress up, if just a bit."

That 'bit', to Rush, looked perfect. A cream blouse with gold flecks and a scarf, blue and gold mixing artfully. He couldn't see what was below the table but could only assume that Marielle was wearing a matching shade.

"When I checked in I wondered if I should have trusted your friend to book a hotel for me. My company has limits on what they reimburse in expenses but then saw the billing, it was very reasonable so I assume I'm getting a cut rate. My room isn't cut rate; it's really very nice, roomy with a small sitting area."

Rush finally joined the conversation rushing to add, "You should..." A silent bell warned him not to finish with 'You should see mine!'. He covered, finding other words, "...have given David some credit. Perhaps to make up for the little battle between you two."

"You warned him about me, about Antioch's problem, didn't you?"

"No, not at all"

The waiter was at his side with the half bottle of the white. Rush asked Marielle if she would like a glass of Chablis. Her answer was quick, "Certainement." Rush at first confused the waiter, who thought Rush was refusing the wine, but Marielle's Spanish quickly clarified that Rush now wanted a full bottle. "Of both Senor?" Rush nodded, silently thanking Jose but wondering if his very attractive dinner partner might think he was using wine as a step to seduction. If she did, she kept it to herself.

The wine was brought quickly and ceremoniously shown to Rush then a little poured for tasting. Rush sniffed, then sipped, allowing the expected few seconds that suggested he was an expert, before nodding his approval. The Chablis was at a perfect temperature and, as wine does, soon smoothed over any bumps or barriers that might have pre-existed between Marielle and Rush. They began a comfortable exchange of impressions of their brief hours in Republica's Capital City, then broadened to their individual knowledge of different countries. Marielle's was wider than Rush's and he was a little surprised when she explained she was born in Connecticut but raised in France, not far from Paris, until she was twelve, then returning to this side of the Atlantic.

"And your Spanish? How did that happen?'

Marielle, from practise, never wanting to reveal much about herself, remained vague, "I became part of a family that spoke Spanish and French at home, English and French at school. Fortunately languages came easily, being young."

Rush had studied French enough to be able to read, but he'd never been able to converse fluently. He wanted to ask more questions about her past, and if he could manage to do so, about her present status, but the waiter was back to their table, ready for their order. Based on a first glance at the menu, Rush had considered having the male reliable: Caesar Salad, then Surf and Turf. Marielle had opened her small purse to slide on half-rimmed glasses, then had taken time to review the menu and after a few questions, in Spanish, concerning the fish entrees, she chose one, preceded by a small salad with blue cheese. Rush decided he'd have the same.

Marielle now took up the questioning, pressing Rush on the reason he was at Isla Cresciente. Rush didn't want to be evasive but did slide around the truth, without actually lying. Marielle had to accept simply that there was a problem, the problem hadn't yet been resolved, but Rush hoped that his stop in Miami would clarify matters.

"And, after Miami, you're heading home, back to your desk at Police Headquarters?"

Rush then had to admit he was under suspension and would be mostly sitting at home awaiting a decision. Without too much prompting, he covered the disappearance of yet another young woman in their City and how a normal follow-up interview found him accused and, for the time being, shelved. Marielle asked a lot of pointed, intelligent questions about his duties in general and then specifically about the suspension and why he hadn't hired a lawyer to represent himself. Rush pointed out he had yet to be formally charged but didn't add that, if the charges disappeared but the stigma didn't, he might simply resign.

He'd joined the Force as an expedient, to provide for Ana and their coming child. It wasn't his first choice as a career and he wasn't really sure why he'd stayed, long after Ana and Stefan had disappeared from his life. As their salads were placed down, Rush now realized that Marielle had been asking about his life. He needed to talk about hers.

"You left France at twelve. Did you ever go back?"

"Mais oui. Three times. The first to take my mother's ashes for burial in the village where she'd been born and raised. The second was with... with a friend...and back again, alone, just two years ago. And you, you've must have seen Paris?"

"Only there once...by myself. I'd been in England for David's wedding, then had a few great days, all spent in Paris. I must have walked miles and miles. Even when it rained I just kept walking. I committed cardinal sins though. I didn't go up the Eiffel Tower, only saw the exterior of the Louvre, didn't take a boat trip on the Seine, and never used the Metro. I just got lost admiring the architecture, the markets, the people. I fell in love with thousands of women of Paris, of all ages, although I never had the courage to use my halting French on them."

"I'll bet that your good buddy would have…" She slowed to erase her intended words choosing instead to make a statement within a question. "You and David are...well…quite different, aren't you?"

"His mother always said I was a good influence on her son but really... he gave me a lot in return."

"Such as?" asked Marielle.

"Well, he gave me confidence, supported whatever I wanted to do."

"Were you needing support?"

Their salads arrived just in time to relieve Rush from answering a question that he would have had trouble doing. They then reviewed the people they had met on Isla. They agreed that both felt that there should be strict criteria for assisted death but neither could really fault those who had flown only one way to the island with them. As much as Rush enjoyed the food it was her company that had him enjoy every minute and, when she remembered something pleasant, seeing the smile that accompanied the thought. Rush now had his first sip of the Bordeaux and Marielle's glass was refilled with the Chablis. Her meal choice had been more than just tasteful and whatever the Chef had mixed gently with the fish was artful. Rush, content as a king, as much with Marielle as with the food and wine, didn't want the spell to be broken but, as they both set aside their forks aside to sip more wine, Rush asked.

"You told me earlier you had a sister. Do you live together?" Rush thought this a subtle question would determine her current household arrangement.

"Not now but we did live together after Maman died. I was just eighteen, Sylvie nearly eleven. My mother asked me to keep us together, not be separated even though she gave me fair warning, it wouldn't be easy. She was accurate in calling Sylvie's mind a drawer 'plein de chaussettes' but I suppose most young teens are the same."

"You weren't?"

"Not quite the same...but hardly perfect."

Their waiter was again hovering, trying not to be too intrusive but anxious to offer dessert menus. Marielle simply set hers aside giving a polite but firm negative nod.

She reached for her glass but the waiter, seeing the white gone, quickly poured the Bordeaux into a clean glass.

"I don't often drink red, despite being French, but …" She sniffed the rim, "...the bouquet is nice…" now taking a sip then smiling "...it's like drinking violets. What is it?"

"French. Bordeaux. More accurately Margaux. Perhaps my favorite wine."

Marielle took a few more sips, obviously enjoying them but then placed her glass down. "Rush, I really do thank you. This has been a lovely dinner but I never did sleep well on the island and tomorrow will be busy so I think I should catch up on my sleep. I do hope your Miami investigations are successful and that your problems back home clear up."

Then she was up. Rush rose as well and turned to watch her walk away. He noticed a table of four middle-aged men also had their eyes fixated on her body as she walked by. He gave them what he hoped was a warning glare but two of them smiled back as if congratulating his choice of a dinner companion. Perhaps they also wondered why she had left him alone. Rush knew. He'd been 'quite nice' but obviously boring. He sat there, after convincing the waiter that he didn't need dessert, cognac or coffee. Even with his glass topped up there was still half a bottle of very good Margaux left. He then noticed a young couple sitting at a table a distance back of the view of the city outside. The man was studying the massive wine list. Rush suspected that this may have been a first date and guessed that the prices were intimidating. He called over his waiter, requested two clean wine glasses and, on arrival poured the rest of the red wine equally into each. He hoped his waiter understood what 'with compliments of the house' was in Spanish as he directed they be taken over to the young couple. Rush didn't watch their reaction as he pulled out four twenties to leave beside his plate. He knew that there would be no charge for this sumptuous dinner.

Back in his room he walked outside to enjoy the view. The city spread out to provide a blanket of lights leading to the sea, there to mix with the moon's brushstrokes that tipped its waves. Although impressive his mind reverted back to the dining room. He turned back into the suite and decided he wouldn't dwell on what he could have said to keep Marielle's interest, to have her stay with him just a little longer. She must have found him too dull to want to linger. He would just have to be content with the remembrance of what there was and not the might have been. He pictured her peering at the menu, the small glasses low on her nose, looking almost like a school teacher. If she had been, he could imagine all the boys in the class being secretly in love with her. He stopped, now asking himself if he was as well. He quickly set this aside, dismissing the thought. He hardly knew her. Simply finding her attractive wasn't enough for love. He certainly was no expert on what would qualify as love. Thinking back to Ana he had been sure he was in love but, his mind scanning the past, he now had to assume he must have been, but there were no embers, only ashes, left to stay in his memory.

There was a sudden buzz at the door and for just a second his imagination pictured Marielle but it was a maid bringing his laundered clothes, ready for Miami. Another reach for a bill then she was gone. Thinking of his early flight, he called to have a wake-up for five-thirty. He flipped on the television scanning the available movies, only a few of which he had ever heard of. Seeing the titles of the pornographic movies they were crude enough, by themselves, to dispel any further interest. The news highlights again suggested that nothing was imminently dangerous, at least in the Western Hemisphere, and Rush was soon into the bedroom where the covers were drawn back and a ribboned package of two chocolates lay on the pillow. He put them aside before undressing. They wouldn't be needed tonight.

CHAPTER FOURTEEN

At the airport he had only time to grab a cup of coffee, drinkable, and a bagel-like bun, tasteless, before his flight was called. The airline's inflight 'breakfast snack' had a better bagel, with cheese, but disgusting coffee. Before long he was landing in Miami.

After Customs, he found a payphone to call Edo's school. Yes, the Director, Senor Artur Arrendi, had been notified and Rush was expected this morning. The cab took time to extricate itself from the airport but soon was cruising through traffic, passing palm trees and neon signs, to pull into a commercial park with a group of similar two-storey buildings. The school's sign was a discreet 'Academy/Academia' with arrows pointing up the driveway. His driver pulled into one of the few spots available to the side of the front entry. Not knowing how long he might be he paid and tipped the driver. In response the driver said he needed gas, a washroom as well as a coffee and would come back in an hour, just in case he might be needed. Rush gave him a thumbs up sign, pulled out a five, "Here's your coffee."

A young slim woman, perhaps twenty, greeted him with a smile. The interior was cool and bright. She directed him down the hall to a half opened door signed: *ARTUR ARRENDI, Director*. Rush thought it interesting that the name was more dominant than the title. Artur literally sprang out from behind his desk, his hand extended, "Buenos Dias...Good Morning Senor Sterne. Be most welcome. Would you like coffee?"

Without waiting for an answer, Artur buzzed his phone and ordered some. While waiting, Rush was asked about his flight, whether he'd been in Miami before, how long he planned to stay, which stretched out the few minutes necessary for fresh coffee to arrive. Normally Rush wouldn't have even tried to have three coffees in a day, let alone before lunch, but he found this cup rich, tasteful yet mellow. As they drank Artur slid a folder over to Rush: #1419-EDO VANTAR.

It contained the original of his application to the school. Then there was a photocopy of his EU Passport. Only the front page was copied, giving no clue from any internal pages as to other countries he might have visited. Scholastically there was a transcript from a 'Technicali' then his marks through his first two semesters at this location.

"I see his grades were not good to start with but then improved."

"Yes." Artur replied. "At first it seemed as if Ed, that's what we called him, had not made a good choice of this profession. It's not easy you know...to be dealing with the...the deceased. It can be...a bit messy. After his first few months I called him to my office giving him an opportunity to reconsider whether he should stay in our programme. He said it was important, very important for his family, that he continue. We gave him some additional assistance and, as you can, see his marks improved."

Rush now asked, "Was it well known that a semester was available at Isla Cresciente?"

"Indeed. We have no crematoria facility here. Local Regulations don't permit it. It's common for one of our male students to be accepted, although other schools, connected to us throughout the Caribbean, can put forth applicants as well. It's always a plus to have crematoria experience on your resume. Normally we wouldn't have sent Ed, not having completed his first full year here, but an opening arose and he was anxious to go so he was sent."

"An opening?"

"Yes, our first applicant was accepted but, almost at the last minute, well...a few days before he was to go, he decided not to. Then Ed came to my office and made a strong case that he be sent and so that was that."

"I assume you have classes today and that I can interview Edo... er...Ed?"

Arrendi frowned: "Senor Fuentes did not inform you?"

"Of what?"

"He resigned from the school. You see, in the folder, his letter?"

It was the last page that Rush had not yet reached.

Senor Assendi, Director:

I must inform you that I will not be able to continue my studies at your illustrious Academy. This very much disappoints me but is unfortunately necessary. My family needs my immediate attention and I must return to them. I thank you and your staff for the instruction and guidance provided to me. Please give my particular thanks to Senor Pacqueso.

Most Sincerely........Edo Vantar"

"Did he deliver this here? To the School?" asked Rush

"It was left in our mailbox, at our front door. I presume by him."

"Have you tried to contact him?"

"I asked Senor Pacqueso to call him but he informs me he was unsuccessful."

"May I speak to Senor Pacqueso?"

"Certainly. Let me check whether he has finished teaching his class. If so he'll be at lunch."

After a brief phone call Rush was advised that Humberto Pacqueso was available and would meet him at the school's cafeteria. The Director took Rush out into the hall, then down a stairway. The smell of food and the buzz of conversations met him before he turned the corner into a compact cafeteria. After introductions, After Rush declined an offer of yet another coffee, they sat down. Humberto was eager to answer Rush's questions. Yes, he'd called Ed's phone number but there'd been no answer. The next day he drove to Ed's apartment but he wasn't in and the building manager was unavailable so he had left a note on Ed's mailbox asking him to call. That was four days ago and there'd been no call. Humberto had asked some of the other students where Ed might be but no one could help. He said that Ed's English was not fully fluent. He read and wrote it well but often was lost in any extended conversation. Combined with his serious nature, as well as his very limited Spanish, he was a bit of a loner, no real close friends among the other students.

Rush, recalling the Director's comment that Ed had not originally been qualified to transfer for a semester at Isla, asked Humberto about this. All he could say was that the original candidate had, only a week before he was to leave, asked if he could postpone this assignment. In turn, he had recommended Ed, a friend, as his replacement.

"I thought you said Ed had few friends."

"He had some although I wasn't aware that Mike was one of them."

"Would Mike be available?"

Humberto looked around, "Yes, he's just over there."

Rush was introduced and pulled out a chair to sit opposite Mike. Two other students who'd been sitting with Mike took their cue from Humberto, so that Rush was left alone with Mike, an athletic young man, looking more like a potential Phys-Ed teacher than a Mortician.

"I'm told you decided not to go to Isla Cresciente and recommended Ed as a replacement. You were good friends?"

"Well, you get to know all of the students here, some better than others, so yes, I guess you could call us friends, but not outside the Academy, just in here."

"May I ask you why you decided not to go?"

"Uhmm…well …" Mike looked around, then at the floor and then, in a softer voice carrying only as far as Rush, admitted, "...perhaps I shouldn't tell you. You won't tell anyone else, will you?...Good...Well, Ed came to me...told me he really wanted to go there and was willing to make it worth my while if I agreed to withdraw and recommend him."

"What was the offer?" asked Rush

"I'd prefer not to say how much but the deal was that he'd pay me half of it to go to the Director. If I'd recommend Ed and he was accepted I'd get the other half. Even if he wasn't I could keep the first bit." Mike stopped, perhaps looking for approval. "I needed the money and a girl I'd been seeing...she wasn't promising to wait for three months while I was on Isla. Ed was so keen to go, so it was a deal that made sense, all around, like, you know, everyone ended up happy."

Humberto asked if there was anything more they could assist with but Rush thanked him but said 'no'. Soon he was out of the Academy and into Florida's midday sun. A cab was parked under the shade of a tree. It was his driver, windows open, seat back, taking a nap. Rush thanked him for waiting.

"No problem, Senor. Where next?"

Once seated, Rush checked the address that had been listed on Edo's registration card.

"No problem, Senor. It's not far."

Ten minutes later the cab pulled into a parking lot. The building was a two-story Six- Plex. Inside a mailbox still labelled Edo's name on it. Rush could see, stuffed inside, papers looking more like advertising than anything else. There was a buzzer over the Box. Rush tried it four or five times. He was about to try again but there was a quick staccato of heels coming down the stairwell. An attractive young woman didn't stop but, seeing Rush's finger over Edo's box, blurted "He's left" over her shoulder before she was out the main door and gone. Rush stuck a foot out to keep the interior door open then turned back to the letter boxes. One was 'A. Miranda, Mgr' and he stretched to press this buzzer and waited. As he was pressing a second time a door clicked in the hallway and he turned to see a tired looking woman, still in a housecoat, calling out.

"Wha'da you want?"

Rush quickly went into the hall towards her half opened door, the blare of a television ad backing her.

"Hello, I'm here to see if Edo's in."

"You mean Ed? No, he's not. He's gone."

"When was that?"

"A few days back. Let's see…five or six."

"Where did he go?"

"He said back home."

"Where's that?"

"Jeez, I don't know what it's called. Back there. Somewhere in Europe."

"Did he say he'd be back?"

"No. He's paid up to the end of the month. If he's not back by then I'll clean it out. It's furnished but they always leave a mess. He was a quiet guy. Good tenant. I had no problems. You interested in renting?"

"No, but did he leave an address, back home, so you could send him his mail?"

"No...nothing. Anything else?"

There wasn't and Rush let her get back to her television show. Back into the waiting cab his driver asked, "What now Senor, where to?"

As they headed to the Airport, Rush realized he reached the end of the trail, at least on this side of the Atlantic. If David, Jose, or the authorities in the Republica wanted to go further they'd have to find Edo and question him, but this wasn't his call. In reflection, he now considered it better that he'd not found Edo, a young man who clearly had a purpose to reach Isla, and then, after leaving it, immediately went further, presumably back to the safety of his native country. In between these two moves was the disappearance of Vuk. The connection of their upbringing imprinted a pointed finger at Edo being somehow involved in Vuk's disappearance. Rush had no authority to take his investigation any further and was now glad to leave the questions and the eventual answer behind him.

He tipped his driver well and wandered into the cavernous avenues inside Miami International with an hour before boarding time. He bought a copy of the New York Times then remembered Jimmy, his 'Little Brother'. It wasn't hard to find a sportswear store and he bought a Miami Heat Jersey. He'd overpaid but it would be worth it. Jimmy was crazy about most sports but particularly basketball, even dreaming one day, as young boys do, that he'd eventually be playing in the N.B.A.

As his plane waited its turn, a just landed plane taxied across the runway, he wondered if that was a plane coming in from the Republica and if Marielle was on it. Then as his plane noisily lumbered onto the runway, gaining momentum, he thought about her planned stay in Miami. Would she dine alone, or not? Would she sleep alone, or not? Then the jet, with one hundred and ninety three people encapsulated, lifted aloft, its wheels clunking to nestle underneath, its nose pointing them towards New York City.

CHAPTER FIFTEEN

He called his father from the airport asking if he needed any groceries. Russell was emphatic in his usual denial that he needed any assistance. Since it was now nearly eight Rush knew his father had already finished his supper and would be sitting in front of the television watching his usual choice of news, documentaries, sports and old movies, rarely watching anything else.

Rush stopped at the local delicatessen for soup, salad, a fresh roll and milk. Soon he was in through the rear entry to his lower compact apartment at 167 Waterburn Drive, his home since he was brought back by anxious new parents from the hospital. After his mother's death, his father had suggested that they trade places and Rush move to the main level. Neither needed the extra two bedrooms but Rush was content to stay below so that arrangement remained unchanged. They did continue with the twice a month cleaning service that had been arranged for the last few months of his mother's weakening life.

After a quick visit upstairs to say hello to his father he was back downstairs. He and Russell didn't hug; only a wave from Rush, a nod from his Dad, seemed enough. Eleanor had showered affection on both of them, with her words, her arms, her smiles and after she died, neither father nor son had been able to fill the void she had left in their family.

Rush's father had left his mail on the table. There were two bills, the rest junk mail. He checked his voicemail. Lou's message asked that he call once he was back but added there were no new developments in either finding Birdie or word that Rush's suspension might be lifted. Rush decided he'd call Lou in the morning. His email had more junk, pleas for money and a reminder to renew his membership at the Badminton Club. He immediately wrote a cheque and added a note of concern to the Club's Secretary/Treasurer, the delightful but ailing Anstey Fairchild. He then heated the soup and soon was sitting, as he often did, well accustomed to have dinner alone, listening to the Jazz station. After cleaning up, he laundered the clothes that he brought back from Republica.

It was now close to ten and it had been a long day so Rush took his borrowed book, having Catton as his bedmate, reading only a chapter before putting it aside. Now his memory scanned back over the week: meeting Manuel at the Casa, then the Sandersons, Winston, Jose and Marielle. Despite the morbid weight of Isla, he was glad he'd gone there and wondered now, if by chance, here back in the City that he might meet or at least catch a glimpse of Marielle as she passed him on the street. Before he sank into sleep he chided himself with "Dream On." Within moments he was.

***

Next morning, fully rested, Rush was quickly dressed and up the stairs to begin the preparation of breakfast, a full breakfast, as if this was a B&B out in the country. The smell of bacon drew his father to the kitchen with "What's the occasion?"

"Nothing special. Just thought we should catch up with each other."

Russell's week had been uneventful, only if you could ignore the stock market had lost nearly two percent. Rush's review of his week engrossed his father who stored up his questions until his son finished with his meeting with Jose Fuentes. Rush made no mention of Marielle Lebow

"This guy...Vug...Vuk..whatever...he's dead, right?"

"Ninety-nine percent dead."

"Suicide? An accident?"

"Possibly...but, in either case there should be some trace of a body."

"Maybe carried away by the storm?"

"Again possible, but to me, unlikely."

"Leaving murder...by...?"

"Edo is the prime suspect but he'd need to be questioned and that's not within my control."

"Uhmm...You need Agatha Christie to help you. She always ends a mystery with a solution...but let's leave yours unsolved. So tell me...how's that devil David doing?"

Russell and Eleanor had only met David three times, both quickly falling for his adventurous charm although they had private concerns that their son might be too much under David's spell so Russell calling David a 'devil' was not totally in jest.

"Well he seems temporarily satisfied...only giving injections." Rush now fully explained the purpose and function of Isla Cresciente and David's dominant role there. Afterward his father then posed the question, "You sound as if you're not in agreement."

"I'll admit that assisted dying should be available. I have trouble making it too available." Rush then questioned back, "What do you think?"

Russell leaned back, stroking his cheek, before answering. "As you get older, you get closer to death. Some fear it but, I think, most accept it as long as they have a reasonable quality of life before it ends. Now when I attend a funeral...which is getting too common...those my age say the suffering is over if there had been months or even years of dying but if someone drops dead on the golf course we say, with a bit of envy, what a way to go. So I guess I can say that you don't have to be terminal to make a choice. As you get older the queue ahead of you gets shorter. I can't object if someone has a valid reason to jump in ahead of me." He then asked, as if a little embarrassed by the direction the topic was going, "So how is David really doing?"

"I think he's treading water, but not sure where to go next. He's simplified his life. He feels he is helping people, even though now his Hippocratic Oath has gone one-eighty. His self-control lasts just shy of a month and then he compacts all his excesses into a few days at a nearby resort. It's a little sad to see his talents diverted and, I guess, also diluted but then again I wouldn't want the pressure of high risk surgery, someone's life in your hands. He's never told me ..." Rush's father knew his son would never have asked. "...what messed up his marriage and why he left London to volunteer with Medecins in Africa, but that was sure to burn out someone like David."

Russell gave that a moment's thought then gave his opinion: "So David thinks he now has control of his life by keeping a safe distance from real life."

His son couldn't disagree with this summation so, after a few minutes silence as Rush cleared up the breakfast dishes, they moved their conversation back to their own lives. Rush confirmed that his suspension might last a bit longer but he had hopes for reinstatement. He then asked his father his plans for the day.

"Nothing at all, but tomorrow I have an appointment with the dentist."

"Any problems?"

"No, just a usual check-up but did I tell you that Harry was retiring? Selling his practise to a young guy." He stopped to think. "He's not yet seventy but when your hands start to shake then messing in a mouth with a drill isn't a good idea, is it?"

***

That same evening Walter Starbuski had arranged his stop at Dr. Arnold's office directly at six, both to catch his women coming to start their cleaning as well as to see Larry Arnold as he was finishing the day at his dental clinic. The timing was perfect as Larry was just putting on his coat.

"Hi Doc."

The dentist's face showed he was not pleased to see Walter.

"Doc, I need some more scripts."

Larry hesitated. "Look I can only give you a few..." He was immediately interrupted by Walter's "I need more than just a few."

"Sorry, I can't risk it. There's word out there that the College and the Police will be setting up...maybe already have...algorithms with the larger pharmacies' computers to check on the volume of opioids prescribed. A check might flag my name. Then we'd both be in trouble."

"Both? Doc you'd be in double trouble if you spilled my name."

Larry had always been afraid of both this man and their 'business' arrangement but his debts from Dental College plus buying a retiring dentist's practice forced him to give blank scripts in return for cash. He still needed the money but he'd sleep better if he could cancel, then walk away from their deal. "O.K. I'll give you six, for the month, but spread out the dates. Use them with the smaller independent druggists. There will be less chance of a computer check."

He went to his office and was soon out with an envelope. He didn't say good-bye, "Lock up. You have the key. I'll expect your...um...envelope in a week."

"No problem, same as usual Doc. My girls will be here soon…" He looked at his watch and said "...they're already late" as Larry was shutting the door and was gone.

Ten minutes later the lock was tried, the door clicked open, and two women were surprised to see their employer who only pointed at his watch. Immediately they set to cleaning the office avoiding his eyes bearing on them. He thought he might dock them a half hour's pay just to make sure they knew who was boss. Then he left.

***

With all his domestic duties done, his desk cleared of invoices and dues now paid, Rush sat down at his small desk to compose his report for David and Jose. He scanned the notes he had compiled in Real Republica. He really didn't need to refresh his memory; it was only to settle on a logical order to follow. Then he clicked on his computer, opened and titled a new file to begin typing, efficiently but short on speed. His fingers had never blurred with dexterity at the keyboard but they unfolded his thoughts, assembling letters into words, sentences into paragraphs for an orderly review of what was known and, more difficult, to assess the relevance of the assumptions that could be made from the holes left in the loose fabric woven from facts and suppositions.

Finished, he pulled his chair back, went to the fridge, poured out a glass of cool water then returned to his seat. Normally, after doing the first draft of a report, he'd prefer to wait then revisit and revise to the extent necessary. However this wasn't a normal report designed for Police Records, but one that might only be read by David and Jose but also might, after translation into Spanish, be read by many. Could this open Rush to criticism, even censure, by the Authorities in the Republica? Could he be called back, subpoenaed by officials there, to give evidence of a crime?

He reviewed his own words but now as if he was a critical analytic outsider. He was cognizant of his bias in protecting David's supervision of his staff and, by extension, protecting Jose's founding and funding of a secluded island whose function ran contrary to the mores of a Catholic country. After a final review he felt he'd followed the line of facts with no proveable accusations or misdeeds but very clearly leaving the gate wide open for the necessity to interview Edo Vantar. This was needed to rule out

Edo's potential involvement in, or knowledge of, Vuk's disappearance. If none, the storm was the vehicle that had conveyed Vuk's body away into the waters of the Caribbean. Whether Vuk had volunteered himself or fought the elements would remain as a matter of conjecture.

Although not entirely satisfied, wondering whether the report should be more aggressive, he printed out three copies. Purposefully and protectively he left it without any acknowledgement deciding to only attach a short letter, simply noting that the report covered his brief investigation on Isla Creciente in hopes that it would assist any further inquiry into the matter, should that be necessary. He did sign the letter but only as 'Rushton Sterne' with no acknowledgement that he was a Police Officer.

Rush left the report and letter on the table, still not comfortable with its avoidance of any concluding opinion. His apartment was small but still large enough for him to see the elephant sitting quietly in the corner, looking directly at him. He acknowledged its presence by admitting "Yes, not only did I not find what happened to Vuk, I'm copping out of making a conclusion. Yes, I'm passing the buck back to Jose. If he wants to search Europe to find Edo, that will be his decision."

The elephant remained silent as Rush sealed the report to be expressed to Real Republica. He suspected that, once received, it would be filed away, only to be used if Vuk's absence was brought to the attention of the Police. Vuk had no known family, certainly no friends, no one to miss him. He would be a Missing Person who might remain missing.

CHAPTER SIXTEEN

"Hi Rush, it's Lou. Got a bit of info on Birdie"

Lou then conveyed what he had heard from the Drug Unit. They had a 'Robin Partridge' in their Data Bank. Never charged. Found in a raid on a Meth house. Whatever she had bought she'd ditched before the officers had a chance to interview her. A second note was when she was suspected of selling opioids on the street. The squad had stopped a buyer who pointed Birdie out as his supplier but Birdie was one step ahead; they'd found nothing on her. The Unit's opinion was that she was a meth addict but probably went 'Doctor Shopping' to get a supply of opioids that she could sell to support her Meth addiction.

"Thanks Lou for the update. Everything O.K.?"

"Sure. Fine. I'll keep going on this. Hope to see you back at your desk...soon."

Rush hung up appreciative of the update as well as hearing from Lou. In the last few months Rush had noticed a slight change in Lou. He seemed to be preoccupied with something.

Lou Contile and Rush, rarely met outside the office, but they had established a solid comfortable friendship within, despite the pressures of work. They had different upbringings and lifestyles. Lou had been raised in a large family and, after his lusting for the shapely Maria had been successful, but requiring matrimony, then had fathered three children. The two older girls had been raised, with some brief episodes as teen-agers, successfully but their now sixteen year old son aggravated his parents almost daily.

Lou had more pressing problems than his son. One was solvable but at a financial cost. This was the upcoming marriage of his eldest daughter. He knew it wouldn't be a small wedding but every day the list of guests became larger and the wedding more costly. His wife was insistent that no close relatives could be left out, without giving offense. The problem was that all relatives were 'close'. Lou had no choice but to agree, grumbling but defeated, especially since he had a second problem. It was not as easy to solve.

Gabriella Lucci and Lou had known each other since she had married his cousin Marcello. At their wedding Lou wondered why such a good looking woman, said to be smart too, had married Marcello. It wasn't that he was ugly or dumb, but his lack of self-control was well known to the family, the neighbourhood and some of the local cops. Five months later a baby daughter answered his question. A progression of Marriages, Baptisms, First Communions, Funerals all guaranteed that, connected by family, Lou and Gabriella would meet, exchange polite hugs but nothing more. Last summer, at a Sixtieth Anniversary Celebration, they suddenly found themselves alone at a table. As Lou looked into her sympathetic face, seeming so attentive to his words, he suddenly became embarrassed and self-conscious. Maria had shown little interest in him lately. She was consumed by the constant needs of her widowed mother, the wedding plans, their troublesome son, as well as her efforts to lose weight, so far showing little success. As a result, most evenings, Lou disappeared down stairs to his workshop, crafting interesting but rarely used items.

A month later they met again by chance. Lou had stopped to pick up a coffee then saw Gabriella sitting alone looking out the window. He could have walked away but instead, after a deep breath, he walked over to her table. Her immediate smile encouraged him to sit down. At first they chatted about their family connections, then their children. They avoided any mention of their spouses. Finally Lou was surprised to check his watch. Nearly an hour had sped by, his coffee only half gone, now cold. He stood up abruptly, apologizing for taking so much of her time, saying a quick good-bye.

Lou began to stop at the same coffee shop whenever he could manage. He felt like a school boy recalling his teenage days when he hoped to intercept or, at the least, cross paths with that good looking girl from the nearby Girl's School but she was always protected with a crowd of other girls and he never had a chance to meet her or even learn her name.

Three weeks later Gabriella came in, as he sat at the same window seat as she had done. She had ordered a coffee at the counter and turned to leave but then saw Lou. He was only expecting a brief smile, a finger wave, but she came over and sat down, facing him. Again time passed all too quickly until they both sat back, glanced at their watches with guilt, said their 'Ciaos' and left by different doorways. He realized that what he was feeling was more than a school boy crush. He wasn't sure what to do about it. If it continued at the same innocent enough level he'd accept it; he would be happy enough. Yet he continued, whenever he could, to be drawn towards the same coffee shop.

On the fourth of these 'accidental' meetings Lou summoned up his courage and looked into her eyes. "Do you think that people are beginning to notice?"

"Notice?"

"You and me...that we meet here."

"You're right." She sipped slowly from her cup raising her head to look directly into his eyes. "I suppose we could meet somewhere else, in case we've been noticed here."

Three weeks later they arranged a meeting, in Room 1122, at Hotel Royale. After closing the door Lou turned to face her, unsure of what his next step should be. Then he took off his jacket, pulled off his tie, unbuttoned the top button of his shirt. Gabriella stood, facing him, then began to loosen the top of her blouse. Button by button they continued. Slowly, neatly folding their clothes and putting them aside, smoothing out any wrinkles, they stepped back into their original positions, each taking a further step in the procedure. As he pulled off his shorts he was not embarrassed to have his readiness show. Then they took careful, almost measured, steps towards each other's bodies.

Lou felt he was dreaming as he explored her face, her lips, her hair, her arms, her breasts until he finally became lost in the forest of her thighs. Finally, both panting, as their passion momentarily subsided, they remained intertwined to slowly rejoin the world but then, only minutes later, needing little stirring, launched off into orbit once again.

That was three months ago. They had managed to find reasonable excuses to meet again, sometimes twice but at least once a month. There would be anxious and excited hours before they could close the hotel door and immediately throw off their clothes, no neatness now, to find the bed. They soon realized that this was not just passion that bound them. They found a deep interest in each other's lives and characters, laughing at the common joys they shared. However, they accepted the realization that other than these few furtive hours together their romance had no future.

Family and religious bonds were too hard to break so they lived and loved for a few hours each month. It was all that their lives allowed.

The joy of those hours would wash away when Lou came home but his guilt did not prevent him from planning, with anticipation, when he would next meet Gabriella. When he came home one evening Maria and Marta, the bride-to-be, were at the kitchen table with papers, brochures, booklets spread out. To Lou it seemed that planning a wedding was on par with planning the Normandy invasion. He stayed out of these deliberations, knowing he had little to offer other than the financing. Maria looked up."We'll clear this off soon. Your supper's still warm in the oven. You want it now?...O.K…Paulo's Report Card is on the desk…" She gave him a warning glance "...and it's not great."

Lou scanned it. No it certainly wasn't. Paulo did well all through primary school, with lots of time for sports, friends and also had time to spend with Lou. High School and puberty changed him into a different person, distant, often surly with grades that were only consistent by their downward direction. His daughters had been typical teenagers, drama was commonplace, but they maintained good marks, good friends and, underneath it all, good values. Paulo wasn't following in their footsteps.

"Where's Paulo?"

"Out--with friends."

"He should be home. Studying."

"He said he would study when he got home."

Lou knew that Paulo, Maria's 'baby', could too easily get his mother's concessions. He went to the oven, took out his dinner, grabbed a beer. "I'll watch T.V." Maria and Marta were too consumed in wedding plans to even acknowledge his words. Finishing his meal and disinterested in the hockey game he retreated to his basement workshop where he spent his time crafting both useful and useless articles. Purposefully he had no clocks to remind himself of the time so that he could work as little or as long as he wanted. He didn't like to be disturbed but couldn't ignore the raps on the door. It was his daughter.

"Dad, there's a guy on the phone. He says it's important."

He went up to the kitchen phone. "Hello."

"Lou?'

"Yeah."

"It's Mike, at Sixteenth."

He and Mike had been rookies together.

"Lou, we've had a hit and run. No injuries, minor damage to a parked car. We stopped the suspect vehicle minutes later. Four kids in the car."

Lou knew what would be next.

"One of them is your son."

"The driver?"

"No. Rear seat."

"Alcohol? Drugs?"

"No and maybe. Car smelt of grass. No evidence."

"Charges?"

"Only the driver. Failing to remain. His dad won't press for unauthorized use of the car."

Joy-riding was a common coming-of-age ritual. "Can you come? Pick him up?"

"Yeah. Be right down. Thanks Mike."

He was halfway out the door when Maria, now in her nightgown and robe at the top of the stairs, called, "You going out?"

"It's Paulo. He's fine, not hurt." His mind, not his mouth, thinking "...but I'd like to..."

His emotions settled, now short of anger but not that much short. What could he say or yell at his son to straighten out, smarten up, not screw up when you're nearly seventeen. As he waited at a stop light he thought back to his seventeenth year. He nodded to himself, acknowledging he had done a few dumb things, nothing that was too serious, at least nothing that he'd been caught at.

He was breathing more calmly when he pulled into the parking lot at Sixteenth Division but still reviewing how he could get his message across to his son. As he walked inside he wasn't sure how he would handle the situation but he had decided yelling at Paulo wouldn't be an answer.

CHAPTER SEVENTEEN

Ellen Lougheed was on a fast track up the promotion ladder. Since a pre-teen she had wanted to be a Police Officer. She went to College, studying Criminology, Psychology, plus Administration, but she realized she'd have to pay her dues, start on the streets but only to get experience. She didn't plan to stay there. Now, less than ten years 'on', her latest advancement was an assignment to the Missing Persons Unit. She heard it was well led but understaffed. Before arriving she learned that it was hurting even more with it's supervisor away on suspension. Within her first few hours she was quickly updated by the two loyal clerks as to the details, all untrue according to Grace and Theresa, for the suspension. Lieutenant Lou Contile was now in temporary charge, but clearly wishing he wasn't. He was trying to keep up with the pressures and doing reasonably well but, within a few days Ellen realized that he was slipping slowly behind. She wanted to be proactive, to dive right in, alligators and sharks be damned. However, Lou was pleasant but paternal in having her review the basics, how the Unit was connected to the Field Divisions, what they could expect from them and what they couldn't . He'd also given her a few unsolved files to review. One was from five years back, two within the last year, and two more recent. Lou asked Ellen to be critical, looking for what had been missed, what areas would merit further investigation. Despite wanting to be more involved on new matters she did feel that Lou had accepted her as an asset, not a liability. A lot of the senior male staff weren't as kind to female officers.

One of the new files was: LUCY MARIE FAIRWEATHER.

She suspected there was a purpose in Lou assigning this case to her as this was the trigger to the current suspension and the empty desk of Detective/Sergeant Rushton Sterne, who she was yet to meet..

The Fairweather file wasn't that thick.The reports covered the first call, from Lucy's apartment mate, who hadn't seen her for four full days, nor had anyone else. The preliminary investigation was at the local level. The

Division that started the probe was like all others, busy with traffic, break and enters, domestics that took their immediate attention, leaving little time left for the more time-consuming investigations. Experienced officers were promoted, if they deserved it; the less deserving stayed in the ranks, accumulating seniority as they plodded to early retirement and a decent pension. Ellen, as she reviewed the initial reporting, would have wanted more detail, more depth, more leads.

The two officers who checked Lucy's apartment neighbours seemed to cover only the basics. Lucy had been a tenant for just over eight months. The manager said she was the primary leaseholder, paid her rent, caused no problems, no loud parties. Her roommate confirmed that she and Lucy were not really friends. MaryLou was normally away on flights, overnight stays and when back, often stayed with her boyfriend. She estimated she only slept in the apartment on average ten days a month, which is why she didn't pay a full half of the rent. She, nor anyone else, were aware of Lucy having a boyfriend, or even knew of any friends at all. She was a private person, now missing.

These same two officers had interviewed the two doctors, the brothers who employed Lucy in their small clinic. Their report again covered the basics. Lucy had been hired from an employment placement agency when their long term receptionist retired. It appeared to Ellen that only one of the brothers, Isak Warsiak, supplied all of what information there was. The other brother, Ludlo Warsiak, had simply said that Isak handled the hiring. Isak told the officers that Lucy knew a lot about record keeping, computers and due to her hospital experience had a good knowledge of medical procedures and medications. Isak admitted that they became reliant on her to handle the reception desk, patients, appointments, the pharmaceutical salesmen and a lot of the paperwork. He admitted that he and his brother were both a bit old fashioned and their primary focus was on being physicians. Like the brothers themselves their patients were mostly seniors, most having a litany of recurring aches and pains.

The lead to Robin Partridge came from Isak. When asked whether he knew any friends of Lucy the only name offered was Robin's. Isak said that Robin would often come to the office, even when she didn't have an appointment for her chronic spinal pain, and would sit, close to Lucy's desk, passing the time. Isak recognized that they both had Native North

American heritage and assumed that was why Lucy was tolerant and friendly with this older woman. It was Sterne's interview with Partridge that had landed him in hot water and now left his desk unoccupied, leaving the Unit even more understaffed than normal.

One of the officers at the Clinic had obtained a copy, once Isak had finally found it, of Lucy's job application. Ellen could see that Lucy had ambitions. She had to check the computer map to locate the small largely native village where she was born, where she attended primary school. Ellen guessed that school only went up to Grade Eight as Lucy's High School was in Fort Teddington, nearly a hundred miles south. After graduation, Lucy went a bit further south to College in Chassington where she obtained an Assistant Nursing Diploma, then worked at the local Hospital for two years before coming here to the City, to work in the Warsiaks' Clinic.

Ellen went over to Lou's desk, his head and eyes focussed on his computer screen. He had asked her to call him Lou, not 'Sir' nor by his rank, but she was hesitant to do so. She simply stood there until she ventured a " Hmmm..."

Lou looked up "Yes?"

"The Fairweather file. Would there be any problem if I made a few phone calls?"

"No. No Problem. Run with it."

Ellen decided to start with the Chassington General Hospital. beginning with H.R. Department, but Ms. Labelle who was wary of discussing anything from their records over the phone, even though Ellen explained her position and the reason for her call. The careful Ms. Labelle took her number, explaining she needed approval from the Hospital's Administrator first. Ten minutes later she was back to Ellen, now friendly and cooperative.

"Did you know Lucy ?"

"Know her? At first...really not. I was on maternity leave when she was hired and it wasn't until the issue...the problem...arose that I was able to put her name to her face."

"So there was a problem with Lucy?"

"A problem developed over prescription drugs. Let me think back... yes it was when Dr. Martin, a young surgeon on our staff, noticed quite a few of his patients, who had been prescribed opioids for pain relief while still in hospital, were coming back within a week or two after being released asking for renewals, claiming they had run out of pills. At first he thought that they were overusing the daily dosage and was concerned about addiction but he began asking how many pills they had when they got home. He was able to conclude that someone, here at the hospital, was removing pills from the patients' supply before they left us. Quietly we tried to determine if we could make a connection between those patients and what staff would have access to their opioids.

We could narrow it down to a handful but nothing conclusive that we could act on. We had to tighten up our internal controls and record keeping and have a check made on the numbers of pills for each patient being released. At the same time, after consulting our lawyers on a wording so it wouldn't sound accusatory, we issued a bulletin to all staff outlining these new procedures without any suggestion that there had been any specific suspicions to trigger these new rules. We did have a final sentence indicating that the authorities would be called in if there was any contravention."

She paused, allowing Ellen to ask the obvious: " So Lucy was one of the handful that could be involved."

"Yes and also...I know this sounds racially incorrect but we do know that opioids, really any number of painkillers, have a street market value and...well...the prices are highest up north, in the remote communities, like on the Reserves."

Ellen could see the connection. "So Lucy coming from there could mean she might be the one pilfering the pills and sending them back home for big money."

"Well, that was a suspicion but one that we couldn't confirm." She then added, "Our Nursing assistants aren't highly paid and it was noticed that Lucy parked her shiny red pick-up truck in our employee lot."

The Fairweather File had all the details on this vehicle except its current location; like Lucy Marie it was still missing.

"When Lucy left you, was it voluntary?"

"Yes, she resigned but it was in the same month as our new controls were instituted. We can't say whether these problems ceased because of the new rules or whether it was Lucy leaving but, in any case, we now have no issues with missing drugs."

"Do you have any idea whether these shortages preceded Lucy's start there?"

"No. We couldn't say. We had no way of knowing."

"Well thanks for your help. By the way did anyone check back as a reference for Lucy?"

"Let me check. It might take a minute."

As Ellen waited, she wondered how easy it might have been for Lucy to access any pills or drugs from where she last worked, the Warsiak Clinic.

"Yes, a week after she resigned. It was from your city. An Employment Agency there. Do you need me to send that info onto you?"

"No, that's fine. Again thanks for your help."

"You're most welcome. I know that she left here under...what can I say...a bit of a cloud but since she's missing I do hope that she is safely found."

Ellen wondered if she was being too optimistic in hoping the same.

***

Marielle was late getting back to her office after her lunch with Sylvie. This wasn't unusual to lose track of time with her sister. Marielle could frame a novel, not a happy one, on Sylvie's life, more accurately her love life. Years younger, and with different fathers, they started as sisters in France, where their mother had returned to when Marielle was still pre-school, where she had met Carlos, a worker from Spain. Their coupling produced Sylvie. Carlos wanted to give her a Spanish name but her mother was insistent it be French. Carlos conceded that point but was just as insistent that his daughter speak Spanish. As a result Marielle added another language at home plus the English she was learning in her school. After Carlos discarded the family, her mother chose to take her two daughters back west over the Atlantic where Marielle's English quickly acquired depth and fluency to match her French and Spanish.

Sylvie had chosen a dark corner of the restaurant and it took time for Marielle's eyes to become accustomed to the dimness to see, under the make-up, the bruising under her sister's left eye. At first Sylvie denied any problems but soon admitted that there had been a fight but lied saying it was the first time this had happened. Marielle had never liked Remi but then again she'd never taken to any of Sylvie's men. Sylvie had not made good choices although, admittedly, Marielle's was open to a slice of the same criticism. Sylvie would always insist that despite their faults her partners could be cleansed of their spots. Marielle's opinion was that 'une fois un chien, toujours un chien'. The luncheon didn't solve any of Sylvie's problems but did stretch out their lunch so that it was nearly two when Marielle got back to her small office.

There was a note on her desk from Harry Hubbart, her boss and Antioch's In-House Counsel, "Come to see me when you get back. Luv, Harry." He had started his career with Antioch's Head Office in London before being transferred here. He still retained his accent and British joviality. When she knocked on his door and entered she was met with his usual beaming smile.

"Congratulations, Luv. You saved this blessed company a quarter of a million dollars. I'd buy you lunch but my budget won't allow it, sorry Dear."

When Marielle had returned to report on her inquiries in Real Republica she was disappointed on the extent of her findings. She had been able to obtain a certified copy of the Death Certificate in Spanish which had been filed with Republica's Bureau of Births and Deaths. Dr. Newton's English copy submitted by the plaintiff's lawyer confirmed physician assisted death just after the two year 'Contestable Death' period in the Policy had expired. This gave Antioch no legal defense to deny paying out the half million to the two beneficiaries. Antioch suspected, but lacked proof, that a diagnosis of lung cancer was known but never acknowledged on the original application. Marielle's investigation did uncover a history of high blood pressure, again not disclosed. However the Republica's official 'Causa de la Muerta' listed 'Insuficiencia cardiaca' on Dr Newton's submittal for Governmental Certification. This was medically vague enough but sufficient to be more acceptable than "Suicidio" in Republica..

Armed with this, Hubbard had informed the lawyer for the beneficiaries that Antioch would defend on the basis of "Non-Disclosure" of a pre-existing cardiac condition and would fight the matter for as long as the Courts would allow. The Plaintiffs quickly decided a bird in the hand was worth two in the bush and called to negotiate. After he hung up the phone and sent out a confirming email Hubbard wondered if he should have been tougher but he knew Antioch was glad to get out of it at $250,000. They would have had to hire outside counsel who would have been only too glad to drag out a protracted defense, their hourly rates clicking over to the delight of all their senior partners, but with no guarantee to Antioch that they'd be ultimately successful.

Marielle's position with the company and particularly with Hubbard and his staff was on solid ground. Nonetheless she was glad that her efforts had helped. In the bargain, she had a brief few days, hardly a true holiday, but a more than interesting visit to the Hospice on that strange small island, plus a brief visit to Republica Real's capital city and then a day in Miami, all expenses paid. True she hadn't met any tall, dark handsome men but she had one of those for eight years of her life. Looking back she admitted Luis wasn't that tall but this Argentinian musician had charm and a passion that led her to his bed. There were some very great days, a lot of good days, but these were at the front end of their relationship before it slowly simmered then soured.

Then she thought back to meeting Rush Sterne. The ride in the beer truck was, in its own way, memorable and their dinner at the hotel was enjoyable, certainly the food and, she had to admit, also his company. He wasn't tall, but like Luis,tall enough; not dark, but no receding hairline; not an Adonis but nice looking, especially when he smiled. She guessed he would be about forty and definitely single. He was certainly a gentleman, almost old-fashioned in manner, and never posed any threat to make any move to an intimate relationship, even an overnight one. She had to smile at her recollection; perhaps she should be insulted by his inaction.Then she wondered, if she had been aggressive, whether he would have responded. She doubted he was gay. He had a pleasant reserved manner that made conversation easy but he seemed hesitant for whatever reason. All in all a nice guy but she wasn't in the market right now for any man, platonic or otherwise.

As she left Harry's Office she was hoping that, within a few days, when she had her final marks from the College, they'd be high enough to apply to Law School. She had confidence as she'd earned her degree, after five full years of night classes, but there were only so many places open to study for a Bachelor of Laws. If accepted, this would mean full time attendance. She had been saving money but still needed some continuing income. Her plan was to talk to Harry, explore some way of working part-time for Antioch

Life. She felt sure Harry would be agreeable but the decision would have to be made higher up the chain; nonetheless it would have to start with Harry, assuming all the dominoes fell properly into place beforehand.

***

The island was now back to normal. Vuk had now been replaced. At first David had some concern as Joseph's scribbled application had some glaring gaps. David guessed that he may have spent some time in jail, probably in his native Jamaica, but he was genial, friendly and quickly grasped the responsibilities of keeping the island's pieces of machinery functioning as smoothly as he could. David had also to assume that anyone wanting the solitary life on Cresciente was running from somewhere. It was a common thread.

The clientele kept arriving, flying in from Porto del Norte. David still conducted his interviews, to confirm that decisions were rock-solid, but now on a more detailed level, making more notes in each file. He never wanted to face a misuse of their function again; the memory of the Dan/Victor set-up still rekindled his anger, still leaving him questioning whether he made the best choice.

Today he had already seen and approved the upcoming deaths of another elderly couple, in their eighties. They were still healthy enough but, like many before them, couldn't envision a life spent together ending with the death of one, to be followed by lonely grief for the surviever. The next patient was young, a very attractive slim woman. As soon as he had seen her get off the plane he wondered why she was here. She seemed totally out of place as if she had flown here by mistake. Immediately he wanted to tell her to turn back, get back into the plane, try to find a life back home or anywhere else in the world. Instead, as he waited for Heidi to bring her to his office for her interview, he reviewed her application. A name as attractive as she was: Alicia Blanche Brookfield. Age forty. Reason for applying to the Clinic: "Sick of Life". How could such a fine looking human being be ready to end her life? He took it as a challenge to make her change her mind. If she wouldn't then he would refuse her application and send her back, off the island, to face the world again.

There was a small quick rap at his door.

"Yes, come in. Please be seated. Can I get you something to drink? Perhaps iced tea?"

She shook her head, her eyes not finding his. There was no smile.

"Alicia. . .may I call you that? Good...well your application is quite different from any I've seen before." He waited for her to ask why. She didn't, so he continued "You know that I ...we...here at the Clinic have a responsibility to respect human life and only agree to assist in situations where there is sufficient reason, acceptable to us, that the choice meets our criteria." David was glad that she didn't ask what that criteria actually was; he would have a hard time objectively defining it. Slowly he asked gentle questions. In return received short, emotionless responses countering any attempt that he could make to sway her, at least give her doubts, give her time to rethink her position. He suggested that they have another meeting tomorrow. She finally looked straight at him. "Doctor I've made up my mind...I want...I need you to assist me in dying. If you refuse I will take my own life here, right here on your island. I brought with me two scalpel blades. I've now hidden them. I doubt you'll find one if you search, but certainly not both. If you force me to use one on myself it will be messy, in more ways than one, particularly since you'd have to notify the authorities. From what I've researched about your island I don't think that you would like that, would you?"

Her eyes bored coldly into his face, "Now Doctor. I'm ready, whenever you are. This afternoon?"

She didn't wait for his reply but simply stood, turned and was out his door. David sat twiddling his pen in his fingers.Then he threw it against the wall. Slowly rising, beaten, he walked out of his office to find Heidi, to have her prepare the Clinic. He forced his mind to project, now just eleven days from now, the anticipated month-end break from the Clinic, his escape to one of Jose's resorts an hour away up the Coast. There he'd wash this cloud away with a bottle, a body and a beach to blackout Isla Cresciente, at least for a few days.

CHAPTER EIGHTEEN

Edo trudged up the hill. Behind and below him was a once successful small town. Since the atrocities, now nearly twenty years ago, the ghosts of the victims walked the streets and the echo of the guns still stuck to the bricks, the walls, and had settled deep into the memories of the surviving families. This shroud still hung heavy, sustained by those still scarred. It discouraged many of the young to stay; if they did it was only to care for the aging, mostly mothers or grandmothers.

He had been up to the communal gravesite many times before he received his assignment and left for Florida. He had no real memory of his father, his older brother, two uncles whose bones were intermingled below in the green grassy hillside. Edo had been too young to remember the day of their slaughter but his mother had raised him with the memory of their bravery and how they were butchered, high up on that sheep meadow. Their grim faces were captured in family photos; custom never allowed men to smile at the camera. His mother and aunts worked hard to ensure that Edo's blood simmered with the need for revenge.

As soon as he was old enough to understand the massacre he made childish promises to avenge these deaths, at first merely to give solace to his mother who he loved deeply. As he grew up his promise evolved, becoming a certainty, a vow that became part of his life and his very being. Now, back home from Miami, he stood feeling the sweet breeze all the way from the Adriatic sweeping eastward from the coast into the hills to where he stood, solemn but proud to address his father, brother and uncles: "You have been avenged!"

Working his way back down the twisting path, he worried that he'd be asked to do more and receive a further assignment. He hoped not, but they could come back to him, pointing out that he'd lost four members of his family and had credit for scoring only one life in retribution. Two summers ago he'd agreed to go up to that secluded training camp, to bring 'justice' to their heritage, and revenge for his town and his family. He was there with three other trainees but, from the start, his target was Sergeant Vuk Losavik, now tracked to a small island in the Caribbean. Edo's English, mainly learned from watching American TV, had been good enough to have him chosen to go Miami. Now back home Edo knew that there were other 'Vuks' from that squad of killers who were still at large. Edo had already been trained and been successful once. Would they ask him to do more? He shuddered at the thought. He still had nightmares, reliving that moment when he had raised the hammer aiming at the back of Vuk's head. No, he'd done his duty. His mother didn't know the specifics of what happened on Cresciente but she knew the results and was satisfied that her prayers had been answered. If they asked him to do more he'd have to find a way of saying 'No'.

***

Rush was happy to be able to sleep in, have a leisurely breakfast, time to go up the stairs to see his father and take the sections of the newspaper Russell that had finished with. Back downstairs he thought about the coming weekend. His monthly visit with his 'Little Brother' was this Saturday. Rush felt that finally he was earning Jimmy's trust and as much a friendship as could be achieved, given the circumstances. Where to take Jimmy was now a question. They had been to the Zoo, the Museum, the Amusement Park and other places that Jimmy had liked. Although Rush had clearly met all the criteria to be a 'Brother' there were still limits where you could go, what you could do. Well he'd think of something.

He also planned to call Morris. They'd met in Law School and after Morris graduated he joined a large firm, there meeting and marrying a fellow lawyer. Now their lives were busy with two children. Gillian's thriving law practise allowed Morris to return to Law School for a Masters of Law, then to stay on as staff. Morris had never felt comfortable being an Advocate of Law yet pressured to maintain monthly quotas of billable hours for the firm. He enjoyed teaching much more than practising Law. Rush could envision that he soon would be called to take a seat as a Judge. They maintained a friendship over the years, meeting for lunch when their schedules allowed. Since Rush was single he had been invited, to what became the one and only time, by Gillian to a dinner party. There was a recent divorcee, a lawyer, that Gillian thought might 'click' with Rush, but polite attempts at finding points of mutual interest sagged and the 'click' became a 'clunk'. Now only Rush and Morris met, usually at the same delicatessen near the Law School.

Since his suspension Rush had been re-evaluating his future with the Police Force. He doubted he would go much further up the ladder. He wasn't interested in a full-time administration desk. If the accusation of beating Birdie wasn't totally cleared from his record he foresaw a declining or, at best, sideways role. Since his return from Isla he had been considering his options. His father had never brought up his son's words from over twenty years ago. Then, with Ana pregnant, he had never gone back to finish his final year at Law School but Rush remembered saying that he could always do that later. Was that 'later' now?

Then his phone rang. It was his Superintendent's secretary informing Rush of a meeting at three this afternoon at Headquarters. It wasn't an invitation; it was a command. It was a long morning then the early afternoon hours dragged by until, at five minutes to three, Rush stepped out of the elevator on the floor housing the top brass of the Force. He was neat in a suit and tie, looking better than he felt.

Thirty minutes later he was back into the elevator, getting out on the second floor, walking down to the entrance to the "Missing Persons Unit". Lou must have recognized his footsteps.

"Rush, what the hell! They've let you back in?"

"Yes...but with strings." He explained the decision that had been made. There was no negotiation on the terms. Rush wasn't happy with them but at least he would be back at his desk by agreeing to the conditions of his reinstatement. He explained to Lou that he wasn't to be handcuffed to his desk but any investigation outside the office would involve being accompanied by Ellen Lougheed.

"You mean that they couldn't trust you and I to go out together?"

"They didn't come out to say it but they couldn't take a chance that our history together wouldn't compromise us."

"Jesus. A trusting bunch aren't they. How long are these rules in place?"

"They only said this was conditional, which could mean anything."

Lou was more upset than his partner; Rush was only glad to step back in as part of the unit. Ellen wasn't in at that point so he asked Lou about her. He conceded she seemed O.K. and, after Rush asked him more questions, admitted she seemed to know her stuff.

"Good. Then as long as she doesn't mind being saddled as my monitor, we can work it out. If she's back this afternoon tell her I'll look forward to meeting her. Don't tell her about having to be my guide dog. I'll spring that on her tomorrow, unless upstairs has already told her. Que sera. See you early tomorrow morning."

Feeling much better than he did an hour ago he looked forward to home to give Russell the good news, already suspecting that his father would grumble that the 'brass' were playing it too safe by putting Rush on a tether.

***

He had to wait, seated with the few patients left at the end of the day, before the receptionist nodded to him, "The doctor only has five minutes to meet you. You can go in now."

"Hello Doctor. Thanks for squeezing me into your busy schedule. Here's my card.I'm Walter Starbuski and as you can see I represent 'Star's Office Cleaning Services'. I realize you already have a cleaning company but, as I waited to see you, just examining the waiting room I could see that whoever does the cleaning isn't doing a great job, probably overcharging you too. Now here's what we'll do. We'll send you a quote to clean all of your office, all rooms, and I'm sure that the price will please you. You'll save hundreds of dollars every year. You'll have our quote in the next few days. Give it a good look. Again, thank you Doctor, have a nice evening."

After Starbuski left, Dr. Mendorf realized he hadn't opened his mouth, even to say goodbye, which was just as well as he had two more patients to see. He'd wait for the quotation and at least take a look at it.

Outside Walter considered he'd have a fifty-fifty chance of taking over the cleaning of Dr. Mendorf's office. The previous evening he waited in the parking lot to identify who was currently doing the cleaning. When he saw the company logo he knew he could easily undercut them in pricing. All he had to do after that was to keep pressure on Mendorf. He liked the set-up. A single practise family doctor, probably sixty or so, would be more dedicated to his practise than administration. He also guessed that he still kept patient files in his own writing, not wanting to pay for an expensive upgrade to a computer program. This usually meant a lack of controls and limited security in the office. This was perfect for Starbuski's other business. The cleaning company made a bit of profit but it was still his mother's company. She had started it years ago. Walter and his brother's first jobs were helping Mom wash and wax floors.

What Walter made his real money, cold cash, no taxes to be paid, was from prescriptions. He could sell anything on the street for a profit. Right now it was opioids. Oxycontins and Percocets were ready money but even lesser pain medication could still find a market. Walter had been dealing since high school starting with marijuana and hash. It was almost by accident that he'd found, in the waste-paper basket at a Clinic where they did after-hours cleaning, a drug company's sample of Percocet that was still intact. Later evenings, with more searches in the refuse, were half written discarded prescription scripts. Walter took these to a buddy who was always good in art at school, but little else. It then was easy to use this real prescription from this doctor, use it as a template to counterfeit his signature for more Percocet. It was quick easy money but also quickly spent by Walter.

Walter then began marketing the Cleaning Company at similar small doctors' offices, dentists too, expanding his sources of scripts. He got lucky with two newly graduated dentists, needing immediate cash to live on, while their practises built up. He didn't have to look in their waste baskets but now Larry Arnold was backing off. Coupled with Lucy's supply from the brothers' Clinic now history, as well as the few opioids he got monthly from Birdie also gone, he was running low. He was getting complaints from his street dealers.They had customers and they needed product to sell.

Walter still lived with his mother, in the same old bedroom next to his brother's, currently empty until Lenny finished his sentence. His mother cooked and fed him, did his laundry, but not for free. Still, he was happy with his situation, except for privacy. For that he needed to rent hotel rooms and tonight he'd booked an expensive room at an upscale hotel. Tonight he was dealing with a new escort service, guaranteeing high class 'sophisticated ladies'. That came at a much higher price than he normally paid for a hooker. So, as much as he was excited at the possibilities, it still lingered in his mind that he had to find more ways to secure the product his dealers needed and, in turn, their cash back to him.

He wasn't yet thirty but was proud of the slice he'd carved for himself in the competitive cut-throat drug trade. Purposefully he kept a low profile, staying away from both organized and disorganized crime circles. He had developed his own small supply chain keeping his risks as low as he could. The cops would reel in and put pressure on the little fish in this sewer, get names and go after those up the ladder. Walter tried to keep his ladder short but strong. So far as he knew, he had avoided any police investigation. His eighteen month stretch, when he was still a teen-ager, was on his record but that was for two counts of car theft, nothing to do with drugs. It was there that he picked up his 'street' nickname. They first called him 'Starbucks' but that soon was simplified to 'Bucks'. He didn't do the street himself. He had runners that he had reasonable trust in, as much as you could trust any in this game. If they were caught he hoped that they take their licks as small-time dealers and not name him. If they did there'd be no usable proof. They'd find nothing at his home. All they'd find was a hard-working stiff, gainfully employed, running a small office cleaning company.

Still he had to do something soon but that was for tomorrow. Tonight he was going to meet 'Eve' and he was more than willing to bite the forbidden apple with her.

CHAPTER NINETEEN

The previous evening, on his way home, Rush had stopped at the local Italian Bakery to place his order to be picked up early in the morning. He wasn't going to rely on the too common practise of dozen assorted donuts for his staff when they came into work on his first day back after nearly a month. Lou certainly appreciated Rush's choices; he knew the Italian name for each of the pastries. He ate three.

Ellen and Rush were introduced to eAch other by Lou, exchanged polite handshakes, and then went to their respective desks. After clearing the back mail on his computer Rush slid his chair over to Lou's desk, "O.K. what are the priorities for today?" Lou tilted his screen half towards Rush and started his concise review. Rush stopped him, "We need Ellen in on this." He called her over. Somehow they squeezed their chairs into a huddle to view the screen as Lou scrolled through the priority status of open active cases.

It was nearly eleven before they arranged who would do what on which file. Ellen was ready to fly out the door with her assignment when Rush stopped her, "Can you handle another coffee? We should talk."

Once seated in the cafeteria Rush toyed with his cup, spilling coffee into the saucer, as he composed his words, " I'm sure that you've been told of our new...let's call it an arrangement...haven't you?"

"Sir..." She saw him wince and open his mouth to correct her so she went on, "...sorry...Rush...yes I've been advised and I'm as uncomfortable with it as...I'm sure you are."

"No. I'm O.K. with it. I see the reasoning but my concern is how it affects you, just starting out with the Unit, having to chaperone me."

Then they exchanged interrupting half-sentences with each assuring the other that there was no ill-feeling for this peculiar role that was now necessary. Rush was her supervisor in the office but in the field she would oversee him. They both seemed satisfied that it would work and, after a quick handshake, Ellen was on her way to interview a fifteen year old runaway to ensure there'd been no criminal history of abuse at home that had caused her to leave.

Back at his desk Rush saw a sealed envelope propped against his screen. Opening it he found an engraved invitation from "Mr. and Mrs. Louis Contile" requesting his presence at the wedding of their daughter.

Lou had been waiting for the opening and called over, offering an apology, "I'm saving where I can. Besides you can't always trust the mailman." Rush chuckled but had, over the last few months, realized that the cost of the wedding was a worry for Lou who had no control over the size of the wedding. His wife and daughter knew what their heritage, the extended families of both bride and groom, demanded of them and they planned to ensure the wedding matched those expectations. Rush had not been to many marriage ceremonies but few had been simple. The most interesting and most memorable was David's marriage to Victoria Longhurst. It wasn't a Royal Wedding but, in Rush's estimation, it was only a few rungs lower.

David and Rush had stayed in touch with each other even after David continued his medical career in England but it was a surprise to Rush to receive the invitation as he thought of David remaining single and beyond the grasp of marriage. He decided to attend the wedding and then go on a short driving trip in England and Wales, to be followed by a trip to Paris.

David arranged a hotel reservation and the rental of 'formal' wear required for the ceremony. Feeling very much overdressed Rush found his way to a large church in the English countryside, then following the service, joined the entourage of cars driving to the Reception Hall. After the hurried exchange of pleasantries in the receiving line, Rush's first contact with the bride, he found his way to find the table he had been assigned to. It was the furthest away from the head table. Once seated he found himself sitting between two middle-aged women who were distant relatives of the bride. They obviously hadn't seen each other for some time and spent the majority of the dinner catching up, talking through Rush as if he was invisible. Indeed he felt invisible and after a four course dinner with fine wine he sat as a spectator listening to the lengthy speakers. He thought David's was the best, respectful to both families, glowingly of his wife's beauty and intelligence, a few humorous references and, best of all, David had kept it short.

Finally a dance band appeared and started with old favorites, a few waltzes and foxtrots that satisfied the over seventy segment. This allowed more bar-time for the younger guests, topping the dinner champagne with whisky and gin. Rush sat back, like a fly on the wall, amused by the overall scene of the upper ranks of British society, young or old, new or inherited money, mixing together, most seeming to enjoy themselves. The wife of one of the couples at his table, her husband deep into a political discussion that obviously bored her, looked over to Rush, flicked both her head and eyes towards the dance floor then reached out her hand to pull Rush out of his chair. Above the music and babble of voices she began to give Rush a running commentary on those just out of earshot. It appeared very few met her approval. At first Rush assumed her criticism was based on elevated morals but as she began to bump into his pelvis more than just accidentally and as her comments on others verged on salacious, he realized it was an invitation for more than just dancing. He would have to bail out. She wasn't pleased when he led her back to their table. The younger guests then took over the floor and the band led them into a swirling, bouncing madcap of arms, legs, heads flailing about, fueled by alcohol and, Rush suspected, non-legal substances.

He excused himself and headed to the washroom. Passing a window he saw that fog was drifting over the parking lot. He decided he'd better try to find his way back to his hotel before it worsened. He collected his coat after deciding his exit didn't need any explanation or apology. Outside, in the thickening mist he found his rental, perhaps the smallest car in the lot. As he turned on the headlights he caught a glimpse of white and heard a raised voice, "Charlie, Charlie, where are you? Where the hell are you?"

The white then came within the reach of his headlights. It was a young woman, clearly very concerned about 'Charlie'. He got out of the car and went over to her.

"Can I help?"

"It's Charlie...Charlotte...I thought she was in the Ladies Room...but when I went to check on her...she's had too much to drink...she wasn't there. I think she came out here...to be sick. Charlie! Charlie! Answer me." She turned to Rush. "Can you help? You look over there. I'll try over here."

It was dark and the edge of the parking lot was hedged but Rush saw a gap and went through it. He saw the satiny sheen of a dress in the grass and then called, "Over here. She's over here."

"Oh my God! Is she alright?"

Rush was careful turning her over, trying to remember his paramedic training, too busy to answer. She was unconscious but her vitals, though weak, were working. Her rank breath was weak and halting. Rush guessed she had ingested some of the vomit that was splashed over the front of her dress. He pulled her halfway up and applied pressure to her ribcage from behind. He expected the choking response but was still concerned about blockage. He laid her back on the grass and, despite her spittle and acrid alcohol sour taste, started to suck out the mess that was left in her mouth. Her breathing then steadied but was still shallow so he began mouth to mouth resuscitation. It helped and her lungs responded.

Getting up, spitting to the side, then wiping his mouth, he turned to her anxious friend, asking, "Any idea what she had tonight, other than alcohol?"

"I don't think...but I'm not sure...she had a tiff with her boyfriend. I think it's only champagne and gin...but then again…" Her voice trailed off.

"Well I think we should call an ambulance. She needs to have her stomach pumped out." Although this seemed obvious to Rush, Charlotte's friend was hesitating before answering. "Let's drive her there. Pull your car over here. It will be better if we take her right now."

Rush still thought an ambulance was the answer but the friend now seemed to have taken charge. They managed to settle Charlotte in the laid back front passenger seat; her friend sat behind Rush giving instructions as they drove out from the lights of the hotel lot into increasing fog. Within minutes Rush had no idea of what road they were on or their direction as all he could do was avoid the ditches at the roadside. The woman in the back seat was confidently instructing Rush where to turn, when to slow down. Finally, while they were still beyond any lights, she told him to look for two large pillars on the right. Seeing them he braked, "Here?"

The tires now crunched on gravel, curving up a long drive towards two dim lights, becoming brighter as they cut through the fog. As they drove closer Rush saw them illuminating a wide expanse of front steps but not looking like the entrance of any Hospital. "Blow the horn" were Rush's next instructions. As they were extracting Charlotte from her seat there was suddenly a man illuminated by a now opened front door, in a dressing gown, not all looking like a nurse or intern, asking, "Miss Alexandra! Is Lady Charlotte ill?"

"Michael...I only hope she's just drunk. Let's get her in the library."

Rush was full of questions but stayed quiet as Alexandra was very much in control of the situation. He managed to carry the still limp woman up the steps into a very large, panelled entrance hall and followed Michael into a book-ladened library to gently deposit Charlotte on a plush leather couch. He then noticed a woman, also in a dressing gown, at the doorway. Alexandria was giving her instructions on what would be needed, adding a final, "Alice...better bring an extra basin, just in case."

Rush and Michael stood in the background as Alexandria and Alice stripped Charlotte of her sodden dress, washed her face, covering her with blankets. Again Alexandria was giving instructions, "Call Dr. Atkins, will you." It wasn't a request and Michael turned immediately to leave the library to make the call.

Rush by now had retreated to the massive entry hall wondering whether Dr. Atkins would welcome the call, find his way in the fog, to attend to Charlotte. There didn't seem any doubt in Alexandria's voice to suggest the doctor would mind. Rush turned towards the front hall, intending to quietly leave.

"Where are you going?" Alexandria came over to touch Rush's sleeve." I'm sorry, I don't even know your name. I'm Alex...Alexandria Hepworth. You are...?"

"Rush...Rushton Sterne...a friend of the groom."

"Rush, thank you so much for your help." She saw his face turning to scan the hallway, "No, it's not a hospital. It's her home...or at least her family's home. She has a flat in London. Look...I do apologize. I misled you but you don't know the exposure that might have resulted. I could see that someone from in ambulance service or in the Emergency Ward would realize who she was, make a call to the Press to collect fifty pounds or more, and tomorrow morning there'd be a big story of Lady Charlotte Darlington, drunk and drugged, lying in Hospital, in a life and death situation. Sorry, I just couldn't let that happen."

"Well as long as she's fine I guess it's sensible. This Dr. Atkins. Will he come--to check her?"

"You can expect him within minutes. Hold on. Where are you going?"

"Back to my hotel."

"You know the way...in this fog? You'd end up in Scotland." She turned. "Michael, Mr. Sterne will be our guest tonight."

"Certainly Miss Alexandria." He turned to Rush. "This way, Sir."

He trailed obediently behind Michael up the long curved staircase, along a hallway that must have taken a dozen craftsmen to create a century or two ago. Then Michael was ushering Rush into a drape-laden bedroom, pointing out to Rush what he might need before retiring or on waking. There were new shaving utensils and a toothbrush waiting in the well tiled ensuite. Rush saw a mouthwash bottle and immediately used it to swill away the acrid bile from his mouth. Before leaving Michael asked, "Sir, can I bring you a nightcap? No. Very well. Please leave your clothes and shoes on the silent butler outside your door. We'll tidy them up for you. If you are in need of anything please use the bell." He pointed to the bedside button. "If you don't mind me saying so Charlotte's parents will be most appreciative of your assistance this evening. They are expected back from London in the morning. Breakfast will be served at nine. Very well. Good night Sir."

The room was much more than twice the size of his hotel room, now some unknown distance away in the fog. Rush saw a pair of pajamas lying on the edge of the large bed. He wasn't surprised to find that they fitted him. He left his soiled clothing, muddied shoes, outside his door and turned to the curtains that covered the window. He pulled them apart to see a flash of lights curving up the driveway then stop. Dr.Atkins must have arrived to take care of Charlotte. Now feeling tired, he pulled back the brocaded covering of the bed, then the sheets, and after clicking the room into darkness, snuggled under the bedclothes. As he reviewed the events of the evening the most lasting impression was of Alexandria, both her poise and her face. She seemed a bit older than Charlotte, certainly more mature and sensible, really quite lovely and, with this warming his memory, he quickly settled down into the comfort of the bed, then into sleep.

He awoke to a room still dark except for a sliver of light from a crack in the drawn drapes. On opening them he saw the morning's light wasn't sunshine but showed no evidence of fog. He checked outside his door. Shoes shined, clothing cleaned as he wondered how much sleep Michael or Alice had overnight. His formal wedding attire was inappropriate but, less the tie, was his only choice to start the day. He left the room as tidy as he could and quietly tiptoed down the wide echoing hall to go downstairs. The library door was open. A blanket was lying on the floor along with a pair of high heels. Charlotte and Alexandria must have found their beds during the night. He tried the front door and as he opened it there was a buzzing signal down the hall. Turning to close the door as carefully as he could, he heard hurried footsteps coming down toward the door. It was Michael, now more suitably dressed than last night.

"Sir, you aren't leaving?"

"Well yes...I have to check out this morning, preferably by eleven."

"Yes indeed, but his Lordship and Lady Darlington are driving back from London. They will be back by ten. I'm certain they would want to meet you, to express their thanks for the assistance you gave to their daughter."

"I assume she's on her way to recovery."

"Indeed but I expect she'll be nursing a headache today. Dr. Atkins will be back to check her later this morning."

"Good...but I still need to get back to the hotel." He stopped then asked, "Could you give me directions to Colonel Burton Inn?"

Michael did his best to have Rush stay but reluctantly gave him understandable directions back to his hotel. Rush's route passed by many imposing gates but tall hedges blocked any view of the estates beyond. Finally, at the hotel, he ordered a quick breakfast, much to the disappointment of his waiter who wanted to serve a full classic English breakfast. He had a quick shower and shave, packed his suitcase and then checked out, leaving the rented clothing to be picked up. The sun was now shining as he placed his bag in the trunk of his car, trying to remember what the British called it. Shoe? No. Boot, that was it, the boot.

He hadn't planned exactly what roads he would follow. He wanted to avoid the 'Motorways' and only use a compass to find a meandering path westward, to the Cotswolds, then into Wales.

He was examining his roadmap when there was a rap at his window. It was the desk clerk. There was an important phone call for him.

***

“Hey Rush! Wake up. No sleeping on the job.” It was Lou. ”It’s Ellen. She thinks that the runaway was abused at home. I’ve told her to call in Family Services.”

Rush wasn’t really surprised. There was often a dark reason lurking when dealing with juveniles who fled their homes. Family Services would now take over to protect the girl if returning her home would endanger her but Rush knew, from experience, that there would be a long rough road ahead for her but hopefully better than the one behind her.

CHAPTER TWENTY

Bucks woke to the sun slanting off the mirror on the far wall onto the bed and into his eyes. For a second he hoped he wasn't alone but Eve had left. He only vaguely recalled her leaving as both his mind and body were so fully sated it left him in a cocoon of half-consciousness. As he now became more awake, his mind floated back, first to the impact of her arrival. She was total class: young, beautiful, slim everywhere but for her prominent breasts tipped with protruding nipples. After the first practicality of payment she had taken command. She had him sit on the edge of the bed as she paraded, needing no music in stripping down to a black lacy bra and thong. She stopped to take his hand to stand up then she slowly undressed him, easily teasing his semi-erection into fullness, before pushing him onto the bed. He had no idea of time after that. Eve took him to the Garden of Ecstasy and he and Eve were the only two on the planet, a world of gasping excitement coming in waves to almost drown him, her mouth resuscitating him time and again.

Her scent still lingered in the bed and, when he finally found the washroom, he was reluctant to shower, to lose the layer of lust she'd left on him. As he towelled off he realized he was hungry and wondered if he should order breakfast to his room. He then thought about that cost being added to the expense of the room and Eve. Most of his mind said it was well worth it but niggling was the concern that this was too expensive a habit to carry unless he found ways to add to his cash flow, at least bring it back to its normal level. There was a coffee maker in the room and he was soon sipping, looking out the window at a world of concrete and glass, reviewing his options. His business plan had always been to minimize his exposure, both to the law and, just as dangerous, his fellow lawbreakers who'd stamped out their specialities and territories and would retaliate harshly for any invasions. However there might be room for him to branch out, beyond seeking new sources of addictive prescriptions, to some other low risk cash scheme. Maybe he could help one of his buddies expand their business. That would avoid any conflicts. He began to review them.

Antonio worked the airport in the baggage departure back rooms. Although his union wages were decent he supplemented them by rifling suitcases for jewellery, cameras, cell phones, whatever his cousin, who scanned the bags at security, saw was available, leaving a small identifying mark that Antonio would recognize. The security requirement to leave luggage unlocked made it a simple quick procedure for Antonio. Bucks concluded that the only fit into this enterprise was to market the goods that Antonio had stolen. He didn't want to be a dealer in hot items, overlooking the fact that he already dealt with stolen pills.

Santos never admitted to anything but it was no secret that he dealt in high end car thefts. Santos operated much like Bucks. He was never directly involved in the thefts himself. He was the middleman, hiring thieves to nab specific models. Then they'd either be slipped into a shipping container and off to somewhere in Africa, or serial numbers erased and re-coded, cars repainted, re-registered, and out to a special market, usually many miles away. Bucks knew he could make money with Santos but the work wouldn't be steady and the risk elevated. He already served time for car thefts when he was nineteen. He learned a lot while inside but shivered at the thought of being back behind bars.

Then there was Howie who ran his body shop just outside the city. It did legal collision repairs but was also a chop-shop, disassembling stolen vehicles then selling them to other shops as replacement parts. Bucks had, after his early hours trip out in the country to bury Lucy Marie, taken her red pick-up to Howie, after first going to a self car wash to ensure there were no traces left in the back. Howie didn't ask any questions but sensed that Bucks wasn't in position to bargain. So Bucks got only a thousand along with Howie's promise to cut it up right away. Bucks decided it was best that he distance himself from Howie.

Bucks had dealt in hash and weed while still in high school. He bought his supplies from his father who, for years, left before six each morning, sandwiches made by his mother and sister, lots of hot coffee, taking his canteen truck to construction sites, serving breakfast or the morning break along with the illegal sales. Most of these buyers were the young workers who wanted or needed a lunchtime lift. Bucks knew there was money to be made in marijuana but you either grew your own or bought it from the gangs, either biker or Asian. He avoided gangs. They were predictable trouble.

There was also the option to pimp. The money could be good but Bucks knew his own strengths and weaknesses. He could be strong enough to control most of his impulses but his temper, fueled by his urges and anger, could erupt when dealing with women. There had been others before Lucy Marie and Birdie and he couldn't count on self-restraint if he had to keep control of a stable of whores.

Then there were the scams, either by phone or using the Internet.The scammers were mostly international, in Eastern Europe, India or other countries that Bucks would have trouble finding, even with an Atlas. He had heard that Joey-D and his girlfriend were still pulling in some dough phoning retirees claiming to be Bank Auditors, the Income Tax Department or a distant Police Force, demanding immediate monies 'or else'. They never asked for anything big, not like the Nigerians, usually less than two thousand and you only needed two or three successes a week to keep smiling.

Bucks thought that this might be a game to look into but he'd need help to set up untraceable phone numbers as well as a protected money drop. He wondered if he could talk to Joey-D and get some advice. Then he considered Joey-D. Would he help set up a potential competitor? Slim chance of that.

His mind floated back to Eve. He would need to see her again despite the price.

So far in his life he had been smart enough not to use drugs or alcohol seeing, at an early age, how addiction screwed up your life. He had no problem selling the products but he avoided being a user. Now he admitted to himself he was hooked; he needed Eve. He shook off these thoughts now recognizing another need--food. He considered breakfast at the hotel but best to save thirty bucks. He'd go home. His mother would give him a big breakfast, no tip needed.

***

The start of the weekend had kept Rush active. Friday night was round-robin badminton followed by pizza and a beer. This morning he picked up

Jimmy, firstly for lunch, then in the afternoon to visit the City Art Gallery. It was now nearing a year of their Big Brother/Little Brother relationship. Originally he had volunteered as he'd been told they urgently needed more 'Big Brothers'. He was quickly approved as he was a Police Officer. It was only later that a question came to his mind. Was he subconsciously seeking a replacement for his own missing son? He thought not. Stefan would now be nearly twenty, not twelve. Rush felt that Jimmy had begun slowly to trust him. He was becoming more open about his interests and his life. Jimmy lived with his mother on the seventh floor of a subsidized apartment building in an area of the City heavily populated by single parent families in cramped quarters. It was a section of the City with a higher crime rate. Jimmy had been delighted with Rush's gift of a Miami Heat jersey. He had put it on right away. Rush wondered how he might like the Art Gallery. So far they'd gone to the places that Rush thought might be of interest for a twelve year old boy. He was running out of ideas so why not try the Gallery. He was sure Jimmy hadn't been there before.

Jimmy seemed to like some of the paintings displayed, eyeing the female nudes with interest. He also was interested in some of the sculptures, preferring three-dimensional art. Jimmy would circle the sculptures, slowly viewing art from all angles. Leaving the gallery they stopped for a milkshake, before returning Jimmy to his mother and then Rush went back to his small apartment, on the lower level of the family home.

There was a two-way intercom connecting the levels. It buzzed. It was his father.

"Rush, there's a young man at the front door. He's asking if you live here...wanting to see you."

"What's his name?"

"He hasn't told me. He has a bit of an accent and...oh yeah...he has the biggest backpack I've ever seen."

"Okay I'll come around, from the outside. I'd like to see who he is first...to check him out."

It was his Police instinct to be cautious of any unknown situation so Rush went out his own door, walking around the garage, out to the street to see a tall slim light-haired young man, a large backpack lying on the front step beside him. Russell was just inside the front door waiting for

Rush's next move. Rush's voice startled the visitor, "What do you want? Who are you?"

He turned to face Rush then tried to find the words he had practised beforehand.

"Mr. Rushton?…Good...I think that...that we are...related."

Even before he finished these faltering words Rush had recognized Ana's features in this young man's face. He knew. It was Stefan. It was his son. The two of them stood there, six feet apart, both frozen with the reality and both unsure what to do next. Rush finally stepped forward, grabbing the youngster's broad shoulders pulling him to his own chest, only able to murmur, "Stefan...Stefan." Russell now realized who this was. After Rush and Stefan released each other, he took a step down to hug his grandson. Then the threesome awkwardly stood together with no one with enough emotional self-control to try to say anything. The silence continued until Rush put an arm over each shoulder pulling Stefan and Russell inside the door. Stefan turned to retrieve his pack and pulled it inside. Then they found their voices and all began to talk at once. Stefan declined anything to eat or drink but Rush, seeing a bit of a grimace asked if he needed the washroom. There was a momentary blank before Stefan nodded, "Yes, the toilet."

Rush led him down the hall then returned to Russell. He walked over to embrace his father, "Isn't what we always wanted?"

They could hear Stefan walk back slowly back down the hall. Rush knew he'd be looking at the photos that his mother had half-filled both walls with. Stefan's own photo in the arms of his grandmother was prominent. As he came back into the room he asked, "Vecamamina ? Grandmother?"

Both Russell and Rush shook their heads simultaneously. Stefan asked, "When?"

When told he said, "I'm too late…I'm so sorry...Mate...my mother said she was a lovely, beautiful person". Then he summoned up courage to ask, "Do I have any brothers...sisters? No...You never married? No?"

They now began a flurry of questions at Stefan. He, with occasional searches for the proper words, explained he had finished his Academia schooling in Latvia and was on a trip to North America before starting University. He had been accepted at the University of Uppsala. He saw his grandfather's eyebrows form the question. He answered, "It's in Sweden, a bit north of Stockholm. Very old, very prestigious."

Rush asked "What will you take?"

"Economics and International Studies."

Rush did know a little about the University. It was highly ranked and Rush had to presume that his son must have high marks to qualify and felt paternal pride. He was tempted to ask about Stefan's finances for tuition but felt that was, at this point, less than an hour of meeting, too soon. Instead he asked, "How's your Swedish?"

Stefan gave a shrug. "Not as good as it should be but I'm improving. I have a good ear for languages. Uppsala has some courses taught in English. Mate was insistent that I learn English starting when I was three, from Mate, from books, from television."

Rush again held back. He very much wanted to ask about Ana. On one hand he hoped that she'd forged a happy life on returning to Latvia. On the other he still felt the sting of her rejection of a life with Rush. He decided to wait until Stefan and he had progressed further in their relationship. Stefan explained that he started his trip with a school friend but they'd met other Latvians in Paris, hooked up with them, then on to London, flying to Montreal for a few days, then bussing down here to the City. The plan was to go to New York City, then on to Washington before heading to Florida, finally flying home for the summer weeks before starting their college studies. Stefan said his friends had gone from the bus depot to a youth hostel, but he, with the address that his mother had given him, asked directions and took the subway then a bus to find the home where he had spent the first six months of his life, where he might to find his missing father and his grandparents.

Although these three generations were becoming more comfortable in asking as well as telling about their respective lives the subject of Ana stayed in the background. Stefan, when Russell asked, said she was healthy and busy as a receptionist working for a dentist.

Russell and Rush both volunteered their home but Stefan politely declined, saying he was committed to staying with his friends. He explained that they would be a bit lost without his ability in English. He said one of his new friends did well in French, which helped for their few days in Montreal, but that wouldn't work here. Rush had suspected there was a woman involved, waiting back at the hostel. Stefan went on to say that the next morning was a pre-planned trip. The group was to spend the day going to Niagara Falls but he would call the morning after so they could arrange to see each other again. Stefan apologized he couldn't stay longer but Rush felt that a gradual assimilation would be best; take one step at a time before sorting out the future of this new found relationship.

Rush said he would drive Stefa back to the hostel so Russell gave his taller, slimmer grandson a final hug before the backpack slid into the backseat with Stefan into the front. Rush had taken out his Police business card, identical to the one that he left with Birdie, jotting both his personal cell number as well as Russell's home number to hand it over to Stefan. As they drove downtown, with Rush concentrating on busy traffic, Stefan, after clearing his throat, asked, "I'm not sure what to call you...you and my grandfather." He left the question hanging.

"I'm fine with Rush. I'm sure that Dad will also be fine with Russell. Does that suit you?" Rush was glad that Stefan agreed. There were too many years separating what could have been and what there was now. Then they were stopping in front of the Hostel and Stefan slid out his pack then came back to the still open passenger door, extending his hand inside to grab Rush's. He was about to close the door but reopened it, reaching down into his backpack. "Oh, I nearly forgot. This is from Mate...from Ana... for you." Then he was gone inside the hostel's front door. Rush held the envelope for a few seconds but decided he'd read it when he was alone, back home, downstairs in the small rooms that he and Ana shared throughout her pregnancy and the first half year of Stefan's existence. He slid it into his pocket and then began his drive home.

***

Marielle had her evening arranged. It would be a quiet one as she stopped to pick up a spinach salad and a crusty roll for dinner. Afterwards she planned to dig deeper into the first year law book she bought in hopeful anticipation of hearing soon from the Law School. She was crunching on her salad when her phone rang; the display showed her sister's name.

"Merde" was her reaction.

She couldn't ignore her; she'd never been able to.

"Hi Sylvie... how's it going?"

"Marielle. I need to see you...tonight...right away...can I?"

"Sure, come on over. Have you eaten anything?"

"No, but that's okay. I just need to see you." There was a pause as Sylvie knew she had to tell her sister sooner or later. "He's at it again. I need out. I'll be right over ...sure that's okay?"

Sylvie had called before about her problems with Remi. Marielle had given her the same advice then as she would, without doubt, have to do so again tonight. Marielle thought back to her sister's boyfriend before Remi, another live-in, who had also taken advantage of Sylvie's placid nature. The problem with Remi was his temper and his emotional, often physical reaction, with Sylvie being the recipient. She would tell her sister to leave him but knew in advance Sylvie would go back to Remi.

Although biologically just half-sisters, Marielle had never thought of Sylvie as being less than her adorable little sister, watching, helping as she grew, only ten when their mother was diagnosed and within months had died. Marielle took on a new role, as maternal replacement, a role with both a burden and the satisfaction that Marielle, then eighteen, could legally take responsibility for Sylvie's upbringing. The alternatives were placing Sylvie in a strange home or worse, that an attempt would be made to find her birth-father, who skipped out before Sylvie's sixth birthday. At least he taught them his native Spanish but little else before suddenly leaving. Mother then uprooted her two daughters to pack and fly west, re-crossing the Atlantic, to start life anew. Marielle didn't consider her own upbringing overly traumatic when compared to her sister's life, which Marielle suspected, had left her too anxious to please, so wanting to be wanted.

Hearing her footsteps coming up the stairs Marielle opened the door and, without words, enveloped her sister in her arms. They stood, hugging, only Sylvie's sobs mixing with Marielle's, "Ma petite...Ma petite..."

Over the next half-hour Sylvie haltingly recounted the details of this last episode in the real-life melodrama with Remi. It had started when he had come home, finally admitting his bank balance wouldn't cover the month-end rental of their apartment. This wasn't the first time. Marielle knew the reason. Remi was a gambler. He didn't smoke, didn't do drugs, drank only on weekends, but figuring out the odds every day consumed most minutes when not otherwise occupied as a Used Car Salesman. He didn't follow the horses. He thought they were too unpredictable and their trainers and jockeys too venal. He bet on teams: baseball, soccer, hockey, basketball. He didn't do this at a machine at a corner store. Their payoffs were too controlled, too limited. He dealt through his cell phone, calling bookies. Their odds were wider, paying more for winners. Remi had tried to quit but each morning's Sports Section had him calculating, assessing, relying on his 'instinct' to pick the winners then make the phone call.

Against her better judgment Marielle offered a 'loan' to her sister, to cover the rent.

Sylvie thanked her but said this was her problem to solve. Silently Marielle disagreed. As long as her sister was having problems she knew these would spill over into her life as well. At times love involved more worry than anything else. She wondered how her sister could cover the rent. She hoped that it wouldn't involve the loan shop, neon lit with the words, $TOP 4 *FA$T CA$H*, near their apartment. She repeated her offer to Sylvie and now there was hesitation then finally a tearful admission that this would really help but she'd be paid back soon, with interest. Marielle wrote out the cheque directly to the property management company. She wanted to ensure the money was not somehow diverted by Remi to his own needs as Marielle could guess that if he was short of money he undoubtedly owed some to his bookie.

Finally, despite Marielle's attempt to have her stay over, Sylvie left to return to Remi.

She admitted she wasn't strong enough to leave him. She did promise Marielle that she would work harder this time, urging Remi to enroll a Gamblers Anonymous group. After all this Marielle tried to concentrate on the Law book without success. She decided to do laundry and some ironing. With her hands occupied her mind might be diverted from her sister's comment that she wasn't strong enough, "Not like you Marielle. You're the strong one. I inherited the boobs...you the brains." Marielle could only hope that these 'brains' continue to be strong enough to carry both sisters into the future.

***

Remi did feel badly about Sylvie and their argument. He felt he hadn't actually hit her but realized that if she hadn't ducked there could have been contact. Maybe her move was self-defence, a teaching born from the past when she hadn't ducked in time. Well she was gone now. Most likely to her sister's. Remi knew that Marielle didn't like him; he didn't think much of her, too damned confident of herself and her job. Still Remi wasn't too worried about Sylvie. He expected her back, maybe tonight, certainly tomorrow. No, right now his worry was about money. He'd been cut off from any further betting until he paid up but how could he get the money if he couldn't bet?

When Buddy said he had a week to find the $900 owed he also slipped a name to him.

"Remi, you are in the car business aren't you? O.K. there's a guy also in that business too. Maybe you should talk to him. You could help him, he could help you. His name is Santos. Should I ask him to call you? At work? Maybe tomorrow, around noon? Forget that I called him Santos. He would prefer you didn't know that. I shouldn't have told you his name...forget I did." Buddy stopped waiting for a response from Remi. When he heard a quiet "Go on" he did. "Well, if he's interested and has something for you I'll get him to call you at work tomorrow. Let's see...I'll tell him to be... Sonny...yeah...Sonny Liston. Okay? You got that? Good. Just remember I'm giving you only a week."

Remi's commission on this month's sales wouldn't be great, unless tomorrow's month-end was spectacular. Even then his commissions weren't paid until the tenth.

He had to hope that Sylvie, if she'd gone to her sister's place, had been able to get money to cover some of the rent owing. He'd have to wait to see if this Sonny Liston would call tomorrow. He had little choice.

CHAPTER TWENTY-ONE

It was the next morning but thousands of miles away as Edo prepared to go shopping with his mother. He preferred to shop on his own but she was insistent they take the bus that morning to Govennia that had more shopping options than their much smaller town afforded. Edo would also have preferred to have jumped on his motorbike instead of the slow jolting bus. The bike, not new but smart enough, was one of the first purchases he'd made with the money that he had 'earned' by completing his assignment on that Caribbean island. There'd been enough money left over, coupled with living free with his mother, so that he'd been able to relax, take his time looking for a job. They were hard to find but then again he really wasn't trying that hard. When he came out to breakfast in jeans and an old shirt his mother sent him back telling him she'd be ashamed to be seen with a son that looked like he was a Roma. When he came out she didn't seem overly pleased at his choice of shirt. She said they'd buy a better one this morning.

In Govennia he shuffled around dutifully following his mother while she shopped. She picked out a conservative shirt that Edo wouldn't have chosen but acceptable enough since she was paying for it. Furthermore, she insisted he try it on and then was just as insistent he continue to wear it, stuffing his older shirt into the bag.Then she announced that they would have lunch. Good, thought Edo, as he was now hungry. Instead of heading to a restaurant she led Edo down a sidestreet to a small but neat house announcing at the door that Helina, her old friend, had invited them. She ignored the sour look from her son and rang the bell.

Helina had prepared an elaborate mid-day meal that more than satisfied Edo's stomach. Competing with his appetite was the pleasing company of Helina's daughter.

Elania was quiet and shy but Edo was more than pleased when, at her mother's urging, she took food to Edo, bending over so that the view of her firm ample breasts were temptingly revealed. As she walked away, back to her seat, her shapely hips weren't hidden either.

While eating delicious dessert pastries, again served with a flash of flesh, Edo suddenly realized what was happening. This 'shopping trip' was the first step of matchmaking between two old friends, one with an eligible son, the other with a marriageable daughter. This realization didn't cause him to suddenly run out the door.

She certainly would be a luscious choice and Edo was astute enough to note that her mother was still comparatively young looking, much more so than his mother's other friends. This promised that whoever took Elania as a bride would not have age and food fatten her too early in life.

Edo was quiet as the bus bumped its way back home. His thoughts flitted back between Elania's breasts and the possibility of another phone call, insisting that his duty to his heritage and his family wasn't yet complete. It was over a year ago that he had been approached to respond to that duty. It hadn't been difficult for him to answer that call, especially when his mother realized what was happening. There was no doubt in her mind and if there was a slight doubt, a sliver of fear within Edo, he ignored it and soon was on his way, deep into the hills, for his training sessions. Only first names were used between the three trainers and three recruits. The first two weeks were hard physically, running up and down the hills carrying backpacks, a few pounds heavier each day. Then came the combat training, man on man battles, finally the usage of the daggers, cords, the quieter ways of killing. Finally they were ready. Edo didn't know what the other two received but he had to think his assigned target, Sgt. Vuk Losavik, who'd been in charge of the squad that took his father, brother and uncles up to that meadow that morning, was the most important. It also had the added adventure of going to Miami, enrolling in school, so as to gain eventual access to the island that Losavik was hiding on. The idea of dealing with dead bodies at the school wasn't appealing but he had somehow managed to overcome that.

Now as the bus took the road's final curve back to his hometown he had to find a way, should they call him again, to convince them that he'd done enough, that the family's revenge was satisfied, his duty done. His mind went back to his meeting with Elania. Clearly the stage was being set, between the mothers, and he didn't mind the prospects of snuggling in beside her body, particularly if being a married man, responsible for a wife, would be enough reason to disqualify him for further assassination assignments. He now would work at getting a job, maybe in Govennia, and begin calling on Elania.

***

A few time zones westward the cab pulled up to the spacious entrance of the resort, the more upscale of the two which Jose Fuente owned. It was over three hours since David had left Isla Cresciente. This was the start of his month-end getaway, a chance to regenerate, to re-invigorate his mind and body, but first requiring his usual regression into his excesses before he was able to revert back to a more normal level. The staff at the tile and marble front desk were busy until Jaime looked up, "Doctor Daveed!" He came from behind the desk to hug David. The two female staff behind the desk gave the new arrival shy smiles. He was well known by the staff for his monthly visits. There was usually a room, sometimes a suite, that wasn't in use and David soon had a key and was pulling his case along a pathway leading to his room overlooking the beach. Later he'd check in with Sandro, the resort's Athletic Director, with a handsome face and tanned steely body, who was immediately noticed by most of the female guests, married or not. For now David simply wanted to stretch out in the shade, with aged rum in his glass, to feel the sea breeze, to begin his unwinding. He'd see Sandro later for his recommendation on the best of his also-rans.

As he relaxed in the sunshine he thought back to his childhood, back to the similar warmth of Trinidad. As a child it was his mother, never his father, who would tuck him in at night telling bedtime stories. They were not the usual fairy tales. She knew her son wanted more realistic stories than old worn fantasies. David remembered she never used a book, she just created scenes and dialogue as she went along, smooth strains from her imagination infusing his own, until contentedly, he was asleep.

He had a hard time getting to sleep on his first few days at boarding school in England. It was the same school that his father and grandfather had attended. He was just fourteen and clearly missed the comforts and friends at home. He wanted to return to Trinidad's warmth in the winter. For David it would have made more sense to summer in England then to winter in the Caribbean but that's not how his, otherwise sensible, parents arranged. After a few weeks in class, out on the pitch or field, despite the weather, he settled down. Normal sleep returned.

He returned home for the hot summers. He was just sixteen when the summer heat steamed higher as he and Lisa Parsons, who knew each other as children, reconnected socially and then much more intimately. It was the first time for both. David and Lisa didn't feel that they had discovered sex; they felt that they had invented it. There were many tears when he took the flight back to England and boarding school.

At midterm his pain was eased when he met Evelyn. She was a year older and a trainee nurse at St. Hilda's Hospital twenty miles from his school. Halfway between both was a country pub, very lax about asking for proof of age. Evelyn's group of girls along with David's friends met one autumn evening. Neither David nor Evelyn were virgins and their libidos propelled them, after a few sessions of groping, to a successful coupling, repeated as often as they could manage. There were no promises of a future together; the present was enough for both. After sex they'd talk and David became fascinated with her tales of the inner workings at the hospital, its successes, its hidden failures, the god-like position of the doctors, mostly male of course. This may have been the match that lit his candle for Medicine.

He did very well both scholastically and in sports. His family, considering their English heritage, assumed that he would go on to university in England, preferably Cambridge or Oxford but David, without their knowledge, decided the New World would be better than the Old to study to be a doctor, most likely a surgeon. When he presented his choice, cemented with notice of a University acceptance, they had to agree it had a fine reputation and seeing their son's mind was set they accepted, with minor grumbling, his decision.They were also surprised at his choice of Medicine instead of Commerce or Law. They assumed that their only child (for his mother one childbirth was enough) would follow the same family path but accepted and that September David enrolled in a Science programme as a prerequisite for Pre-Med.

He was in his third year at University, now in Pre-Meds, when he was told that his replacement roommate would be a freshman. This is how he met Rushton Sterne and their friendship began. David came to appreciate the stability that Rush's common sense gave him. David knew his strengths and his weaknesses; how easily he could veer off course. Despite being three years younger, Rush could steer him back. After four years as roommates their paths separated. Rush was back to live at home, now into Law School. David was finishing his medical degree then decided to go to England for his Surgical Internship. On parting they didn't make any solemn vows to keep up their friendship; they just simply shook hands, then embraced, with David's height and long arms enveloping Rush. They both knew they were friends for life.

Naturally the miles between them lessened their contact. Sometimes there were many weeks, even months between. Rush had his schooling diverted by Ana, the Police, then parenthood. Although David's life was busy with his internship then on to his residency he still found time to burn the candle at both ends; fortunately it was a long candle.

At the hospital as David was guided by a mumbling senior resident surgeon, doing the usual morning rounds, he saw Evelyn swishing by in her starched uniform.They later had tea. She was now married with a year old son and a husband, a civil servant. Afterwards David was struck by her choice of domesticity, a concept that was a stranger to him. Two years later, now a fully recognized specialist but still too young for Harley Street, he met Victoria Longhurst. She was over ten years younger and part of the active party set in London, a would-be designer but not yet overly successful. It was not surprising that they ended up in bed. What was surprising was that it wasn't a passing one night fling. It lasted over a month then a predictable conflict of egos split them.

It wasn't for long. A not totally accidental meeting, engineered by Victoria's girlfriends, reconnected them, soon back to bed and, within another month, news of their engagement spread quickly through those in the know, in and beyond London. David's mother was more than delighted and was soon flying to Heathrow to meet the bride-to-be. Just as important was to meet her family. The Longhursts were noticeable higher on the social scale than her own lineage. This made the marriage more than acceptable to David's mother, perhaps a little less so to Victoria's family. Still Dr. David Newton was a handsome, mature, and recognized surgeon. There was still concern as to his resources. A quick check confirmed that his father's family had deep rooted connections to Trinidad's sugar and rum history. Edward Lewis Newton had been a lawyer, then a teacher, now a seated Justice in the Lower Courts, a rank noticeably less than a High Court Judge. The Longhursts were advised that the Newtons had an old, stately home but it was doubted that the family's fortunes were deep. It was common knowledge, at least within the family, that Victoria would be the prime beneficiary of her childless aunt, who was nearing eighty but, due to continuous smoking, was already connected to a portable oxygen canister. The Longhursts' worry was ensuring that their daughter's assets would not be split in the event of the marriage floundering. They already had their solicitors working on a prenuptial agreement. Perhaps they were prescient about the prospects but, regardless, they prepared for a large wedding, asking only nominal input from the groom's side.

The wedding was considered to have been a success and the newlyweds honeymooned in St. Barts then onto Trinidad for a few days. Back in London David stayed very busy at the hospital. Victoria was less busy but split her day between her designing assignments and seeing all her friends. These were intermingled as her first customers were those she knew, those who would support her, give her a chance. For the first few months of marriage their ardour still consumed and carried them but then this passion only heated their bedroom. Outside of it their lives gradually took divergent paths. David usually had morning surgeries and his need for reasonable sleep and abstinence beforehand began to conflict with Victoria's social life. Her designing career now was slowly ebbing, due both to lack of talent as well as application. Their differing paths widened as Victoria began spending more time with her friends while David became more immersed in the demands of surgery, seminars, and conferences. This dedication was, to Victoria, a competing mistress and gave her more reason for her reverting to her pre-David lifestyle.

One evening David returned home to find a note from Victoria. It was simple. There was a dinner to be heated in the microwave and that she might be late so he shouldn't wait up. He didn't but when his alarm rang at six he was alone in their bed. During the morning he attempted to reach her both at home and on her cell. Finally, at four, she answered their home phone. She apologized but said she'd stayed overnight with friends, claiming she had too much wine to attempt driving and, oh yes, her cell phone had run out of charge. David hung up wondering was it only wine that had prevented her from coming home? Why had she not, at the least, arranged to leave a message on his?

In the weeks that followed they attempted to patch up 'a fuss': Victoria's words. She dutifully accompanied David to the various hospital or medical functions trying to hide her boredom of being encircled by people the age of her parents. David, although he'd met Victoria in the younger party scene, began to both feel and see that their age difference, outside of bed, now made him uncomfortable in the alcohol/drug powered partying that Victoria had been part of her young adult life, one she seemed continuing to need.

Then there was another evening when she wasn't at home. Again a note, *"Sorry darling. Out with friends. May be late. Don't stay up. Sweet dreams...Love...Victoria."*

David had worrisome dreams not helped by an empty bedside. She did call him at the hospital, leaving a message of apology that her friend had OD'd and she had to stay the night with her. That evening Victoria was very affectionate, then passionate, making up to David for his night alone.

So their lives, like the tides, ebbed away or surged together. David was never sure what he would find when he came home at night but there were more uncertainties than sureties. If he found himself alone, after finding something to eat, he would find something to drink, whatever his morning schedule.

Yet another morning waking alone, David took off to hospital with worry and a Scotch-induced headache. His first surgery went well. He went for coffee and another analgesic. There was no message on his cell.

At lunch he double checked his messages. There was a new one:

> *Subject: Your Mother.*
>
> *David: This morning your mother suffered a stroke and she is in the hospital in Port of Spain.*
>
> *I'm told she isn't conscious but little else. The head doctor here is Peter Ewart. You might remember him from school and you may want to call him to find out more than they are telling me.......Father.*

He tried the Hospital in Trinidad first and was promised that Dr. Ewart would call back 'as soon as it is convenient'. He did reach his father who could only tell him that his mother was fine the evening before but, in the middle of the night, he heard a crash in their hallway to find his wife on the floor, unconscious. It seemed hours waiting for the ambulance but David realized that his father would count seconds as minutes. Before he finished this call there was a beep to indicate he was receiving another call. It wasn't Peter Ewart. It was a curt message from Victoria, "David. We need to talk. Tonight. I'm at home."

His mind was only partially on patients as he then went on his post-op rounds. Finally a call. It was Peter Ewart. David listened, then began his questions to learn that his mother's condition was poor but a prognosis would have to wait until further tests could be done. In the meanwhile they could only keep her as stable as possible. Whether she would have a reasonable level of recovery, be a vegetable, or survive were questions that were yet unanswerable. Ewart promised to keep him updated and would email David the test results once known.

At home Victoria was waiting, a wine glass in her hand, but silent. There was ice, a glass and Scotch waiting on the table. David sat opposite his wife, poured a stiff shot over a cube before lifting his glass, a mocking salute, "Welcome home."

The following half hour had no screaming or shouting but each exchange of words was ice edged, ending hurtful to both. David hadn't told her about his mother but his phone buzzed. It was Peter Ewart, "David. Sorry to tell you. Your mother has died. I haven't called your father yet. Should I...or would you prefer...?"

After thanking Peter he looked up to see Victoria's questioning face. He told her but it didn't seem to register at first. She didn't ask any details, only getting up to go to the kitchen. As he dialed his father's number he could hear her pouring more wine into her glass. His conversation with his father was stilted, non-emotional. It was as if David was giving sad news to a relative of a patient who had not survived surgery. He promised to be home as soon as he could rearrange his surgical schedule and book a flight.

To Victoria he simply said he would be leaving for a while. Before he began calling to arrange matters he thought he heard her say, faintly from the kitchen door, "I'm sorry", but he couldn't be sure.

Twenty-four hours later he was high over the Atlantic thanking the attendant for the ice-cubed glass, and the plastic bottle of Scotch, that she'd brought him.

CHAPTER TWENTY-TWO

Birdie's legs were already aching, her lungs panting and her cravings still calling for meth. Just a touch, that all she needed. She tried to think back. Was it a month, maybe two? Her teeth and jaw still hurt, didn't seem to work as they should, but her memory was clear enough to remember Bucks and his fists. Then there was the hospital, the cops, the need to get away, as far as she could. Now she was miles and miles away, safe from both Bucks and the police but she couldn't outrun her addiction. Her new friends were trying to help, keeping her busy. Here she was trying to keep up the pace to follow the eight year old daughter of her niece along the path, up the grade, towards the look-out clearing. There she could rest before heading back down the hill, back to her temporary refuge here high in the hills. She really did appreciate the help that she'd been given and, she had to admit, there were times now when the craving didn't call but there were just as many times when it shouted, demanding to be satisfied. She was ten miles or more from the Reservation. She knew that there she'd find meth, or at least something available for sale, that would quench this hunger. She didn't have any money left. This had been used up for bus fare, a bit of food and some hash she'd bought along the way. She considered stealing from her niece's purse that hung behind the kitchen door. As well there'd be the keys to the pick-up parked outside. She'd never learned to drive but thought she could steer and brake enough around the curves in the road but she already looked inside the cab. It was a gear shift. She didn't think she'd be able to handle that or, even if she managed it, how she'd handle the disappointment of her niece for wiping away the slow progress of all her efforts. She took a deep breath and trudged further, behind the skipping girl, the crest of the hill now in sight.

***

The unopened letter was still pinned to the bulletin board in his kitchen. He wasn't sure why he was avoiding it. Perhaps having gradually, over the years, moved the remembrance of Ana and Stefan into the recesses of his mind, he was unwilling, a little afraid, to open both the letter and all those memories. It was now the evening after Stefan had thrust the letter into his hands at the curb of the hostel. Hesitantly he walked over, unpinned the letter and opened it.

Dear Rushton,

Stefan was very wanting connecting with you. To see his father. It is his wish and if this letter find your eyes then you have meeting. I pray you like him. He is a fine man, a fine son. We did good. Didn't we? We are fortunate to start him.

You Rushton --Rush --I am sorry for many matters but me pregnant… what should I do? I did in my heart love you. But here in Latvia I also had a love. I had choice --very hard. Big problem. I came home, taking Stefan to see--to feel what best. What I decide would hurt one. Hard… it was you. I pray you wonder mother and father well. I pray you well.

If you have wife? Tell her? Maybe No.

Rush.--you best man for me--Pray you good.
Loving--------Ana
P.S. Sorry my English speling not practise.

He re-read it then carefully replaced it in the envelope to store it at the rear of his lower desk drawer. He had a fleeting thought to try to compose a reply for Stefan to take back to his mother but decided not to, not sure of what to say. Leaning back recalling their first meeting on that Spring afternoon, Ana's one day off from her au-pair duties. Their mutual initial shyness along with her limited English did not suggest anything but, after a third afternoon meeting there was sudden eagerness to be shared, which led to his bed within a week. He wondered now, once again, if he had been seduced. Her urgency, with his predictable response, neither with any thought of the consequences, brought a reality. She was pregnant, but so radiant, so happy with every increase in the size of her belly. Of course she lost her job but moved into the small downstairs apartment of his parents' home with him. What was intended as a bachelor pad became married quarters, with the large closet converted to a nursery. Rush progressed through his first year as a rookie cop to become a proud father. He had anticipated, during pregnancy, a decrease in the level of physical intimacy with Ana. After the delivery he also expected to wait until Ana signalled a resumption of passion but, when it did, the passion was noticeably one-sided. He now had to think he had been merely a pawn, only a paternal necessity. Well, even so, he was proud of Stefan and looked forward to his call, to arrange to see him again.

***

Remi was out on the lot trying to gauge how serious this elderly tire-kicker was to buy one of their 'pre-owned' cars. Remi had seen him pull his old Buick in *'Customers Parking'* to then shuffle over towards Remi's side of the lot. Although he needed sales, he felt he was wasting time, but right now, he had time to waste. He knew, from experience, that this potential customer would bargain for the lowest purchase price and expect a high trade-in value on that old clunker that had managed to get him here. There would be little profit at either end of the deal. Then the loudspeaker crackled "Remi, a call for you on line two." He excused himself and picked up the phone at his desk.

"Hello. My name is Sonny Liston and I'm interested in a car. Not new but low mileage. Something with class and extras, not a basic compact. What do you have?'

Remi was nervous but played out the game describing a few of their higher priced models that 'Sonny' would be interested in.

"You recommend the Caddy? What's the mileage? What are you asking?"

The end result was that 'Sonny' was interested and would like to see it, test drive it, but he was really busy right now. Would it be possible for Remi to drop off the particulars of the car, plus maintenance history, at his office? It was only a mile away. Remi said he could do this at lunch. Sonny would meet him in the lobby of his office building and they could go next door to a fast food joint. "Would that be O.K.?" That was fine with Remi but he could guess, if Sonny did have a real office, it wasn't at the address where they'd meet. After he hung up he looked out the window to see the old guy still there. So Remi, with no high hopes, walked back outside.

An hour and a half later he was munching a hamburger as they discussed the deal. Remi had a specific plan in mind when he promoted the Caddy. Remi explained that their Sales Manager was continuing his affair with Roselyn. She'd been the assistant accountant fired by their straight-laced owner for both the affair and some unaccounted petty cash funds. It was no secret that the affair continued with regular trysts on Thursday afternoons at four. A few weeks ago Remi had carefully followed his boss, curious as to where he picked up Roselyn, then further to park in the rear of a small hotel down by the river. Remi knew he 'borrowed' the Caddy each time. He liked to drive the best, to impress both himself and Roselyn. He had to assume that this would be the same deal this coming Thursday. Sonny liked the plan. All he needed was a copy of the registration and the key coding in advance. Sonny said he had a guy who would cut a key to fit. All Remi had to do was to call Thursday when he saw the Caddy leaving. Sonny would do the rest. Remi was pleased when Sonny slid an envelope over the table. "This is a bit of an advance." Remi hadn't asked what his end of the deal would be. He was in no position to negotiate. He'd take what he was given. A few minutes later, back in his car, he opened the envelope. There were eight fifties. He was tempted to place a bet on the Euro Cup soccer game being played tomorrow. The odds were really good for an upset. Instead he thought of Sylvie. He'd give half towards his betting debts and the rest to treat Sylvie, out for a little shopping then a nice dinner. He knew she'd like this and he might be rewarded when they got home later.

***

After his son had gone back downstairs, Russell Sterne thought back to Ana. Rush had only told him that Stefan had given him a letter from Ana that, obvious to Russell, didn't wholly explain why she'd left, taking her infant son, his and Eleanor's only grandchild, with her. Perhaps partly due to the language and age divide Russell hadn't had a lot to say to Ana while she was living just below them. Eleanor certainly tried and simply doted on Stefan, even when just hours old. Russell, with his own newborn son, was never totally comfortable until Rush had begun to focus, to smile, to slowly find his way to mobility, before he felt a real bond. Eleanor had enjoyed each day of Stefan's progress and was disappointed but understood why Ana wanted to see her family back in Latvia. When it was clear that Ana and Stefan were not returning she hid her anguish from her son as he had enough to deal with, but she couldn't hide it from Russell.

They didn't hide much from each other throughout their marriage, only little harmless things. She did keep one big secret as she didn't tell Russell about her first series of visits to their family doctor. Finally, after referral to the specialist and receiving the lab results, she told him the truth. The tests showed the cancer was already at Stage Three heading to Four. She started treatments but, after five months, she told Russell and later Rush that she would have to accept what she'd been dealt with and would not be having any further treatments. It took less than half a year, the last few weeks in a Hospice, before she was gone. When her heart stopped, the heart of her home stopped with it, leaving her husband and son numb and without any want other than merely to carry on, existing as best they could.

That was over four years ago and although the memories of Eleanor now hurt less Russell still replayed them in his mind, finding some smiles and, at the least, solace. He remembered their first meeting with exacting clarity. He was nearly thirty-five, slated to be an established bachelor for life. He had been a supportive son for his widowed mother. His father was buried in a military cemetery, amongst hundreds of his fellow soldiers, marked with a cross, graves tenderly cared for by those still alive to remember their liberators. Russell had always been proficient with numbers and easily gravitated to accountancy. He was taken on by a firm with connections to investment interests. When he opened his own one-man office it was both as an accountant and as an investment advisor. Clients didn't barge in but didn't trickle in either. He hired an assistant. She handled his appointments. "Mr. Sterne, remember you have a ten o'clock appointment with Mrs. Rushton." This recently widowed and financially confused woman had brought her niece along. As Russell reviewed the material and began to give preliminary options on a financial plan it was the niece, Eleanor Rushton, who began to ask pertinent questions. Russell listened and answered each but as he was doing so he took off his reading glasses to finally notice how pleasant this woman was. He guessed she was not yet thirty and he saw no band on her left hand. He found his mind wavering between two points of interest. It was finally decided that Russell would fully review Mrs. Rushton's portfolio of assets and investments and would prepare an analysis and his recommendations. An appointment was set for the following week.

Eleanor came alone. Her aunt felt unwell, a migraine, but insisted her niece go, "You'll understand it better than I could." Russell concentrated on looking down as he was presenting his summary to Eleanor. Again she asked pointed relevant questions, matching Russell concentration on the subject. Once finished Eleanor thanked him, saying she'd discuss the matter with her aunt but would recommend that Russell be her advisor. Before she could leave Russell asked if she'd like coffee, apologizing that he hadn't offered it sooner. She accepted and Russell learned that she taught a Grade Six class. There were shy silences as they sipped their coffee. Then Russell remembered something he read that morning so he asked, "Do you like Restoration Comedies?" She did. He then said he'd been given a gift of two tickets to a local production of '*She Stoops to Conquer*' for this Friday night. Would she be interested in going? She would.

After she left Russell retrieved the copy of the theatre flyer that he found among this morning's mail that he had consigned to his wastebasket. He quickly called and was relieved to find that tickets were still available. He bought two.

They married six months later, much to the relief of her mother and aunt. "Finally" they said. Better start a family soon but soon didn't happen. After a few years they had tests done. Some issues with both but nothing major. The doctors said to keep trying. They were happy to follow these instructions. Fortunately, it takes only one determined sperm to wriggle its way to success. Now Russell would be a father.

***

David's eyes finally fully opened. There was just a glimmer from the rising sun against the wall. As he waited it spun more crimson and gold into his room. He glanced at the clock. Not yet six-thirty. He now refocused on his day ahead. He needed to be back to Porto del Norte to meet the new batch of clients and be ready for the flight back to Isla. He hoped all of the island's staff would be there and further hoped they were, at this moment, in better shape than he was. As he swung slowly from bed he was relieved to see the other side empty. He tried to remember her name. Wanda? No, that was the night before. He did remember that she was from Maryland, worked in Washington but her name escaped him. If it had rhymed with rum he might have received a hint from the almost empty bottle beside the bed but it stayed quiet. A fast shower helped to revive him. After leaving money for the maids he was soon down to the front desk. The morning shift greeted him with smiling 'Holas'. He did not need to check out as there was never any bill for his stay; he was the guest of Jose Fuentes. He knew Sandro would still be asleep, unlikely alone. David would have liked to thank him for his 'cast-offs'. Instead he found a sleepy cab driver outside. He knew David, knew without asking that he would now steer towards Porto del Norte.

As they drove the sun was soon clouded over and a light rain began to intensify so that the wipers provided the cadence as they followed the coastal road eastward. It began a steady consistent rain, not the usual tropical downpours that might only last minutes. It reminded him of the rain in England and his mind floated back. Was it six, seven, maybe eight years ago that his mother died? He didn't stay long in Trinidad. David was soon landing back at Heathrow, grabbing a taxi, welcomed to London with drumming rain. He remembered rehearsing what he would say to Victoria. He would apologize, then suggest they work out a way of keeping their marriage together, with counselling if necessary. He hoped that his week away gave her time to consider how they could patch the holes. Pulling up to the sidewalk the driver accepted the fare but offered no assistance with David's bags. He was well soaked before he fitted the key and entered the front hall. It was quiet. He called her name. No answer. He only stuck his head into the front sitting room to see half the furniture was missing. He went upstairs, again calling her name. There was no furniture in the upper hall and he wondered if there had been a burglary but entering their bedroom seeing only the bed, his dresser and one lamp, he dismissed that idea. The envelope was conspicuous, set in the middle of the bed. David set down his bags, took the envelope and went back downstairs, settled in the sparse room and opened it. Victoria offered no hope of reconciliation, no let's talk it over, no let's seek counselling, no trial separation. Victoria's message was cruelly clear. This marriage had collapsed.

David had sat there, letting her letter fall to the floor, staring at an empty wall that once featured a floral watercolour, now gone, that they found at an estate sale in the country. Finally he slowly stood up realizing he still wore a wet coat. He went to the kitchen. Most of the counter appliances were gone. He hung his coat over the back of a chair to dry. Seeing the phone he wondered if he should call some-one, call one of her friends, find out where he could contact her. What would he say to her? Did he really have hopes that she would ask to come back. The letter said no, that wasn't in the cards. He then thought of his friends, someone to call, go out to a pub, find sympathy. He had friends but most were married and would be busy. He wouldn't bother them. He saw the cabinet in the corner, at least she hadn't taken that. He opened it. There were a few of his old friends inside. He shook hands with one, from Scotland, and carried it, after grabbing a glass, to the sitting room. They would spend the evening together.

The cab was now nearing Porto del Norte but the rain persisted as did his memory of distant London with Victoria gone. The few months that followed were ones that he would prefer to forget. They were a muddle of days, worrisome weeks that blurred together. He became a robot following a regular regime at the hospital and whisky at home. Week-ends involved less work, more whisky. There were no friends, no women. He did take long lonesome walks but scarcely noticed the views. Sometimes he would end up lost, needing to flag down a taxi to take him home.

Then came the problem of Mrs. Darcy McDonell, the wife of an Under-Secretary at Westminster.The operation to remove her tumour would be complex and with risks which was why her husband demanded the best surgeon. It would be Sir Roderick Lee-Barton, Senior Head of Surgery. Dr. David Newton and Dr. Lionel Reverton would assist. It was a lengthy careful procedure as was usual with Sir Roderick commanding the operating theatre. Also, as was his custom, when he felt his involvement was complete, when he felt the procedure a success, he left the theatre, leaving his assistants to 'mop-up'. Unfortunately, as she was being wheeled to the Recovery Unit, Mrs. McDonell's vital signs beeped warnings. Despite best efforts she was pronounced dead by nightfall. This was hardly the first death at the hospital but it was the patient of Sir Roderick and the wife of the Under-Secretary. The post-mortem was not totally conclusive but there was a suggestion of a surgical error. All of the surgical team were intensely interviewed. The entire Hospital buzzed with opinions, some based on facts, some without. A male nurse did testify that he had seen Dr Newton, in the pre-op washroom, use mouthwash and swallow what appeared to be a pill. When asked about his prior evening preparation for surgery, about alcohol and hours of sleep, it was the considered opinion that his responses were, perhaps, less than forthright.

David received the service of the writ, in which he was named a co-defendant, alleging negligence for the death of 'Anne Lucerne McDonell' the same day as he received notice of the commencement for Divorce Proceedings from Victoria's lawyers. The Hospital and its Insurers clearly didn't want to defend the Civil Action and quickly proceeded with settlement discussions. David also told his now necessary Solicitor that he would not contest the Divorce process. In the meanwhile his status within the Hospital was such that he was only assigned to the simplest procedures. He was aware of the cloud that followed him as he walked the halls. Although he was clever in covering his drinking problems, he couldn't avoid the intense inspection and speculation of the staff. Finally the Head Administrator of the Hospital called him into his office. A Leave of Absence was suggested with the clear expectation that it would be agreed to by Dr. Newton. David could see his days at this Hospital were at an end and he wondered whether any other would welcome him. He considered returning to Trinidad to practise but that had no appeal. He needed something entirely different from his current lifestyle and he knew where his services would be more than welcomed and much needed. Leaving his Solicitor to conclude the Divorce and tidy up the other ends of his London life, he caught a plane to Cairo, the first stop in joining 'Les Medecins', heading to the Horn of Africa.

This much shorter trip in the Republica now ended as his taxi stopped at the dock in Porto del Norte. He was back into the present and would soon be back to the reality of Isla Cresiente.

***

Ellen was home before Sydney and she had time to review the mail, throw out the flyers and put two new bills on the desk to await payment. Sydney handled their finances. Then Ellen's partner was in the door with an affectionate hug and kiss to share. They both busied themselves in their accustomed roles to set out the table, share the dinner preparation duties and pour two glasses of Chardonnay. Seated, facing each other with contented smiles they began, simultaneously to ask each other about their days.

"O.K. You first."

Ellen started, "Good and bad I guess. We had a Missing Child alert first thing but although we get the notification, it's the frontline who does the work. They found the girl by ten, scared but safe. Then came the second alert. We think it's just another worn-out wife. Not all runaways are teen-agers. We'll find her."

"And the bad?"

"Surprisingly, no new cases but the bad are the files that just sit there... unsolved. I get to help on the new ones but my main job, other than locating runaway teen-age girls, is reviewing old files. It really gets frustrating."

"How's Lou?"

"You know, I think he's warming up to me...but it's as if his mind isn't always there at work...it's somewhere else. I'm the same way..." she looked over at Sydney "...when I think about you."

Sydney decided to bypass the compliment. "So, what about your boss, this Rushton guy? Still on your side with you being his chaperone?"

"Oh yeah. It doesn't seem to bother him. He's made me part of the unit since Day One...I'd heard a rumour, before I got there, that he might be gay...which...of course..." She smiled at Sydney, "...is fine by me but now I don't think so. They say he lives with his father. No known special friend of either sex. He's just a quiet decent bright guy who would be perfect for someone who wants a quiet decent bright guy. Know anyone at the Research Library who's looking?'

"Umm...I'll post a notice on the bulletin board tomorrow morning."

Ellen put down her now empty wine glass. "You know this partial suspension must bother him, even if I don't. I have no idea how long this arrangement will last. The upstairs brass haven't put a time limit on it. Technically he was only accused of beating a woman, this Birdie character, but she disappeared before laying charges."

"So she's a missing person, isn't she? Is your unit looking for her?"

"No. No one has filed a MP report. We don't have a file open on her."

"So who is looking for her?"

"I guess that Internal Affairs should want to talk to her. Remember her injuries were to her face. She couldn't talk but only nodded when Rush's card was shown to her."

"If you found her what would you do?'

"Go over her story, hear what she'd swear to, but even if she said Rush beat her silly I wouldn't believe her. Rush is not that type...no way."

"Well." Sydney took a final sip to empty her glass. "What if I help find her? We Research Librarians can do many things, sometimes unsanctioned. All I need is as much personal details you have on her then give me a few days. I'll give it a try."

"That's a deal...now let's cook dinner."

***

Rush was cleaning up the dishes after dinner with his father. Russell was now settled in front of the television when Rush's cell buzzed. It was Stefan.

"How was Niagara Falls?"

Stefan and his friends were impressed. So much water thundering over the edge to crash and swirl before eventually, downstream, calming to become a river again.

"What are your plans for tomorrow?"

Stefan said he and his friends had planned a day of sightseeing in the city and tomorrow night they would be going to a rock concert featuring the 'Ghast House Ghang.'

Rush had never heard of them. "What time is that?"

His son told him that they wouldn't be on stage until after nine but they wanted to see all of the bands, right from the start.

"How about dinner? Any plans?'

There weren't any so it was arranged to meet. Stefan agreed with Rush's suggestion of Thai food. There was a decent restaurant only six blocks from the hostel and Stefan took down the directions. As they spoke Rush had tried to remember Stefan's friend then it came to him.

"Will Simona be coming? Great...but by the way... how's her English?"

"Not so good. Still poor but she's good in French. How are you?"

Rush's French was limited to reading. He had only tried a few attempts at conversation when he was in Paris after David's wedding. They had not been successful. "Sorry Stefan, not fluent but I'm sure we'll manage. I look forward to meeting her."

After disconnecting Rush asked his father whether he wanted to join them for a Thai dinner. Russell hesitated before declining as he thought it best that Rush have time alone with Stefan.

As he went back downstairs Rush wondered about Marielle. She said she was fluent in French having spent part of her childhood in France. He certainly would like to see her but doubted she'd be interested.The dinner they'd had on his last night in Santo Vincenza was still strong in his memory but she had, at the end, only thanked him giving no encouragement that she'd like to duplicate the evening. But then again, all she could do would be to say 'No'. Since he didn't have her home number he'd have to wait until tomorrow. Perhaps he'd try then.

***

As Lou went to his workshop in the basement, he had left his wife and daughter at the table still reviewing plans for the wedding now only two weeks away. The current problem was that the seating capacity of the Banquet Hall was limited at two hundred. More invitations than that had been sent out. Maria patiently explained that not everyone invited would attend although it was expected that all would send gifts. Now they were receiving the acceptance cards. They weren't quite at two hundred but they were getting close. Some of those who were expected only to send regrets now planned to attend. Yet just another problem. Lou had more.

One problem was worrying about the cost of the wedding day. He certainly hoped that the marriage would last. Even if it didn't, he wasn't going to pay for a second one. He wasn't that keen on his son-in-law-to-be or pleased with the thought of him being on top, humping away, with his daughter underneath. Maybe Maria's father felt the same way about him, twenty-six years ago. The need to find a speck of blood on the honeymoon sheets was history now. These days even Catholic couples were well practised by the time they reached the altar.

His second worry was the prospect of having Maria and Gabriella in the same room. He was hopeful that she and his lousy cousin wouldn't be on the list but wasn't surprised when he saw their names. He could hardly object. They were family and his objection might have raised suspicions. He and she would have to meet, certainly in the reception line, where there would be the obligatory hug. No--he wasn't looking forward to it at all. He wondered if he'd get any enjoyment from the wedding. He'd just have to smile, grin, and bear it.

***

The following morning Rush, Lou and Ellen, having no separate table in their crowded office, pulled their chairs together in a loose huddle to review the status of their current files and what the next best step would be. The most recent was the file for 'Leila English'. All three of them thought she'd be located, returned to her family, relieved but puzzled why she left them with no warning, no note. Their Unit wasn't required to answer the 'why', only to find them. Her photo had already been identified by a bus driver who noticed her frightened face when she got on at the depot. She'd only gone as far as the resort area in the hills and the local force was checking with all the hotels and B&Bs. They'd be sure to find her soon.

Rush turned his chair back to his desk. He had decided to call Marielle. He checked his screen for Antioch Life's number and, still not sure if he was being foolish, dialed it. He reached her voicemail, her taped voice pleasant but businesslike, simply asking that a message be left.

"Hello...It's Rush Sterne...you remember me? From down in the Republica? Well I have a favour to ask you. I have a…a relative visiting... from Europe and he has a friend who doesn't speak English but she's fine in French...which I'm not. If you like Thai food and are free tonight, at six, we...I would very much like it if you could help...with the translation. If so we'll be at the Tastes of Bangkok restaurant on Elm Street just north of Seventh. Very informal. You don't need to call me back. Just show up if you're not busy and are hungry. Thanks."

Purposefully he didn't leave his number although she could easily find the number to the Missing Persons Unit. If she couldn't or wouldn't come he didn't want to bother her to call with an excuse, whether invented or not. He was perhaps deluding himself that she'd arrive but if he knew that hope would buoy him for the day.

Back in her office just before lunch, Marielle checked her emails and phone messages. She quickly typed three replies on her keyboard but there was only one taped message that didn't ask for a reply, not even requiring a response or an excuse.

She headed to the cafeteria quickly to find, then to sit with her usual luncheon companion, Marjorie Dempster. Marjorie was known throughout Head Office and even at some of the branches. Now, just less than fifty years with Antioch Life Assurance North America, she was a unifying force connecting with the newest employees as well as the Executive Floor, treating all with the same kindness and, when necessary, concern. She had started as a dicta-typist, still a teen-ager, rising to be the Personal Secretary for the President. After he retired, with Marjorie almost sixty-five, there were plans for a big retirement presentation. She wanted no party because she had no intention of retiring. She pointed out that there was no rule or regulation, merely custom, requiring she should leave. So she stayed, officially with Human Resources, but finding many roles, hard to define under any 'Job Description', but an integral cog in the workings of all floors at Head Office.

Marjorie was her middle name. Her first was Willow, named after a favorite aunt. When she was thirteen, on a Grade 8 'Nature Walk', the teacher was pointing out all signs of the coming Spring. She only had to point out the pussywillows once before the boys in the class reversed that word's segments. She heard the snickers and she saw their eyes glance not only on her blossoming chest but also to that spot below her waist. Fortunately she only had to endure this embarrassment for a few months before her family moved to a town miles away. There she registered at school as Marjorie, never allowing Willow to re-emerge. She was hardly conventional in her personal life. She'd been married three times, wanting but disappointed with no children and, although currently unattached, had a series of 'male friends' but only on her terms. She had no plans to be attached to a fourth husband.

She and Marielle, despite the age gap, became friends. At first Marielle was cautious in forging too close a relationship, concerned that if she disclosed too much then her personal life might be spread about the office. Marjorie wasn't a gossip and always ready to offer a shoulder to cry on for anyone needing it, without revealing any secrets. She did encourage Marielle to have more fun in life. She felt Marielle had so much to offer any man but, with the exit of Luis from her life, it was clear that Marielle wasn't wanting any new relationship. Marielle was focused on her current goal of Law School; a man would complicate matters. Still Marjorie's advice was that even 'one-nighters' had benefits.

As they ate their luncheon salads Marjorie updated Marielle on the plans to celebrate the upcoming anniversary of Antioch's expansion from England to North America. The Chairman of the Home Office was flying over. Marjorie was on the Committee making arrangements and was busily involved. Now thinking of the big dinner planned she asked "You're entitled to bring a guest, any thoughts on who?"

Marielle said she would probably go solo but then, thinking of Rush's message, she told Marjorie that she did have an invitation for dinner this evening but had doubts about going.

"A dinner date! Why not?"

"Well it's someone I hardly know and I'm only wanted as a translator so it's hardly a date either."

"O.K. There's a story here that you haven't told me about. Now spill it!"

Marielle grudgingly gave her the brief details and the name of who she had met on that island when she'd been on assignment there. More reluctantly, she admitted to having dinner at her hotel with him, a Police Officer living here in the City. Marjorie managed to drag out a few more details then scolded Marielle, "So here you are, at dinner, looking out over the city and the sea. Great food and wine with a man across the table paying attention to you. Whoever he is he'd be a fool not to fall in love with you, at least for one night. Did he try anything to entice you up to his room?"

Marielle only laughed. "No...he was a real gentleman but I'll admit I gave him no encouragement."

"So go tonight. Have a nice dinner. Be a translator. What's the harm?"

She headed back to her office, only telling Marjorie that she'd think about it. At her desk she reconsidered the invitation. She had no plans for this evening. The restaurant was within walking distance of her office. Rush was a decent pleasant guy and it sounded as if he really did need someone who spoke French. She also liked Thai food. She looked up the Police number for non-emergencies.

"Hello Rush. It's Marielle. I received your message...is your suspension over?"

"Oh hello. I'm glad you called." As he said this he thought he should have been more assertive, telling her that he was more than glad, but instead only managed "I'm at my desk but with restrictions. It's not cleared up yet. How are you?"

"Fine, thank you. I'm glad you called as I do need to thank you."

"For what?"

"Remember why I wanted to interview your friend? Well it was either on the plane or in that beer truck...we were seated together and you suggested I get a copy of the official registered death certificate as it might be different from the English version supplied by your friend. Well it was and gave us, here at Antioch, ammunition to work out a deal. So you helped save us a quarter of a million. Sorry for both of us that there was no reward offered." She couldn't resist asking, "So how is your friend? Doctor Death."

"That's a bit harsh, isn't it?"

"Well I guess it is but you have to admit there's a comparison to Dr. Kevorkian."

"Perhaps. I didn't know him but I do know David and, at least for the present, he feels he's helping those who, by their own choice, want to… want to advance their due dates."

"Rush, I'm not against euthanasia. I gave up on religion years ago. I only wonder what satisfaction a physician gets running such a setup whose focus is solely on death. I prefer to have a doctor deliver babies, cure illnesses, prolong lives...to follow that Oath thing."

"Well I can tell you that David has done all those things but he had a marriage dissolve, then was with Medecins in Africa, back to a hospital in the Republica before deciding to take over at Isla Cresciente. I really hope he doesn't stay there. It's a waste of his talent."

"Alright...you have a point. I'll stop calling him Dr. Death."

This momentarily dried up the conversation so Rush asked, "I did ask if you were free, for dinner tonight?"

Marielle suddenly took a defensive position deciding to use the well used 'white lie' of many women when asked out by a stranger. "I did have some other plans but...perhaps I can change them. Can I leave it at that?"

Rush had to leave it like that with the hope that she'd show up.

***

Bucks called the Escort Service number, waited to be connected to a woman with a liquid voice. He asked for Eve. The next available 'appointment' with Eve would be next week. That would be fine with Bucks. Yes, at the same time and Hotel as last time. Then this woman added that the price was now a hundred higher. Bucks protested but he was reminded that now he was making a specific request for one of their top escorts and that was the price. Bucks hung up after agreeing to the new terms but he again realized the need to generate more cash, not just for Eve right now but for his other expenses. Still, in his imagination, he saw her body; Eve seemed his most compelling need right now. Tomorrow he would figure something out to get more money. He knew that it would require him to take more risks.

CHAPTER TWENTY-THREE

To be certain he would be there to greet Stefan and his friend, Rush was at the restaurant early. He sat there the sole occupant at the table, nursing a beer. Half an hour later his beer was gone. As other guests arrived he received a few glances, some guessing he'd been stood up by his date. Finally Stefan and Simona were there, all smiles with a brief apology for being a bit late. They had turned the wrong way on their walk here. Just as Rush was mispronouncing French in his attempt at welcoming Simona another voice came from behind him, smooth and fluent, with warmth, "Bonjour...je suis Marielle...Marielle Lebow...et vous?"

Simone answered with a broad smile showing she was more than pleased to be able to converse without halting translations. Stefan introduced himself in commendable French leaving Rush, for a minute, as the outsider. Once they were all seated, drinks ordered, they comfortably settled, using French, English and Latvian, translations inserted when needed.The two young backpackers gave a colourful review of their travels to date and where they hoped to go to next. The groups they had met up with seemed to always be in flux, meeting here, separating there, then perhaps connecting somewhere else, a mixture of nationalities and languages, all sharing youth.

Rush checked his watch and suggested they order their selection from the extensive choices of Thai food. This added up to a wide range but once served they all concentrated on the dishes, now spread on the table. Rush was not surprised at the appetite of Stefan but the slim Simona almost matched him. Rush and his son then became involved in world politics with Stefan covering Latvia and the Baltic countries perched precariously on the border with Russia. Rush mainly listened, pleased with the extent of Stefan's knowledge and opinions. Beside them the two women conversed steadily in French with no lapse of topics. Only Marielle and Rush ordered coffee as Stefan, with apologies, said they were meeting friends to attend the concert and would now have to leave. Then there were 'Adieus', then kisses on both cheeks before they were off. Rush suspected that Marielle and he wouldn't be exchanging kisses later; a handshake was his best expectation.

They were both quiet for a few minutes before Rush opened the conversation in hopes that Marielle wouldn't rush off. "Thank you for coming. You certainly made Simona more comfortable, Stefan too...nice to be young, to be so adventurous, isn't it?"

"I'm sure that they felt we were a bit ancient."

"Certainly me, hardly you."

Marielle sipped her coffee, placed it down, then eyed Rush directly. "When you left the message for me you said it was a visiting relative, not your son. Is this the one you told me about...down in the Republica...that you hadn't seen since he was a baby?"

"Yes, it was a bit of a shock, but a nice one, both for me and my father."

"Your mother is…?"

"Yes. She would have been thrilled to have seen him. She, all of us, only had him for six months, before his mother...well...she left."

"Yes, Simona filled me in on Stefan and his family but it must make you very proud that he wanted to see you, to fill in that void in his life. He seems like a solid, thoughtful twenty year old."

"Well, I wish I could take some credit for his upbringing."

"Well his two mothers obviously did a good job."

Rush was momentarily stunned."His two…?"

"Oh my God! You didn't know." Marielle stopped, hand to her mouth trying to take back her words, not knowing what else to say. She could see that Rush was slowly absorbing this new revelation. Finally he looked up at her, "Did she tell you anything else?"

"For a couple only connected for a few weeks, Simona seems to have learned a lot about Stefan. I think it's a little deeper than just a woman's curiosity. She obviously likes him; perhaps more than a passing young fancy."

"So…?"

Marielle hesitated. "Perhaps Stefan should be telling you...not me." Seeing that Rush was desperate for more details she continued. "Stefan has told her that his mother...Ana?...has told him that he was conceived out of love but...Ana…"

After another hesitation she decided, since she'd gone this far, she'd tell him what else she'd learned, piecing together from what Simona had told her with the addition of her own assumptions to fill in the blanks. As teen-agers Ana and Karla, that was her name, had met, found that their difficult differences with both sexes gave them something in common. Slowly, probably both with pain and promise, they experimented and explored their emotions and bodies. Their society and religion required secrecy but there was a slip-up. Their families suspected. Ana had to leave.

"So, she came over here, as an au pair, found me, tested her...her sexual preferences...became pregnant...or maybe it was their plan...that I was simply a sperm donor for Ana and this Karla."

"Rush, I doubt it was just that...clinical. This would be something that only Ana could tell you, if she even knew herself. Remember she was what...not even twenty...probably confused and unsure of herself. I doubt you were just...well. . .a producer. I think you should give her more credit than that."

He listened to her careful words but still his mind was searching for answers. He felt confused, puzzled at his place in Ana's, Stefan's, as well as in his own life. His face showed Marielle his confusion but then he collected his thoughts and apologized, "Sorry that you've been dragged into this family melodrama."

"Well." She answered with a smile. "I'm glad that you haven't shot the messenger."

"No...no...not at you...really not at Ana. . ." He paused. "I guess I need a little time to sort this all out."

Then Marielle pushed her chair back, in preparation of leaving. "You know,at the very least, you helped, voluntarily out of love to bring a bright young man into the world. One could do worse...but now it's time for me to go. Another busy day tomorrow. I wish you and Stefan well, whatever you and he work out together. Thanks, once again,for another lovely dinner."

Rush stood, mumbling his thanks, asking if he could arrange to see her home. Before she walked away she said that was taken care of. He sat down, watching her leave, reminding him of her exit weeks back, from the dining room at the hotel in Santo Vincenzo. He stayed in his seat, facing three empty chairs that had held individuals who had now become significant in his life.

A few hours later, Marielle was preparing for bed with the choice of either a new novel or a law text to be her companion before sleep. Instead her mind reviewed the dinner with Rush and her unintentional part in telling him about Ana and Karla. She could again picture his face on learning Ana was a lesbian. Did it make it worse or less damaging to his male pride that she left him for a woman rather than a man? She would never meet nor ever know Ana but could sympathize with her, running away from Latvia, coming to a strange land, meeting a caring young Rush, probably losing her clinical virginity, to find herself pregnant. Then Marielle connected the dots to her own mother's young life who had also left her native country. Her mother had never told the exact reason why she suddenly left France but, like Ana, became an 'au pair' helping feed, shepherd the two younger children of a lawyer and his second wife. There was an older son from the first marriage, just eighteen, who would visit, then came to spend the summer, working at a nearby golf course, before he would be away to college. Her mother never gave her any details of her conception other than to say it was not forced.

When the son came back for the Christmas break he was told and to his credit immediately accepted responsibility although his father wanted a test to prove the paternity of his son. Marriage was out of the question by all concerned, including Marielle's mother. A financial arrangement was made to cover the costs of birth and upkeep for future expenses. These ended when her mother, ever homesick, finally returned to France. As far as Marielle knew her birth father never saw her, never held her, didn't know her. However, she knew him. Before her mother died she had disclosed the name to Marielle. Out of curiosity, with no other intention, she used the Internet to research his name. He, like his father, was a successful lawyer with three children, perhaps already a grandfather. As she now picked up the novel to read, she recalled Rush saying that he and Ana's brief history was a melodrama. Marielle's mother's life certainly could be called the same. She could qualify as well: a father she'd never know, a step-father who only had shown affection to his own daughter Sylvie, their mother dying too young, then having to forego a college scholarship to raise her sister. Then there was her love life: losing her virginity in the library of the rectory next door to her parish church, a few short-term romances, the long term, but hardly steady, relationship with Luis-Philipe whose wife and daughter were back in Argentina, then last year her brief fling with her English Lecturer. Maybe she should start to write a book, or at least a soap opera. Instead, here alone in her own bed, she tried to fix her attention back to her book.

***

Rush returned home to see his father's living room light on and, against the wall, the flicker from his television. He decided not to bother him as he might reveal the reason for Ana's leaving him. As much as it dominated his thoughts he didn't want to put a voice to them right now. So he puttered around in his small apartment below, finding things to do, as his mind couldn't shake this new realization, this new aspect of what happened twenty years before. Finally he simply sat down, trying to sort out his emotions from his rational thoughts. Eventually he came to a resolution, an acceptance. Her letter spoke of love. This wasn't a contrivance, a deception. It was a reality for her, different than his, but still real.

He remembered Marielle's words pointing to his share, with Ana, in the creation of their son, a talented human being that would be an asset to the world. This is how he should and would look back on their brief time together. With this thought he settled into bed but before slipping into sleep he wondered if he should somehow thank Marielle, not only for her translating assistance. Perhaps flowers? A dozen roses? No, certainly not roses. They were sent either as an apology or as a personal expression signifying some degree of affection. He felt that would be pushing things on his part and perhaps push her away from any further contact with him. Well, he'd leave the choice of something appropriate until tomorrow morning.

***

Remi heard again from 'Mr. Liston' who suggested they have a quick lunch. This time they were to meet in the lobby of a different suburban office building and, as before, there was a fast food franchise nearby where they found a table to munch on the same excess calories that thousands of others were also digesting. Remi didn't open the envelope that was slid across to him. It was better that he waited to see how much he'd been rewarded than open it now. Whatever his piece, it was not negotiable. Remi was told that there could be more deals, another 'arrangement', at no risk to Remi. Mr. Sonny Liston was interested in any late model imported cars with low mileage. Remi knew that there was a deal in the works with a newly separated wife who wanted to trade-in the car that her affluent husband, prior to his departure, had bought for her, possibly out of guilt for the affair he was having. Remi had been told that the deal hadn't been finalized but the issue wasn't money, the lady simply couldn't make up her mind on the options in the new car. Her loaded AMG should be on Remi's side of the dealership lot within days. Remi didn't give Sonny any specific details but said he expected a car that would 'fit the bill' soon. In turn, Remi was told that they were thinking of doing things a bit differently this time by taking the car right off the lot. Sonny needed full details of the coverage by the security cameras around the dealership.

"We may be in luck. These cameras have had too many breakdowns and we've been told they are scheduled for replacement very soon. I'll probably not know exactly until they show up and begin the job. That would be a good time to take any car you want."

"Remi, remember we don't just want any car. We want one that's worth the effort. Do you know if they have to shut down the entire security system or can they replace each camera one at a time?'

"I'm not an expert but management wants it done when all of us are there so I'd guess that it'll be a complete closing of the system, at least for three hours, maybe more as there are a lot of cameras."

"That sounds A-1. Here's what we'll do. As soon as you see the security company show up, before they start, call me on this number." He stopped to scribble out numbers on the back of his fast food receipt. "That is, if there is something on your lot that's going to be a goody. What I'll do is send a couple of guys around.They'll be interested in buying this goody. They'll want a test drive. They'll give you the usual identification you'll need. You can copy it, tell your manager you are taking these guys out for a test drive. If he doesn't like the idea or wants to meet my guys then we'll scrub the whole thing. I want my guys outside, at a distance so they'll be hard to identify."

“Then what?” questioned Remi.

“You go out with them for the test drive. They’ll want to test it at high speed so they’ll go out of the City to a secondary highway. You’ll tell the cops later that they claimed to hear a noise from a rear wheel, maybe a bearing? The guy driving pulls over. Your story is that you all get out to look at the rear wheel then suddenly you’re on the ground. They take your cell phone. You can say you were stunned, couldn’t fight off two of them. Then the car takes off. You lie there at the side of the road for...maybe twenty minutes. I doubt anyone will stop right away but even if they do then stall, as my guys will need twenty minutes to be on the safe side before the alarm goes out. That’s enough time for us. You got all that?”

“What do you mean by ‘stunned...fight the guys off’?”

“Remi...look...so you might have to take a knock on your coconut, just to leave a mark, a little bruise, to make your story hold water. See...there’s nothing to worry about. You’ll get an envelope with a lot more in it than the one I just gave you.”

Remi wasn’t happy with the bruise part but had to admit that it was needed to keep him in the clear when the Police questioned him.

***

The hot weather on Isla was fortunately tempered with a continuous breeze. This also helped direct the smoke from the crematorium out to sea. On the rare occasion the wind shifted one-eighty they would shut it down.

This morning David scanned the list of clients to be interviewed. First was Matthew Bernard Olmstead. He recalled seeing, shortly after the latest group’s morning arrival, a gaunt-like figure striding up and down the beach. David thought back to when the plane first unloaded its passengers at the jetty. There was this rail thin man, greying his limited hair and moustache, wearing a blue blazer, white shirt and a regimental tie. Now for this solitary parade on the beach the jacket was gone, the tie loosened, shoes and socks off, pants rolled up. David smiled to think that this could have been a photo of holidays on a beach on either side of the English Channel nearly a hundred years ago.

David quickly reviewed Olmstead’s application. His submittal clearly asserted that he was ready to defeat his enemy, this cancer, that he’d been battling now for three years. These few words, to David, spoke of action, not resignation. He went to his door seeing Olmstead a few steps away ready for his interview. He smiled and called him in asking him to sit and, as he did with all prospects, suggested he relax. Olmstead's posture, standing or sitting, gave no hint of relaxation. Always on the look-out for some type of disqualifying dementia, David began his questions but Olmstead was lucid, concise and intelligent and clearly had a mind steeled with determination.

David noted the application stated Olmstead was a widower, two married children, four grandchildren, 'occupation' listed as retired.

"Mr. Olmstead have you discussed this...choice...you are making with your children?"

"Well yes. Partly. I advised them that I was going south to a clinic to supplement the chemotherapy I have been taking in my continued battle with cancer."

"...and what did you not tell them?"

Olmstead paused. "Well I didn't tell them that my oncologist advised me that the cancer cells had gained a distinct tactical advantage."

"...and so?"

"I learned of your clinic, your services, and thought it would be ideal terrain to close out my battle with these cells that have invaded my body. They need to be repulsed, repelled, defeated."

"You know our procedure is irreversible?"

"Oh certainly, but once this enemy is destroyed that will be the final victory." He sat back, smiling, satisfied with his plan.

"Mr. Olmstead. Can I ask...what about you? The rest of you? The good cells?"

He leaned forward and in the most matter of fact voice stated, "Doctor, that's merely collateral damage."

This last clue prompted David to continue, "Mr.Olmstead, can I presume that you have a military background?"

Olmstead grinned, now more relaxed. "Now I suppose I should limit myself to name, rank and serial number, shouldn't I?"

"I know the name, forget the number, what is the rank?"

"Major General. Should have been at least Lieutenant General but…" He seemed to sigh. "...not enough wars for that."

"May I ask about your military career?"

"Sandhurst of course. Then up from Lieutenant, Captain and so on. Mainly stationed in Europe with NATO. A bit in the Near East. Nasty business there, worse than Ireland. Finally some real action in the Falklands. I received my M.C. there as well as a Mention in Dispatches but after that a lot of staff work...quite necessary but boring. Then retirement. A position on the Board of one of the Veterans Hospitals...St. Boniface... heard of it? Then my wife died, I should have been first to go but then this mess which brings me here."

David then recalled a Bart Olmstead, part of the younger crowd that Victoria swirled with in London, so he asked, "Are you related to a Bart Olmstead, a red-haired young man?"

"You must be referring to Bartlett. Yes, that rascal is my eldest grandson. Did you know him?"

"Only in passing. He was a friend of a...friend...Victoria Longhurst."

"Uhmm...Longhurst...Victoria." The General's mind was in review. "The Longhursts of Dutton had a daughter. As I recall...very pretty. Would that be her?" He received David nodded confirmation so continued. "I now remember that she married a friend of Bartlett's. I think that was her second marriage but that also ended in divorce. Then she was in a number of those places...treatment centres...for addiction of some kind...costing her family a lot. A sad situation that, but I can't tell you more. Hopefully she's improved, cured. However that is all I know."

David looked again at the papers on his desk." I see that you want half your ashes sent back to England, the other half to the C.O. at H.Q. in Stanley, Falkland Islands. You have prepared instructions for him?"

"Yes. I want them scattered on Hill 53. That's where we were caught in a trap. Very nasty. I lost three of my men there before we managed to extricate the company to safety. The next day, with better preparation and better info from overhead surveillance, we took the hill, with only two minor casualties." He stopped to reminisce for a minute. "Mind you there's probably no plaque or marker with their names on it. Should be. Good men those. Now there's only sheep."

Then David reviewed the procedures necessary before entering the clinic. The General either nodded or said "Agreed" to each point. He would be ready this afternoon.

"Will you be having lunch then? Perhaps the staff can prepare..."

"No thank you. No luncheon please. Is that all?"

They both stood and David half-expected an exchange of salutes but it was only a firm handshake. At the door General Olmstead turned to David, "Doctor, we'll see each other at 15:00 hours." He left, closing the door with a firm click.

David thought about Victoria. Looking back, as he had done many times before, he came to the same conclusion: their relationship was based too much on passion. There was not enough mutual respect for each other's lives to counterbalance and steady them. It should have only been a brief bonfire for both. He didn't blame her as he should have known better, particularly about himself. His own history should have told him that he wasn't ready for serious commitment, perhaps he'd never be.

CHAPTER TWENTY-FOUR

Throughout Europe's long history its internal boundaries regularly shifted, or were obliterated entirely, whether small Duchies or large Empires. The Balkans were certainly no exception but the Twenty-First Century did bring about some geographical stability. However, there was continued turmoil within and without those lines drawn on a map. They did not form themselves into separate protective cocoons. There were webs from history that criss-crossed these new countries and old enclaves to entrench already deep seated memories. Forgiving and forgetting were alien concepts. Whether loose communities, organizations, or close-knit families, blood still coursed from hearts to heads with scarring stories, often even true, of a past indignity or atrocity.

One such organization were the Loyal Patriots. They kept and protected their own ideology as well as its faithful adherents. One of these was Vuk Losavik. Only a few knew of his hidden location. Vuk had arranged for a letter to be mailed out every month to confirm he was still safe. His leadership of his squad in two similar 'incidents', that resulted in mass graves for men and boys, had marked him as a target for those bent on retaliation. The Loyal Patriots tried to keep his exact location a secret knowing the broader the knowledge the more chance of it being uncovered.

Three matters now gave them concern about Vuk. One was that there had not been any letter from him now for over two months. The second was confirmation from Vuk's sister that the usual monthly money transfer from Vuk had stopped.The third was a report from an informer who had heard gossip. There was a quiet celebration in a small town which had supplied the men and boys for one of those mass graves on that hillside twenty years ago. Further inquiries in that town narrowed down the source of this whispered pride to the mother of a young man, named Edo Vantar, who had been, for nearly a year, in Florida which was close enough to where Vuk had been secreted. Not needing absolute proof the

Loyal Patriots concluded that Edo Vantar had been the instrument that had eliminated Vuk Losavik. They set their own plan in motion to correct this situation. They called upon the son of one of their loyal comrades to be their weapon of retaliation. This was Tomas Ludlosh. He was twenty-two, the same age as his intended target. He was also the champion small arms marksman at the Patriot's sporting club.

***

Marjorie had developed small but helpful ways of assisting Antioch Life's operations. She had for years read a newspaper's 'Obituary' section first. It wasn't just a search of people she knew but she also enjoyed these capsulized glimpses summing up the lives of strangers. Of course these obits were all sanitized. To Marjorie it seemed that, on dying, one's blemishes, faults or even sins were airbrushed away, as if the grieving families were granting a public absolution, sometimes a beatification. She wondered who might write her own death notice; she thought it would be vanity to compose her own.

Now, each morning at her office desk, Marjorie would access the Obituary Columns on her computer. She would compare the names of the recently deceased, their ages, known or estimated, to a list of the lives that Antioch insured. It wasn't a perfect system but worked well enough. Where there was a match Marjorie would then notify the local agent or broker who had written the policy so they could be of assistance to the grieving family. This personal touch pleased Marjorie's sense of the 'right thing to do' as well as giving positive public relations and a better corporate identity for Antioch.

Sometimes she even expanded this to checking the names of those killed in traffic accidents. Only months ago she saw that a single car accident had taken the life of a William Lloyd Hedwick, age 44. A click of her finger confirmed he was insured with Antioch and the policy was for $300,000 and had only been in force for sixty-five days. Marjorie saw the red flags and immediately notified their Legal Department for the involvement of Marielle Lebow, Senior Investigator. Marielle found more red flags as she dug into the matter. A credit check showed that Hedwick was in financial difficulty. Interviews with the Police confirmed that the tire marks were in a straight line after leaving the highway directly into the bridge abutment. Furthermore there was a witness, a driver behind Hedwick, who had seen him begin the same off-highway path towards an abutment a mile before the one he actually hit. The assumption was that he lost his nerve on his first try but succeeded on his second. Marielle's conclusion was that it was suicide which would vitiate the insurance policy. Antioch's only exposure would be the return of the premium, with interest, pennies in comparison to a double-indemnity pay-out of $600,000 for 'Accidental Death'.

The problem was that there was no suicide note and the widow's lawyer, pressing for payment, had advised that Hedwick had never expressed any suicidal inclinations to the family. Discreet checks with co-workers and neighbours found no hint that Hedwich had given any indication that he was planning to end his life although there were rumours that the marriage was having its troubles. Antioch's defences could only rest on details of the accident, his indebtedness as well as another fact that they couldn't introduce into any trial. Marielle had identified his employer's Group Insurer and found that their drug plan had paid for antidepressants. However this was a legal non-starter but gave Antioch no doubt that it was a planned death. The heavy legal onus required that Antioch bear the burden of proving that this was suicide. Their legal beagles advised that a Court might not agree with them.

Marielle had just received confirmation but kept quiet that she had been accepted for First Year at Law School. She'd now have to work out the arrangement, only briefly discussed with her boss Harry, for her to work part-time while at school, to cover some of her expenses. She planned to do that but first wanted to wrap up the Hedwick file. Her recent review of law texts gave her the thought that Antioch's inability to conclusively prove suicide wouldn't automatically also allow the extra $300,000 for 'Accidental Death'. The legal onus was squarely on Antioch to prove suicide but the proof of it being 'accidental' would switch to the plaintiff, the widow. This would be her approach in this morning's meeting with the widow's lawyer.

The lawyer's offices were not in a high office tower downtown but on the second storey of a small building only three blocks from the Hedwick's home. This didn't mean that he was just a local yokel lawyer but did mean that he wouldn't handle any litigation, nor earn big fees, if a lawsuit was necessary. Marielle handed him her business card now noting a "B.A." behind her name. She accepted his offer of coffee and they exchanged opening pleasantries before the opening salvo.

"Now why the hold-up? My client is a grieving widow, with two teenage children, now without a father. You can't prove suicide. Antioch is just playing a game and, if it keeps up and we have to litigate, we'll claim Punitive Damages, big-time."

Marielle took her time before replying with confidence. "We don't have a weak case at all. If we have to defend an Action, you will find we can play a tough game. In Court we can apply for full disclosure of all his medical history. We suspect we'll uncover facts that will supplement the overwhelming physical evidence at the accident scene to prove it couldn't have been anything else but suicide."

She stopped, hoping that this bluff made its mark. The other side of the table showed no outward sign of concern. But he realized that if it were known that the widow-to-be had approached him over a month before the crash to consider separating from her husband, then this might be an adverse factor. Clearly this was privileged information to him but what if she had told one or more friends and Antioch could introduce this into Court?

Marielle continued to outline Antioch's position. "We grant you it's our duty to prove the Exclusion in the Policy for the $300,000 but it would be up to your client's high priced legal team to convince a Court that it was "Accidental" in order to get the additional $300,000." Marielle was subtle in reminding that the local lawyer's fees would end if litigation became necessary. "We could argue that driving his car, on which our credit check showed he was behind in payments, was with an intent to wreck the car for Insurance proceeds, not necessarily suicidal but intentional, not accidental. Obviously we would try to convince the Court that he had another intention, even though he left no physical note." She waited before continuing to ask a question for which she already knew the answer, "And what about the Life Insurance on the mortgage on the house? Have they paid it yet?"

The lawyer didn't answer that but shuffled some papers in front of him before looking up at Marielle."So what are you offering?"

"Well I'd be willing to suggest to my Head Office..." Marielle was conveniently overlooking the fact she was part of Head Office. "... that it might be possible to settle this for $300,000 only. This avoids unnecessary legal costs on both sides plus, I would suggest, clears the way for having her mortgage Insurer pay off her house, once they see that we have settled."

So it was left that he'd discuss this potential settlement with his client, although it would not be his recommendation to accept it. Marielle suspected he would recommend it. Returning to her car she thought about the widow's impending decision. The usual bird in the hand versus two in the bush. She also considered her part in this possible compromise. Was it calculated cruelty to deny the widow and her children the additional monies? Her answer to this was simple. It was her husband's illegal connivance to defraud Antioch. The need of Life Insurance was to be as protection not a scheme to get your beneficiary rich. Hedwick's family would still profit from his death. His plan, at least half of it, could work but, to Marielle's mind, was still unlawful.

While driving back to the Office she again thought about Mrs. Hedwick. How well did she know her husband before her marriage? Did it start out well? How long were they happy? Just another marriage doomed to crumble? Then she considered William Lloyd Hedwick. Was it courage to sacrifice his life to give money to his family, even if a scam? Or was it cowardice to run away from the responsibility of the problems that he had created? She arrived back at Antioch without fully answering these questions but did ask a question of herself. Here she was about to study to become a lawyer. Some lawyers become Judges. She doubted she would ever want to be a Solomon, sitting on the Bench, weighing evidence, making Judgments.

Passing the main floor front lobby the receptionist called out, "Marielle, a delivery came for you. I've sent it up to your Office."

There she found a colourful Spring bouquet of flowers with a simple note, *'Thank you, RS.'* She went to the cafeteria to find something to put them in. They'd be nice on her desk but she could foresee Marjorie coming in to begin the questions. She was surprised that Marjorie's antenna hadn't already detected the delivery. She wouldn't leave the note in view; instead she tucked it into her desk drawer.

***

Rush felt his career was in limbo. He was still in charge of the Unit but restricted in field investigations. He didn't mind Ellen's required involvement as the necessity of their partnership added a two-way benefit. Her presence was a guarantee that he wouldn't be the subject of any more false accusations. In turn he was able to offer quiet advice on improving her investigative abilities and techniques. Rush had accepted H.Q's response to Birdie's still unspoken accusation and the leash imposed as better than a suspension. The problem was how long it would last and, even when dropped, the lingering odour that would be attached to his name. If so, he saw no advancement for his future within the Force.

Again he thought of returning to law school after a hiatus of over twenty years. If he resigned his position with the Police he was sure to get some return on the contributions he made to the Police pension fund. His father handled all of his financial affairs. They'd have to talk about the possibility of Rush living without a paycheck for three years plus the expenses of tuition and books. He wondered if he would get any credit for some of the courses he'd passed, with good marks, years ago. He decided it was time to do something now, not simply sit and wonder. He'd call his old friend Morris.

He dialed the Law School's number and was connected to a secretary advising that Professor Newman was currently in the Lecture Hall. Would he care to leave a recorded message? He did:

> *"Hi Morris. Rush here. It has been a while since we grabbed lunch.*
>
> *At your favorite deli. Check your schedule and call back. As well think about a question. If I applied and was accepted back to Law would I have to start in Year One or could there be some way to get some credit for my past history there? Anyway, give me a Call...we can talk about it over lunch."*

***

She stopped again at the usual spot where she needed to catch her breath, regain some strength, to continue up the trail to the clearing. She did feel much stronger now as her body and mind slowly were shedding the dependencies that had, for too long, ruled her. As she stood there, this time alone, she inhaled the fresh air. The scent of the trees took her back to being a child, when she could run for miles. Other remembrances flooded back to a time when she could go all day, both helping her family but with time to play with her friends. That time seemed so long ago and seemed as if she was a different person then. She had changed, hardened by life's problems and temptations, some of her own choice, some imposed on her.

She then began pushing her legs into a stride that would bring her upwards to the lookout. She now did so with a purpose so that she could get to the viewpoint where she could scan the land that, centuries ago, belonged only to her people. This gave her a sense of belonging, a connection that she had lost when she left to go to the confusion of the City. She didn't want to go back there. It would just be trouble not just with Bucks and the Police but the hurtful memories of her young friend who, in Birdie's mind, was now probably dead. She'd need to talk to her niece to see how she could earn a place here, not be a burden, remaining safe in this new found sanctuary.

***

Far away, back in that City that Birdie was trying to forget, Bucks had registered under a false name, pre-paying for the room in cash so that the desk asked no further questions. Once in the room he e-mailed the escort service to give them his room number. Then he undressed, had a quick shower, giving his body a splash of lotion. Earlier in the day he bought a silk-like dressing gown that he now slipped on. As an eight year old he'd started to relish all the photos of *Playboy* but tonight, in the gown, he felt as if he was Hugh Hefner, in his mansion, waiting for Eve's knock on the door.

***

Jimmy, as always, was hungry. When he unlocked the door and entered the apartment his mother was on the phone but gave him a smile and a wave. Jimmy looked in the refrigerator. There wasn't much as they were still a few days short of his mother receiving her welfare money. There was peanut butter so he opened the bread box and soon had a sandwich to munch on. Then his mother hung up the phone.

"So, how was school today? Get your test mark?"

"Yeah, a 'B'."

"Only a 'B'?" His mother was forever urging him to do well in school. So far her son had not turned against school but was too easily distracted by friends or dreaming about basketball. He needed a dedicated teacher to keep him focused. This year he had a 'B' teacher in an oversized class that wasn't having the results his mother wanted. She didn't want to be always on him so she steered off that subject. "Your brother was here today. Says hello."

They had different fathers and a six year separation in age. At one point, still impressionable, Jimmy thought that Jayden was great, someone to follow and imitate. Then Jayden's combination of puberty, school problems and dumb friends led to the inevitable squabbles, then shouting matches with his mother. Jimmy sided with his mother and was glad when his brother left to live with his older girlfriend with Jayden only having an unsteady minimum wage job to support his many needs. Jimmy knew that Jayden's visits to his mother only meant he wanted to 'borrow' a few dollars. Then a thought of worry flashed into Jimmy's mind as he ran to his small bedroom and checked the bottom corner of his closet.

"Mom! Mom! Was Jayden in my room?"

"Well, I guess he could have.The phone rang so I was busy for a bit…"

"Mom! My new shoes are gone. He must have grabbed them."

"What new shoes?"

Jimmy was almost sobbing as he explained that he saved up his money, from helping deliver flyers, picking up bottles for deposit cash, anything to get the money to buy these special basketball sneakers that looked just as good as the NBA pros had. When his mother was told of the price she reacted .

"That much! Just for sneakers to run up and down at the gym! Jimmy I could get you two, maybe three pairs of shoes for that. You always need new ones, the way your feet grow."

Jimmy didn't wait for her to finish. He was running out the door, not sure where he was going, but tears mixed with anger as he had listened to his mother's stinging words. It was as if she was defending Jayden instead of comforting him. She shouldn't have let Jayden into his bedroom. The shoes were brand new, still in the box along with the invoice. He had only tried them on at the store. He was waiting until his team was in the playoffs to wear them, to show them off. With them on he'd be able to play his best. Now he could see Jayden outside the gym selling them for quick cash. Yeah, that was where he'd go...to the gym.

***

Lou didn't slam the phone down but it was loud enough to get the attention of the rest of the unit as they began to switch down their computers at the end of their day .Within minutes Rush and Lou were alone. Rush ventured a question, "If it's work related tell me. If it isn't then it's your choice"

"Sorry Rush. It's this damned wedding. Just a week away. After all the planning there are still problems. Now the banquet hall tells me that they can't fit in a few extra chairs for the dinner. Fire Regulations! So now we'll have to ask a few people to sit on someone's knee all because Maria sent out too many invitations!"

Rush hadn't heard Lou criticize his wife before so he tried to simmer down the conversation. "Lou. Look...airlines continually overbook. They survive. You will too. There'll be no-shows." He waited a few seconds. "I can be one..." He saw Lou about to react so continued. "Face it Lou. I don't speak Italian. I'm way too old for the bridesmaids and too young for the widows. Maria probably didn't know where to seat me anyway. Seriously Lou let me, at the least, be one less problem for you. Now pack up. Go home."

Lou didn't object and left, unsmiling, at the door before turning, "Thanks Rush."

At the same time that Lou was leaving his office and Jimmy was running towards the gym, Russell Sterne hung up from the second of two telephone calls. The first had been to the family lawyer Ted Stanton. Irene, his secretary who, it seemed had been there forever, answered with her normal formality to ask how both Mr. Sternes were doing. Russell didn't tell her about Stefan, knowing he would face a barrage of questions from Irene if he did. The offices of Stanton and Stanton had been started by Ted's father and uncle. Leonard Stanton was pleased when Ted joined and, in turn, Ted's son Anthony followed the family tradition so that the firm's name required no change. Anthony, only in his mid-thirties, had contracted a unique type of virus that quickly invaded his body and attacked his organs so that within a week he was dead. Russell still felt a tinge of guilt in knowing his own son was alive but Ted was without his. In his call to Ted he explained that he wanted to revise his Will, now to include a now found grandson.Ted said he could fit him in at ten the next morning.

The other call had been to arrange an appointment with his Doctor, whose office was in the same block as Stanton and Stanton. The receptionist asked if Russell had any specific medical issues. Russell lied a little in replying that there were just a few minor matters that he wanted looked at. Indeed he did have a few minor pains that he, now eighty-five, simply felt came with his age. However there had recently been some other issues that were noticeable. He did take a walk, on a regular route, often stopping to chat with Alberto at his Deli. He'd order coffee but rarely emptied his cup; the problems of the planet, city or neighbourhood all needed solving by Alberto and Russell. Twice last week ago,on leaving the Deli, he had felt unsteady more than just a little off balance. This morning, while shaving, he noticed a slight numbness on the left side of his face, but it was gone by noon. Still he'd better see the doctor. Although Eleanor wasn't physically present he still heard her soft voice with protective advice, "Russell, you need to call the Doctor or should I do it for you?"

CHAPTER TWENTY-FIVE

The very next morning, at first light, Bucks stumbled back from the hotel bathroom to the empty bed, Eve was long gone. He was still in a torpor, half awake, half dreaming of having her body on his. Through half-lidded eyes he saw his robe thrown against a chair. He smiled at the thought of what his mother might say if she ever saw it. He would have to hide it from her as she did clean his bedroom at home. If she found it, she might think it was a surprise gift for her.

Less than two hours later Rush, a bit earlier than normal, was at his desk, clearing some reports plus procedural revisions. He had immediately switched on his computer, checking the overnight activity around the City. Nothing commanded immediate need for his attention so he concentrated on the reports. Ellen was next in, almost immediately followed by Lou. Rush looked up and returned their simultaneous greetings as all three faced their screens.

Lou was the first to say anything. "Rush...that 'little brother' of yours... Jimmy. What's his last name?"

Rush was quick to answer, "Destin...Jimmy Destin. Why?"

"Well...if he lives down at Sandwich Place he's been reported as missing!"

Rush switched screens to view the first reporting and immediately called the investigating officer P.C.Halliwell. He'd remembered her from a previous case. She'd just returned to her desk after interviewing the anxious guilt ridden mother and was supervising the search by the on-duty officers at that division. She concisely gave Rush the background. Jimmy had run out, before five the previous evening, being upset over his missing new basketball shoes and his mother's criticism as to why he spent so much money on them. His mother assumed he'd be back, had just gone to one of his friends, but admitted she'd been watching T.V. and fallen asleep. Before she went to bed she looked into Jimmy's room and swears she saw his body bundled under the bedclothes. That morning, getting no response to her 'get up' calls, she checked to only find a lump of bedding but no Jimmy. After a few calls to his friends she called the Police. Rush realized that Halliwell was covering all the obvious bases to locate Jimmy and, without saying he was Jimmy's 'Big Brother', only asked that he be kept in the loop.

Hanging up, he reviewed what he knew, and might guess what Jimmy might have done and where he might be. Jimmy's father's identity was known but, wherever he might be, he wasn't part of Jimmy's life. There was an older brother who wasn't living with them and there wasn't, as far as Rush knew, any brotherly bond. He thought of where Jimmy might have gone. He would like to think that he might have called his 'Big Brother' but, by the rules, Jimmy wasn't allowed that contact information. Then he thought of the cause of the problem. The basketball sneakers! This sport was almost all-consuming for Jimmy, whether following the N.B.A or playing for his team at the local gym. The gym!

As he was leaving he told Lou to keep him advised through his cell phone then ran down the stairs to his own car heading towards the recreation building a few blocks from Sandwich Place. It wasn't yet eight-thirty but Rush found the door unlocked but the front desk empty. There was a bell that he punched, once, twice, then again. A young woman came out of the Ladies Washroom drying her hands on a paper towel.

"Hello, can I help you?"

He told her how she could. She reached down to open a drawer then hesitated.

"I'm not sure if I can release the number for the coach of your friend's team, or any name at all, without permission."

Rush then pulled out his wallet showing his identification. Despite this, she still decided to call the Director. Rush waited but only to hear her leave a concise message asking for permission to release the coach's number. Then she turned to Rush, "He's probably on his way here but I know he doesn't answer his phone when driving." She looked at her watch. "He'll be here soon. He's usually in before nine, depending on traffic."

Checking his own phone Rush found no messages. He turned to wait for the Director's arrival but, seeing the door to the Men's Change Room, his morning juice and coffee signalling a need, he pushed open the door and used the urinal. He walked back to the sinks to wash his hands then heard a noise from one of the cubicles. Bending to look under the partition he saw a bundle and from them protruded a worn sneaker.

"Jimmy! Jimmy!"

Rush pushed the door open and grabbed Jimmy from the floor into his arms. Jimmy's surprised look changed to recognition then to sobs as he clung hard to Rush. Holding him, calming him, Rush was suddenly aware that this was the first time they had any intimate contact. After a long minute he released Jimmy to take him to the sink to clean up his streaked face then, both smiling, went out into the reception area.There the young woman's face showed her confusion so Rush immediately gave her assurance. "He's fine. I'll call his mother and get him home."

In the car he called Halliwell to say that the search was over and to tell Jimmy's mother he was unharmed and would be brought back to her in about an hour.

"Tell her it will be before ten. I'll meet you in the lobby just before then so you can take Jimmy up to his mother. I'm taking him for breakfast. Is that O.K. with you?"

That settled, Rush drove Jimmy to an all day breakfast diner, cleaner than most, to get some food for his hungry 'little brother'. He also wanted to get the full story of why Jimmy had left home and why he stayed overnight on the hard bathroom floor. Rush had another coffee while Jimmy began to dig into a full breakfast. Between munches Jimmy gave his account of the new shoes he bought, his brother stealing them, his mother's sharp words over spending too much money, and his reaction to go out, try to find Jayden before he could sell the shoes. He thought this would likely take place either in or near the Rec Complex and he hung around waiting but Jayden didn't show up. It was getting really dark and he planned to go home but, needing to use the washroom, he then, still upset, decided against home so he simply curled up for a long night on the floor.

Rush knew that Jimmy had an older brother but he already left home before Rush's involvement with the family. He asked where Jayden lived. Jimmy only knew he lived with his girlfriend. He did know her name and knew they didn't live far away. As Jimmy worked on his breakfast Rush called Lou asking him to scan that name on their computer files. This was not the National Data Bank but the controversial 'Local Listing'. Any contact with City Police could involve name-taking, even if no suspected crime was involved, which meant a name and an address were entered on their computer. There was disagreement between local politicians and the Chief of Police as to whether this helped control crime or whether it helped enforce a quasi-police state but now it gave Lou an address for the girlfriend that he passed onto Rush.

"Thanks Lou." Rush then had another thought, "Isn't your cousin's son a rookie attached to this division? The big guy?"

"That's Rickie. Why?"

"Can you check to see if he's on duty right now. If he is, give him the address and ask him to go there. If he finds Jayden, demand he give him his brother's shoes. Call me back. I'll wait here."

Rick Despario was on duty and, not sure of why he was doing it, was soon banging hard on an apartment door. Finally awake Jayden shuffled to the door, opening it a crack to see a tall broad shouldered uniformed cop there, yelling at him.

"Give me your brother's shoes...now...and fast!"

It wasn't far from this apartment building to the one that Jimmy lived in. At the entry door Rick, carrying a box containing basketball sneakers, met P.C Halliwell, Detective Sterne holding the hand of a skinny boy. Halliwell didn't ask any questions as to how the box got there. Jimmy excitedly opened it to find the shoes still inside. Rush thanked Rick, tousled Jimmy's hair, bent down to eye level, giving him an instruction: "Remember to apologize to your mother. She's been very worried about you. Offer to take the shoes back for a refund so that your mother can decide best as to what you should buy. Your birthday is in a couple of weeks. If you still need good sneakers then...that would make a good present...from me, wouldn't it?"

Jimmy, still a bit dazed by all that was happening, was led by Halliwell inside to be reunited with his mother. Rush thanked Rick a second time and decided he'd better get back to his desk. There was sure to be other missing persons to locate, but not as easy.

***

Two trucks and crews from the Security Company showed up just after ten to the Dealership. Remi strolled outside eyeing the overhead cameras.

There were no fluttering dots of light showing they were operational. The entire system was off so he went to the first bank of used cars facing the road. He dug out Sonny's number and used his cell confirming that the cameras were disconnected and the shiny almost new AMG was there, only a few feet from where he stood. Sonny went over the procedure making sure Remi fully understood it.

It was nearly noon and Remi was now in the front seat of the AMG with a small thin older man at the wheel and a young muscular guy in the back. Remi's manager, busy assisting the Security crew, saw no problem with the prospective buyers of the car taking it out for a test drive. Remi had photocopied the fake licences of both this 'father and son' and left them on the manager's desk. No words were exchanged as the driver headed out of the city to a secondary, but paved, road.

Almost with a snicker, the driver, acting out the script, looked back over his shoulder, "Hey Bud, do you hear a noise back there…from the rear right wheel?"

Bud at first missed his cue but then, half laughing, played his part replied, 'Yeah man...I hear it too. Maybe it's a bearing or something...better stop to check it out."

They stopped on the roadside, no houses nearby, no traffic speeding past. Remi was wondering why there had been a need for these two to pretend the noise was real. He also was worried about the bruise that would be necessary as proof he was a victim not an accessory to the theft. This younger man was a big guy. Now only the two of them were outside the car on the narrow shoulder between the car and a row of rocks lining the road side of a deep ditch. Without any warning, but reacting instinctively to turn his head, Remi saw an arm strike towards him.

As the AMG sped away the driver asked "You hit him pretty hard didn't you? All we needed was a bruise, not a concussion."

He'd been in lots of fights but had never planned to cold-cock anyone before. He hadn't been sure of how hard he needed to punch but this idiot turned away and his fist connected to the side of his head, propelling him forward so that his head hit hard on an angular rock, his body slumping over suddenly still on the ground. He seemed out cold. Too bad, he shouldn't have ducked.

Back at the Dealership, as one o'clock neared, there was anger at first then worry about both Remi and the car. Finally at one-thirty the Police were called.

***

Antioch Life Assurance North America was about to celebrate its Seventy-Fifth Anniversary. The parent company came into existence in 1883 from very humble beginnings. Albert Delberford was an Undertaker in a Borough at the then limits of London, England. His small shop was only just managing to provide sustenance and support to his growing family. In part this was due to his inability to deny grieving, but penurious, parents a decent burial for their children. Whatever they could afford to pay often didn't cover Delberford's costs. He then conceived a plan. Parents could pre-pay, even farthings or ha'pennies a week, towards the possible and probable funeral costs of a child's death. As both health standards and the disposable income of families improved, the concern of parents, particularly mothers, for their children stayed the same. Soon these pennies a week became sixpence then shillings a month and Delberford found that this new plan was as profitable as his basic undertaking services.

He was astute enough to incorporate as a 'Beneficial Society' gaining support from various denominations' support which, Church by Church, Parish by Parish, Diocese by Diocese expanded his base. He soon sold his funeral home and with the assistance of a shrewd solicitor expanded, county by county across England, as a registered Assurance Company. Its range of policies widened to cover more monied lives than infants but, true to its roots, it still sold basic policies designed only to cover basic burial costs. All lives were recorded longhand in large leather bound ledgers at their expanding Head Office location. When computerization arrived these details were transposed. If an insured life achieved one hundred years of age without any claim made, Antioch Life responded by locating that policyholder, if still alive.

Marielle had done a few of these searches before. They all came from policies written in England but where those insured were found to have relocated then the closest Antioch Office became involved. Marielle was reviewing the file of Maude Adeline Rigby born just over a century ago. The Antioch office in Southampton hadn't located her but had determined she'd married a First Special Service Force soldier in 1945 named Lars Engblum and, as a war bride, sailed west a year later.

Her computer screen quickly connected to Special Forces and then to Lars Engblum. He enlisted in 1942, saw action in Norway and Italy until decommissioned in December 1945. Marielle searched further on the history of this Special Force discovering it to be a joint U.S./Canada Brigade of elite troops, better known as the 'Devil's Brigade'. She wondered how an Englishwoman, with the delicate name of Maude, had met then married the battle hardened Lars from Bemidji Minnesota. Another screen gave his date of death in 1996 and the last known address of Lars. She now was able to trace a Maude Engblum to an address in Minnesota. There were quite a few Engblums in that state but this was the only Maude. She transferred the file to their St. Paul's office wishing that Maude, if still alive and hopefully alert, would have been within driving distance of her. She would have loved to have time to sit down, have a cup of tea or a glass of sherry, to hear about Maude's life, before and after Lars. Her daydream was interrupted by the buzz from her cellphone. It showed that it was Sylvie.

Her sister's first few words were just understandable but then it was a mingle of sobs, gulps and garbles that Marielle pieced together. The secretary at the dealership had called her. Remi had been hurt, was unconscious and in hospital. Sylvie was still at work. Marielle told her that she'd pick her up out front of her office in twenty minutes, then take her to the Hospital. She clicked off the connection before her sister could hear her mutter: "Merde! Plus de merde!"

At that same time, less than a mile away in the Missing Person's unit, Rush reached for his ringing phone. He said little but his face set into a frown that Ellen, glancing over, could only interpret as hearing bad news. As he listened Rush was clicking the keys bringing a file onto his screen. It wasn't a new file; it originated a year earlier when Brittany Loretta Lewis was reported missing. There had been a previous file, when as a juvenile, she'd run away from home here in the City. By the time she was found, reasonably safe, she was old enough to choose to stay on the street but contact was resumed with her mother and that relationship improved, with concessions on both sides, so that she moved back home, resumed schooling and was, at twenty, enrolled at a Beauticians Institute. She still needed her freedom and her mother granted it knowing she had no choice. Brittany studied hard during the week and partied hard on weekends. On a Monday evening her mother hadn't heard from her daughter. She hardly slept that night, hoping to hear the front door being unlocked. She called the police next morning.

Rush and Lou worked hard, with the help of other officers, on the case but any leads left suspicions but no answers. Brittany had a range of friends going back to her mid-teens as well as the many she'd just met. Rush's only conclusion was that she hadn't disappeared voluntarily which left only one likely conclusion. The mother would call either Rush or Lou on a regular basis but they never voiced their suspicions. While she still had hope they tried to keep optimistic as well. Today he wasn't totally surprised when the lab had found a DNA match to the remains found by hikers a hundred miles away in the Black Hills Resort Park. Brittany had been found.

"Ellen you and I need to make a call to see Mrs.Lewis. Do you know that file? Brittany Lewis?"

Ellen had only a recollection of seeing that name on an abeyance file but no specific details.

"No? I'll give you the details as we drive."

Concentrating on the busy afternoon traffic, eyes fixated ahead, Rush outlined the frustrating investigation that had hit dead ends. This was now a true dead end. They could now close their file and let Homicide take control.

"Have you ever done a next-of-kin before?" asked Rush.

Ellen had been on Traffic Detail for two years but fortunately had never been the bearer of death before. Rush reviewed the procedure. Ellen's function would be to assist in offering sympathy as well as to obtain names and contact numbers that would give further support. This would range from a doctor, to clergy, family and friends. Ellen had steeled herself to tough times before, such as post-mortems and gun-drawn confrontations, but she would have preferred not to make this visit. They parked and walked to the front door. She choked as she looked over at the front window. There was the glimmering light of an electronic candle showing. Now she and Rush would be the ones to snuff out any hope that was left in that candle.

CHAPTER TWENTY-SIX

The following morning Rush was at his desk before eight happy to see no new assignments requiring their involvement. Ellen arrived next and Rush quietly asked how she was doing. It was his subtle way of enquiring how she'd managed after the emotional visit with Mrs. Lewis. They had only left when others arrived, needed to console the distraught, now childless, mother. Ellen only offered a masked, "Okay, I guess" before she settled at her desk.

Shortly after nine Rush received three successive calls.

The first was from Morris. He apologized that lunch would have to wait as he was flying off to Washington later today for a conference on Modern Jurisprudence. He had checked the Law School records to review Rush's courses and marks from the past. He thought that if Rush was really serious about applying then special consideration could be given, as a mature student, for acceptance into Year Two providing he could re-write and pass all Year One courses as then pass all his Year Two Courses. Morris pointed out that Rush could study now and write the August exams on two entry courses which would lessen the load for the Fall and Winter sessions. Morris would be quite willing to add his letter recommending Rush's application. It would be Rush's decision but one that would need to be made before the end of the month. Rush said he'd have an answer for him when Morris returned next Monday.

Rush then sat considering whether he really wanted a career in law and would be willing to spend the grunting hours necessary to get his degree, as well as whether he could afford it. He'd talk to Russell tonight about that. Then came the second call.

It was from Stefan, whose road to romance had hit a rock. That morning, on waking at the hostel, he found Simona was dressed and just finished packing. She explained that she had the chance to catch a free ride down to New York City with that trio of new friends they'd met at the Rock Concert. Her mind seemed set, saying that she'd keep in touch with Stefan so he could catch up with them later. Stefan tried to change her mind but soon, looking out the window, she said their car was down at the curb and, only giving a wave then blowing a kiss from her fingers, she was gone.

Rush, from memory, could sympathise with his son's rejected state and immediately suggested he come up to stay at the family home. Stefan immediately accepted and would come in the afternoon. Before he could call to advise his father there was the third call.

"Hi Rush. It's Marielle...fine...no, not really…sorry it's been a long night. It's my sister, Sylvie."

She concisely explained that Sylvie's live-in partner had died early this morning in hospital. She knew few details but already Homicide Officers had interviewed her sister. They had only confirmed that Remi had been found roadside yesterday afternoon, unconscious. He had never recovered. She was apologetic in asking Rush if he could somehow find out what had happened and what would happen next.

"Remi? What's his full name?"

"Uhmm. I think Remi comes from something Latinish...maybe Remilios...anyway his last name Estavan."

As he listened to Marielle, Rush was already clicking screens to find the case. He saw the Investigator in charge was someone he had dealt with before and with whom he had retained a friendly connection. He told Marielle he would do what he could and would call her back. She gave him her cell number. He didn't tell her that his own phone had already identified her number to him. Not trusting memory he scribbled it down on paper slipping it into his wallet. One never knew when he might want to call.

Homicide was only one floor down and Rush entered the much larger confines of this department. Detective Sgt. Dom Scanelli's chair was empty so Rush left a short note on his desk asking him to call when not busy. Walking back up to his office Rush thought it was a poor choice of words. Homicide was always busy.

He then called his father who was delighted to hear that Stefan would be coming.

"Any idea for how long? Okay, but I'd better go out now to get some more food, snacks and maybe some more beer. Is there a Latvian beer sold here?"

Rush doubted it but suggested any European beer would do. He also asked that he get some steaks. The weather forecast was good for a barbeque dinner on the patio.

Later came another call.

Hey Rush. It's Dom. You left a note for me. What's up?"

Scanelli didn't press Rush as to his reason for asking about the Estavan case. He gave a concise summary of what they knew which was only that Estavan was out on a test drive with two men who left phoney driver licences and then he was found unconscious on County Road 210. The medics suspected a cerebral hemorrhage when his head hit a rock at roadside. There was also a contusion on the other temple to suggest that the thieves who stole the car had whacked him, probably harder than necessary.

"Probably didn't mean to kill him but whether the skull is thick or thin we'll press for first degree when we catch them."

Dom sounded confident on this point but now explored Rush's interest, "You knew this guy?"

"No but my...friend's sister lived with him."

"Sylvie? Good looking piece of woman there." Dom's interest in the opposite sex didn't stop at the neck. "This Remi wasn't the MVP at the dealership. He did just enough to keep his job, never enough to be fired, according to the owner. What's interesting is that the security cameras were being replaced that morning so we have no videos. Also interesting is that there was an earlier theft of another high-end used car, that's what Remi sells, less than two weeks ago...not the same MO but still... what with a rumour than Remi played the odds with bookies...this may have been a setup that went bad. Who knows? Remi might have been in deep and needed a piece of the pie. Well, whatever the why, we have to get the who."

Rush thanked him, asking to be kept up to date. Dom said he'd be happy to.

Marielle answered her cell right away. She'd brought Sylvie back to her apartment and settled in her bed hoping she'd sleep.

"How about you? Have you had any sleep?"

Marielle conceded that she only had only dozed a little throughout the night at the hospital while hugging her sister as they sat in vigil awaiting any news. They were not allowed in Remi's room as his mother and sister had taken over as immediate family. Marielle said her sister hadn't cohabitated with Remi long enough to qualify as his wife. Marielle said that was, to her, fine as Remi's mother had never accepted Sylvie as family anyway.

"Rush, I know this sounds calculating but it's best they look after all the funeral arrangements especially since I called Remi's company this morning and found out that Sylvie was not the beneficiary on his Group Insurance. When he divorced his wife he changed it to his mother and left it there. I hope that I can convince Sylvie not to go to his funeral." She stopped before asking, "Does that make me a controlling witch?"

"No, never. You are just protecting your sister." Rush then gave her a redacted summary of Detective Scanelli's information emphasising that it was car theft that went wrong and Remi was the victim without adding that he wasn't necessarily an innocent one.

After Marielle's tired voice thanked him there seemed little else to say and so they disconnected their conversation and, to Rush as he looked at his phone, possibly the contact between their lives.

***

As the taxi drove David westward from Porto del Norte towards the resorts, each passing mile scrubbed the scales from David's numbing month, scattering them onto the road behind. As they came nearer he looked ahead with relief and anticipation. He was sure Sandro was already evaluating the current crop of unattached, or those who wanted to, women who would more than warm David's bed over the next few days. Sandro always had first choice but David, with only immediate needs, wouldn't be disappointed.

The front desk staff again were exuberant in welcoming him with both hugs and kisses.They had a nice room available and clipped on his wrist tag for 'All-inclusive" services although he was so well known now that it wasn't really needed. As he left the wide foyer he glanced back to see the back of a woman walking out from the interior office away from him.

Well, he thought, if the front was equal to the rear, that was someone he had to meet.

After a shower and a light lunch at the beach enjoying what sun, sea and sand generously gave plus the view of bikinis as a bonus, he shed the last kinks from Isla. Wandering back towards the main building he saw at the desk the front profile of the woman he had seen earlier. He neared to easily overhear her dealing with complaints from an overweight couple, hands waving, opposite her at the counter. With each step forward towards her he became more appreciative of the view. He waited until the couple, now seemingly satisfied, shuffled their bulk away giving David his opportunity.

She looked up."Senor. Can I assist you?"

"Not at all but I must compliment you on your diplomatic handling of Mr. and Mrs. Grumbles. Let me guess...were they from New York?"

"Close. New Jersey."

"Ah, birds of a feather."

She laughed, followed by an engaging smile, "Again, are you in need of assistance?"

He now saw her name tag. "Senorita Andy...my only question I have is when you can get away from this desk?"

Her smile faded quickly, cooling the distance between them. David was rescued by Sandro's arrival.

"Hola Andy. I see you've already met my friend, the good doctor David. The one who gives free medical services to our staff."

"Ah si, the end of the month visit by the doctor I had been told about. The doctor's reputation is...ah...interesting but I did expect someone who looked more like a real medico."

"I am a real doctor...and what's wrong with my looks?"

"You're too tall, you still have hair on your head, and don't wear lentes."

"My eyesight is still good enough to enjoy the view."

She backed off the bantering and resorted to formality, "Unless you need any of our services Doctor, I do have other duties to attend to."

At that, she turned to enter the interior office. David turned to Sandro who had a definite smirk on his face. "David...amigo...you are not the first to be shot down by Andy. She's a cool lady. If you want female company tonight I have a few suggestions. Do you want to meet them now?"

As they walked back together towards the beach David asked about Andy. Sandro could only say that she'd asked for a transfer from their associated resort in Palm Beach. She had been pleasant and got along well with the staff as well as guests but, off duty, kept to herself, frustrating Sandro, as well as a few male guests, since her arrival.

"Since I've backed off, we get along well. I'm guessing she's running away from something to ask for the transfer. The Palm Beach Resort is top of the line. Here we get economy class tourists, there they get the money crowd. Take my advice, go easy with her, don't crowd her or she'll close down. It's better I introduce you to two ladies from Cleveland."

"Maybe later Sandro. What time does Andy get off?" Sandro checked his watch, "In twenty minutes, amigo."

David took a position near the employee doorway exchanging smiles and 'Holas' with staff coming on duty. Then she came out, saw him and turned to leave. Two strides and he was at her side.

"Andy, I must apologize. I was crude, gauche and...er...churlish."

"Churlish? Isn't that medieval?"

"Yes. Off with my head?"

"Unfortunately that's no longer allowed…"

"I promise to behave. I was brought up properly but sometimes forget."

"Fine. Forgiven." She resumed her pace up the path to the staff quarters as if the conversation was over. He gave it another try.

"Look...I'm just human, a male of the species. You're human too but clearly not male. We, at least in general, are coded to be attracted to the opposite sex. I won't apologize for that but I do, very solemnly swear, that, should you agree...even condescend...to meet me whenever...coffee… drinks...dinner...your choice...then I'll be a perfect gentleman."

"You are aware that there is a rule prohibiting socialization between guests and staff, are you not?"

"Andy I'm not a guest. Remember I work here, granted unpaid, donating my professional services."

"Rumour has it that your services are not necessarily medical."

"Ah. Yes. Guilty as charged." He stopped, gently gripping her elbows, turning them to be face to face. "Andy that's true but...when you're running away...running from life then you seek relief wherever you can."

They stayed there together, momentarily still, until he asked. "Perhaps you're running away too?"

She seemed to struggle with a reply before answering. "David. You're here for a few days. Let's leave it for now. Let's see what tomorrow brings."

As she walked away David was satisfied. He hadn't been shot down but was struggling to gain any altitude.

***

Rush found his father and his son on the patio enjoying the fading afternoon sun and cold beers. He stopped at the refrigerator to pull one out for himself but he stayed quiet as Russell and Stefan hadn't finished their discussion on the future of the world. There were some differences in their viewpoints but Rush could only sit, listen and be pleased that they were exchanging and considering each other's opinions.

When Russell excused himself to use the washroom Rush asked, "How are you doing? A bit hurt?"

"Yeah." Stefan shook his head as if to clear his thoughts. "Yeah...a bit. I thought Simona and I had the start of something, even though we had known each other for just a month. We got along really well. We could be serious or just silly...it didn't seem to matter but maybe I became too serious, a little possessive, frightened her off. Still, being dumped hurts doesn't it?"

Rush didn't think this was specifically directed at him for the past precedent set right here in this home. It was just a comment, not requiring a response but it was, to Rush, ironic that he and his son had both been discarded. He hoped that Stefan's hurt would only last a few weeks, not the years that it had lived within him.

Russell was now back, "Rush, if we're having steaks and no one is driving tonight why don't you dig out a red from that little cellar of yours."

He left grandfather and grandson to resume their political discussions, going into the kitchen. His father had already laid out the steaks on a platter. Rush added a little seasoning and then went down to select a Napa Cab for dinner then back to the kitchen to mix a salad and prepare garlic bread.

The food, the wine, the setting evening sun all combined to bond this newly formed family unit closer. Rush sat back, fully content and very proud of the two men sitting with him. He knew his father would feel the same and hoped Stefan did as well.

Rush brought two candles and three dishes of chocolate ice cream to the table then decided to risk ruining the easy feeling at the table by asking, "Do you have any siblings?"

Stefan didn't understand the question.

"Brothers or sisters?"

"Oh yes, a sister, Elvinda. Just fifteen.right now she's...how do you say it in English? A ...mouth...no...a handful."

"Is she...is she Ana's too?"

"No. She's adopted." He reflected for a few moments, "I think that she's started to feel like an outsider, sort of an intruder to the family. She's fully a part of us. She is my sister. Maybe it's the age to be rebellious whether adopted or not. We all hope she'll level out as she gets older."

Rush decided to push further. "When did you know I was your...birth father?"

"When I was young I never questioned why I had two mothers instead of other families until we started to have sex-ed in school. I asked who had, you know, contributed to my being. Ana still had photos of all of us together. She told me what a good man you were and…" He looked over at Russell, "...how nice your parents were to her. She told me how lucky I was to have the genes of such a wonderful family. When I told her my trip would come close to here I said I'd try to find you. She wondered if I should. She thought you'd be married now, other children. She didn't want your life upset but I said I wanted to so she gave me the only address she had...leading me right here."

"Did she give you an explanation of us...Ana and I...why you were conceived here?"

"Yes. I was a little older then, maybe twelve or thirteen. She said she did love you as much as she could love any man and tried to be a good wife for you but...she couldn't change her nature and it would have been a...what would you call it...a fraud, a deception, a lie for her to pretend. She told me she was really sorry for what she did to you but…" His voice trailed off before finding words, "…she knew Karla was waiting."

Rush realized that this had been her real love affair, first started in Latvia, interrupted, then resumed with a child, his necessary contribution to the loving family. He also doubted that Stefan saw him as a parent as he already had two, and whether, in these few days of meeting, that Stefan felt the beginnings of a father/son bonding. This wouldn't upset him as he only had the memory of holding Stefan as a newborn, cuddling and comforting him through those first few months of his life. All Stefan had was a photograph. Rush would accept what he was given and, for now, wouldn't ask for more than the joy of sitting here, with both his son and his father as company.

***

In their condo on the other side of the city, Ellen and Sydney had spent the hours between seven and ten, emotionally but rationally, before, during, following dinner considering whether they were ready to start a family. They had been together now for three years and both felt that this was a permanent loving union. Neither were religious, not needing a ceremony to legalize their love but if the next step was to either adopt or bear a child then a marriage certificate should be considered. Sydney had always offered to be the one to carry then deliver their child. Ellen had never told Sydney that she was not only unwilling to volunteer her ovum but was also hesitant about parenthood. Her own upbringing had been a roller-coaster and the two and a half years she'd been attached to Juvenile Crime was a negative shadow. However she had known, within the first few months of her loving Sydney, that motherhood was inset into her partner's being but Ellen, trying not to be contrary, felt this still might be too soon.

It was hard to convince Sydney otherwise. They were financially stable in a committed relationship. Sydney could get maternity leave and benefits. She was now twenty-nine, prime for motherhood. The question of the sponsor-to-be gave them concern. Did they want a child who might, from an anonymous sperm donor, have unknown and unnumbered half-brothers or sisters in the world? The alternative would be to seek a volunteer, someone they approved of, but how could this be done? They shared, over cleaning up the dishes, a lot of laughter naming various males as to how they would be approached, enticed, seduced into fatherhood. Sydney wasn't averse to the standard method of procreation. She'd lost her virginity, out of curiosity, at seventeen and continued bi-sexual experimentation until twenty. She was quite willing to "think of England" if necessary. Not having resolved all the issues and having an early meeting Sydney was ready for bed. Kissing Ellen she headed to the bathroom then turned. "Oh. I almost forgot. I think I may have a lead to your missing lady through one of her relatives. I think I can trace her then maybe find this Birdie for you."

Ellen stayed up for a while, switching on the television, but her mind kept reverting back to having the responsibility of a child to rear, a child that wouldn't bear her genes. She also thought about finding Birdie and helping to clear Rush from the accusation hanging over him. Then she thought about Rush, as a man. She had few male role models who impacted positively on her life. In the short time that she had been attached to Missing Persons she had growing respect for her supervisor even though she knew little of his life. No matter what outward confidence he might show she imagined he was only accepting, not really enjoying, his day-to-day existence. She suppressed a chuckle as she pictured approaching Rush to request that he, either self stimulated in a clinic, or aroused in a bed, provide paternity for she and Sydney's child. It was a perverse thought of 'Selling Sydney' but, she smiled again, if it was Rushton Sterne who volunteered, she'd fully endorse his candidacy.

***

Tomas had to be careful. A stranger was easily remembered here but he felt confident that he'd identified Edo without being noticed himself. He ruled out any attack in Edo's little town for various reasons. He knew he could eliminate his target with ease but there was only one paved road he could use as his escape route. It connected to Govennia, from where three paved highways led outward to safety. Clearly he needed to find Edo in Govennia, await his chances, act quickly, then speed away. It would take patience but he had time to spare. He would have to keep surveillance on Edo's road leading to Govennia. Saturday and Sunday would make sense. He headed back to his own home to consult with his father, assuming he would get approval for his plan.

CHAPTER TWENTY-SEVEN

Stefan slept upstairs in the room his father once did. From the master bedroom he could hear his grandfather's snores, coupled with an occasional snort, during the night. In the morning there'd be breakfast with Russell as Rush was usually off to work early. Each day Stefan would explore the City, sometimes alone, other times meeting other backpackers. He'd messaged with his parents in Latvia and Ana was very pleased that he had been accepted by his father and grandfather, although sad he wouldn't meet his grandmother.

When Rush was home for dinner all three settled into a contented routine as if they'd been a family for years. Rush saw how much his father enjoyed Stefan. He wasn't jealous but clearly felt there was a stronger quick setting bond between them than between him and Stefan. As he sat back, whether on the patio, at the dinner table, in the living room, just watching them and listening to their conversations, he wondered whether Stefan had forged with his grandfather, in just a few days, as much as he had in his forty years with his father. Again he thought of his mother and the glue that she had been to the three of them and how sad it was that she wasn't here to share Stefan. He also thought about his father's brief relationship with his own father, a grandfather Rush had never known. There were only his photographs which hung with other family remembrances in the hallway of their home.

On the fifth night of his stay, Stefan said he had received a text message from Simona. Her involvement with her new German friends was wearing thin and she'd be willing to wait in New York City if Stefan could come now to meet her. With hesitant words, not wanting to offend, he said he would be leaving. Rush guessed that he might want to resume a lot more than just sightseeing with Simona. Russell's face, quite openly, showed disappointment. Stefan had rekindled some of the emotion that had become lost in him when Eleanor died.

After Stefan's announcement there was silence until Rush affirmed

Stefan's right to continue his travels. "Have you checked the bus schedules to New York?"

"Yes, there are three during the day, one overnight."

"Available seats?" Stefan then checked his pad. "One tonight, none until three tomorrow."

"Stefan, I'm not trying to push you out the door but why don't you grab the one for tonight. I'm sure Simona is anxious to see you. Why don't you book it?"

Stefan's fingers staccatoed across the keypad then he looked up, almost apologetic, "Got it."

Then he looked again to see the two serious faces, "Maybe I should wait a day or two, stay a bit, before I leave?" He let the question hang. Russell answered it, "No, you should go. You've left enough memories here for us. Just promise to keep in touch, won't you?"

They all stood and slowly hugged each other, avoiding words that might have lodged in their throats. Rush pointed to the bedrooms managing a "Better pack."

Russell gave a final hug at the doorway and then Stefan and Rush were heading to the Bus Station. With purpose Rush didn't look for a parking spot but pulled up outside the entrance. His son slid out the seat, pulled his pack out the rear door then back to the open passenger door, hand extended.

"Good luck. Let's keep in contact...and...when you get home give Ana a hug from me."

Then they were apart starting with just a few feet that would widen like ripples in a pond and eventually into waves across an ocean.

Back at the house Rush went upstairs where Russell immediately clicked off the television. He asked how the parting went. Rush gave a succinct reply, "Well I guess as well as any. We kept it brief."

"I wonder if I'll ever see him again…" He waved off Rush's attempt to deny it, "No, let's be realistic, it's entirely probable...and while we're on that topic I want you to know that I've made a change in my will to include Stefan, an equal amount to Sis's son out west. Don't worry that still leaves you a lot, even after taxes, bequests and expenses. Of course you'll inherit the house too."

"I should amend my will as well to include Stefan. Right now it all reverts to you."

Russell almost shouted, "To me! That's not a plan at all. You need to call Ted Stanton at his office. He'll give you good legal advice."

"Dad." Strangely Rush rarely used this term, "Speaking of a plan, I'm thinking of applying to go back to Law School. The question is whether I can afford two or three years without any income, without giving you my contribution to expenses here."

Since Ana and Stefan had flown back to Latvia Rush had continued to live at home. Although his parents had not asked for his contribution to household overhead, Rush calculated his fair contribution and gave his father a monthly cheque. He was pleased that there had been no argument from Russell for it nor for the annual increases he added. He contributed to his Police Pension Fund and if he resigned now, he would get some return but that would be heavily taxed. With his father's advice he also directly made monthly contributions to a mutual fund as a retirement fund. He now asked his father which fund would be the better to cash now for his education expenses.

"Your mother and I felt that the monthly cheque you gave us was excessive so I have, in your name, been investing most of it in equities and a few bonds over the years. You've done quite well. I can give you the numbers now. I should have done this annually but you never asked." He stood up and took a step towards his office.

"No, that's not necessary. All I need to know, should I apply and if I'm accepted, whether I can handle it."

"Rush, let's sit down, tomorrow after work, to review your anticipated expenses but I can guarantee you'll be able to handle it and with ease." He stopped to give a brief smile. "Also, by tomorrow, I'll have prepared a long list of reasons why you should apply to Law school, right away." He glanced at the wall clock, "It's nightly news time." He reached for the remote. Rush realized this wasn't a dismissal but only his father's way of making sure Rush accepted his decisions and would quietly leave without any further questions. He waived a 'Good Night' and retreated down the stairs.

***

It was a very different first morning at the resort for David. When his alarm went off at six-thirty he was as sober as he had been when he'd fallen asleep and he was alone in his bed, with no lingering scent of a stranger. He saw the sun was up and ready to begin another day of burning those below. After showering, and as he was finished shaving, now looking in the mirror, he wondered what Andy might see beyond his face, see the person that lay behind it. He asked himself why he had so suddenly been attracted to her. Certainly her appearance demanded any man's notice and David had rarely ignored the attraction of any woman he met. Somehow Andy, in a total of only sixty minutes, without any physical contact, had triggered a compelling need to have her as part of his life. It was, for David, a strange and new sensation. Was it Isla's constant umbra of death that was propelling him to want her? To renew himself? If she did respond to him would he revert to seeing her as just another conquest? To be bedded, then discarded?

His answer was definite: No. He now made a vow that if he felt any wavering of these best intentions then he'd leave the resort, leaving Andy unspoiled, at least by him.

Whistling a somewhat offkey melody that he couldn't remember either the title or the words, he strode towards the staff kitchen, hoping to find her there. He had only two days to break through her protective shell, to convince her that, whatever her past, her future should be with him.

***

Bucks now patrolled the areas that tourists, even some of the locals, avoided. These were off the beaten track: coffee shops, all-day breakfast restaurants, seedy bars needing renovation, strip joints needing younger bodies, places where Bucks might find answers to what was stirring in the subterranean market that never paid any taxes. Although he kept a low profile he, as well as his brother currently serving time, were known to past contacts and, in this business, one contact could lead to another. He'd nod, wave, hi-five to a number of men he slightly knew and sit down with those he half trusted. One of those was Sol Lucas.

"Hiya. How's your brother? " Bucks replied that he was doing O.K. but counting the weeks to his release. They spent a few more minutes exchanging words that meant nothing until Sol ventured a seeming innocent question, "All's well with you, you know, business wise?"

Sol had heard that Bucks was a supplier with a few runners even if he didn't exactly know the range of his products. Sol also knew Samson, whose territory was on the other side of the City from Bucks. He accepted the reply that all was fine but then cast out a line slowly spooling the words.

"Well, if someone was wanting, you know...to branch out...expand a bit...I hear that someone is looking for a...well...a sorta partner. If you know somebody who...who might be interested let me know...but soon... who knows...my friend might have already found somebody."

Bucks was careful only to suggest there might be a 'someone' and, should that 'someone' be interested, he asked what the next step would be, also asking what Sol's personal expectations might be for being the go-between.

"You know me, Bucks, I wouldn't ask anything up front and I wouldn't expect any percentage but I'd think it fair that some consideration, from both sides, be agreed to. Anyway here's the cell you...or your friend...can get me--but better be quick."

Bucks didn't want to seem too anxious and waited until early evening to call Sol telling him that he had someone who might want to look into something new. He suggested a meeting with all those who might be interested in doing a deal. Sol said he'd check on his end and call back. It was after nine and the meeting was set for tomorrow at two at a picnic table next to the river at Central Community Park. Sol made it clear he'd be there. He wanted to make sure that his end would be worth something. The bigger the deal, the bigger his cut.

***

The wedding ceremony wasn't without minor hitches. The best man almost dropped the ring. A baby cried until taken outside. Someone sneezed just as the priest gave his blessing to the newly wedded couple. Maria sniffled through the service but as the procession proceeded outside the clouds had cleared and, as a good omen, the sun shone on the church steps.

Lou hadn't seen Gabriella or Marcello in the Church and half hoped that some reason prevented their presence but, standing in the lengthy receiving line at the Banquet Hall beside Maria, he saw them shuffling towards them. Gabriella leaned her unsmiling face upward to give him the customary kiss on each cheek and to whisper, startling Lou. He hardly paid attention to the remaining guests coming down the line. What did "Gotta talk" mean?

As he sat at the end of the head table, with Maria beaming like a neon sign beside him, he concentrated his mind on the wedding, forcing a smile to the festivities, trying to blot out the worry over Gabriella's words. When his turn came he somehow managed a short speech gaining laughter as he gave a warning to his new son-in-law to look after his daughter or "the law will come calling."

He hardly tasted the meal and only sipped the wine until it was time for the dancing and socializing to start. Maria started circulating around the many groupings of friends and relatives. Lou started in the opposite direction and saw Marcello approaching. The fear that had been in his mind, that Gabriella's husband now knew of their affair, was snuffed out quickly with a hearty handshake and embrace, "Well how's the proud, and I guess much poorer, father of the bride? Congratulations."

The music became louder and faster. The younger guests took over the dance floor. The dinner wine was now replaced by booze and beer. Maria floated from table to table repeating and hearing the same words of compliments on every aspect of the wedding. Lou's shoulders were repeatedly slapped and his cheeks were lipstick stained as he rotated around the room. As he neared the open doors leading to the balcony outside he saw Gabriella. Her eyes flicked a signal and he followed her to the far unoccupied area overlooking the parking lot.

"Lou, listen...we have to stop. It's wrong. We'll get caught, sooner or later. We're heading to a disaster." She saw the look of disbelief on Lou's face as he took a step towards her. "No Lou. Don't say anything. My mind is set. Our love doesn't have to end but it can only be memories. Don't try to call or contact me. Please respect my decision. I'll manage somehow. You will too."

Then, giving no time for any protest, she quickly turned hurrying back inside, away from Lou.

He should have run after her but he seemed numb, frozen by her words. He wasn't sure how long he stayed there, eyes open but not focused, with his mind, his emotions roiling within the stiff shell of his body. Finally, still in a trance he headed back to the lights, the laughter and the music inside, into the crowd. Maria, seeing him, hustled over, "Where were you? Drink too much? Have you been sick?"

He mumbled something about only needing fresh air.

Maria was quick with a reply, "Good. One sick person is enough. When Gabriella left feeling ill I wondered if there was something wrong with the food. You had the chicken too. Wasn't it rubbery? And what we're paying for it! We should call tomorrow and complain, get a discount."

She grumbled further before hurrying away leaving Lou standing, feeling lost and lonely. He stood for a minute then turned to head purposely to the bar. It wouldn't be any surprise that the father of the bride got drunk at his daughter's wedding. What would have been the surprise was the real reason he needed to blot out this night.

***

That same Saturday, Sydney had worked on a project at the Library and it was after six when she came home. Ellen was already sampling a new choice of Chardonnay she picked up earlier. Sydney flopped into her chair and extended her fingers to hold an imaginary glass. Her partner responded, pouring then placing the wine glass within those fingers, "Beat?"

"Just a bit. Too long in front of a computer. It was probably easier before they were invented, at least we'd get exercise going to and from the shelves carrying material."

She swallowed and tasted, "Hey this is good. Expensive?"

"No." Ellen paused with a sudden thought. "When you get pregnant and can't drink alcohol does that mean I have to stop too?"

"Damn right." A malicious grin enforced the words. Then suddenly serious, "That Robin Partridge...the missing Birdie...well I think I found out where she may have gone. I've traced a relative, a niece, way out west. If your lady was on the run, wouldn't she seek family, as far away as possible? The info is in my case if you want it now."

Ellen scanned the print-out seeing it had a phone number. The time difference would only have it mid-afternoon out west. She decided to try right away, immediately taking a positive approach.

"Hello. I'm Ellen. Could I please talk to Birdie?"

There was a pause but no immediate denial so Ellen pushed on, "It's important."

It was obvious that whoever answered the phone was being cautious. Finally after seconds of silence." Well, I might be able to get a message to her. Can I ask exactly why you want her?"

"Just tell her it concerns Lucy Marie. Her friend. I'm a friend too." Ellen lied a little, a necessity needed from time to time by a Police Officer.

"Maybe leave your number. I can try to pass it over to her."

Ellen quickly guessed she'd probably never hear back, "Why don't I call back. Say in an hour or so?" The response was a brief and noncommittal "Maybe."

Almost on the hour Ellen was talking to the same voice, "Hi. Ellen again. Are you Birdie's niece?" She didn't wait for a reply. "Well, thank you for looking after her. She needed help. I'm guessing she still does. Right?"

The words worked and the ice was broken. Charleen, the niece, listened to the reason for the call then demanded a promise that Birdie could stay safely where she was. She wouldn't be dragged back east. Charleen didn't ask for identification. She accepted Ellen's statement that she was a friend of the man Birdie may have unintentionally accused of assault. She said that she'd talk things over with her aunt. She promised nothing but it was agreed that Ellen could call back the next day. Perhaps Birdie might talk to her.

Ellen hung up smiling from her achievement, then walking to the fridge to open the second bottle, "You're not pregnant yet, are you?'

"Not unless you believe in immaculate conception. By the way, my glass is empty."

CHAPTER TWENTY-EIGHT

On Monday morning Ellen, Lou and Rush were all at their desks before eight with two new missing person reports awaiting them. One was a senile octogenarian who somehow slipped out of his nursing home, in slippers and pajamas, and the search was already well organized with police, volunteers and dogs. Rush checked on the availability of a helicopter with heat seeking scanner capability in case that might be necessary as the nursing home was at the edge of a conservation area. The other was yet another fifteen year old female. Her mother had last seen her Saturday afternoon but only called 911 at seven this morning. Ellen was in touch with all hospitals as well as the downtown detachments to check all the usual alleys and hallways frequented by frightened or stoned youths.

All three had arrived that morning preoccupied with differing dominant intentions.

Lou's was to concentrate on his work to push away the continuing ache left from Gabriella's words at the wedding. Drinking too much had only given him a headache that lasted all day Sunday and still lingered this morning. It had given him an excuse for tuning out Maria's re-runs of almost every minute of the day before. Gabriella told him that he'd have to accept the fact that her decision was final. He'd have to share the same hurt that he felt Gabriella was also feeling.

Rush's plan for this Monday was to call Morris and, at lunchtime, go to the Admissions Office at Law School to take that first step towards a Degree, over two decades late in the waiting. His father had been totally supportive and was emphatic that Rush's stock dividends would provide sufficient monthly income to finance three years of study, should that be necessary. He dismissed his son's concerns that he wouldn't be able to give him a monthly cheque. He pointed out that the vast majority of those past monies had been invested, by Russell, into accounts in Rush's name. He summarized the issue by stating that this would only be a levelling out period, simply to maintain Rush's holdings, not an unrecoverable loss.

Ellen was disappointed she'd have to wait before sharing the news that she'd spoken with Birdie yesterday who admitted it definitely wasn't that Police Detective who'd assaulted her. Ellen had been apprehensive when, on Sunday just after lunch here in the east, she called Charleen. Again she promised her Birdie wouldn't be hauled back to the City to testify, to negate all the success her aunt had achieved so far. Finally the phone turned over to a cautious Birdie and Ellen, just as cautious, began her interview, firstly reviewing then praising Birdie for her recovery, not only from the injuries suffered from the beating, but also her withdrawing from her addiction. Birdie was slow and hesitant in responding but when she finally gained confidence she made it clear to Ellen that she was staying where she was, where she was safe. She limited her admission to confirming that no Police were involved in her beating. She wouldn't go further and Ellen didn't push it. After hanging up she thought it would have been better to have called from the Office so she could record the call but, to have proof of Rush's innocence, she'd need more than a tape.

Finally, as the threesome took their earned coffee break Ellen was able, with justifiable pride showing on her face, to announce her success. "I've found and talked to Birdie! She confirms that you didn't touch her!"

Without identifying Sydney, as she hadn't asked nor wanted to know if her research was entirely legal, she only admitted to having a source assist her. Neither Lou or Rush asked who this was. She concluded by asking if there could be funds available for her to fly out west, hire a car, drive up into the hills to obtain a signed or recorded statement. She made it clear that she would be the only one to have Charleen and Birdie's trust.

Rush said that he couldn't authorize that without approval from 'Upstairs' but even if this was denied he then would advance funds and make sure she was fully reimbursed for expenses although she might have to use a few days of her holiday allowance.

"You can also tell Upstairs that there's a good chance I can get whatever Birdie knows about Lucy Marie. We all suspect she was murdered but perhaps we can keep this out of Homicide's hands, at least for now." At this point Ellen didn't reveal her promise to ensure Birdie could remain safe in her far off sanctuary but it was a promise she intended to keep.

Rush realized that if he were to resign within a few months that fully clearing his name within the Force might not be needed but, even if he had to pay for Ellen's trip, it was simply the proper thing to do. There was another thing to do.

"Ellen I won't ask about your source but I do thank you, and your helper, for tracing Birdie. It'll be nice to get this off my back. I do owe both of you a favour."

Her mind flashed back to her thoughts of Rush fathering their child but that was too much of a favour, one she couldn't ask.

***

That same Monday morning, also at coffee break, less than a mile away from Police Headquarters, Marielle pulled up a chair beside Marjorie in the staff cafeteria.

"How's your sister doing...and, just as important, how are you doing?"

Marielle sipped the too weak coffee and reviewed the slow progress Sylvie was making. She hadn't yet gone back to her small apartment but this morning had returned to work.

"How long will she be staying with you?"

"I guess as long as she has to."

"Well don't make it permanent, remember you have a life to live too. Speaking of which you're still coming to the Anniversary dinner on Thursday aren't you?"

"Umm...I'd forgotten about that...maybe I should stay at home with my sister."

"Are thou thy sister's keeper?" sermonized Marjorie. "I think not. You need to get out. It's almost a command appearance for all senior staff to be there, to meet his Lordship, our illustrious Chairman of the Board from across the waves." Marjorie now stopped before going on. "There's also something you need to know. Word has it that Reg Hathaway, in Accounting, has been asking about you, whether you are going alone or with someone.To me that sounds as if he's trying to get the courage to ask you to go with him."

Marielle had spoken to Hathaway only a few times. He was a tall, somewhat shy, and sad faced probably due to the fact his wife had left him, as well as their two young children, to run away with the husband of one of her, at the time, best friends. This was four years ago and word was that Reg was looking for a wife and a stepmother for his children. Marielle wasn't currently interested in either role. At Antioch she had a reputation for independence and had no compunction to repel any advances of on-the-prowl men, married or single. However, the thought of saying 'No' to a man, who'd still be hurting from the ultimate rejection, wasn't a pleasant thought.

"Can't you use your resources to let it be known I already have a date?"

"Oh sure when he sees you on Thursday...all alone...won't that send a nice message!"

"So it's probably best I don't go at all."

"Well the obvious solution is to have a date. What about that cop you met down south, had dinner with a few weeks ago. What's his name? Rush or something? Anything wrong with him?"

"O.K. Nothing...he's presentable...maybe not Hollywood handsome but, in his own way, handsome enough...but if I call him aren't I just encouraging him to a relationship that I'm not looking for?"

"You mean he needs to be discouraged?"

"Uhmm...maybe." She thought back to think back to their meetings. Rush had been more than a gentleman but, recalling his admission about the women of Paris, she guessed he was a romantic at heart so added, "I prefer not to test the waters."

"Well if I remember correctly, he asked you to help him out as a translator for his son's girlfriend. You can make it clear that you now need a favour returned. Tell him it's a one-off."

"I'll think about it but somehow get the word back to Reg that I'm unavailable. You've been a matchmaker here before. Isn't there some single thing on staff, anxious to be a mother without going through childbirth?"

***

Marielle wandered back to her office at the same time as, many miles away to the South, David arrived back in Porto del Norte ready to begin another few weeks of helping patients come to terms with death. However, his mind was on what he had left, not on what was ahead on Isla.The last two days had been spent exclusively with or thinking about Andy.

He had been persistent but didn't crowd her. There'd been twice when she told him to 'Get Lost'. The first time had been serious and she'd stomped away but the second time had been said with a smile. The only physical contact they had was on the last night walking on the beach, when he reached to hold her hand and she returned the squeeze to his. In the hours available to him he had told her a lot about himself, almost a confessional. In turn he'd learned only a bit about her. He'd guessed wrong about her name. It wasn't Andrea. It was Andromeda.

He had asked, "Isn't that a star?"

"No. It's a galaxy. The nearest one to Earth."

"You were well named. Out of this world and unattainable to mortal man." She couldn't tell whether he was being serious or just kidding. He learned her father was Greek, hence her surname Makaris; her mother Catalonian. They'd met and mated, conceiving a daughter, while working on a cruise ship.

"I suppose that's why I've gravitated to the Hospitality Industry."

What David hadn't learned much about her past life. She didn't even give her age or birthday but David's estimation was about ten years younger than he was. She'd given no clue as to why she'd transferred from Florida to this resort. She was interested in hearing of David's life, ranging from childhood in hot Trinidad, to boarding school in rainy England, to a university with ivy covered walls in the north-east, onto the granite clad London hospitals, then to the frail tents in scorching Africa, and now to a self-imposed exile on a small island. At first she reacted on being told Isla's function but as David gave her vignettes of his patients' lives and the myriad reasons they chose to end them, she became less critical, becoming more understanding of David's participation.

Still, it was almost a one-way street of personal revelations. David could only hope that his honest self-exposition would show Andy what made him a person, warts and all, and crumble the wall she had built around herself. He wasn't asking or in need of Andy revealing her past to him. He couldn't explain to himself why this was of no importance; it was simply a feeling he had that she had no evil nor shame to hide and whatever was in her past would have no bearing on their future.

The stuttering start of a Pratt and Whitney engine had jolted his mind to the reality. that he needed to shepherd a handful of applicants to their chosen destiny. Now,on Isla Cresciente he could only count the days before a return flight would give him the chance to see Andy again.

***

The Community Park had originally been built, after an empty factory had been demolished and the ground cleared, as a much needed play area for the many children living in low income housing and run-down homes nearby. It was the only grass close to them. Now there'd been a partial gentrification of some of the nearby streets so the playground that afternoon had both single mothers plus a few nannies minding the children.

The picnic table with three men seated was well out of earshot and unwanted surveillance. Sol had arrived there first. Bucks was next and he wasn't totally surprised to see Sampson amble over to sit with them. They knew of one another but had never connected before. Each had their turf, miles apart in the City, and that distance had not made them friends but avoided making them enemies. Their products also didn't overlap enough to cause conflict. Sampson dealt in heroin and Bucks in opioids. For the first few minutes they all played a game, as if they were emissaries representing far off potentates. Slowly Sol brought them to the point of the meeting, to get some type of agreement that would benefit all three. Once it was conceded that all was not going as well as liked in their respective markets it was Samson who steered the conversation.

"Hey Bucks, know anything about China White?"

Bucks, who only remembered recent whispers about it, gave a pretence of knowing."Maybe. Why?"

"Well, I have a chance to buy a bundle but it'll take some financing. I need a partner."

He glanced over at Sol. "Since we will be discussing dollars maybe you should take a little walk. Give us fifteen minutes. Don't worry, if there's a deal made we'll work you into it."

Sampson was vague on his supply source but clear about the cost. "They want two-twenty five but I think we can buy at a hundred thou each. I'm told his stuff is dynamite. It's like candy to a kid. I figure that it'll be easy to get a return ten times the cost and, out on the street, they'll love it, be calling for more.Without admitting his ignorance Bucks asked, "Tell me more about this stuff."

"Well I'm not a chemist but it's a kind of fentanyl. I guess about the same. This stuff we can get is already bagged, small, easy to handle."

"Tried any?"

"I've heard you stay clean of the stuff. So do I but if I... if you and me do the deal we'll ask for a sample up front. It'll cost maybe ten thou just for a sample. That's really being squeezed for what we'll get. It's a gamble but I've done a few deals with this guy before and I haven't been bagged yet. Once we get a few packets we can try them on the street, test the market. At worst we might lose, at most, five each but if it's what they say is true then our only worry is where to hide the million."

Bucks wasn't sure if he could fully trust Samson and, in turn, trust his unknown supplier. He guessed it was probably a biker gang but didn't ask as he knew he wouldn't be told. Taking a chance on losing five was one thing he could handle but risking a hundred thou was another ballgame, especially since he'd have to borrow off his mother.

Sol, who was waiting, worryingly too close to the kids in the playground, was now signalled to return. Bucks and Sampson had an agreement on five each for the sample but no cut for Syd until they were pulling in dough from the bigger deal. Sol wasn't happy to be put on the shelf but shrugged and agreed to wait for his piece for brokering a deal.

CHAPTER TWENTY-NINE

It was late afternoon when Harry, with a broad smile across his face, called Marielle into his office.

"Have I got a deal for you! Well, maybe. First tell me, after you get your degree, where you intend to practise law?"

Of course Marielle had given this thought before. She certainly didn't want criminal law but beyond that would have to see what opportunities existed three years from now.

"I don't have any irons in the fire. I have to get my degree first. I suppose my best bet would be to try the firms that I already know, that I've been dealing with here at Antioch."

"Ever considered in-house Counsel? Stay right here, at Antioch?"

"Will there be openings?"

"In a few years I'll be retiring so there'd be an opening and I have to make sure there's going to be someone ready to take over when I do." His face became serious as he explained, "I've talked to the VP who will undoubtedly soon move to be President and I explained how valuable you are now and how much more valuable you'll be with a law degree." He paused then went on. "Look we don't expect you to sign a contract but a handshake would be enough to keep you on the payroll providing we get first call to give you an offer to stay with us." He let all this sink in. "As soon as you start school you'd be demoted here, lose your title, your office, and go down to our lowest salary level, whatever that is, but you get some pay every month and do the occasional assignment, field work for us. Anyway, think it over."

Marielle, without hesitation, rose from her chair reaching her hand over the desk. "Let's shake now before you change your mind."

The handshake was followed by Harry rounding his desk to bear hug Marielle.

Still beaming she returned to her desk knowing she'd have difficulty concentrating on anything in front of her. Then her cell buzzed. She saw it was Sylvie.

"Sis, I'm at my apartment, to pick up the mail. There's an envelope with a dozen fifties in it. Nothing else, no note, no name. What should I do? Should I call that detective? Tell him?" She hesitated, "Will he take the money from me if it may involve Remi? I sure could use the money."

Marielle told her not to touch the envelope or money further but wrap it carefully and bring it back to Marielle's apartment. After disconnecting from her sister she sat for a few minutes before calling the Police Department.

Ellen was out interviewing the young friends of the still missing fifteen year old when Rush received the good news from upstairs to pay expenses, within set limits, to allow Ellen to fly out west to get Birdie's statement. He was just about to call her cell when a call came in. He saw it was from Antioch Life.

"Hello Rush. It's Marielle...again...bothering you."

Surprised, Rush mumbled it was no bother at all, as she quickly updated him on her sister's mysterious envelope asking if this was something that should be passed on to the Homicide Unit. Quickly Rush considered the possibilities. This could be a bookie simply paying off long odds to Remi. It could be an anonymous generous gift to Sylvie to cushion her loss. He remembered Scanelli's comment that Remi could have been part of a scheme that turned bad. It could be Remi's posthumous cut of the profits. He suggested he would call Homicide. In the meanwhile have Sylvie avoid leaving any more of her fingerprints on the envelope or money.

"I've already told her that and to bring it back to my place. I guess we'll hold it until we hear back from you or Detective Scanelli."

"Yes, one of us will call you...by the way...how is your sister doing? You too?"

"She's managing. My problems are minor in comparison."

"Any minor problems I can help you with?"

Marielle didn't immediately respond but Marjorie's words at coffee break came back to her. She hesitated before answering.

"In fact...I do have a problem this Thursday evening. There is a company event and I need...an escort...just for cocktails and dinner.Are you...er...interested...available?"

"Let me check...let's see...yes the Rushton Sterne Escort Service is free... and at no charge this Thursday." As he finished he wondered if he'd gone too far with his attempt at humour. He immediately changed his tone, "Seriously I would be happy to. How formal is the dinner?"

Marielle explained that Antioch Life was having its North America's Anniversary Banquet also emphasising that she was only avoiding someone at the office and that's why she needed an escort. She told him suit and tie, no corsage, was all that would be needed. She would meet him in the lobby of the hotel about six. Thanking him again she left Rush extremely pleased, even if it was very clear that he'd only been summoned from the end of the bench as a last minute substitute when the game was almost over. What the hell, he was still in the game, in her life.

It was a full five minutes later before he remembered to call Ellen with the other good news of the day.

***

"Walter." His mother had never heard his street name. "That's a hell of a lot of dough. Do you have any idea of what you're doing?"

"Ma...it's still not sure I've got a deal, or want to take it. If the sample sells then I'll have to make up my mind real quick or Sampson will go to someone else. I'm just asking if you can advance me, say seventy maybe eighty, like fast, if I decide to go in big."

"You know Walter, you could go to a bank, maybe offer to pay points way above prime but you know when you tell them what it's for, then the door will hit your ass hard on the way out. What you're looking for is risky venture capital. That comes with a price. If I were interested and dealing with a stranger I'd want a big return. However, since you're family I'd take ten percent paid within sixty days, fifteen over ninety and twenty over six months."

"Mom I'm your son! That's a hell of a lot...for family."

"Walter, you can take or leave it. I'm not sure if your brother would let me if he knew. Speaking of your brother he gets out in six weeks. I'm going up to visit on Saturday. Maybe you should come along."

The walls, locks, doors, guards as well as the overall smell of prison brought back too many memories for Bucks. "No Ma. When he gets out then I'll see him. We can throw a party." When they were growing up Bucks got punched by both his father and older brother. He wouldn't be unhappy to have Lennie stay where he was for another year or two. If Bucks made big money on this deal with Sampson he could foresee his brother trying to muscle in somehow.

"Ma...Instead of seventy thou why don't I get a loan on my car and only borrow sixty from you at...let's say...thirteen percent over six months."

"Walter. Thirteen is an unlucky number, better make it fourteen...over four months. Now let's have supper."

Bucks knew that this was the end of the negotiations so he dutifully followed her into the kitchen.

***

Russell had been seeing Dr. Nathan Green now for nearly thirty years but still thought of him as just out of medical school. Russell had answered the doctor's questions but slightly discounted the frequency of the vertigo episodes having that in his own estimation, were simply a natural consequence of the continuing aging process. Nathan thought otherwise and suggested that he schedule a number of tests at the hospital for Russell.

"Do you think that all this is necessary?"

"So your time is that valuable that you can't spare a morning downtown among all those pretty nurses?"

"Fine. You're the doctor. Let me know when it will be. Thanks again."

***

Sylvie was sitting watching television, looking up as Marielle entered the apartment then to simply point to the paper bag on the side table. Marielle picked it up delicately, as if it was contaminated, carefully placing it on the higher shelf of her entry closet. It would stay there until she'd heard from either Rush or Detective Scanelli.

Sylvie stayed engrossed, eyes fixed on the screen as Marielle set the table and began to prepare dinner. Although it was admittedly easier to cook for two than just one she would have to, perhaps tonight, ask her sister if she intended to return to the apartment that she had shared with Remi.

If Sylvie insisted on staying, Marielle couldn't object but this compact one bedroom plus a small den would be inadequate in September, when she'd need a quiet separate room for studying.

At dinner she raised the question. "Any ideas what you will do about your apartment?"

Sylvie slowly considered the point, as if it was the first time she'd given it any thought.

"Sis...I really don't know. I don't think I can afford it on my own. It's on a month to month lease so it'll be easy to get out of but...can I stay with you...for a while...until things sort out for me?"

"Well, if it's long term we'll need a bigger place. If it's only for a month or two we can manage."

"That's really great. I'll give my notice tomorrow. There's only a few pieces of furniture I'd want to keep, the rest is junk. Do you have any room in your storage locker?"

As they cleared the dinner dishes Sylvie began to realize the imposition her stay might cause.

"Thanks Sis. I've never liked living alone. I don't know how you manage. Coming home to an empty place each night." A thought came to her mind. "Unless you've got something going? A man in your life?"

Marielle gave a negative shake of her head. No, the last man in her life had been her English lecturer nearly a year ago. The affair was limited to his small office, both of them thrashing on the couch or on the floor. It lasted only a month, ending when Marielle sighted a much younger woman hanging possessively to his arm. Over a year before that was the end of her eight years with Luis-Filipe. She had met him at a club that pulsed with the South American rhythms where he and his group belted out music six nights a week. At a break he and another guitarist came over to the table she was sharing with girlfriends. He was paying more attention to the blonde beside Marielle exchanging gross comments in Spanish with his band mate. As Marielle got up to leave for the washroom she hurled a few words of gutter Spanish back at him. At the end of the next set he came to quietly sit beside her and, in Spanish, apologized for the crudity of their remarks.

After that he was very much the gentleman and thereafter followed weeks of almost formal courtship before Marielle's acceptance of a serious relationship. His friends called her his 'Tangerine', after the old song; her friends called him her 'Don Juan', after the old movie. It was an atypical existence of cohabitation. She'd be in bed asleep when he came home from the club; she would leave in the morning while he slept. They really only had Sundays. He was occasionally out of town on gigs and every year, for two weeks, he flew back to Argentina to see his daughter. At first Marielle accepted his comment that he was divorced only later learning it was only a mutual agreed separation. Marielle never felt had the sense of comfort in their relationship as both seemed to need the up and down drama of fiery arguments followed by torrid sex to co-exist but as the years went by there were less sparks but with nothing solid to replace them.Their times apart became more wanted than times together. It slowly faltered until Marielle ended it. Luis-Filipe didn't protest.

Sylvie was stacking the dishwasher "Well maybe you should."

"Should what?"

"Have a man in your life." Marielle left this advice unanswered. Instead she was now thinking of her invitation for yet another spur of the moment dinner with Rush. Looking back to each of the previous two they were enjoyable enough but neither were intended to lead to another. She would have to make it clear to Rush, as nice as he was, that this was the end of the line in their relationship, if you could even call it that. Right now she needed no further complications in her life

***

It was Thursday at four-thirty when Rush arrived back home carrying his dry cleaned best suit, a new shirt and a tie that had cost as much as the shirt. The salesman had insisted it was a perfect match to compliment the shirt and a dark blue suit. He placed a towel on his kitchen table to use an iron out any wrinkles from the shirt and tie.

He shaved, showered and was beginning to dress when his father came down the stairs. "You don't look sick."

"No. Why should I?"

"It seems, anytime you're home early, it's because you have the flu, or something."

"No, I'm feeling fine. It's just that I'm going out for cocktails and dinner."

"A Police thing?"

"No. It's a banquet, an Anniversary Dinner for Antioch Life. You know...the company that you're insured with."

"So they invite the sons of their policyholders and not the ones who have been paying them premiums for all these years."

Rush glanced at the clock, "I don't want to be late. I'll explain later."

This didn't seem to satisfy Russell's curiosity.

"Look...it's sort of an assignment...just helping out a...a lady...that I've only met a few times and she needs...well...just an escort."

"So it's not a real date."

"No Dad, it's more like an accommodation."

"If your mother were here she'd want more than you're telling me but O.K. Get dressed and get going."

He turned to go back upstairs then glanced back, "Nice tie."

***

The Hotel was busy, the large lobby crowded with a few going out, many more coming in. Rush saw the signage to the Antioch Life reception and there was Marielle, not gowned like some of the other women, but very stylish and attractive, not in any need of a flattering outfit. He tried to think of something complimentary to say but she was first.

"Nice tie."

They entered to mingle inside the Liberty Room. Rush let Marielle lead the way, only stopping a waiter to reach for glasses of white wine, before reaching a group of Marielle's friends. Rush was introduced to Harry and his wife Muriel, Lorraine and her husband Martin, and another couple whose names were blurred by the noise of the crowd. Rush smiled and nodded while trying to nibble, without dropping, a variety of hors d'oeuvres that were being constantly presented, while managing a napkin and his now nearly empty wine glass. Then an attractive silver haired woman joined them. With the noise from all the elevated volume of voices in the room, again he missed her last name but her first was Marjorie. Her questions focused to show more interest in Rush than Marielle had shown so far. She had begun a mild interrogation of Rush and he, as politely as possible, deflected questions without revealing anything too personal. In turn she was positive in pointing out how lovely looking Marielle was and that she was both an asset to Antioch as well as a good and trusted friend. Marielle had disappeared through this conversation but as the first bell rang in preparation for dinner she was back.

"Sorry. You're probably totally bored, aren't you?"

"No, not at all."

"Well. I think I'll find the Ladies Room before sitting for dinner. I warn you, there'll be speeches. Oh, we're at table twenty-two. Meet you there."

It seemed many others had the same washroom idea; Rush as well. Looking around he saw an 'Exit' sign and slid over to push a door open to see an empty hallway. He guessed he'd find a washroom somewhere down it and turning a corner he saw a door signed with the frontal masculine outline. As he opened the door a tuxedoed younger man was in his face.

"Sorry. This is a private V.I.P washroom."

Behind him, drying his hands on a plush towel, was an older, tall, grey haired man also in a tuxedo. He turned, "Gerald, we're finished in here. Let this young man use the facilities."

Rush stood aside, muttering a quiet 'Thank you' and, as they passed, the older man glanced at Rush and, in return, Rush was doing the same at him. Then the combination of the accent and the face combined to give Rush a recollection of a day ten years ago.

He was back at table twenty-two well before Marielle arrived. "Sorry, as always a line up for women."

Purposefully Rush had taken the chair to face away from the front but as he rose with the crowd to applaud the entrance of the Head Table, all the men and women formally attired, he saw that the gentleman who'd afforded him washroom privileges was arm in arm with another face he recognized.

For a hotel meal it was quite good. The soup was hot enough, the salad crisp with a dinner choice of chicken or beef. Wine was served, but only once. As dinner was being cleared it was announced that dessert and coffee would be served after a few "short" speeches. For once that promise was correct. The President of Antioch's North America operations gave a succinct summary of the past successful seventy-five years and the forecast that the years ahead would promise even more expansion. The C.F.O followed with a blurring string of numbers, all positive, buttressing the

President's earlier comments. Then Lord Caldington, Chairman of the Board from the parent company, was introduced.

After the usual complimentary remarks to the current executives beside him he gave a brief historical review of the simplicity of the Company's founder and his dealings face to face with his neighbours, its first policyholders, and how important it was, despite the thousands now involved, that this personal contact should remain a constant in Antioch's philosophy.

"Finally I have two apologies to make. Firstly I will be unable to continue my visit here with the events scheduled for tomorrow to meet more of you than I have already. As some of you might know, as a member of The House of Lords, I have Parliamentary Duties to uphold, in addition to my duties at Antioch Life. I've been informed that there is going to be an important vote demanding my quick return. So it is with regret that I must leave early tomorrow morning. I'm pleased that I've had a chance to meet so many of you, although, a second apology, I haven't been able to remember all your names. As my lovely wife, Lady Caldington, will attest I have a good memory for faces, less for names."

He stopped, looking at his wife as if for approval to continue. "In that regard earlier, before dinner, I recognized a face but needed to have Lady Caldington assist me in recalling his name. I did ask if he now might be an employee of Antioch. No one here…" Lord Caldington waved his arm along the lengthy head table "... knew of him so I assume he is a guest. My wife and I would be very pleased, should he still be present, to have him, and his companion, join us here, we'll make room somehow, for coffee and dessert." He paused again catching the eye of his wife. "Oh yes. His name...Rushton Sterne...that's Sterne with the extra 'e'."

Rush chuckled. Lord Caldington had remembered him. He looked over at Marielle.

"Your mouth is open."

She shut it quickly to ask. "I guess there couldn't be two Rushton Sternes here tonight, could there?"

Rush stood up reaching out his hand. "Let's go to meet the Lord and Lady Caldington."

He navigated Marielle around tables, every eye on them, toward the Caldingtons. Rush thought that, for once, he had an advantage over

Marielle. She still had a puzzled expression until she changed it to a shy smile on being introduced by Rush before chairs were rearranged to have them sit between the eminent Lord and Lady. Marielle stayed silent as Rush asked about two women, Charlotte and Alexandra, and was told that both were now married and mothers. He also asked about a Michael and an Alice and was assured they were still running Caldington Hall efficiently. Marielle only ate half the dessert and felt the continuing glances from Antioch executives at the Head Table as well as other faces within her view. She heard Rush being asked about his life and his Police career which he modestly answered. Then after less than a quarter hour Lord Aldington extended his hand to Rush signalling the end of the conversation. Returning to table twenty-two Marielle saw Marjorie's thumbs up, a sign of success, plus eyebrows raised, questioning what was the real story behind all of this. Marielle couldn't have told her then but she was determined to get Rush to tell her.

When the Banquet was finally concluded she steered Rush to a corner seat in the Hotel bar, ordered two glasses of wine.

"Now tell me all about this High Society business."

Rush had only recounted the story twice before, once for the amusement of his parents and later to David. Tonight there would be a third, for Marielle. He started with the surprise invitation he received to attend David and Victoria's wedding which he decided to stretch into a side trip to the Cotswolds and the Welsh border then back to London for only two days before taking the Chunnel train to Paris. He told of leaving the wedding reception to hear a woman's voice calling out for 'Charlie'. He omitted details of his medical attention but told of this woman, Alexandra, taking control and delivering a still drunk and comatose Charlotte to her stately home and due to the fog having to stay overnight only returning to his hotel the next morning.

"I was just about to leave there when I was called to the phone. It was Alexandra insisting that I return as Lord and Lady were just as insistent that they meet the man who helped get their daughter safely home. So that is how I met the Caldingtons. I had a delightful lunch with them and Alex. Charlotte was still in bed but did send down a brief note of thanks. You know I think I still have that somewhere at home. I do recall that the four of us sat in a room that could seat at least forty."

Marielle asked more questions forcing Rush to fill out the story with more details. He didn't tell her about leaving as Alex had accompanied him to the front steps giving him an embrace and a kiss of thanks that still lingered, now years later.

Marielle had noted his change of 'Alexandra' to 'Alex' and now her instinct interpreted the wistful look on Rush's face. "She made quite an impression on you, didn't she, this Alexandra."

He had never admitted this to his parents or David but now his secret had been uncovered. "Yeah but there was never any chance for me although…" He halted, "...I did dream of it back then. Silly...to think of the impossible."

They then remained silent, their glasses still half full. Marielle signalled the waiter and as Rush fumbled to pull out his wallet she already had cash ready. She slid out of her seat.

"Rush this has been an...interesting evening...and you are an interesting person. I do thank you, for tonight, and for your help with the Remi business but it's a work day tomorrow, meetings all morning and I should be home to bed. My car is downstairs with valet parking. I'll be fine. You stay, finish your wine. Muchas gracias."

He could only half rise and wave to her as she left. He sat back, and following instructions, reached for his glass. Yes, it had been an interesting evening.

***

It was early morning, a continent away. Edo was awake thinking ahead to tomorrow, a Saturday afternoon with Elania in Govennia. She had invited him to her cousin's engagement party. He knew that this would send a signal to all her friends and relatives but he didn't mind the message it might give. He wasn't committed as he'd only seen her a few times, protectively chaperoned, allowing only hand holding and a few quick kisses when backs were turned. Tomorrow's party would give him much more opportunity to explore Elania's lips and embrace.

Suddenly his cell phone buzzed. The display showed an area code that he hadn't hoped to see again. It could only be his handler. He was tempted not to answer. It might be a new assignment. He'd done enough.

He decided he'd simply tell them that. What could they do? He pressed the green button.

He listened only answering in monosyllables until asked if he'd told anyone of his elimination of Vuk Losavik.

"No. No one, not a person."

This wasn't entirely true. He'd never given his mother any name nor any details but he had assured her that the tragedy causing her widowhood had been avenged. He clicked off his cell and settled back, uneasily, on his pillow. The call was a warning. One of his fellow trainees at that secluded camp in the hills had been killed, a murder with a message. It was suspected that there was a leak within the Organization who knew names, knew who had done what. Edo was urged to be extremely careful, lay low, perhaps move to the safety of another country.

No. This was his community, his people. He would be safe enough here, staying close to home and close enough to keep seeing Elania.

CHAPTER THIRTY

Although Rush had told Ellen not to bother coming to the office that morning she was there before eight. Her flight west to see Birdie didn't leave until after two but she said she was packed, didn't need a drive as she would take the bus to the Airport and--thank you just the same--need any assistance. It was a busy morning for the unit and Rush was glad she was there.

Shortly before noon Scanelli called. The envelope and the bills inside were clean of any fingerprints, except Sylvie's. They now had Remi's cell phone calls over the last few months. They'd traced many calls to two known local betting operations and were working on a call he'd made just before he'd gone on that last fatal ride but so far without success. He said he had already called Sylvie, told her the money would be returned to her as they had no proof it was connected to the crime. Rush had hoped he could call Marielle with the news but that was now not necessary. Instead he thought about the interview Morris had arranged for him with the Admission Officer at Law School. He realized, but wasn't apologizing for, the advantage of knowing people of influence.

He'd had only a quick lunch in the Cafeteria and was heading back through the reception hall to the stairs when his name was called.

"Detective Sterne. There's a package just left here for you...by a lady." The receptionist laid heavy emphasis on the 'lady' part. Rush picked the oblong box to bring to his desk, sliding it into a drawer, hopefully out of notice to any staff. He was tempted but didn't open the small card, held underneath the ribbon on the box.

***

Knowing that Bucks would be worried about getting his fair share Sampson hadn't yet opened the package. He had just paid ten grand for this sample of China White and had met Bucks in the rear room of a buddy's bar to split it equally, fifty-fifty, which was the exact math for sharing the one hundred small plain paper packages. Bucks thought there'd be more and wasn't happy with the cost of a hundred a shot thinking these were single doses. He couldn't see buyers forking over a C-note, they might be lucky to get fifty each.

"Bucky..." Bucks scowled, he never liked being called Bucky, but didn't interrupt Samson who continued "...look on this as a loss leader. I told you we'd pay heavy for the sample but, if we take the rest, we can charge ten, fifteen, twenty, whatever the market will take after we re-package it into smaller cuts. Let's face it I'm not sure of what the takers out there can handle. We want them coming back for more not getting OD'd on their first buy. Maybe, just to be safe we should cut them in quarters, maybe smaller, before we put them out on the street."

This made sense to Bucks, preferring to cover his costs rather than take a loss. "Fine with me. How long do we have before we decide to go for broke." He missed the potential irony of his words. If Sampson recognized it, he passed on any correction.

"He wanted a week, I tried for two but we settled for ten days. It'll be tight to make sure this stuff sells but if we decide it's a go you'll need to have the cash ready. Will that be a problem?"

"Nah. No problem at all." Bucks hoped his mother was onside. If she had changed her mind there would be a problem, a big one. As he angled back to his pick-up then drove home, driving as lawful as a Sunday School teacher to avoid any violations that might risk his cargo, he now considered the best way to introduce his new product to his street. He'd start with Willie Tomic. His allotted territory wasn't large but populated with the newly upscale high rise apartments and condos as well as the older sections with subsidized and low income residences. It was an interesting cross-section to start with, to test the response to this new stuff on the users, out there on the streets..

***

It was nearly two when Marielle entered the lobby of Antioch Life's North American Head Office. There was the usual greeting of the girls behind the desk as well as a friendly warning, "Watch out. Marjorie's been hunting for you all day."

She was only at her desk five minutes before Marjorie's radar found her.

"Just where in the hell have you been?"

Marielle explained that she and Harry had been in a morning long meeting at their legal counsel's offices.

"Honey, Harry was back here by twelve."

"Well, I had a few things to do and since I was already downtown, I had a nice lunch. No insult to your company, I do get a little tired of our Caf by Friday."

"Baloney! You are avoiding me. All morning I've been pestered by questions about you and this Mister extra 'e' and your tete-a-tete with Milord and Milady. Give me the details."

Marielle did, but in condensed form, simply saying that Rushton had, by chance, assisted Caldington's daughter a few years ago. It didn't totally satisfy her friend but seemed enough before she returned to the topic of Rushton Sterne.

"So this Mister extra 'e' is the same guy you met on this deserted island, had a romantic dinner at a fancy hotel, had another dinner here, back in town, the morning after which a bouquet of flowers arrives at your desk. Right. Then, pressed for a reason to avoid an invite from Reg in Accounting you reluctantly call a date who, in my estimation is a good looking guy, maybe not leading man material, but good enough for my taste..." She stopped to catch her breath, "...who then...last night, elevated your status, at both ends of the ranks, to the 'Employee of the Month', maybe the entire year. So I hope you will send him a bouquet or, at the least, a posy of 'forget-me-nots' as a Thank You."

"Marjorie you know that I don't want to encourage anyone. I'm not on any dating sites, or hanging around bars. I'm not looking for Mr.Right. If my life isn't quite heavenly bliss, at least it's a life that I'm in control of. I'm not looking for a romance or marriage or babies. It's not that those couldn't be nice, in an ideal world, but I doubt they will be, at least in the foreseeable future, in mine." Her smile took any edge from her words, "Now, get back to earning our Antioch some dollars."

As Marjorie left, with a pretended expression of hurt, Marielle now wondered if she really meant all of those words, and whether she should have permitted that surprising impulse to deliver that parcel to Police HQ.

***

Ellen had decided not to deduct hours from her watch face. She'd only be here for twenty-four hours and thought it best to stay on EST which now conflicted with the sun's position, still high above the foothills leading to the Rockies. Leaving the airport, proceeding to 'Auto Rentals', she began to notice the differences from the City she left a few hours ago and this new, to her, land that sprawled ahead. The strangers she was seeing seemed taller with tanned, sometimes leathery, faces and had a confident stride in their step along with the noticeable absence of ties and suits.The few people she had spoken to seemed to have genuine, not forced, smiles. It took only minutes as she drove further west before the horizons widened and the concept of space, room to roam, overtook her mind such that she wanted to steer off the uncrowded highway onto the stretches of land on either side. Forcing her attention back to the road that began to climb upward beyond each bend, she felt she was simply a spectator viewing the display of Nature's supremacy that mocked mankind's attempts to control it. There was evidence of civilization spread as the miles passed by but it had not yet come close to overcoming the vastness of the land, all in contrast to the city where she was raised and now worked. Back East it was concrete, bricks, asphalt to dominate with dwindling grass and scattered trees as reminders of what was once.

Ellen was surprised that her attention had been so easily deflected from her planned meeting with Birdie Partridge by her new surroundings. Would this be a better place to raise a child, Sydney's and her child, than back east in the City? Would there be less crime, conflict and confusion here than there? Her experiences told her that some people were better than others, some cities safer than others but impossible to find somewhere that hadn't tasted that enticing Apple in the Garden.

The dashboard's GPS easily led to her B&B and the freshest air she'd tasted in months blew down from the sun splashed far off peaks to greet her. She stopped before leaving her car to look westward. The white tipped mountains might be miles away but their magnitude brought them closer and made them more intimate. She now wished she'd had time tomorrow to chase after them but now only forty odd miles away was Birdie. It would be better to refocus on tomorrow morning.

***

Rush managed to extract the oblong box from his desk drawer and attempt to hide it under his arm to the safety in his car as if he was conveying state secrets. He chided himself for his subterfuge, not sure why he had been so secretive. As he drove the final block to home he waved at the neighbours out on their front yards, trimming gardens, cutting grass or just tracking those passing by.

After entering through his own back door he went to open the doorway leading upstairs. He could hear the evening's telecast was on and he pictured his father sitting back, engrossed in the latest news. He'd go up in a minute but his curiosity demanded he open his present. He read the note first:

My turn to thank you. If I remember correctly this is your favorite wine… ML

His memory scanned back to the first of their dinners in Republica Real. Nice that she remembered the wine. He remembered her very clearly from that night. He saw that the label and vintage promised a special bottle. He would have to save it for a special occasion.

Going upstairs he saw his father's easy chair empty. The kitchen was as well. Turning down the hall he saw only slippers, toes down, just outside the bathroom door. With sudden panic he sprinted to see his father, face down on the tile floor. A quick check detected a weak breath, weaker pulse and half-lidded unseeing eyes. He reached for his cell phone to punch 911 now noticing a patch of blood seeping out from the underside of his head. Quickly and with a surprisingly controlled voice he gave the 911 desk what information they asked for. Then he reviewed his paramedic training considering what he could do, without endangering his father. His first decision was to cover Russell with a bedspread then carefully raise his head just high enough to slip a hand towel underneath. He tried to think what he should do next but then heard the faint wail of a siren and ran to the front door out onto the steps to wave at the approaching ambulance then let the medics inside.

He stood back letting the two attendants proceed professionally through their practised routine. One was relaying their findings to a central station, the other quiet and careful in assessing the necessary priorities. Then with a nod of agreement they turned Russell on his back. Rush could now see more of the bloody abrasion to his temple. The female paramedic asked, "He's your father? Name?"

"Russell Sterne"

"Age?"

"Eighty-five."

"Health problems?"

"No, nothing severe. Just the usual aches and pains."

"You live here?"

"Yes, downstairs."

"Do you have a list of your father's prescriptions? No? Better check his bedside table and dresser. After we get him off the floor in here check these cabinets. Make a list. Bring it to the hospital. We'll be taking him to Northside General but first hold the door. I'm bringing in a stretcher."

Soon their procession, his father prone between them, went down the steps. Rush saw concerned faces of neighbours on the sidewalk. After the ambulance had left he saw the questions on their faces. Those he couldn't answer as he went back inside to complete his assigned task. Although he thought his father was in good health he was surprised at the list of prescriptions he had compiled. Perhaps his father wasn't as healthy as he had believed, or wanted to believe.

He drove carefully but exceeded the speed limit on finding open stretches and was soon at the Hospital Emergency Entrance, frustrated in trying to find a parking spot. Finally inside, he found any time saved by his haste in arriving served no practical purpose for any update on his father. The busy woman at the desk thanked him for the list of prescriptions but could give him no details on his father's status. She could only ask him to wait. Soon he was resigned to sit among all of those others waiting, all sharing the same worried faces.

***

It was a sunny Saturday morning as Tomas took a commanding position, hidden in a clump of trees, to wait in the event Edo would be taking this, the only main road to Govennia. He was glad of the shade as the temperature rose in sync with the sun as it rose towards its daytime height. There had been a few motorcycles on the road. Tomas could predict the size of their engines just by the sound. Even before he had peered through the leaves he was certain this one approaching would be Edo. He kicked his own bike's engine alive and followed at a safe distance.

Fortunately Edo didn't drive through Govennia's shopping area and it was an easy trail to follow before Edo stopped at a small but neat cottage. As Tomas drove past he noticed Edo was wearing a jacket and tie which suggested he'd be back out soon. He was fortunate to find another observation post less than a hundred metres away. Judging from the position of Edo's parked bike he presumed that his future route would take him past where he waited so that it would be easy to follow him. Within minutes, Edo emerged holding hands with an attractive young woman. She slipped onto the seat behind Edo and as they passed Tomas he appreciated the view of her legs and thighs as her dress billowed out. Again it was a simple matter to follow them as they pulled in among an already crowded cluster of cars and motorbikes beside a plain one story brick building. There were groups of young people on the steps who waved welcome to Edo and his girlfriend.

Tomas cruised by before pulling into a vacant section of grass separated by a short stretch of head high shrubs and small trees from the building hosting whatever party was being celebrated. He found an easy path into this copse to hide his bike, facing it outward to the road as a precaution. He then unlocked his side bag pulling out the wrapped package, the instrument he hoped to use to fulfil his assignment today. It would all depend on chance, on fate, but he had a premonition that today was the day.

Carefully he threaded his way to a position about fifty metres from the rear door, already held open, of the building. To keep hidden he would have to crouch looking slightly upward, not his preferred position for shooting. Still he'd been in tough situations before and always ended up with the best scores. This time would be different. The target was flesh.

The pistol was new to him, a long barrelled .25 calibre equipped with a small scope. He'd never used a scope in competition and somehow doubted he'd need it now. He slipped six shells into the pistol.They said they could kill even at hundreds of metres. Now he would have to wait hoping Edo would come out to this back verandah seeking fresh air or a chance to smoke.

He waited patiently crouching, ignoring the discomfort, reminding himself that he was a warrior committed to the cause. There were, as the afternoon and the party inside progressed, a number of people, mostly men, who came out that rear door. Once he thought he glimpsed Edo but only for seconds before he went back inside. Another half hour went by and suddenly Edo was outside, a beer in one hand, his other pulling his girlfriend out with him. Tomas readied the barrel in the crotch of a small tree and waited for an opportunity. He now was using the scope and the crosshairs showed Edo's face leaning over to the girl and his mouth was on hers. Tomas gently pressured the trigger three times in quick succession. He now didn't need the scope to see both bodies crumple, blood splattering the wall behind them. It only took him a minute to find his bike, wrap the gun before locking it in his side bag, slip on his helmet and lower its tinted screen. His bike started immediately and he tried to minimize the noise from his engine as he accelerated, heading north, out of town, to the busy highway where his bike would be only one of many going towards the Capital. As he mixed in with other traffic he finally felt safe and was certain the job was done as was expected of him. He was truly sorry that the girl had to be included but if she was a potential breeder of the children of his enemy then best she go too.

CHAPTER THIRTY-ONE

Ellen's flight left in daylight heading east. Looking out from her window seat she soon saw the encroaching night darken then display emerging stars. She thought back to her interview of Birdie Partridge, happy that she had the statement that would now lift the suspicion off Rush's head. She also thought about the promise she'd made not to involve Birdie in any further dealings with the Police, as well as hoping Birdie's life had now stabilized and her days of addiction were over.

Across the aisle a young mother was trying to quiet a fussy child, still young enough to be coddled and cuddled. This now set her mind to Sydney and their future child, hopefully a daughter. Would this child only want her natural mother to hold her? To comfort her? Where would Ellen be in this family?

Her thoughts then spread, her worrying wider. Would Sydney's maternal instincts smother all the passion between them? As alarming, what if Sydney chose intercourse rather than clinical insertion and enjoyed an orgasm better than the ones they shared? She shook her head to dispel these troublesome thoughts trying to find a distraction, to fill the remaining miles, from the small screen in front of her. It was past midnight as her flight landed and nearly two before she crept into the bedroom where Sydney was curled, sound asleep. Trying not to wake her she slipped into bed, snuggling up to Sydney's back, slipping a hand around to gently cup her breast. Now secure she slid solidly into a contented sleep, then to wake up after nine to the aroma of a Sunday breakfast being prepared. At times throughout the day she wondered if she should call Rush's cell, with the good news, but decided Monday morning would do.

Now it was Monday and, entering the unit, she saw Rush's chair was still pushed tight against his desk. Lou was huddled over his phone, listening with a solemn face before turning to her.

"That was Rush. He's at the Northside General...has been there all week-end. It's his Dad."

Ellen was full of questions but Lou could tell her little. Russell's condition was very serious but still short of critical. He was stable, comatose, but unresponsive and this morning they planned a series of tests. All signs pointed to a stroke complicated by another brain injury from when he had fallen to hit his head. They both sat silent until Lou remembered.

"How was your trip out west?"

She had been looking forward to sharing the excitement over her good news but her voice was flat as she updated Lou.

"Well, it isn't as if we were in any doubt...but...get your report together and deliver it to Internal Affairs this morning. At least we'll have one piece of good news for Rush."

It wasn't until she returned, report duly filed, at mid-morning that she told Lou about Birdie's clarification. She had slurred the word when Rush first saw her. He thought she had said 'Lucky'. Birdie had told her that it was 'Bucky' or 'Buck' or maybe 'Bucks'.

Lou and Ellen would have preferred to have Rush's involvement in plotting their next steps but having no option they reviewed the connection of Birdie to Lucy Marie. A given was the medical clinic run by the Doctor brothers. The second connection, a good probability, was illegal traffic in prescription drugs. If they could sew this 'Bucky/Bucks' in as part of a pattern then this might be an opening to a solution. The first step would be a visit to the clinic of Drs. Isak and Ludlo Warsiak.

Lou suggested Ellen to call at the clinic, giving no advance notice. She wasn't sure she should do this alone but Lou said he'd have to stay close to his desk, with Rush being absent. She waited until late in the afternoon before walking into the clinic. She didn't show the receptionist her badge or indicate she had a medical problem. She simply stated that she would wait until the doctors were free and walked over to take a seat among the patients already waiting. She sat beside a young woman trying to soothe her baby. Beyond her was a whiskered man continually blowing his nose with the same rumpled handkerchief. Next to him, trying to lean away, was a woman continually rubbing her arm. No new patients arrived but it was nearly two hours before Ellen was the only person waiting. Finally the receptionist looked at her, pointing to the door that the whiskered man had just left. It was the only door that patients had used; the other door had remained closed. It was clear that only one of the brothers was here today.

Ellen took a seat opposite a partly bald head as the doctor was leaning over making notes on a file. As she waited she glanced at the framed degree on the wall behind him. It was in Latin, but the name decipherable to indicate this was Dr. Isak Warsiak. After a few minutes he looked up to see Ellen's credentials displayed in her hand. She began to state that this was a further step in the investigation of Lucy Marie. The doctor shrugged his shoulders and with a slight accent stated, "We have already told the Police what little we know...knew about her. She was a nice young lady and we still hope she's come to no harm."

Purposefully Ellen led the doctor over questions that he'd been asked before in the initial interview, receiving his same short answers, before she narrowed down the scope of her inquiries.

"You had a patient, a Robin Partridge?"

He agreed so she continued "...and she and Lucy Marie were good friends, weren't they?"

"Friends? I suppose so...but good friends...that I don't know."

"I know you're not allowed to disclose patient information but we do know that you were prescribing strong pain relieving drugs for Ms. Partridge's complaints. She complained and you prescribed opioid patches. A lot. She didn't need them. She'd sell them for money to satisfy her meth addiction. Did you know that?"

He looked down, as if reading what was in front of him, before looking up, "If patients don't tell me the truth...if they hide facts from me...how am I able to look inside their heads?"

"Lucy Marie was doing the same." Ellen didn't add that was only a suspicion before pressing forward. "You don't track the overall opioid volume, either per patient or total prescribed by you and your brother do you? What about samples, are they kept secure? Your computer system is probably archaic."

It took a full minute before Dr Isak composed his reply, " We... my brother and I...we are two old fashioned physicians, maybe too old fashioned but we don't see our patients as potential criminals. If they tell us they are in pain we have no machine that measures the extent of their pain. We only prescribe what we feel will relieve them, make their lives more comfortable." His voice trailed off and he sat back, extending his hands outward, as if saying we do the best we can.

Ellen didn't doubt their dedication but they should have realized how dependent their patients become on pain medication as well as having some awareness of the dollar value of these drugs out on the street. She half wanted to continue with her lecture but came back to the prime reason for her visit.

"Do you have a patient called Bucky, or Buck, maybe Bucks?""

Dr. Isak looked up at the ceiling to consider the question before lowering his head to face Ellen, his frown answering before his voice did, "No...but that sounds like a child's nickname. Is this a boy?"

"No, a man. Is there anyone that you know with a name that could be shortened to Bucky?"

Again another ceiling inspection before the head shake, "No, no I don't. Not at all."

"Your brother isn't in today?"

"Ludlo was worn out, working too hard. He's older than I, now seventy-four, so I insisted he take a holiday. He's visiting a retired classmate of his, in San Diego. He'll be back on Sunday."

"I'll come back on Monday. He'll be here?"

Another move of his head, this time in affirmation.

***

As Ellen had been sitting, waiting in an uncomfortable chair of the Ludlow's small clinic, Rush was also waiting. It was another day of sitting, eyeing the minutes drag by on the clock on the wall opposite. He now felt like a permanent fixture although the waiting had moved from that first overnight in Emergency to his present chair outside the Critical Care Ward. He had gone home twice, setting his alarm for just four hours of rest, then a shower. A stop at the deli for a breakfast sandwich to eat in the car as he drove back to Northside General for more waiting. He had seen two doctors who gave him limited information about his father. They weren't hiding anything; they didn't have all the information for a complete diagnosis.

A pleasant, concerned, and sympathetic Dr. LaMarche had called him into a consultation room on the evening of that first full day of waiting. This small room had two chairs squeezed close to her desk, a faded Monet print on the wall behind her. "There are two problems. The first is that your father has had a stroke, fortunately with no major paralysis but he is still comatose. Then there's the second problem caused by the trauma of hitting his head after the stroke caused him to fall. Deeper behind a subdural haematoma is a clot. We hope that a scan will give us a better picture and we can decide on future steps after that. I'm sorry I can't tell you more but even if we had a more complete diagnosis right now...I'm sorry...I couldn't give you an accurate prognosis."

"What are his chances...of a recovery...of a reasonable recovery?"

"I can't give you a guarantee for that...it's much too early. We are simply in a day to day situation. If the swelling subsides we can re-evaluate remediative procedures. If it doesn't and if it worsens...well that would..." Rush didn't ask her to finish the sentence.

Now it was seventy-two hours after finding Russell unconscious. They'd reduced the swelling but this afternoon's scan still didn't fully answer the concerns over the clot. The potential, good or bad, from the stroke was also an unknown at this point. Rush thought David, if he could somehow be here, would ask better questions than he to clarify the situation. Thinking back to the Isla he remembered that each of them had asked as to the health of the other's father, giving almost the same answer "Doing well, for his age". Rush had never thought that David and his father had a strong relationship. He'd been a bit closer to his mother but his parents, repeating their own restricted emotional upbringing, had only reinforced that pattern. Rush had always appreciated the security and comfort his parents had provided, without smothering or controlling, for his upbringing. Now he was asking himself if he had shown them enough appreciation for that love. He hadn't had the chance to be a father to Stefan and the distance between them now didn't afford much of an opportunity.

In the first few days of worrying and waiting at the hospital he had only considered his father either recovering or dying. Now he thought of the third, of not dying yet not quite living. He remembered, just a few years back, his father had spoken of visiting Art Enfield. The Enfields were not close friends but they lived near enough for his parents to stop to say hello and ask how they were doing. Then suddenly Art wasn't doing well and after months in hospital returned home but only after a ramp had been built to their door and a special bed had been delivered. Russell had seen this and, passing Art's home after a walk around the neighbourhood, had stopped there. Rush remembered his father's description. "Face half frozen. Stiff like a board. Slurring his words, saliva dripping. Propped up. A pack of diapers on the side table. Good God!" Russell turned directly to face his son, "If I ever get that way you know what I'd want you to do...don't you?"

Rush knew he would never be able to. David had that ability but Rush wondered if even David could, if asked, snuff out his own father's life. Still he thought back to Isla, to Jose's founding and funding for those who sought it, accepting the choice that the island offered. He now also remembered his father saying that in the event of any infirmity which prevented him from continuing to service his tax and investment clients that these accounts should be turned over to Arthur Ransome and Eli Dunlop. Rush now thought that time had arrived and he'd have to call Arthur and Eli tomorrow.

Although he sat with others in the waiting area, with some family member bedded inside beyond those swinging doors, he sat apart in the furthest chair, preferring solitude as he considered how he would be able to handle the logistics of Russell incapacitated and in need of constant care. Their home would have the space for any special bed that might be needed plus room for an overnight nurse. It might be necessary to forget about both the Missing Persons Unit as well as Law School. He could accept all of this but his mind simply couldn't picture his father only technically alive but almost dead nor could he wish for death itself. Rationally he accepted the statistics, in keeping with the Biblical formula, that sons bury their fathers, yet emotionally he shoved this probability away to the furthest reaches of his thinking. Both his mind and body were numb from the wearying hours of frustration, sitting here not being able to help his father, not even having faith in a God to whom he could direct his prayers.

***

Willie Tomic had been a street dealer for Bucks going on three years. At first he didn't make a lot of money but it was all tax free to add to his monthly disability pension. His income improved when Bucks supplied him with Percocet or, better yet, patches of Oxyies. He could cut these in portions without letting Bucks know. He hadn't been sure what to do with this new stuff, that sounded as if it came from China. Bucks told him to cut it into quarters, see what highs it would bring to his usual customers.

He had separated this first small supply into separate doses but he forgot to mark them accurately, now not sure of their potency. He would have to rely on the feel of his fingers to gauge each package.

Now, just over two days of what Bucks said would be 'trial marketing', his regulars were out looking for him. They wanted more and his supply was soon gone. Using their safe messaging system Willie asked Bucks for more. The next morning he found another supply, half what he first received, at the drop point at the back of a toilet in 'Donna's Donuts' on Fifth Street. That day he was back on his usual route of those who now looked out to find him and those who Willie had yet to find. One of the first of his regulars that had taken a sample didn't answer her cell that morning. He could usually reach her before noon, when she normally woke up. He could only guess at what she did at night but whatever she did, she was drop dead gorgeous.

Willie was one of the four dealers that Bucks used and the other three came back with the same message. They needed more of these new packets. Bucks reached Sampson on his cell who told him his own pushers were also asking for more. They agreed to go ahead for the whole deal by offering two hundred thousand. Bucks now needed his mother's money. Bucks still worried what cut Sampson might slice off for himself before the product came into Buck's hands. He expected it might not be an equal share even though he would be paying for half. He knew Sampson was taking more risks both in doing the deal and transferring the thousands as payment. Buck's financing would pass the smell test as he would exchange ten money orders payable to a registered company that Sampson had set up. If the Police or Tax Department came calling his prepared answer was that it was merely a speculative investment which, in truth, it was. Now he had to call his mother who he expected would have him sign a promissory note outlining the interest conditions.

The next two days would be busy completing the transfer of money coming from his mother to direct it to Sampson's shell company. He knew that Sampson would need to pay cash to his supplier which meant, once that was done, there should be no further delay in Bucks getting his end of the deal. He already paid for rental on a storage unit. He'd moved in some of the cleaning supplies there from his garage along with some older cleaning equipment. He planned to stash his supply in the underside of a heavy floor polisher, hidden behind the brushes. He didn't want the risk of stashing at home and he figured regular trips to the unit to pick up supplies was a good cover. Once everything was settled and smoothed out in a few days, he would call the Escort Service. He would be able to afford Eve and he felt he deserved a reward to top all of this, the biggest deal he'd ever made.

***

Arriving home, first checking her mailbox, it was unusual for Marielle to meet any of elderly tenants in her apartment building. They'd have been downstairs to the lobby within minutes of the morning mail delivery. Tonight she was a little surprised to meet both of the Bentley sisters, almost as if they'd been waiting, both with forlorn faces.

"Hello dear...well we thought you should know...although it's not confirmed but..."

The other sister broke in "...we have it on good authority, through Millie David's nephew...he's in the real estate business...and he says..."

Like a tennis match the ball was onto the other side, "... he's sure that this building and the two on either side will be torn down and a large condo will be built. It's very distressing news isn't it? We aren't sure of what we'll do...where we can go...we've lived here for eighteen years...wanted to stay here until..."

Marielle tried to comfort their anxiety but only able to suggest they wait until there was more than rumours to deal with. She could only pat their shoulders and tell them not to worry. As she then walked up the stairs, avoiding the cramped and unreliable elevator, she realized it would be easier for her to find a new place than the elderly Bentleys. If Sylvie planned to stay with her then they would need to find a bigger apartment in any case.

As usual Sylvie was engrossed in watching television but, not as usual, she switched it off at the end of the talk show.

"Sis I've found a place to move to." A friend at her work had a roommate that, due to a pregnancy test and an honourable boyfriend, would be moving out by month end. She had asked Sylvie if she would share her apartment. Marielle made polite protests that moving wasn't necessary but both knew that it really was.They moved towards each other for a hug and promises that they would always remain sisters.

Preparing supper, with Sylvie back watching television, Marielle now hoped that the Bentleys' source was wrong. She had moved here after she and Luis had separated and she enjoyed the old fashioned high-ceiling rooms, the stable sensible occupants on all three floors only having to cope with the aging elevator and outdated laundry room. Nearby was a park that was reasonably safe, even for jogging after dark. She was comfortable here, her privacy respected and had assumed that her next three years at Law School would have her remain here. Well, if there had to be changes, she would want them settled before her first term in early September. She would have to take what life would give her.

***

DUNBAR, Evelyn (Evie) Eliza, age 23.

Suddenly and cruelly taken from her loving family: Beth and Gordon, brothers Luke (Joanne) and Jay, grandmother Amelia, cousins and many friends.The service will be private followed by cremation. In her memory please consider a donation to any organizations that support, care and assist those lives troubled with addiction.

CHAPTER THIRTY-TWO

David had the cab's windows wide open to allow the sea scented wind to attempt to blow away the cigarette odour embedded in the seats. He counted the mileage signs as the cab followed the coast road to the Resorts, back to Andy. He had wanted, in the nearly four weeks since he last saw her, to text or send her a note showing that he hadn't forgotten her and that he needed very much to see her again. However, remembering her guarded reticence, he thought it best to not overwhelm her with his enthusiasm. She had to know that he was a regular visitor at each month end so he shouldn't need to announce his arrival.

Finally he was striding into the wide, flower laden lobby of the hotel to see that Patrique was on duty at the desk.

"Hoya amigo!"

They clasped each other reaching across the wide counter. "You have, I hope, a spare room for me?"

"Si senor, I will find you a room." Patrique turned his attention to scan a screen.

"Look up when Andy is next on duty."

Patrique stayed with his head down, focusing on the computer, before answering. "La encantadora Andy? Lo Siento, Senor Doctor. Andy is not on duty. Andy...gone. Vamos. Back to America."

"When..." David felt panic "...did she leave?"

"Maybe tres, maybe cuatro dias, señor."

"Where did she go?"

"Dice nada."

He turned to wander away stunned as his anticipation, his expectations slowly crumbled at his feet. Patrique called, "Senor Daveed! Your room. Numero Ocho, by the beach."

David returned to the desk to be handed his card and then Patrique slapped his own forehead. "Madre mio. Una carta. A letter...for you."

He had never seen her handwriting before but knew this was from Andy.

Pulling his suitcase down the pathway his slow steady steps belied his racing mind to reach and open the door to Number Eight. Once inside he threw the letter on the bed and immediately went to the mini bar. Although it was stocked he wondered whether there was enough there to help him withstand what he was sure would be in Andy's letter. Leaving the letter untouched he emptied two small bottles of Scotch into a glass and walked out to the patio only steps from the beach. Settling into a chair his eyes saw the bodies tanning in the sun but his brain only saw Andy.

Over the last few weeks since he'd returned to Isla Cresciente he spent most of his spare time reviewing the changes he would have to make to his life in order to convince Andy to share it. Clearly he would have to resign from Isla. Jose would simply have to get someone else. If Andy continued to keep working for the same hotel chain he could try to convince the corporation that an on-hand qualified doctor would be a selling point. If she wanted to return to the United States then he could apply for a license to practice in whatever State she chose. In his mind there was a slight worry that the British Medical Society may have put an asterisk beside his name for that past problem. Well whatever was necessary he would handle and they could now plan a life together.

In these last few weeks the feeling of having a future, rather than simply exist in the day-to-day present, gave him enthusiasm that he could leave the past, take this sack off his back, loosen the chains around his ankles. He couldn't really explain it but knew this optimism centered on Andy, his Andromeda, if she chose, if he could convince her, to share her future with him. He had known many women, bedded dozens, loved only a few and now Andy, whom he had never even kissed, who he had only known for hours, this was the woman he wanted to spend the rest of his life with, in thousands of new hours, hundreds of new days.

Now, noticing that his glass was empty he slowly pushed himself up, out of his chair, back into the room seeing the envelope alone on the empty bed. He emptied two more ponies into his glass and reached for the envelope carrying both back outside.

Whether from courage or resignation he opened it.

Dear David,

This letter will tell you I've left the Resort and, by doing so, avoided seeing you, for necessary reasons.

If I had stayed I couldn't trust that my resolve, to stay independent, to avoid any relationship, would be strong enough if I saw you again. If I stayed and we talked this over I doubt if you would quietly go away, back to your island or wherever, leaving me alone. I also have doubts that I would really have wanted you to. Please don't take this as any encouragement to seek where I've gone, to find me.This letter is difficult enough, hurting me and hurting you, but the written word is often easier than the spoken.

You have been honest with me, telling of your past successes and failures, making you a fascinating, even captivating, person. You know that I don't approve of your current occupation but I'd guess that you'd swear to leave it behind you. If so, thank you for your willingness to do so. I'd also guess that you might promise me to forgo your womanizing ways and days. I'd probably believe you but I've been hurt, perhaps damaged, and also I've hurt others, deeply. I've learned that promises wear thin.

I haven't told you my story, my history, why I am what I am. If I did, you might say it doesn't matter to you but it matters, very much, to me. I am simply not ready to share my life and perhaps never will be. You must accept my decision. I can't hide on a desert island; you could probably find me. Please don't try. I wish you find some happiness in whatever world you choose to seek, or seeks you........Sincerely..... Andy.

In the morning a litter of mini bottles covered the floor, David's inert body hanging half out of bed, still in the clothes he'd worn yesterday when he had hopes of seeing Andy. Even when his eyes half opened and the reality of yesterday came back to burn, he stayed splayed out on the bed, hoping sleep would revisit and blot out the morning.

It half succeeded and it was mid-morning that brought incessant banging that wouldn't go away. He commanded his legs to function towards and a hand to open the door. It was Sandro.

"How goes it Amigo?" He looked around the room, "Not well. I see. It's Andy, isn't it?"

After David used the toilet and splashed water over his face he returned to face his friend.

"David, you have to remember that as lovely as she was, she was only just a woman. There are millions out there.You tried marriage. Did it work for you? No. You and I are not husbands, we are only lovers, making many women happy, if only for a few hours and not hurting ourselves either. Remember there are so many women, tan poco tiempo."

David reached down for one of the small empty bottles to throw at Sandro's face who didn't even flinch as it sailed wide.

"Sandro you are a lump of mierda!" He stopped before adding, "Me too."

After a few minutes of silence Sandro tried to reinvigorate his friend. "Come. Let me introduce you to a couple of very lovely ladies, in need of a man. You will have first choice."

David's head had cleared enough for him to see the easier pathway on offer, at least for the moment, for an escape from his lingering painful emotions. He'd done this before, many times, allowing his groin to show the way forward, suppressing any other feelings.

"All right. Let me shower and shave first. I'll meet you out front in a half an hour."

The shower helped clear some of the sludge from his brain and he felt a little better as he found fresh clothes.Then he noticed the flashing message signal on the face of his cellphone.

It was a Trinidadian country code. He dialed.

"Good morning, Dr. Ewart's Office. May I assist you?" The friendly rhythmic lilt of her accent brought Trinidad immediately into David's room but her tone became more subdued when he identified himself. "Oh yes. Please hold and I'll try to locate him."

It took a few minutes before, "Hello David. It's Peter...with some bad news…"

***

Rush had gone to the cafeteria for another cup of coffee, half hoping they'd improved the taste from his last cup. He really didn't need it but gave him an excuse to get up and away from his chair in the waiting room outside the ward. He would have another excuse soon to take the only half drunk cup to the washroom to empty it. It was now the fifth day of just sitting, worrying and wondering about his father's condition, but now his earlier optimism of a reasonable recovery was tempered with reality. His mind rewound the scenarios that had played in his mind over these past days with different finales but none with happy endings.

"Mr. Sterne." He was snapped back from his reveries to see Dr. LaMarche smiling down at him. The waiting room, for once, was almost empty so she didn't suggest the consultation room and sat down beside Rush.

"We've completed all the tests we can do at present and had a conference, reviewing our options." She hesitated but still gave a comforting smile, "I'm afraid we have few that promise enough progress for us, again right now, to proceed with. So the situation has not improved nor has it worsened."

"Which means?"

"We expect that he'll remain comatose, but not in any pain…" She reassured him with another smile, "...but the expectancy of any immediate positive changes are, to be blunt, unlikely. His vital signs are steady, not as strong as we'd like, but consistent enough."

"Are you saying he is in a vegetative state?"

"No, not from a medical point of view. He's not in need of life support. His brain, as so often is the case, is managing well enough now to sustain his essential functions. It calls the tune…" She sought for the right words, "...the notes to play. We can only wait to see if the brain can help itself find new pathways to manage some degree of improvement."

"Should I be looking into a full-time care facility or converting our home to accommodate him?"

"No, we don't think that's imminent although we can't say whether that might be necessary...but not now, not at the present. Let's keep him here and we can continue to monitor him."

Pausing again, putting her patient aside for a moment, seeing his son's anxious eyes, she offered him some solace, "It's simply a waiting game. Although we have many tools and procedures that may be needed…just right now they're in reserve...so we wait. I can't really say what your father may be conscious of but why don't we make room for you to sit with him. Holding his hand, squeezing it, telling him what's happening in your family or out in the world. It may help and may, if I can say so, help you, rather than sitting alone out here."

So Rush's hours were now at his father's bedside. At first, the sight of a trussed immobile figure, wired to small screens that with numbers and pulses confirmed that his father was alive but not living, was distressing but within minutes at bedside Rush felt more at ease. He did hold his father's inert hand, squeezing and stroking, thinking that this was the hand that had guided and steadied him as he grew up. At first self conscious, Rush began to talk to Russell, only a few words, separated by long silences, but with hopes that some part of his father's senses recognized his presence.

These hours gave him ample time to review his own relationship with his father. There was always a comfort level of respect and affection but he now asked himself whether he ever demonstrated actual love for his father. He certainly had for his mother. Those last brief months of her life were painful to remember and, after her death, as the pain eased to numbness, he realized that his father, her husband, her lover, would feel the loss deeper than he had. Now he wished he had shown more support for his father, not that he needed a crutch, but simply to show love. It wasn't as if they'd gone their separate ways but, a masculine failing, they'd continue to live, side by side, both untrained, perhaps afraid, to acknowledge any deeper emotion.

Now looking back at his upbringing and his father's influences he remembered a continued feeling of comfort. Russell's voice was rarely raised to any level of anger although he was also sparse with praise. He wasn't the sports type of father: to play baseball, shoot hoops or toss a football. Russell had never liked guns and Rush wondered if this was a result of his own father dying on a battlefield. Whatever the reason, hunting was never a consideration.They did occasionally fish together on Loon Lake, where his parents rented a cottage for two weeks each summer for ten years. Father and son would sit waiting for nibbles on their lines but rarely landing any fish even though it was never the plan to keep them. Rush was ten when he discovered the reason for their poor record. His father had filed down the barbs on the hooks. When Rush had asked why, his father's response was that it was to avoid hurting the fish.

It was on one of those occasions of sitting quietly in the boat offshore that his father, very hesitantly, began his 'Facts of Life' explanation to his eleven year-old son. Rush remembered how embarrassed he was, looking away at the far shore, as his father patiently gave a factual account of the physical requirements of procreation but ignoring any explanation of the impetus that compelled copulation. Rush, from the street and schoolyard, had already received the basics, but at that stage, with no real interest in girls, sex was merely a word.

At age twenty Rush should have been more knowledgeable but driven by opportunity and passion failed to use protection before impregnating Ana. Tonight, sitting alone in an uncomfortable chair, he had no regrets for that oversight. Conceiving a child was not a thought in his mind back then but now his son occupied a place of pride. Rush had passed the point of the 'what ifs' and 'might have beens' while his son grew up without him. One or both of his mothers would have had to introduce adult concepts and facts into a child's mind. Now, thinking of Stefan, he could only thank Ana and Karla for their nurturing efforts. Although a depth of mutual feelings now flowed from those few days with Stefan, he had to conclude that there hadn't been enough time to evolve from initial curiosity to a deeper level of bonding. Perhaps there never would be enough time. He had taken a semester of Philosophy in his first year at University but one didn't need to be Aristotle or Kant to realize life was full of regrets.

***

The two investigators were always nervous when called to District Polizia Headquarters, more so when directed to Colonel Stavik's large office. They stood as the Colonel busied himself over a file in front of him signing whatever it was with a flourish. Then he looked up giving a welcoming smile that lingered on Arencia Ladoz which made her even more uncomfortable in his presence.

"Sit down, sit down, make yourself comfortable. I've ordered coffee."

At that, the door was opened and a police cadet arrived to set down a pot of coffee along with a clatter of porcelain and cutlery. The still nervous cadet poured three cups then, picking up one, looked for direction. The Colonel waved aside the offered cup and with another wave signalled it towards Arencia. She noted the quality of the China. She sipped and smiled at her temptation to tip the saucer over to read where it came from. The Colonel misread her smile.

"You like the coffee. Good, no?"

"Yes Colonel, very good. Thank you."

His own smile broadened at her response and she noted a gleam of gold from an upper incisor.

"Well now." This time he focused his attention on Lieutenant Craskiw, the senior of the two officers in front of him, "What do we know about this shooting in Govennia ?"

Craskiw was prepared. He reviewed the scene of the crime, the witnesses interviewed, the causes of death, the ballistics until Colonel Stavik held up his hand.

"Your conclusions?"

"Sir, an obviously well planned execution by a marksman, probably due to..." He searched for the proper phrase, "...the past historical incidents near Govennia." He made it sound as if this was ancient history, a position favoured by the current authorities. "The male victim's father and brother died there. The male victim was only a child at the time. He had a normal upbringing, decent marks at school, living with his mother. Then off to technical school. Again good grades. No problems noted. Then, following graduation, a gap in his activities for a few months." Craskiw could feel the Colonel's mind question why this gap remained unknown but he continued, "Then we are not sure where he obtained the funds, but we have our suspicions, and he was off on a Student Visa to study in America, in Florida. Then his passport shows he was off for a few months to Republica Real then back to Florida for a very short time, flying back here to a quiet life at home. He had started to see the other, the female victim, and it was at her cousin's engagement party that they were killed, at the back of the building. Three shots were fired but no noise was heard, little doubt that a silencer used. We found the location of the shooter in the bushes but no usable evidence was found, only a few footprints of a shoe and tracks of tires, both sold by the thousands. Definitely a planned extermination."

Stasik slowly stirred and stared at his coffee as if asking the cup, "By who?"

Arencia expected her ranking colleague to be careful with his words but did expect him to disclose all of the further information they'd so far uncovered. The Lieutenant began: "You will remember that it was a company of irregular troops who took part in those past incidents." Craskiw again followed the comfort of his country's revisionist history with this description. "There was a Sergeant Vuk Losavik involved with that squad and following the settling of hostilities he disappeared but was traced to the Caribbean. Since the male victim was also in that same area we strongly suspect that there may be a connection."

Arencia waited for him to expand on what they learned. There was the tracing of calls on Edo's cell phone.There was the mathematical matching of the only bullet that had not fragmented to a specific type used with a high powered pistol. They traced the few sales of this type and suspected one was still located, but hidden, at a shooting club connected to a 'sporting' association with deep seated nationalistic roots. There were some other interesting items as well but Craskiw didn't proceed to disclose any of them to the Colonel. Instead he gave a slight shrug of his shoulders before adding with a resigned look, "Perhaps just another page from our history."

Colonel Stasik decided to overlook the commentary. The Colonel had long practiced the art of ignoring the obvious.

"There have been no arrests?" The Colonel made it more of a statement than a question.

"No Sir."

"Would you not think that this case should now be turned over to Bureau Twenty?"

Again Stasik only pretended to make it a question. Arencia stayed silent. If the Colonel could read her mind she'd be instantly out of a job. She now realized that Craskiw had been waiting to sense whether Colonel Stasik wanted to hear the real progress of the investigation or had called them in to shelve their involvement. Bureau Twenty was a group of officers, many close to retirement, known for their inactivity and shared political views. It was sometimes called the 'Bureau of Unsolved Cases' as almost all referred files would remain that way. She now fully understood the situation, the Colonel's staging of this farce. He already knew what they had uncovered and didn't want any further progress.

Arencia was not surprised to hear Craskiw's reply. "Yes Sir. I was already considering that."

"Good. Then do so. You may now leave."

Arencia also started to rise but the colonel raised his hand, "Please stay, I'll call for fresh coffee."

She sat back uncomfortable in her chair trying to hide the grimace she felt with a weak smile knowing what might be next, hoping that her career wasn't to be determined in the next half hour with the beaming Colonel.

***

Bucks was on a high that hadn't needed any of his new product as fuel. His customers obviously needed this stuff and, within a week, their demand generated the dollars that gave Bucks the relief that his investment would be a real money maker. Now he would need to find a place to hide his money from being noticed to avoid both the taxman and the law. He also now envisioned moving out of the house, finally away from his mother. He'd miss her daily cooking but could always come back, bringing his laundry, for dinner. He saw himself in a fancy apartment, maybe a condo. With a nice pad he could avoid hotel rooms. He began to dream of having Eve for more than an occasional night. If the dough kept coming in and if Sampson could get even more China White he could even see Eve living with him. Imagine having her every night. For now it was back to calling the Escort Service.

There was the expected brief delay while they checked his history until a smooth, very friendly, female voice welcomed him.

"Good Evening Sir. What can we do for you?"

I'd like to book another evening with Eve."

"Eve, let me see...oh, could I ask you to wait just a minute?"

"Yeah, sure, I'll hold on."

He expected that they were checking her schedule but the voice was now back.

"I am sorry sir but Eve is unfortunately not available but we do have some delightful..."

"What do you mean, not available. I'm a regular customer. Just when will she be available?"

"I am truly sorry but again we can recommend…"

"Are you telling me she doesn't want to see me!"

"No. No. Not at all. It is just that she isn't, at this time, seeing any of her clients, even regulars. We are sure you'll be just as pleased with one of our other…"

"I only want Eve. Why all this runaround?"

"Again, we are very sorry but please do consider…"

"Bitch!" He nearly hurled his cell against the wall and streamed obscenities until his anger faded. He now looked at the clock on the kitchen wall. It was time for him to make some deliveries. He went to the smaller refrigerator, the one his mother left alone for his use. Pulling out the vegetable bin he took out a cellophane wrapped oversized head of romaine lettuce. Taking it to the counter he carefully dislodged the top of the inside core to access the hollowed interior where he kept a small cache of the packages bought from Sampson. His main supply was hidden in the old floor polisher in the rented storage unit only a mile away but this would be enough for tonight. He was only seeing Samuel and later Willie.

The packets were now stuffed behind his seat as he was driving through intermittent drizzle as day darkened towards night. His normal routine, if he was only dropping off a supply, had its risks but then--didn't everything in this game. For Samuel, Bucks would ring Samuel's cell, giving him the signal that his new supply was securely taped under the rim of the dumpster behind his building, awaiting pick-up. When Bucks was exchanging a supply for dollars then that had to be done face to face, hand to hand. In the past this pick up of cash was only once a week but now with accelerated sales it was twice. He and Samuel signalled each other from opposite sides of a small alley and then, if all was clear, would quickly stride towards each other in a transaction that took only seconds. Bucks didn't worry when he moved to meet Samuel. If there was a problem, such as the cops, he could throw the packages away and keep walking, absorbing the loss somehow. He was always more nervous on leaving the alleyway. There was no way he wanted to throw real cash away but Samuel was a small timer; there was never too much in exchange and if necessary he could swallow the loss.

The exchange with Samuel went without a problem as Bucks went back to lock the wad of crumpled bills in the glove compartment of his pick-up. Now he was off to connect with Willie Tomic, who turned over three or four times more than Samuel. Bucks had two set systems also for Willie. If supply was the only need, Bucks would tape the package to the backside of the toilet tank in Donna's DoNuts 'Employees Only' washroom then call Willie who waited less than a block away. Bucks wanted a few minutes to get to his truck before Willie came to the washroom to stash the drug packages into the sides of knee high elasticized socks.

Buck's had free rein to use Donna's for his dealings. His crews did the early five A.M. cleaning of this run down coffee shop, six tables and a counter of eight stools, for almost nothing. Donna and her small staff simply looked the other way from Bucks and his gang coming and going, mainly in and out of the washroom. Donna had taken over the coffee shop twenty years back and given her allergies to nuts, and her preference for women, it became known by the locals as 'NoNuts'.

It was here, at NoNuts, that cash changed hands with Willie. Beforehand Bucks was doubly cautious that neither were being tailed. This involved the intersection of Third Street and Rowlands Road. From opposite corners they would signal if all looked clear. Willie would wear the visor of a Yankee cap frontwards for 'Go', backwards for 'No Go'. If Bucks suspected a problem he would walk in the opposite direction, away from Donna's, and the switch was off for that night. So far this had never happened.

Bucks stayed hugging the wall on his corner waiting for Willie to show. He checked his watch. Willie was normally on time within one or two minutes of eight o'clock. Bucks now felt exposed, just loitering on the sidewalk, as the rain increased. He was considering turning back to go home when he saw the Yankee hat with Willie underneath. He was looking back over his shoulder before he looked across the street resetting the Yankee logo to face Bucks.

Soon, using the rear entrance at Donna's, they were inside the narrow hallway then into the Employee washroom. As they exchanged their small but valuable packages Bucks asked whether there'd been a problem. Willie only said that he was being cautious as he thought he'd seen a couple of men following him a few blocks back as he was coming down Fourth

Avenue. Willie then took to dodging down side streets, doubling back before he was satisfied that there was no need to worry.

Bucks was about to unlock the door when Willie asked, "Tell me, this new stuff, how safe is it?"

"Safe? Wadda mean...safe?"

"I mean is it mixed right...you know...that each dose is the same as the next?"

Bucks had no idea. He wasn't into quality control. Anyone who bought street drugs couldn't expect a written guarantee but, with feigned assurance, he answered, "Sure it's good stuff, all the same. Why, are you worried?"

"Uh maybe. I'm hearing rumours, you know some O.D's."

"Any of your customers?"

Willie had no proof, only rumours. "No."

"Fine, let's split. Give me a few minutes."

As usual Bucks was extra careful on leaving Donna's, only after getting a large cup of steaming black coffee in a double cup. If he was intercepted before reaching the safety of his truck he planned to throw the coffee face first as his defence. It continued to rain as he headed back to his pick-up checking behind and in front of him carefully but had no problems before steering towards home, sipping on the still hot coffee. There he would carefully count the cash from Samuel and Willie to make sure they weren't stiffing him.

Willie fixed his Yankee cap firmly on his head giving him a little protection from the increasing rainfall. He never owned an umbrella, way too gay, but right now he'd take one as he still had two regulars to meet before calling it a night. He knew where to find them and headed, eyes downward, to avoid the now driving rain. He glanced up to see two figures heading towards him. He had a momentary surge of danger but they passed him and he relaxed. The rain pelting against brick and concrete hid any noise and he had no warning before a gloved hand clamped over his mouth and another around his neck. He had no choice but to hope that this was only a hit from another drug dealer. Although hardly able to breath his mind still worked. He doubted these were cops. This was something else. He wouldn't fight to keep his supply. Let them have it. Just leave him alone, in one piece. He realized there were two guys involved, both behind him, one gripping him in a vise, the other whispering in his ear.

"Willie, we need to talk. We hear you do a little dealing...maybe some of this new stuff." They weren't waiting for him to answer. He had to think someone, maybe one of his customers, had fingered him.

"We want you to tell us who supplies you with this crap. You have a choice. It's gonna be you or him who pays. Which is it going to be?"

The glove on his mouth relaxed enough to allow an answer. It was an easy choice; it wasn't going to be him but he still played for time, time to think, "I don't know his name."

A fist drove into the side of his ribcage with such force that he'd have fallen if he hadn't already been supported. "Try a better answer Willie."

Gasping through the glove he at first could only try to shake his head in denial before being able to mutter, "No. I only know what they call him...not his name."

Another rib-cracking punch that travelled into his spine had him want to cry out but the glove pushed it back down his throat. "His name. Try harder!"

"Okay. Okay. I only know him as Bucks." He tried to swallow before gasping for another breath. "Don't know where he lives." Again he paused which only resulted in another punch, adding pain, deep pain.

"Then give us your routine...how and where you meet...everything."

This time it was a blow into his right ear. The guy holding him straightened his body upright again. Slowly they extracted the information they wanted. Willie wasn't becoming used to the pain but he now anticipated the blows and giving more details seemed to lessen their intensity. Finally, from the guy at his ear, came the threat that if they had to trace him again he would die, very slowly. He was slammed into the brick wall, slumping onto the wet rain-washed sidewalk.

He lay there, still alive, but hurting so much that he was afraid to move. He wasn't sure how long he stayed down but hearing steps coming closer and thought they might be back but the steps, now identifiable as high heels, went by with a mutter. "Another drunk."

The sound of the rain was steady but then he heard more steps, more of a shuffle, and someone was bending over him. "Hey Willie. What's up... you fall?"

It was Ricky, his next in-line regular, who'd been waiting for Willie. Ricky managed to haul Willie up on his feet, his back against the wall for support.

"Jesus...Willie...you look like a garbage truck ran over you..." Ricky's concern was short lived "...but...you selling?"

Willie now pattied the side of his leg realizing they hadn't taken his stuff. Painfully reaching down to lift his pant leg he took out a package, took Ricky's crumpled dollars and took hesitant steps ahead. He now knew what he had to do. He'd sell as much as he could, as fast as he could, use the cash to get out of town, far off, before Wednesday, the next time he was scheduled to meet Bucks. He'd told these two guys how the contact was made.They'd be waiting for Bucks on Wednesday. He now felt the rain dripping down his face and down his neck. Yeah, they'd even taken his Yankee ball cap. Then he reached into his jacket pocket. Empty. His cell phone had been taken as well. It made sense. They'd need it to receive Buck's call to confirm the timing of the contact. As he struggled down the street, each breath drawing pain, he wondered how Bucks would be after these two worked him over. There was no sympathy in that thought for Bucks. Theirs was a tough world with no time for feelings.

CHAPTER THIRTY-THREE

David, after thanking Peter Ewart, was still holding his cell phone as he sat down to digest the news of his father's death and began to sort out the necessities of the next few minutes, hours and days ahead. He was an only child so it would be his unwanted responsibility, his obligation to go home to arrange the burial of his father. He also had responsibilities here. This was the second of the usual four day break from Isla but a new group of patients were to arrive on the fifth day. He foresaw that he would not be back in time to meet them. As he considered the various options to deal with the problem he clicked his cell to call Jose Fuentes. Not surprisingly he was told Jose was in meetings and he could only leave a message.

His next call was to Heidi Fermer's cell phone. He assumed that she and Dr. Ernesto Manuel were comfortable somewhere in the Republica for their usual monthly trysts. She answered after the second ring, listening then offered her sympathy. David began to outline the re-arrangements that would be necessary when Heidi interrupted, as always, with professional formality.

"Please Doctor Newton. If I could ask you to wait just a minute?"

David could detect but not understand the exchange of words in the background but Ernesto was now on the line with condolences then quickly assuring David that he could easily arrange to stay a few extra days before returning to Santo Vincenza so that he and Miss Fermer could return to Isla and keep the Hospice functional until David was able to return. A relieved David thanked them both, receiving further sympathies in return. He would have to become used to these expressions, whether sincere or not, in the days ahead.

Next, with surprising ease, was to arrange the flight back to Trinidad catching an early afternoon flight from Bonojara to Santo Vincenza then to catch a five o'clock flight directly to Port-of-Spain. He quickly stuffed his casual clothing into his case realizing his need to buy something more formal for the days ahead. Then he was outside to meet the waiting Sandro to tell him that tonight he'd have to satisfy both of his two lovely ladies-in-waiting. As soon as he explained why he had to leave, Sandro was suddenly on him with a bear hug, tears in his eyes, muttering "su padre, su padre".

At the brief stop-over in Santo Vincenza he was able to reach Jose Fuentes. to receive his condolences. "David, lo siento mucho, so sorry for you and your family."

David didn't interject to clarify that the family, outside a semi-alcoholic aunt and two distant cousins, was only David. Still it was nice to feel Jose's sincerity as well as his assurances that he and Dr. Manuel would ensure all would be well until David could arrange his return. It was only after his flight left the airport that David was able to sit back in his seat, now up in the clouds, sipping a scotch, that his mind could leave the present and look back on the past.

Any sadness he felt over his father's death was more for the passing of an era than for the man himself. There was no pretence, no real grief over the ending to any father-son bond. As David flew closer and closer back to the waiting body of his father, neither his feelings nor his remembrances grew warmer. There had never been hostility; respect was their main tie. He only vaguely recalled his father's father and doubted that there had been any deeper feelings to be passed to the next generation. Perhaps it was a family tradition to leave child rearing to the maternal side; fathers providing discipline as needed. David had no scars, no simmering resentment against either parent. He was brought up in the Anglophile tradition for a son. It certainly had given him independence and, after sink or swim discipline, confidence. He had received more affection from Alma, the long time family cook, caretaker and caregiver, than his own parents. He had been able to call her to tell her that he'd arrive late but she should only come to the house in the morning.

Still, as the miles jetted by, his mind kept returning to his upbringing, and to both his parents. His thoughts saw them as individuals, never as a team, no outward affection shown. Like most children, on learning where babies came from, he couldn't possibly envision their coupling to produce him. He remembered once wondering whether he could have been adopted, never the genetic product of both of his legal parents. He had less doubt of his mother's involvement as she had had her moments of non-conformity. It wasn't until after her death that her sister, his aunt, after too many Rum Swizzles, gave him some family history. The two sisters had, following the war, been uprooted from England for their mother's second marriage. Their birth father, a Major in the Eighth Army, was buried in Egypt. His war widow was still attractive but needing financial security she agreed to marry Gerald Josparth and be transplanted to the Caribbean. Her children had a comfortable upbringing in Trinidad and their mother was keeping track of potential sons-in-law as her daughters came of age. David was told by his aunt that these plans became derailed as his mother-to-be became very involved with a handsome young man. Mr. and Mrs Josparth did not approve. His handsome black hair wasn't straight enough, his eyes too dark and his tanned skin a touch too brown. He might have passed as Black Irish to some but not to many on the island who knew of his mixed heritage. Edward Newman was ten years older, not rich but from a good Trinidadian family that once had been affluent. It was more of an arranged rather than forced marriage; with some effort the bride consummated it on the third night of their honeymoon.

The lights were on at his home as the taxi pulled to the front entrance and, despite his suggestion, Alma was there at the doorway, arms wide open welcoming David. He claimed not to be hungry but quickly consumed the ample 'snack' Alma had prepared.

David realized it had been almost three years since he had last been home. After asking about Alma's family he asked her about his father. She had been more informative on her own family than on his father. With reluctance she revealed that he had aged quickly and had almost become a hermit in his own home, only showing interest in some financial problem but Alma could not give him any details of this. Alma gave no criticism for David's lengthy absence but he now felt the guilt of his disinterest.

After cleaning up the dishes and re-setting for breakfast she said she'd stay over in the small room behind the kitchen. David gave her a heartfelt hug and answered her concern with a promise that he would not stay up too long. She had prepared his old bedroom upstairs and the events of the long day now were felt as he recalled Andy and the pain of losing her. Two sudden losses, one much more painful than the other. He was tempted to see what his father's liquor cabinet held but instead went up to the comfort of his old bed, curling up in the fresh sheets and thankful to slide easily into sleep.

***

Ellen didn't have to ask if both brothers were receiving patients that late afternoon. The entry and exits to and from the two doors confirmed it. Again she waited until the last patient went into one of the rooms. The other, now left open, allowed her to look inside to see Dr. Isak, head down, finalizing notes. She waited until he looked up.

"Oh yes. The lady Police Officer. Do sit down. Anything new... concerning Lucy Marie?"

"Unfortunately no, but of course that's why I'm here." Her eyebrows began the next question, "Any further thoughts about this Buck or Bucks guy?"

He seemed to be trying to remember their last conversation before replying, stretching out his words as his memory unfolded, "Ah. Yes...you were asking if I knew anyone by that name who was connected to Lucy Marie and...as I told you...we did not know her social life, really any part of her life that existed outside the Clinic. Sorry."

"Have you asked your brother about this?"

"No. . .no...but let me call him in. You can ask him directly. Stay here."

Dr. Isak came back with a slightly older version of himself. Dr. Ludlo pulled over a stool from beside the examination table to perch onto before facing Ellen. Dr.Isak had a slight accent, his brother's was more pronounced. "My brother said you are from the Police and want to ask me a question." Ellen could detect a hint of a 'd' inserted into his pronunciation of 'brother'.

"Yes I was asking if either of you had heard of a person with a name like Buck or Bucks, or anything close to that."

With the same fraternal mannerism he looked up at the ceiling, then at the opposite wall, back to his brother with a questioning glance, before returning to Ellen. "No, no one by that name." He now began to get up as if the interview was finished. Ellen, disappointed but with no further questions also arose, thanking them both. As she left Dr. Isak's office, Dr. Ludlo following her, his brother called to remind him, "Ludlo, don't forget to tidy your desk. The cleaners will be in tonight, doing the furniture too."

Ellen was almost at the door when Ludlo called her. "Miss...Miss... just a second."

This time it was the waiting room ceiling that had his attention until he then looked back at her, "I think I now remember that name, or something like it...yes...yes...it was maybe ...what...a year ago when...it was late and I was still in my office. . .when I heard him answer his cell phone. He said 'Yes, it's Bucks'. Yes, I'm sure that was what I heard."

Ellen tried to remain calm. "Who was that?"

"Uhm. I don't even know his name. Isak does. He runs the cleaning service that looks after our office."

Ellen immediately went back to see Dr. Isak. He shuffled a few business cards taken from the back of his desk drawer before handing over one: Stars Office Cleaning Services.

As she left the Clinic, going out onto the street, Ellen wanted to shout 'Eureka' out loud then realized she'd have to be naked to emulate Archimedes. Well--that could wait until she was back with Sydney. She could strip then, perhaps slowly, teasingly.

***

Rush became a regular at Northside General, greeting the same parking lot attendants, the ladies behind the main desk and the receptionist on the fifth floor. He would sit by his father's bed moving aside when nurses did their regular checks and made their notes. Rush and Dr. Lenore LaMarche were now on a first name basis but Russell was their only topic. Daily, sometimes twice, Rush was updated on his father's condition. It remained constant as Rush could see this for himself by tracking the screens behind his father's bed.

"Rush it may be appropriate that you start looking into a permanent care facility."

Dr. LaMarche had just reviewed the possibility that this still stable but comatose condition may continue with no predictable positive change. She didn't need to state the negative possibility. Rush said he hadn't checked on any nursing homes but asked her if she could recommend one.

"Sorry, I'm not allowed to do that. Check the web. There will be some variance in pricing due to location and decor but mainly, of course, on the choice of private, shared or ward rooms. It can, over time, become expensive. Will that be a problem?""

"No. That's not a problem but what's the timeline on this? How soon?"

"That's not tomorrow but it may be in a week or two. Best to start looking now."

After thanking her he decided to go home to his computer to start the search. He then thought about his work station at the office. It must be backed up with emails and memos. He was calling to check with Lou daily and was receiving assurances that all was being looked after, not to worry. Still, he should make an appearance.

At the office he accepted, with appreciation, all the concern and sympathy of the staff starting at the front desk, through the halls and into his unit. A quick scan of his computer clearly told him that they had been as busy as usual. Clearly his absence was creating a backlog. He would need to split his hours between the hospital and his desk. This would allow Lou to get free from the desk and out into the city on investigations, helping Ellen. He asked Lou when she was expected. He would like to see her before he left to go back to the hospital.

"She should be in soon. She called me this morning excited about something but she wanted to do a bit more checking first. I'll call to ask her to come in."

He didn't have to as she came striding into the office with firstly a smile to see Rush there but followed with a frown as she asked about his father. Rush gave her the same response he'd said to all, trying to make it positive by saying he was no worse, remaining stable. Now Lou and Rush looked expectantly at Ellen.

"I think I've found Bucks!"

She went on to relate Ludlo's spark of memory and 'Stars Office Cleaning Services'.

This morning she'd been able to determine it was an unincorporated company registered to a Lajda Starbuski, a widow, with sons Leonard and Walter. She had checked them as well. Leonard had nearly finished his current sentence and Walter had also done time.

"It all fits. The clinic's sloppy opioid controls. Lucy Marie's past history, or at least the suspicion, of stealing drugs at the hospital. The odds are that Walter, our Bucks, was also dealing. The coincidence of Bucks and Lucy

Marie at the same clinic, same time frame, it all fits together. Bucks knows what happened, where she is, where she's probably buried."

There was no doubt in Ellen's mind and both Lou and Rush had to agree that a lot of dots did connect but they fell short of provable guilt. Their unit dealt with 'Missing Persons'. Lucy Marie Fairweather was still missing. The question was whether they would continue with the file or whether it should be transferred to Homicide. Rush suggested that Ellen do a total review of the facts, only adding the assumptions at the end. Rush would take this downstairs. Basically Missing Persons would be asking Homicide if they wanted to carry the ball or not. Given how busy they were Rush would bet they'd pass. He wouldn't mind continuing with the file. He now wanted to see the face of the man who'd probably beaten Birdie and probably done the same, or worse, to Lucy but first he would go back to Northside General for another long vigil at his father's bedside.

***

Marielle decided to tell Marjorie today about her plans for Law School but with the added news that she would still be doing some part-time work for Antioch Life, and that they'd be able to stay in contact, to remain friends. Seeing Marjorie sitting with Lori at the cafeteria table she would have to wait a bit. She could trust Marjorie to keep the news confidential but anything Lori heard was immediately broadcast, not necessarily accurately, to all levels by her network of friends. Lori saw her coming to their table.

"Hello Marielle. How is Mr. Extra 'e' doing?"

Ever since the Anniversary Dinner the hens of the office had fed on the description of Lord Caldington's invitation for Marielle's date to join the head table for dessert. No one seemed sure of his name except that it involved the extra 'e'. That name stuck and from it floated rumours of a romance stretching all the way to the 'fact' that Marielle was living with this man. Marjorie's advice, which Marielle followed, was to ignore the rumours, simply let them ebb away. This didn't mean that Marjorie, one on one with Marielle, avoided the topic but at least she was subtle, or tried to be. She certainly didn't let Rush's name fade from the picture. She reiterated her maxim to Marielle: "A good man is hard to find".

Once Lori had left, learning nothing from Marielle that would satisfy her audience, now Marjorie could be told about Marielle's plans for the next three years. In part it was also her way of telling Marjorie that her studies would take precedence over men. Marjorie recommended otherwise.

"Honey...you're going to Law School, not entering a nunnery. There are no vows of chastity necessary. At least call this Mr. Extra..." she corrected herself, "...this Rushton guy and have some fun. You're both of age, no laws will be broken if you do whatever you decide to do. Let it happen. See where it goes."

One thing was quite clear to Marielle. She didn't know Rush that well but she was somehow certain that he wasn't the type for just a one nighter. She could manage to have a fling and walk away unscathed but for this she wouldn't choose a man like Rush. His pool was too deep for her to disturb with just a quick splash.

"Marjorie, thanks for the advice but really I'm doing fine." As they picked up their dishes heading to the sink she asked, "What about you? How's that new man in your life?"

"He's all talk, no action. Cheap too. Always wants to split the bill. So it will be 'Adios Amigo' for him.

***

David slept deep and, if there had been dreams, they remained below and beyond any remembrance. A quick shower in the antiquated bathroom delivering inadequate hot water sufficed and he was downstairs where Alma was preparing his breakfast, humming a familiar tune. It was just after nine so he had time to call Abrams, Bethune and Cartwright, Barristers & Solicitors. Alan Cartwright already knew of his father's death and had expected David's call. He'd foreseen David's immediate needs which would require a signature at the Hospital for the release of the remains to a funeral home. Bentley and Son was his recommended choice. Then it would also be best to call St. Gethen's to schedule the funeral service.

"You are thinking of a Church Service, aren't you?"

David would have preferred not but he would have been a prodigal son in the eyes of the establishment if he had denied his father, in death, clerical direction for the proper deliverance of his soul. In Trinidad funerals were a necessary social rite: to dress up, see old friends, laud the deceased, gossip about his survivors. Well, thought David, he'd already given the local gentry a lot of gossip in the past. They would have to revisit those stories as he only intended a short stay in Trinidad; no time for new ones.

Arranging to meet Alan for a luncheon meeting after he had finished at the Hospital then with Bentley and Son, he sat down for his breakfast inviting Alma to join him. She wouldn't sit with him but did stand, leaning at the doorway, sipping her tea. He again asked her about his father's last few months as she came daily to ensure he was eating well. She again was reluctant to say much but David did get Alma's kind, but brief, account of the downward spiral, the deterioration of an old man.

"Alma, he never called me."

There was a note of reproach in her reply, "You didn't call him."

"Perhaps you could have called me."

"David, I'm not family." Alma then turned to go into the kitchen leaving David with regret that he could have been a much more caring son to his father but, perhaps defensively, the reverse was also true. Now it was too late to repair.

Peter Ewart led David downstairs to the mortuary for the necessary identification. The room had no softening, no colour. It was either metal or dull grey. The body that had been alive until just over a day ago was pulled out. It had almost the same pallor as the room. David was used to seeing death starting with the grey-white cadavers in Medical School. There had been lots of bodies in Africa but they retained their pigmentation as, out of necessity, they were buried quickly. Those he saw daily on Isla, certifying their deaths, were only minutes without vitality and merely looked asleep. For the record David confirmed to Peter that this was his father as he reached out to touch the now stiff cheek, not as a sign of affection but to confirm that this wasn't a mannequin, only an aged facsimile of the father he remembered.

Peter accompanied him to the Office to complete the paperwork. He saw David examine the Death Certificate as to the Cause of Death and anticipating the usual question answered it, "No. I am sure that it was quite fast and that he didn't suffer."

After thanking Peter for all his help David made the call to the Funeral Home for transfer of the remains and, half an hour later he was inside the quiet confines of Bentley and Son. The burial process in Trinidad was certainly much more complex than it had been in Africa. There were all sorts of suggestions as to what would be "appropriate" with a reluctance to give a firm price on each item. David had no idea what his father would have wanted. He had, that morning, taken a quick look into the large desk in the study but there was no envelope addressed to him or to anyone else outlining any last wishes. Then David remembered that his father had made all the arrangements for his mother's funeral so he asked if they still had a record of it. He was soon reviewing that statement. Seeing the date he was surprised how long ago that had been. He looked at the final price for these services of Bentley and Son which included all expenses from embalming to gravediggers. He asked for a quote on replicating the same today. After minutes of calculation he was given one significantly higher but, other than minimizing the floral tributes, he signed the contract. He was assured that Bentley and Son would immediately contact Reverend Morton to confirm the first available date at St. Gethen's Church. He asked that he be contacted via Alan Cartwright.

Alan gave him a brief commiserating hug and soon they were sitting face to face in a restaurant that was new to David. Alan ordered white wine, David a bottle of Carib. After asking about David's morning Alan approved of the steps taken. After considering their lunch choices Alan became business like.

"You are aware that your father appointed me as Executor of his estate, are you not?"

Alan and he were close to the same age but Alan could seem Victorian at times. David was not aware of any legal or financial matters of his father. He never asked nor was told. Since fourteen his life had only involved Trinidad on an infrequent basis and his contact with his parents followed that pattern. Alan underlined the point, "I'm sure this wasn't any intended reproach but given your...let us say...various changes of addresses and that dangerous spot in Africa. Well...after your mother's passing my father was named Executor and now that had passed onto me." David suddenly realized that Alan's father, the original Cartwright in the firm, was perhaps dead. It seemed too late to ask so David let that question pass.

Now Alan, looking carefully at the adjoining tables as if they might be listening, quietly outlined the cold facts of his father's assets, the limited extent of his Estate. All of this was news to David although he did recall that, after his mother's funeral, his father did mention that he was considering joining in a real estate project. Alan firstly defended his firm, "My father did warn yours that this was a high risk speculation. Yes it would have brought your father the...can I say it...the riches and status that he seemed to want."

The father that David remembered was not a speculator. The family background was solidly based on the sugar plantation of his great-grandfather but that had been sold sufficient to finance careers in law, banking and scholastics for descendants. Edward Apsley Newton was talented and it was easy enough for him to learn Law and earn a degree but he wasn't as successful in actual practise. He had disappointed his new wife with a career change by accepting a teaching position at St. Rostern's, his old school, but the financial burden of a fashion and society conscious wife eventually forced another change.The salary was a little better and his wife pleased at their advancement in status when he secured appointment as a Lower Court Judge. She hoped he would rise to the Bench of the High Court but that didn't happen, keeping her husband content, his wife less so. David had grown up assuming his family, if not wealthy, was well off as they had assisted to support the costs of his education, all the way into Medical School. He had assumed that there was a flow of funds annually from his great-grandfather's estate but Alan was now advising that this had dried up a few years ago. As he listened David realized that he had taken a lot for granted.

Alan continued, "It was after your mother died that your father invested in a new venture, on the east coast. Once, and if, the Crown land was freed to bids there was an opportunity of new resorts, upscale estates, golf courses. I don't know if you followed all this from where you were...no?...well it became a battle between those who wanted the land as a Nature Preserve and the developers. Then came a change in government and the discovery of a new oil field offshore involving politics, protests, money and...yes...lots of lawyers." Alan waved his hands in dismissal. "Our firm was involved on the...call it the periphery of all this...which made it difficult...this being such a small Country...to offer legal advice for all those involved."

Looking relieved to see the arrival of their plates Alan attacked his lunch, either from hunger or the respite from having to explain why David's father had lost almost all of his assets. After scraping his plate clean, finishing his wine, he resumed, "As all of this dragged on there was little choice for the investors, your father included, to get out with, at the least, something. They were forced to continue the fight, but due to the multinational oil interests who needed the shore line, it became a losing battle. Your father had been forced to use his home as collateral to the bank to finance his legal efforts to recoup what he could."

David was a physician, not a businessman, but could almost predict Alan's next words as he explained that David could continue the process, attempt negotiations with the bank, join the legal battle but Alan regretted that his firm would not be able to accept a retainer to proceed further. David was suddenly tired of all this, perhaps the sadness of not knowing his father, not having been made party to all of these events that ate up his father's last years. He put aside his first reaction to question Alan about his firm's potential conflict of interest. It would be a futile exercise. Instead he asked Alan for the real figures that, after taxes and expenses might be left.

"David, other than a legacy to Alma Ferdinand, you are the sole heir under the Will. I'm not sure if you plan to retain ownership of the home, despite indebtedness to the Bank. I've called the Bank and I am waiting for them to give me what they'll expect to get in principal and interest, plus their fees. If you want our firm to handle this we can perhaps negotiate for something but that might not be easy." David's focus drifted away from the drone of Alan's legalese, hearing it only in segments, "...the home has value but primarily for the property." No, thought David I don't want the house. "...I did visit your father before Christmas and quite frankly it's in need of many updates…" Just what did I want to do, he next wondered. "...these would be costly, very costly at today's rates." Now with Andy removed from his life what was there next for him? "David, I suggest we wait to hear back from the Bank before…" He had an obligation to Jose and Isla but that needn't be the rest of his life. "...then of course there's Probate, Inheritance Tax and possible Capital Gains on the property should you…" He was sure Jose would be agreeable to sit down to discuss changes. "...decide to sell." A change to what, where would he go after Isla? "...I do realize this is a lot to digest but David, you need to form a plan and need to give me, without too much delay, your instructions."

The phone buzzed and Alan listened for only a minute before asking,

"The Church is available for a service at three-thirty tomorrow. Is that fine with you?"

David agreed that would be fine. The service would be over within an hour allowing, whatever the number, the attendees to be home, or go to the Club, for cocktails. David thanked Alan for the lunch suggesting he would think things over and an appointment was set for eleven tomorrow. Now, since he was in town, David had to buy a funeral suit and tie. He had to park next to a Police Car near the Men's Wear Store; this triggered his mind onto Rush Sterne and considered that his friend, if told, might try to fly down here as soon as he could.The funeral was tomorrow afternoon and David didn't plan to be much longer in Trinidad. He could write to Rush later, when back on Isla.

***

Maria was, as usual at this time of day, busy in the kitchen. She didn't have to look around to see who'd just come in the door; hearing the first few heavy steps she knew it was Lou.. As she expected there was a muttered 'Caio' and he was up the stairs. There he'd change into, for him more comfortable clothes, but for her too sloppy. She waited for him to come downstairs, check the mail, pick up the Sports Section of the newspaper then to settle into his chair.

She called from the kitchen. "Paulo got his mid-term report. It's on the sideboard."

Lou first finished the article on the upcoming NFL draft before rising to go into the dining room feeling he should show interest but not expecting much. Ever since Paulo entered High School his marks had been slip-sliding downward from A minus in Grade Eight to a C minus. As Lou reviewed the print out he walked towards the kitchen.

"Hey, these are pretty good. Better than I expected." There was grudging pride in his voice. Maria's pride was not grudging. "Damn right. He's a bright boy. He should be getting high marks. I think he could do better yet." She stopped to stir the bubbling pot on the stove then turned back to face Lou, moisture fogging her glasses, "I think that he could even get into college."

Until a few years ago Lou and Paulo had a strong relationship and back then Lou did envision that his son would continue beyond High School but Paulo's marks and his relationship with his father faltered in tandem. Lou had fond and proud memories of a son who would listen to him, respect his guidance yet have time to laugh together enjoying the mayhem that would bother the three females of the family. All that had disappeared.

"College? Is he thinking of College?"

"Well his friends, these new friends he's going with, they'll go on and it's been a wake-up for Paulo. Maybe we should encourage him to go. I know it's expensive but I'm sure we can manage it, can't we?"

Lou still had another daughter's wedding in his financial future but managed to suppress his first thoughts, "I guess we can...if it happens." Now wanting to change the subject he asked. "What new friends?"

"Nice kids. Good parents. Boys and girls. These days they hang out in groups, not like we did but I think Paulo has his eyes on one of the girls. She's at the top of her class, and really pretty. Fortunately she got her looks from her mother, not from your cousin."

"My cousin?"

"Yeah. Your cousin...Marcello...you know...married to Gabriella."

"Sweet Merciful Jesus." Lou's mutter was missed by Maria as she went on. "I saw her at the bakery last week and stopped to chat about our children becoming friends but she said she was in a hurry...like she didn't want to talk about it. Maybe she doesn't approve of Paulo."

Sweet Merciful Jesus.

"I hope I'm wrong. Gabriella used to be so nice to talk to. Over the last while she's hardly said a word to me. Well, maybe it's a problem at home. Marcello is no prize to live with, that's for sure."

Sweet Merciful Jesus.

"Where are you going? Dinner will be in a half hour."

He headed down to his workshop.

Sweet Merciful …

***

After a re-stock from his hidden supply in the base of the old polisher, Bucks drove away from the storage unit, heading out to connect with his street dealers. Tonight it would be Buddy, a lazy small timer, and then Willie, who was now doing bigger volume. Flashing lights ahead blocked the street. He could see fire engines further down the block. He followed the shift of creeping traffic onto a detour route leading down a side street. He then saw what was ahead. It was the block of small apartments buildings where Lucy Marie had lived, where she'd died.

In his mind it was just an accident. He didn't fault himself; he had no guilt. If she hadn't pushed for a bigger cut, threatening to cut off the Clinic's supply from him, then it wouldn't have been necessary to wait for her, in the dark next to her parking spot. He only wanted to bring her back in line, just to scare her a bit. As she opened the door of her pick-up he did scare her but only for a moment. Then she turned tough. Words weren't working so he grabbed her shoulders, to shake a bit of sense into her. The keys clutched within her fingers cut into one of his cheeks, her spit into the other. He drew his arm back preparing to smack her but, seeing it coming she tried to duck to her side. His fist propelled her turned head downward into the metal edge of her truck's rear panel.

Slowly shuttling forward in the line of vehicles approaching her building Buck's memory flashed back to the frozen stare of surprise in her fixed eyes as she slipped to the ground. At first Bucks thought she was faking but giving her ribs a jab with his foot brought no response. He wasn't sure how long he simply stood there, waiting for her to stir, wake up, to curse at him. Finally he stooped down, seeing a small pool of dark red under her temple, then reaching for her wrist. While serving his two years less a day he'd taken a First Aid course, something to do. He'd been taught how to feel a pulse but now wondered if he'd forgotten the drill. He tried the other wrist then back to the first. For confirmation of his fear he stretched her flat on the ground putting his ear to her chest.

His memory continued to run, like a video, frame by frame, back to that night in the dark of the parking lot. No one would believe this was an accident but to leave her lifeless body here would involve a wholescale murder investigation that might somehow be traced back to him. What if she was just to disappear? People, especially young women, did disappear. He decided, seeing no other option, was that she'd be one of them. Today he knew he'd done everything right back then, making a quick decision to pry the keys from her grip then cover her limp body in the back of her truck, drive by his house to get a shovel from the shed, drive the two hours north to the rear quarter of his uncle's farm, a section he knew well from his childhood summers, there to dig the grave, then drive back to his buddy's chop-shop to get rid of her pick-up, get a drive to his pick up before heading home to sleep. He could still sleep soundly. It had only been an accident.

The pace of the traffic picked up and he was soon beyond the block, her building out of sight, her memory out of his.

CHAPTER THIRTY-FOUR

Rush had brought two law school texts to the Hospital but at first felt guilty for diverting his attention away from his father. Certainly his father was in no condition to object, a body still physically living but a mind only functioning on the basics of survival. As the hours went by Rush was able to concentrate for longer periods of time. Despite the absence of adjectives, the cold text outlining past and present laws, the words still held Rush's interest and he was sure he made the right decision. Hopefully he'd hear about his application soon. He saw that it was nearly noon and his father was still in his other world, not in this one but not yet in the next. He decided it would be safe for him to leave and attend the duties of his office.

After complimenting Ellen for her review of her suspicions on the connection of Walter 'Bucks' Starbuski to the disappearance and probable murder of Lucy Marie Fairweather, he then carried the brief to the Homicide Squad glad to find Dom Scanelli at his desk. At first Dom thought the visit concerned the death of Remi Estavan.

"Sorry Rush. Nothing new on that used car guy. Still working on it." He spread his arms wide over his desk, "Plus a few more files as well."

Apologetic for bringing a new matter to Dom's desk, Rush briefly outlined what was in Ellen's case summary. "Dom, I know it's not conclusive. We don't even know if Lucy Marie is dead but I just wanted to offer it to you first. I don't want to get our lines tangled."

In return Dom apologized for taking a pass, leaving it with Missing Persons, at least for now. He kept the file, promising to read it through "when he had time". Rush was just as glad that his Unit could keep it and suspected that Ellen would as well. Tomorrow he would sit down with his partners to plot their next steps in the investigation of Bucks Starbuski.

***

Bucks found Buddy in his usual daze but with it enough to pass over money and take a small supply to peddle. Bucks checked the time seeing that it fit with his usual connection with Willie Tomic. He punched in Willie's number to text a message, "same time, same corner" as a clap of thunder threatened overhead. By the time he reached his corner the rain had begun to unleash mini missiles to explode on the sidewalk, accompanied by more rumbles from overhead.

He peered through the rain to see, across on the other corner, half hidden by an umbrella, a cap showing the white of the Yankees insignia. As he turned to head towards Donna's Donuts he thought that he'd never seen Willie use an umbrella before but, considering the continued downpour, wished he had one himself.

As usual he used the rear entrance, signed with a 'Donna's Donuts: No Parking' to duck into the rear hallway, out of the rain. He shook off the rain from his jacket and opened the washroom door and had taken a step inside when there was push into his back. He managed to turn to see a threatening face under a Yankees cap. "What the hell…" was all he managed before he was grabbed, spun around to face the toilet. As Bucks now stumbled forward a powerful arm under his neck jerked him upright and he did not see the other arm, the other gloved hand and what it held as it thrust towards his chest. He did feel searing pain for a few seconds before he was beyond any feeling.

Jay Dunbar spun Bucks around to dump him into a sitting position on the toilet, seat up, pulling out the knife, uttering a final judgment.

"You son of a bitch...this is for Evie!"

He quietly closed the bathroom door which had been guarded by his brother. Together they slipped out into the rain, bound for life to keep their secret.

***

David's day seemed to be propelled by questions, all requiring his decisions, on the necessary religious, social, perhaps tribal mores and rites of Trinidad that were expected to be performed at the funeral of the son of an established family, even if no longer prosperous. In the Men's Wear Shop, he found no off-the-rack suit that fitted his tall frame so he settled for light grey trousers and blue blazer. He was sure there'd be a usable shirt in his closet and a tie, probably regimental, from his father's that would do. Then he was back in the aged Rover driving to meet the solicitous rector of St. Gethen's who had either earned or affected a pronounced English accent. David was required to listen to his list of what was prefaced as suggestions but were more like requirements. With each 'No thank you', 'Perhaps not', 'Your choice' from David the Rector's face sagged only just managing not to show outright disapproval. In the end it would be a simple service. No choir, no hymns, three readings, no homily, no address to the mourners by David. David's decision to have no pallbearers nor a graveside service clearly troubled the Rector. With reluctance he conceded to have the interment later, after everyone, including David, had left. For his wife's resting place David's father had purchased a double plot and that the small headstone already included his name, only now requiring the date to be inscribed. David did go to the grave not surprised to see a small bouquet there. He thought it must be from Alma. Standing at the foot of the grave David thought it ironic that his parents would be closer in death than they had been in life.

Returning home he did have Alma admit that she had slipped by the churchyard to leave the flowers. He also tried to convince her to sit with him, as family, in the front pew. David hadn't even called his aunt yet. The rector had advised him that an email notice would be sent out to all parishioners announcing the funeral. Still he should call her, hoping that she wasn't too far into her extended cocktail hour. She sounded surprisingly sober when she answered his call. She already knew of her brother-in-law's death. In Trinidad, the ever present heat could slow down physical pace but not local news. She had never had affection for her sister's husband and had been far removed from being a doting aunt to David, nonetheless she advised she would be there to sit with him. If Alma did agree to sit in the front David knew that wouldn't meet her approval.

Alma was reluctant to leave him but David, once alone with a glass of his father's Scotch in his hand, wandered around the house, now his but co-owned with the Bank. The curtains and shutters were drawn against the still strong evening sun but, as he thought back to the years he lived here, they were always drawn. It was a house of darkness, the reason why, growing up, he was only inside to eat, study, and sleep. He envisioned it now as a movie set for some kind of dark melodrama. Well the Bank could have it. He didn't plan to ever return here. His mind was set but no other place that he foresaw as being his next home.

Pouring more Scotch, he went to sit on the verandah. The chorus of birds singing early evensong were backed by the dischords from the cicadas. He sat there closed off from the world. He would be content to remain just as he felt, right now, as someone just drifting, disinterested by life, neutral to the world as it turned without his involvement. He felt no desire to seek a woman only still feeling the ache of what might have been with Andromeda. He now accepted that she wouldn't be part of his future also admitting, with another sip of Scotch, that he could not see a place for himself in anyone's future.

***

As Rush drove home the day darkened with ominous clouds but it was still dry when he entered the house. In his lifetime of living here there were a few times, but only a handful, when it had been empty. Even after his mother's death his father was rarely away. Now the stillness of the rooms, even in his own downstairs unit, felt uncomfortable and a vacuum seemed to follow him, like a silent shadow. Trying an antidote he turned on Classical FM station but it was dreary largo that did nothing to lift the mood.

His voice mail only had two messages. One was a call from his badminton partner asking about his father and suggesting, if Rush needed physical relief, to call for a game. As much as it would be a relief this would, like almost everything else, have to wait. The second message was an authoritative female voice advising that "We are calling regarding your credit card as we have detected unusual activity on your account. We need you to verify these charges. Please call now to this number…" Rush had now detected a slight accent. "...should our representatives be occupied when you call back please enter your card number using the dial pad on your phone…" As Rush deleted the call he wondered how many might fall for this, yet another, telephone scam. He knew trying to trace the phone number would be a useless exercise.

He took a brief shower followed by a microwaved cup of soup and was soon back in his car just as a rumble of thunder passed overhead. The rain began with forceful splatters against the windshield needing the wipers at maximum speed to fight for visibility. Traffic was slowed down, at times to a crawl of brake lights, before Rush reached the Hospital. Even with an umbrella Rush was wet before he reached the entry doors. As he did his cell phone buzzed. The display showed it was the Hospital calling. He ran to the elevator and on reaching the ward heard the call.

"Mr Sterne! We had just called you. It's your father." Rush stopped at the desk front to be told "Unfortunately his vital signs are weak and unstable. Sorry but right now we would ask you to wait out here while he's being attended to."

She regretted that she couldn't tell him anything further and promised that Dr. Johnston would be out as soon as he was free to do so.

"Dr. Johnston? Is Dr LaMarche there too?"

"Dr. LaMarche is at home. Her son took ill."

Rush realized that he had begun to think that Dr.LaMarche was a permanent part of the Hospital, not having a life of her own, not connected to life outside these walls. It was not long before a young man, to Rush looking about twenty, swung open the doors from the ward. Looking at the nurse behind the desk she pointed to Rush. He strode over extending a hand.

"Mr Sterne, I'm Andrew Johnston. Let's go to the Consultation Room."

Before they settled into chairs inside the small room Rush feared the worst. It wasn't quite that, but close. The doctor explained that they were now assisting his father's functions. Technically he was not totally on life support but that might be the next step.

"If that is required then you, assuming you are the one…" He looked inquiringly at Rush who confirmed, "Yes, I am."

"Well, you could have a decision to make."

"Can I see him? Just sit with him?"

"Yes certainly. Let's go."

His father's face was hidden by a mask making him look even less a human being than he had before. There were also now more wires and tubes connected to the body concealed under the sheets. He gazed at what was still his father but now realized he was only a step away from having to make that decision. He knew, if it was possible to wake him up, discuss the issue rationally, that his father would say that he'd arrange to stop living right now rather than have his son bear the burden of ordering the switch be turned off. Russell would want to do it himself but Rush knew enough about the brain that the side that wanted to find that switch couldn't override the deeper core that fought to keep its host alive.

So he sat to the left of the bed, his father the centrepiece, the grim spectre of Death on the right. This scene stayed static with Rush only shifting to find a new position in his chair. At one point he did open his law text but quickly closed it. He couldn't concentrate and also thought it was being disrespectful, even if he was the only one to criticize himself. He had become accustomed to the faint beeps from a monitor on the wall above the bed. Occasionally it would become irregular but he knew that his father was electrically connected to the desk of an overseeing nurse outside the doorway down the hall. The constancy of the room's hush had him close his eyes and perhaps he drifted off until there were two nurses suddenly in the room and, without being asked, he quickly stepped back pulling his chair with him as they moved bedside.

"Perhaps it might be best to wait outside."

He nearly bumped into the young Dr. Johnston as he went out to the hallway. Slowly he went to the waiting room choosing the same chair he'd waited in many times before. It seemed like an hour but was much less before the doctor came slowly out the swinging doors, his young face unable to disguise the message he was bringing.

Rush calmly recognized the words, accepting their reality at the same time that a tidal wave surged up from his bowels, past his stomach, into his chest, up his throat to his eyes, as if to drown him. Somehow he heard the doctor's suggestion of whether he wanted to see his father. He answered without words, to head down the hall into the room, now totally quiet, no signals beeping, only one small screen showing a flat line. Russell's face still showed the marks from the mask but to Rush, perhaps imposing his own wishes, he saw no obvious signs of pain, only a peaceful aura on the pale thin face. Rush leaned over to kiss him, an act not done for decades, then a squeeze of his hand, before turning to Dr. Johnston, standing quietly aside, who with a gentle hand on Rush's shoulder, walked him to the door. Rush took one last glance back as he left the room. Death had left beforehand, taking his father with him.

***

The message on Lou's screen only said that Rush wouldn't be in this morning. It gave no details but Lou thought it was ominous as it had been sent at one o'clock that morning. He called over to tell Ellen that Rush wouldn't be in but withheld his worry from her. It was not long after this that the phone on Rush's desk buzzed. Lou clicked his phone to answer the call, identifying himself .

"Oh...Hi Lou. Dom here. Isn't Rush in yet?...No...Okay...when he comes in tell him that his suspect Buckowski bought it last night...down at Donna's DoNuts. . .you know that dump...down on Fifth. He had a heart attack...helped by a sharp knife...found propped up on the can."

Scanelli went on to tell Lou that there were no witnesses, no security cameras nearby, no obvious clues although Forensics were still busy. The Drug Squad had him listed as a minor player and Donna's Donuts had that reputation so Dom had to assume that drugs or drug money was a motive.

"Who knows who hit him. Chances are we'll never know." Dom paused, "I guess he won't be able to tell you anything about your MP will he?"

No, Lou thought, Lucy Marie Fairweather would remain an open file, still missing. He doubted many would miss Buckowski, maybe just his family. He called over to Ellen to give her the news.

CHAPTER THIRTY-FIVE

David felt detached, as if he were a stranger, as the funeral service began in the heat of the mid-afternoon sun. The main door and two side doors were left open in efforts to create circulation inside. Most women were in frocks, subdued slightly in tone, but allowing bare arms and shoulders and, if the upper slopes of their chests showed, they were accented by pearls. The older the skin, the more strands needed. The men suffered in their jackets and ties. All seemed attentive as the Rector, with his Canterbury accent, proceeded through the funeral service. David half-listened as he heard the reading of the Lesson (...a Time to be born, a Time to die…) through Psalm 23 (...the Shadow of Death…) then the Epistle (...Death will be no More…) until his mind wandered away, back to Isla, thinking of the services that would be needed for all those urns shipped back. His mind refocused to recognize silence then to see the Rector's eyes staring at him, gesturing with both hands, asking him to stand. He realized this funeral was now concluded and he rose to guide his Aunt's elbow down the aisle passing faces that probably were glad the service was brief and a graveside attendance not required. No one seemed upset by the absence of sandwiches and coffee following the service as they filed, with shuffling steps, out through the nave to where David and his aunt awaited for their condolences.

David shook hands, received polite embraces, and a few lips brushed his cheek but he had received only one heartfelt hug followed by a solid kiss. It had been almost thirty years ago when Lisa and David, both sixteen, both fueled with more lust than love, although at the time unsure of the difference, had a summer of secrets, sweat and sex. As David wiped off her lipstick he and Lisa shared a smile of remembrance for those times, with no shame, with no regrets. Then she was off to take her husband's hand and walk away. Peter and Holly Ewart were next with Holly only giving him her hand, not her cheek. David knew why. It was because of her friendship with Liz Easterly. Alan Cartwright of course was there, but alone. David couldn't remember if he was married. David wasn't counting but it didn't take long for the attendees to file by until there was only the Rector, Alma and David at the steps of the Church. David was unsure if his honorarium was expected now or was handled by Bentley and Son but, after a quick handshake, the Rector turned back into his church, which answered David's question.

Alma was insistent that she return with David to the house to prepare his dinner but reluctantly accepted David's alternative. As he drove her to her home he explained he was leaving Trinidad tomorrow afternoon. He told her the situation with the Bank but Alan Cartwright would continue to pay her to maintain the house until the Bank took over. He gave her permission to take the aging Rover for her son plus whatever items of furniture she wanted, except the library books and paintings. His father had left these to his School. He told her, once all the legal issues had cleared, that his father had left a provision for her in his will. David didn't tell her he had, that morning, instructed Alan to also include her in his will. As he pulled the car over beside her modest home he looked over to see streams of tears down her cheeks. Opening the car door he held her hand leading her to her door. Then an embrace that captured all the years of loyalty and affection that Alma had given to David. His throat caught and his eyes watered recognizing these would be their last moments together. Neither were capable of any last words. Alma simply reached out, with tenderness, to stroke his cheek before he turned to drive away, to his home for his last day there.

As he entered the early evening sun let a slice of light into the darkened entry hall. The white envelope stood out against the dark mahogany flooring. It bore his initials: D.A.M.N. He carried it to the study, knowing who it was from before opening it.

Dear David:

I am sorry to learn of your father's death. I also regret that I am unable to give you my sympathies in person.

Thinking of you at your loss,

Sincerely, Liz

David had not expected to see her at the Church service. Her husband would want to lock her up while her former lover was on the island but David could decipher the words of her note. She clearly wanted to see him. Firstly there was the envelope with his initials. Often, in the thrusts of love making she would mutter "damn...damn...damn" but not out of condemnation. He also noted her use of 'regret' and the telling space after 'thinking of you' signalling to him that she would have wanted to end it there, without any further words. Her message was careful enough that even her husband could not have found a legitimate excuse to criticize, even if he ever saw it. He wouldn't. David used one of his father's wooden matches to burn it, leaving the ashes in the large ashtray beside his father's favourite pipe.

Elizabeth. Lizbeth. Liz. She was called all three but to David she was only Liz.

It was now almost three years back. After years in Africa's unforgiving sun, a thin and yellow David returned home to both recuperate and regenerate. Peter Ewart, the younger brother of a childhood friend, had been the doctor attending to his mother and now his father. David hadn't a licence to practise medicine in Trinidad so Peter filled out the prescriptions David needed to regain his health. Peter also suggested exercise, measured at first.

"Why don't you come out to the Club for tennis. It's only mixed doubles, nothing serious. It would do you good."

This was how he met Elizabeth Easterly. Partners were rotated after four games and they were often playing on the same court, together or in opposition. She was tall, athletic and her tennis whites couldn't hide the contours of her body, from calves to chin, a smiling face to match. She played a solid serious game but never became upset at either her partners' or her own fewer unforced errors. David's game came back as he regained strength and when they played together they became, at this level, unbeatable.

Over post game drinks it was Peter Ewart who suggested that they enter, as a team, the upcoming Club Championship. "Come on," Peter urged but not loud enough to be heard beyond their table. "Someone has to give the Drestels a tussle." Dieter and Isobel were perennial winners of Mixed Doubles, in addition to both Men's and Ladies Singles.

It was only after Elizabeth and David lost in a tie breaker to the exuberant Drestels that David was introduced to Edwin Easterly. In shoes he would have matched his wife's height, but only if she was barefoot. David could immediately see from his physique why he didn't play tennis. He hadn't congratulated either his wife or David on their good showing on the court nor did he pick up the chit for drinks afterwards. Sitting back David had a difficult time imagining them as man and wife but he'd seen many dissimilar combinations that seemed to work so he had to assume, given Elizabeth's continual smile, theirs might as well.

It was Peter, walking back to their cars later, who gave him a warning, "I saw Easterly's face when you hugged his wife at the end of the match. I would guess that she'll hear about it when they get home."

"You've got to be kidding."

"Wish I was. He is a controlling s.o.b., extremely jealous. My wife has been Elizabeth's shoulder to cry on. She won't betray her confidence but I'm Elizabeth's physician and I once saw some suspicious bruises on her rib cage. She said it was from a fall but when I mentioned to my wife she said she wasn't surprised." Peter opened the door of his car turning back with non-medical advice, "So be careful David. Someone could get hurt."

Later, at home, David had asked his father about the Easterlys.

"Humph." He looked up from his newspaper to answer his son. "Edwin Senior or Edwin Junior? Really not much difference. Both bullies. Money came from Senior's advantageous marriage. I hear that Junior does well, both at cards and on the market. I've never heard that he has a real job. Do you know him?"

"No. I just met him at the Club. I'd been partnered with his wife in doubles."

"Elizabeth? Met her a few times. Nice young lady." He stopped to sort out his memory. "Her mother came over as an English teacher and…" he stopped before admitting "... I shouldn't gossip but it's said she pushed her daughter to marry into the establishment here, preferably monied."

David then remembered his aunt's revelation about his own mother's parents wanting much the same but didn't raise the similarity to his father who went back to reading his paper.

Perhaps Peter's warning was an enticement for David when he, on seeing Elizabeth in the wine store pondering over the racks, went over to her. He thought he saw a blush on her tanned cheeks as she turned to recognize him.

"You seem unsure. May I help?"

She explained that she was having a dinner party and had selected whites but was unsure of the red wine. Acting as a sommelier he gave her his suggestions which she happily accepted. Carrying both his own small parcel and the much larger of hers, he walked to her car, a shining Jaguar, to place them in the boot. Opening her door she thanked him then asked, "If you're not busy tomorrow night perhaps you might help fill in the twelfth seat at our dinner table."

Certainly David would be delighted but, two hours later at home, the phone rang. It was Elizabeth, stumbling with an apology. It seemed her husband had already invited someone to fill out the dozen at their party and he didn't want to have an unlucky thirteenth at the table. David laughed it off but knew that it was Easterly who had pulled his chair away.

Next week, at tennis, David had immediately waved Elizabeth's start of another apology aside and was careful not to pay any particular attention to her, finishing the set with a polite handshake at a respectable arm's length distance.

Trinidad is large enough to miss and rarely cross paths but within the entrenched Ever-England community it could also be a small island. David would see her at the Club, about town, exchanging polite greetings, nothing more until Peter and Holly Ewart gave a party. Elizabeth came alone as did David, both circulating, but never standing alone together. A not unusual downpour hit as the party was ending. David was driving his father's Rover. Despite its age it ran well having low mileage as it had rarely been outside a fifty mile radius of its garage. It was often less reliable in rain as David learned only a half mile after leaving the Ewarts. Elizabeth pulled her Jaguar up beside the stopped Rover. Through open windows, shouting to be heard over the tropical downpour, David accepted her invitation and settled in next to her. The rain lashed against the car all the way to David's home intensifying as they sat silent there awaiting abeyance. It only took a touch of hands before arms reached over the console and lips met hard, almost hurting in their intensity. As the rain lessened so did their embrace until they were apart, heartbeats slowly subsiding, a return to reality. A question neither could immediately answer: was this only a sudden impulse, best shelved, no real harm done, or would it be continued?

Nature needs to fill a vacuum and Elizabeth and David felt like mere puppets who were being pulled together to satisfy that void, as well as each other's needs. Physically these were subdued by the limitations of opportunities to meet. Elizabeth belonged to a Horticultural Society and this gave them chances to meet at the far corners of secluded Nature Preserves. This didn't satisfy either of them but Liz, as David now called her, said she was flying to New York for a visit with a school friend who lived with her highly successful husband in Hilton Head. She would have a layover in Miami. They both giggled at the entendre as they made their plans for a full night together, their first.

That night was more than satisfying yet only intensified their hunger for each other. This was a frustrating exercise on their return to Trinidad. David had freedom but Liz was not only married but had a husband who guarded his cards at poker and whose jealousy kept an accounting watch on his wife's time away from the house. Sitting calmly, like Buddha, at the gaming table he was sometimes thought to have X-Ray eyes to know what cards his opponents held. It was an extension of this intuitive sense of what they might be holding that carried over to his wife. He knew men found her attractive; he knew he was not. Although it burned, he was realistic enough to suspect that she would be undressed in many men's minds but imagination was all he would allow. So he suspected any man who came too close. His warning antenna had reacted as soon as he had seen David and Elizabeth on the court, smiling at each other, slapping hands on a point won. Then there was that too close embrace at the end of the game. David would be one to watch. Edwin didn't need a private detective to follow his wife. He began to see her smile more, hum as she worked around in their home and he suspected something even before Elizabeth and David knew what was happening between them. So, with time, it was inevitable that there'd be just a small slip that Edwin could pounce on, to confront, confuse, accuse to the point that her sobbing silence was enough proof for him.

David was finishing breakfast when Peter Ewart called from the Hospital. Elizabeth was there, brought by ambulance, badly beaten, just after midnight. Peter chose his words carefully but his use of 'apparently' and 'Edwin's account' left David with no doubt on his suspicion over what Edwin had told the Police. They had told Peter that they had responded quickly to reports of shots in the area and on seeing lights on at Easterly's home, they checked there. Edwin told the officers that Mrs. Easterly had awakened to hear a noise downstairs and leaving her husband asleep had gone downstairs where she was attacked by an intruder. The noise, her screams, awoke Edwin who, grabbing his bedside revolver, rushed downstairs to frighten away the burglar into the garden, firing shots, but missing him. Edwin said he did try to give chase through their yard but returned to assist his injured wife. The Police arrived before he had a chance to call an ambulance.

Peter confirmed that Elizabeth was not in any immediate danger and should recover from extensive bruising to her upper body and face. David suspected that Peter's use of 'immediate' was a warning. Possibly Peter, most likely via Holly, had suspected something between the tennis partners. The hinted warning was clear; Elizabeth may be in further danger if David continued with the romance.

"Right now she's not seeing any visitors. Even the Police haven't interviewed her yet."

Peter chose his next words carefully, "I expect she'll collaborate with her husband's account."

Again David saw his meaning. She would have no choice but to agree unless David came to her rescue, to support her, to promise her a future. She could charge her husband with assault and even if there was no criminal conviction there'd be suitable grounds for divorce. David's racing mind managed a thanks to Peter, then sitting down, needing time to think, he envisioned himself as a Chair Umpire, elevated alongside the net, overseeing a contest between two players, both of them named David A.M. Newton.

He had sent flowers to the hospital, careful to have them signed with, '*From your Tennis Partners at the Club. Hope to have you back playing soon*', hoping she'd know who had sent them, hoping her husband wouldn't.

Four days later there was a brief note:

> *Thank you for the flowers. They have brightened my room. Unfortunately the nature of my injuries mean that I*

might risk further injury if I resume playing with the same intensity as I've done in the past. Again thank you….Liz

Now sitting in that same chair years later, he thought back to that message. Liz had now seen David as he really was. She did not expect him to be a knight in shining armour, charging forth to rescue her from the grip of her husband. David now realized her note had excused him from any further obligations. It clearly confirmed his cowardness to any commitment. Yes, he had once married and now knew, as if there had ever been doubt, that if his wife had not outraced him to infidelity, he would have set upon the same path.

So he'd left both Trinidad and Liz, not searching for any real romance until Andy. If she'd hadn't run away would his infatuation have lasted? It had been only days ago when he couldn't wait to see her. To what end? Just another conquest? If successful, what next?

There was still a few ounces of his father's Scotch left. Sipping it, he wrote down the next necessary steps that were required for the plan now crystallizing in his mind, the course that he decided his life needed. Seeing Alan Cartwright tomorrow morning would take care of a number of items on his list. Next was to arrange a meeting with Jose Fuentes. He reached for the phone. Perhaps that could be done at the airport in Santo Vincenzo when he returned to Dominica Real later tomorrow.

CHAPTER THIRTY-SIX

Miles northward an emotionally exhausted Rush was working on his own list as the morning tolled by. The Hospital had assisted with the completion of the necessary documents there, as well as advising what else officialdom would require and where to go next, some needing in-person filings. All of this was mandatory to transfer Russell Marshall Sterne from a living citizen to a computer statistic. This process was involved but was pre-programmed, tedious, but relatively easy to follow.

The hardest decision was how to commemorate the real life of Russell Sterne, to allow his friends and associates, those who remembered him as a person, the opportunity to show their respect for knowing him. He and his father had never discussed any specifics on funeral arrangements. There had been a church service for his mother. She was not a committed churchgoer but would go alone, always attending at least at Christmas and Easter. Rush had once asked her if she believed in a God. Her answer was 'Yes' whenever she thought of all the love and compassion in the world; 'No' when she saw its cruelty and savagery. Rush was certain that his father, whose prime belief was in logic, would not want a religious funeral.

There was no family to object to his decision. His aunt, Russell's sister, lived too far away and when Rush had called her son that morning with the news he said his mother would not be well enough to travel. His cousin offered condolences but didn't ask to be advised of any arrangements, implying indifference. He had sent a text to Stefan, not having any phone number as contact. It was only a few sentences, emphasizing that Russell had not suffered. He did ask that Stefan text him a phone number and the best time that he could reach him. He would have to call the family lawyer, to arrange a meeting at Stanton and Stanton. He should also call his father's doctor, in case he had yet to hear the news. He recalled his father's scoffing at the usage of the word 'celebration' to describe a service or an honouring. Definitely he would have to organize this now so that details could be given in an obituary. However, this afternoon involved an appointment at Philpott and Linderson, Funeral Directors. He was certain they would be disappointed at the simplicity of the arrangements: no visitation, no service, no interment, only cremation. He fully expected to leave there with some degree of guilt.

As he drove to make these arrangements he saw a billboard picturing a sunny Caribbean beach and a bikinied blonde. David. He'd forgotten to add David to the list. Tonight he would send an email but then he hesitated. Would David insist on coming north to be with his friend, particularly if he knew there'd be a commemoration. Certainly, in reverse circumstances, Rush would want to go to Trinidad. Perhaps better to wait, write a letter, even suggesting Rush might take David's offer to meet him for one of those month-end hedonistic escapes at the resorts on the north shore of Republica Real. He knew he wouldn't be able to match David's extremes but maybe that might be worth the try, to get away from this gloom.

Back at the now even more silent house, he did see that Stefan had sent a phone number that he could be contacted. It wouldn't be that late in Latvia so he dialled. It was a female voice that answered.

"Sveiki."

Rush hesitated then ventured a 'Hello', which was answered with a "Tikai Minuti." Then there was a different female voice, one from his past.

"Hello, is Rush? I am Ana...yes Ana...so so sorry for you, for your father. I cry. Stefan cry. Karla cry. Very sorry...a...good man."

The conversation was halting, slight pauses, words bouncing off an impersonal circling satellite, as Ana searched for usable English words but Rush knew she was crying again. He then felt tears down his own cheeks. Now he was the one fighting to find words. Conversation faltered but not the emotions.

They finally stumbled to say their goodbyes. Ana promised to have Stefan by the phone if he could call at the same time tomorrow night. He then wandered upstairs. The television wasn't on, there was no head of thinning hair visible above the back of his father's favorite chair. There was only the silence. He stood, rooted as if afraid to break it, even with just footsteps. He wondered if he should go down to his father's bedroom. The funeral home had asked for suitable clothing. Their involvement was only to handle the cremation but Rush, anxious to leave, hadn't asked why these were needed. He then realized he would have to pack up all his father's clothing. Most of it was quality but hardly new; he assumed some charity could use the clothes. He would have to clear out a lot from the rooms, not in any attempts to remove the memory of his father, but simply out of practicality. It just was what had to be done. A sudden picture jumped into his mind from an old movie: Miss Haversham sitting in her crumbling dress among the detritus of a wedding table. No, his father would want all of this done now, cleaned out without delay, not find excuses.

Rush then opened the front door to collect the mail. A telephone bill reminded him the need to cancel that service. A phone ringing in empty rooms, never to be answered, wasn't needed. Another letter had his name neatly typed. It was from the Law School. He walked to the kitchen using a knife to neatly open the envelope.

He had been accepted but,at the moment, this felt like a consolation prize

There were conditions. He would need to successfully pass all the exams of Year One while directly enrolled into Second Year. Taking two summer sessions and writing their exams this August would be a start but then he would have to fit classes of the First into the Second in just one year. If exam times conflicted he would have to write them back to back, only with a supervised bathroom break in between. If he managed all that then he could carry over one Second Year subject into the Third. He could see that he'd been given a special dispensation for this. The influence of his friend Morris clearly showed. Was he up to all this? Would a brain twenty years older manage a return to intensive schooling? He took a deep breath, heading downstairs to his own apartment. He would need to use his computer for the Course requirements; he would need to order updated books.

***

David's morning was not rushed as he had awoken early to shower, to shave and then have a brief breakfast, leaving a note for Alma reminding her to take whatever she could use from the house, adding a closing, 'Much Love, David'. His bag packed, his flight back to Republica Real confirmed, he left the still usable Rover in the garage calling a taxi to take him to the offices of Abrams, Bethune and Cartwright.

Alan Cartwright re-introduced his clerk who had been present the previous morning, taking notes as David had explained exactly what he wanted to be done. Alan had voiced some objections but David was firm. Today the clerk, Desmond Singh, smiled, shook hands briefly with David then sat aside at a small escritoire, papers at the ready. Alan was all business, sounding stuffy, as he reviewed the documents, one by one, that were handed to him by his clerk. Alan explained the legal import and consequences of each, concluding with "as required by you" suggesting that Alan still had other thoughts. If so he kept those to himself, clearly seeing David's mind was set. In turn David's mind presumed that Desmond had prepared each of the necessary papers leaving Alan only to make the presentation. David's revised Last Will and Testament, Powers of Attorney, Instructions to the Bank and to Government Departments in Trinidad, various Releases. Eventually all were signed and sealed. As David had requested, the invoice for all these hurried legal services had been readied and David signed a cheque in payment. After further handshakes David left to go to his Trinidadian Bank, leaving a sealed envelope to be given to the Manager. He then withdrew a sizable amount of U.S.dollars that he had plans for. He'd been toting his suitcase and the almost midday sun stuck his shirt to his back. Fortunately the taxi he used to take him to the airport had an efficient air conditioner.

Jose had agreed to meet David at Santo Vincenzo before boarding for the short trip to Bonojara. It was arranged that Jose would be just outside the terminal, waiting in his chauffeured Mercedes. David slid in beside him. Again Jose repeated his sincere condolences as the driver drove to a quiet shady spot at the far end of the airport's parking lot. There Jose came to the point.

"Mi Amigo. I suspect you have something important to discuss with me."

David wasn't certain where to start so began by thanking Jose for all his support and friendship. Jose waived his arms in polite dismissal, both to deflect the compliments and to bring David back to the point. David then advised him that he wished to terminate his position on Isla Cresciente but only when Jose had found a replacement who David would gladly instruct to ensure that the Clinic could seamlessly continue. The timing was totally in Jose's hands.

"David. I'm not surprised by your decision. I think it is time that you moved on. Your talents could be better used in a world wider than a small island. I won't ask what your plans are. All I can do is wish you all success and, if I might add, find a level of contentment that you have not found for some years." Jose paused, "If your plans are set then you will not need any assistance but I have many contacts, not just in the Caribbean, if needed."

David voiced his appreciation for that offer along with another of financial help but 'con muchas gracias' neither were needed. After Jose gave instructions to his driver to return to the 'Salidas' Gates, he turned to David, "Searching for your replacement might not be difficult. The good Doctor Ernesto may be available. His wife has now realized that her demand for a husband to live with her was only a social pretence. She knows he sees Senorita Fermer for a few days each month and, it seems, does most of her friends. Dr. Manuel might be interested and, if so, the Clinic will be in good hands...perhaps not as good as yours David but…"

The Mercedes was now at the busy curb to the airport entrance. David, knowing this would be the last time, and Jose, also sensing that it might be, firstly shook hands then gave each a clumsy embrace in the rear seat of the car. As David took a few steps towards the entry he heard the car accelerate away. David didn't look back. It would be a short flight to Bonojara, a shorter cab ride to Porto del Norte, a night at the Inn, finally back to Isla.

***

Rush was cleaning up his dishes from a tasteless frozen dinner at his small kitchenette sink. He realized he could have used the main floor kitchen but he felt more comfortable, less invasive, in his own apartment. He would need to go back upstairs though. His meeting tomorrow morning was with Ted Stanton. Undoubtedly he would have a copy of Russell's last Will but Rush assumed there would be a copy in the small safe in his father's office. Rush knew the combination was written, in reverse order by design, on the backside of a print of 'The Fighting Temeraire'.

He'd never opened the safe before although his father had clearly made it known that he was entitled to. Rush had never had much interest to follow the Stock Market. Although he inherited many of his father's traits, a following in finance wasn't one of them. After Ana took Stefan away Rush had tried to locate her, at the least make contact and arrange financial support. His efforts were frustratingly unsuccessful so that his Police salary was much more than he needed for regular expenses. He began giving half his income to his father for household expenses and, if any left, for investing. When he had mentioned, just a month ago, that he was applying to Law School and was concerned about finances he was told by his father that there was no need to worry as the returns on Rush's portfolio of stocks, carefully managed by Russell, were doing quite well.

Now the contents of the safe spread out on his father's desk showed that he could now qualify as being well off and, to some, even rich. In addition there would be the assets of his father's estate under which the Will now showed Rush to be the primary beneficiary. There was a codicil adding Stefan plus a smaller legacy to Rush's distant cousin who, in Rush's opinion, was undeserving of it. Rush wondered if he was as well. He was simply very fortunate to be, or soon would be, a millionaire plus the owner of a pleasant home in a desirable neighbourhood. He sat in his father's office chair back thanking his father's foresight and business acumen but willing to trade it for having him in the room down the hall, watching television.

He carefully reorganized all the papers to place them back in the safe when he saw a small velvet jewellery box. Opening it he saw his mother's rings. Her engagement ring, an emerald cut diamond in a simple setting, her wedding ring in matching white gold. He guessed his father hadn't known what to do with them. He now would have the same problem. They were too personal to sell and he couldn't foresee that he would have any need to use them. He settled them neatly in the slots of the box locking it and all the papers back inside the safe, clicking it closed. He then neatly straightened Turner's print on the wall before returning down the stairs. He knew that his planned conversation with Stefan tomorrow evening would be difficult for both of them but knew that Stefan would be honoured by his grandfather's bequest.

***

Detectives Flanders and Rodrigues, both lacking sleep, needed strong coffee for this morning's first meeting. Flanders' fatigue was due to a colicky four month old; Rodriques from a long poker game. On the table, along with their mugs, were the reports on their latest Homicide assignment: Walter Stancius Buckowski, a.k.a 'Bucks'.

Forensics had carefully, inch by inch, scoured the washroom cubicle, the rear hall, the back door at Donna's but there were enough fingerprints to populate a village. Both Detectives doubted that any of them were left by the killer. There were no security cameras either inside or out in the alley. A quick profile of Bucks showed him to be a scrounger around the bottom rungs of the ladder and the Drug Squad already had him on their list suspected of dealing in the new stuff that was sending users both to the hospital and to the morgue. There was little doubt that it was a planned hit, well executed, knowing Bucks hung out at Donna's. The victim had shown no signs of putting up a struggle to survive any attack probably meaning he wasn't expecting any problem. There were loose bills on the washroom floor. Rodrigues suspected that the first to find Bucks lifeless may have helped themselves to a few of them. Still robbery wasn't suspected to be the real motive, killing was the prime.

Buck's pick-up truck was found a day later, two blocks away from Donna's. Forensics were understaffed and were tied up in too many other investigations so they had yet to go over the vehicle. It would be no surprise to find traces of drugs inside. Flanders had interviewed Mrs Buckowski, grief stricken, sobbing that "...he was such a good boy..." repeatedly. If she knew anything that might assist the Police, she wasn't telling. The detectives were waiting for legal clearance to access his cell phone records. Once received they would sit down with the Drug Squad anticipating they might be able to make connections to suppliers, dealers or customers. A coin was flipped to see who would have to drive up to the Penitentiary to interview Buck's brother Lennie. Rodriques lost the toss.

"When's the funeral? Lennie might be allowed an escorted pass for it. Maybe I could see him then. I'll call the mother. It'll save me a trip up there."

Neither detective enjoyed the hour long drive to the Pen to interview a prisoner. There were hard chairs in the cold cramped cell-like interview rooms plus the fact that an inmate was already doing his time meant he would sit uncooperative, silent as if stricken with lockjaw. It was guaranteed to be a waste of time.

Flanders and Rodriques both shared the same but unspoken thoughts on this case. Whether it was solved or not seemed immaterial. A dead scumbag meant one less out on the streets, out in their city. They would do the necessary follow up on the file but neither would be frustrated if it had to eventually filed as 'Unsolved'.

***

Both Ted Stanton and Irene, the firm's faithful secretary, were sincere in their sympathies but then met Rush's expectations of efficiency by laying out and explaining all the provisions, as well as the tax implications, of his father's Will. Ted was very detailed, although not forgetting that Rush did have a past learning of legalities, he still followed his standard professional practise. Now more signatures were needed before Rush put away his pen and left to go downtown to his office. As he drove he pictured himself, a few years from now, on the other side of the desk, explaining the same to some other son or daughter of a deceased. When he had been finishing his second year at Law many of his classmates were assessing their chances of being chosen by the large downtown firms to start their careers knowing that long hours were necessary steps of servitude to climb the ladder. Rush had not shared those goals. He would have been quite satisfied to pay his dues at a smaller firm. He hadn't then, nor did he now, aspire to be anything more than a trusted neighbourhood counsel, covering the wide range of the legal needs of people, small firms and stores, not likely large corporations.

As he entered Police Headquarters he received either a hand shake with a short slap on his back from male colleagues or lasting hugs from the women. Inside his unit Lou gave him both. Ellen seemed hesitant to embrace her supervisor but did so, then back away with sincere tears welling in her eyes. Rush made it easier for both of them, as well as himself, by burying himself into his own work, finding relief from the last few weeks in the demands of his desk. He wasn't sure how management would respond to his decision to resign from the Force but didn't want his work to have any loose ends if they decided on an immediate replacement to take over his chair. His immediate decision was whether to tell Lou and Ellen before he went upstairs with the letter he had prepared last night. Despite security within the building to protect it from outside forces it never had managed to control inside leaks. Gossip travelled fast and he didn't want his unit to hear it from anyone but him.

At four o'clock he decided it was time.

"Damn it, Rush...it's...it just wouldn't seem...seem...you know...real... not having you in charge...not sitting in that chair...not here with us." Lou looked as if he might cry. Ellen's quiet reaction was guarded. Rush wondered if she was calculating her chances of inheriting his desk. That would be a decision for upstairs but, if asked, Rush would support that choice. She had the smarts to match the ambition. They both sat back, a little stunned as Rush checked to ensure the envelope was still inside his pocket before leaving to take the elevator to present it upstairs.

Ellen's attention was not focused on the screen in front of her but on Rush's empty chair. She pictured herself sitting there but even if she did get to head Missing Persons it could potentially a dead end job. The position was both frustrating as well as satisfying, depending on the failure or success of each case, but it wasn't large, even Auto Theft had one officer more. It wasn't as low as Stolen Property yet it could still be one step up to get to the top floor. She would let it be known, discreetly, that she would be interested. It wasn't a huge step but still a rung up.

Then she realized she hadn't told Rush about her further call to Birdie Partridge. She had thought that the news of Buck's death would not only take a huge load off Birdie's mind and that she now might give out more details of what the connection between Lucy Marie and Bucks might have been. Ellen had been disappointed at Birdie's lack of any reaction. Her few words were emotionless. She asked no questions. Finally Ellen had to simply say good bye and good luck. Birdie's response was to disconnect. She wanted no part or memories of her lost years back east. She was now secure, sheltered from her past.

***

As Marielle opened the front door to her apartment building she could see the Bentley sisters standing inside the second door. Their presence was always a harbinger of news. From their faces she could tell that it would not be good. She opened her mailbox. The only envelope was from a law firm.

"That's telling you...everyone here...we're being evicted!" The taller sister's voice had both outrage and hurt mixed together, "We'll all be tossed out onto the street!"

So Millie David's nephew had been right. There was little Marielle could say to the sisters either in consolation or advice. She left them standing there waiting to pass on the bad news to other incoming tenants.

The lawyer's letter showed that new owners were exercising their right under the leases to terminate 180 days after notice but allowing each tenant to terminate their leases with 30 day notice. Six months from now she would be into her first months at Law School. She would be best to find something else before that. As she folded the letter back into its envelope she thought she was glad she had a future position with Antioch Life Assurance. Somehow she wouldn't want to be a lawyer that sent letters to upset people like the Bentley sisters.

She also thought about bumping into Lenora at noon. They had been friends, not close, by both having lived with fellow musicians. Her Luis and Lenora's Diego were both Argentinians, both guitarists and often played in the same group together. She and Lenore didn't maintain any contact after she and Luis separated but Marielle was greeted as a long lost friend with a full embrace. Lenora was insistent that they sit and talk but Marielle really didn't have the time or inclination. She was glad to have a legitimate excuse that she had to get back to the office for a meeting.

Lenore was anxious to tell her Luis was coming back from Buenos Aires to be part of a new group that was being formed. Apparently his daughter, the reason he'd returned home, was now finished school and had taken a job in Mexico City. Now Luis had little reason to stay in Argentina. Lenore insisted they keep in contact. Marielle reluctantly gave her a business card and Lenore promised to stay in touch. Walking back to her office Marielle hoped she wouldn't hear from her. Her life with Luis wasn't a chapter that she was trying to erase from her life. There had been good times living with him, often exciting both in and out of bed, but if it wasn't day to day it was a month to month relationship. Neither made any commitment to the other and, looking back, Marielle wondered why it had lasted that long. Also looking back, Marielle admitted to herself that she hadn't made a commitment to anyone, except her employment with Antioch. That fulfilled her days but not her nights.

***

Detective Rodriques was waiting at the side entrance to the Church. As he expected an unmarked sedan pulled up letting Lennie Starbuski and a plain-clothed escort out. Rodriques showed his identification to both then asked Lennie if he could have a few minutes after the service to "help us with the investigation". Lennie gave him a cold stare then turned his head only slightly to spit onto the grass. The detective shrugged as he hadn't expected much and got even less. Still he walked in behind them taking a side pew with good sight lines. Lennie was slowly making his way down along those seated in front pew, bear hugs lasting more than a minute with each family member before arriving at his mother. She caressed his cheeks, ruffled his hair, as he sank into her shoulders, his body shaking with sobs, hers rigid and firm.

The homily of the priest painted Walter as a loving caring son, a loyal brother giving him attributes just short of sainthood. The solitary man in the side pew wasn't heard as he muttered "Horseshit" under his breath. Unnoticed by the mourners he slipped out of the Church first, taking another position to the side to be able to fix his eyes and memory on the faces of those slowly leaving in the wake of the casket.

Being outside he couldn't see Lennie hold his mother back from the exiting procession, shelter her in his arms, couldn't hear him whisper in her ear.

"Listen Ma. I swear to God I'll find out who did this. You've got to keep after the cops, try to have them tell you what they are doing. I'll be out in a month. Did Walter tell you what he was doing? What was he selling...some of this new stuff?" She whispered back in his ear well below the hearing range of Lennie's escort standing, waiting, allowing a son and mother a private moment. "Dammit. Ma! You gave him that much! Where did he stash the stuff? Have you checked his room? The basement? The garage?"

Lennie saw that his escort was signalling to cut it. Lennie waved him off and with his fingers demanded for two more minutes to grieve with his mother.

"Ma when I get out we have a lot to do. Get your money back. Find the one who killed my kid brother. I'll need to start with who he was using on the streets, to push his stuff. I'll bet Willie was one. I'll start with him. See if you can find him."

Lennie could hear the footsteps of his escort close in behind him, "Get one of my hick cousins to drive you up when I get released. I'll be in touch...Ma...I'll find him...the son of a bitch...I'll kill him...I swear to God!" After Lennie let his mother go he stared at the Altar, crossing himself, commanding God hear his vow of vengeance.

After the family left the church Michael Buckowski walked with his father towards their parked car. "Mike, your aunt asked if you could drive her, in a few weeks, to pick up Lennie and bring him home. She'll call you when she has the details."

Michael wasn't being asked if he would, his father was telling him he would, so he didn't argue. Family was family which is why he was here in the first place. Given a choice he'd be in the College Library right now, studying for final exams. Fortunately they'd be over and done within a month's time otherwise he might have protested. Growing up at the farm he dreaded when his cousins, Lennie and Walter, would arrive for a summer working vacation. They were older, bigger and seemingly took pleasure in threatening, bossing Michael and his younger sister, calling them 'country hicks'. Still Michael was envious when they brought up their 250cc motorbikes and tore over the fields, through the woods, finding or making trails. They soon knew every part of his father's 200 acres. Michael was glad when they stopped coming up to the farm as they became old enough to work the summers back in the city helping their Dad, an uncle who Michael had a hard time believing was the brother to his own father. They looked alike but were so different. Michael's father was content to be a hard working farmer. His brother and his sons, Lennie and Walter, worked in the city's dirt and shadows for their harvest. Well, if he had to go with his aunt to pick up his cousin at the end of his sentence, he hoped it would be the last time he'd see either of them. When he had earned his degree he was heading out west, way out of here.

CHAPTER THIRTY-SEVEN

On Isla it was another sun-filled morning, two patients easily passing David's necessary, if perfunctory, interviews. David had now settled back into his normal routine. When he'd returned his staff had given him sincere condolences over his father's death. He hadn't yet told anyone his intent to resign. He'd wait until he had heard that Jose had arrangements in place..

He and Heidi Fermer prepared for their first patient inside the clinic. Thompson Tillett, age 73, was from Milwaukee.The diagnosis was definite; Glioblastoma was terminal. He could have waited to play the odds, try for six months, maybe even a year but he chose not to. He had enough money for the services of Isla Cresciente. He had made his choice.

David had become so accustomed to Heidi and her quiet supportive competence that he perhaps took her for granted. He respected her privacy, she his. He wondered if her lover had already told her that he might be returning to Isla on a permanent basis. He looked over at her as they prepared for Mr. Tillett and noticed traces of a smile in both her mouth and her eyes. Once he thought he heard her humming but when he turned around she was all business so he assumed he might have been wrong.

Later returning to his office he saw an email from Jose Fuentes requesting he call. When he finally did locate Jose he knew why Heidi had been smiling. Dr. Ernesto Manuel had agreed to resume his post here as Medical Director. Heidi obviously already knew this and was looking forward to working and enjoying each day, living with Ernesto, here on this island of death.

Jose advised David that the changeover could be at the normal turnover at month end. That was only two weeks away. David wouldn't need to do any training. The transition should be smooth. Now he could tell the rest of the staff of this change. All of this made David's plans for leaving much easier, much cleaner. Now with confidence he could chart his own escape from Isla. A sense of order settled on David's world.

***

Marjorie settled back to her morning ritual, reviewing the newly posted obituaries, cross referencing them to Antioch's database of Lives Insured. Fortunately only a few made that connection but she read each brief summation of lives just ended, and relatives left, with interest and compassion. For many it would be the only time they would have their names in print, although unable to see it. There were a lot this Monday, a culmination of deaths from the week before. She worked her way down the alphabet of names before suddenly stopping. She raced to the elevator with a copy in her hands.

"Look. It's your Mister Extra 'e'. His father. It's got to be."

Marielle read it and agreed.

Sterne, Russell Marshall.

Peacefully, at age eighty-five.

Predeceased by his loving wife Eleanor(nee Rushton). Survived by his son Rushton, grandson Stefan, sister Lois Ralston, her son Ralph.

All of Russell's friends, clients, associates and neighbours are invited to meet, to remember, to reminisce this coming Saturday at Madison Hall, 512 Madison Avenue, from 2pm to 5pm. As he would have wished, dress should be informal.

No donations please.

"So, you're going, aren't you?"

"Well...why should I? I didn't know his father...or any of his family." She stopped to correct herself before Marjorie had the chance. "Okay. I did meet his son...briefly...and besides...I hardly know him."

“Poor excuses, quite lame.” Marjorie was trying to compose her sales pitch. ”You do know him. You had how many...four or five dates and…”

“They weren’t dates and there were...” She stopped to count, “...only three.”

“Then go. Offer your sympathies, your shoulder to cry on, your...your... your other body parts.” Marielle’s desk was too wide to allow her right hand to find its target.

“Missed!” Marjorie was laughing. “You’ll miss an opportunity if you don’t see him. Go. Get to know him. What are you afraid of?”

There were a few more attempts at encouragement from Marjorie before she left. Marielle could anticipate a few more before Saturday arrived. She read the obit again. It sounded informal. She could slip in and out. Pay her respects. Satisfy Marjorie. There would be no harm done. She went back to her screen but thought of Rush, now alone without either a mother or father, but she was the same. Mother dead and a father, a birth father she’d never known, never seen, although she had checked the Internet. He was alive and well, successful and living in Connecticut, working in New York City, married with now grown children, her half siblings who were probably unaware of her existence. Well, that’s the way it would stay. She would accept who she was, where she was and where she was heading, rowing her own boat, at least for now.

***

Stefan was glad to be seeing Simona this weekend, not just for the pleasure of her company and the delight of her body, but to help him sort out his feelings after hearing of his grandfather’s death. The telephone conversation with Rush was as much silence as words, neither letting their true emotions show. Stefan now realized, in that week’s stay with them, he had formed a bond with Russell not having as much time to spend with his father. Rush had told him to expect notice from a lawyer as Russell had left him money in his will. He hadn’t expected this and he hoped it would be enough to finance a trip next summer to see Rush. He assumed that his father would want to keep connected with more than just brief emails. Certainly he would do that to keep him advised how he would be progressing at University, those studies to begin in two month’s time.

Stefan thought about Rush living alone in a house twice as big as his own home here in Latvia. Would he stay there? It seemed that Rush was a committed bachelor. There'd been no indication of any woman in his life. Even with that lady at that dinner...what was her name...something French...there didn't seem to be any personal interaction between them. Shame...she certainly was attractive. Simona had said how very nice she had been.

Simona. As glad as he would be to see her for another weekend these were now to be fewer and fewer as his leaving for Sweden came closer. Now it would become an involved trip, costing more than bus fare, if they were to continue to see each other. Their romance, started in Paris, kindled in London, off and on as they tripped through North America, had survived and flourished on returning to Latvia, only a two hour bus ride away from each other. Would their relationship survive? Stefan hoped it would but there would be new friends in the future for both of them, with youth's hormones fighting fidelity. Stefan was now old enough to realize that love, lasting love, was often just a concept, not a reality. Still, he was glad to be alive with a future and a world, wide open, ahead of him.

***

Rush was the sole greeter to those entering into Madison Hall on a sunny Saturday afternoon. He knew most of their names but couldn't recall all and in a few cases had no idea who they might be but he took the time to ask their names and their connection to his father and was content to listen to their accounts. From Ellen a short embrace, from Lou and Morris more manly hugs, telling them he would catch up to them later. Rush had arranged a licence to serve wine and beer and most eventually found their way to the bar.

Finally Rush was free to mingle with each grouping. If he found someone alone or as a twosome he took them to introduce to a larger collection. Eventually he was able to stand between Ellen and Lou just about to start a sentence until he looked at the doorway, then quickly strode to meet a woman who had just entered, alone.

"I wonder who that is?" Ellen asked Lou. "He took off like a startled deer."

Then Rush was bringing her over, introducing her as Marielle Lebow, identifying them as his 'co-workers', then asking Ellen to make sure Marielle didn't leave as it was time for him to give a little speech. Conversations faltered then stopped as he waited to start. Beginning slowly: "Hello again... Thank you all for coming…for being here to remember Russell, your friend...my father. Each of you will have your own set of recollections and memories. Many of you will also remember Eleanor as well...and if so you'll know the deep love they shared. Although, as a widower, my father managed to keep busy I know that a part, a large part, of him died along with his wife. Sadly that is a price paid at the end of a happy marriage…"

Rush paused, swallowed twice, reminding himself not to become too emotional,

"...I am the happy and lucky recipient of the love of my mother and father, as well as their guidance that still also allowed me to find my own way forth. In contrast Russell only had childhood memories of his own father, a Captain killed in action in 1945. Fifteen years later his mother died. I think that you could classify Russell, over the next decade, as a 'loner'. That is until he met and married Eleanor." Rush took another breath before continuing. "Some of you here only knew Russell from the accounting, financial, and investment advice he gave you. If he had not served you well I doubt you'd be here today…"

Fortunately a response of laughter lightened the room and brought a smile to Rush's face as he continued:

"...I also am sure you'll be relieved to know that your investments will not be handled by me." A bit more laughter. "Although I inherited a lot from my father, financial acumen wasn't among them but you should have already received notice that your affairs are now in the very capable hands of Eli Dunlop and Arthur Ransome." Rush waved his hand to point to both men; the younger Eli, slightly balding, the older Arthur almost completely bare. "Please make sure you meet them before you leave."

Again he paused. "My father has left me footsteps to follow. I will try to follow his example. By being a person who is honest, reliable, earning your trust and deserving of your friendship. That is the epithet of Russell Sterne. Simply stated he was a good man."

Marielle stood at Ellen's side as Rush finished. In the brief pause before the applause started, she distinctly heard a whispered "...and so are you." Marielle now looked at Rush who seemed a bit overwhelmed by the affection of the crowd who continued their tribute not just to Rush's words but to the man he'd just described. As Rush became surrounded by well wishers Marielle was being asked by Ellen. "So you're a good friend of Rush?"

"No, not really." Marielle sounded lame. "I mean we've met. I've met his son, once, but never his father. A shame. He sounded like someone I should have met."

This was the first time Ellen had heard Rush had a son. She'd assumed he had never married. She also shouldn't be surprised that he had female friends, perhaps closer than this 'not really' friend, but Ellen wondered if there wasn't more to decipher here. Clearly Rush had been delighted when she came through the door and wanted her not to leave. As well, she thought this attractive woman, Marielle, seemed guarded in answering her question and had quickly switched the topic over to the son and father. Ellen's intuition, as well as taught techniques, made her suspect there might be more to this than casual friendship. She wanted to ask more questions but Rush was now coming over with that man who she was introduced to earlier.

Rush introduced him. " Marielle, this is an old friend...Morris Newman. Morris this Marielle Lebow."

"Enchante Marielle. Can I assume a Francophone heritage?"

"Mais oui, certainement."

"Are you also on the Police force?"

"Certainly not. That's too tough a job."

"Apparently not for Ellen." Morris turned to her." Lou told me you would be taking Rush's desk...when?...in a few weeks?"

"Just two."

"So Rush, what are your plans for the summer?"

"What else? Study, study, study...reactivate the brain cells. Maybe take a brief holiday but I'll take my books with me."

Then an elderly couple came to say goodbye to Rush. Lou and Morris began to talk together so Marielle leaned over to ask Ellen, "Rush is leaving?"

"Yes, back to complete the degree he left half done years back."

Marielle then asked, "Uhmm...Do you know...?" Before she could finish her question about Morris Newman, Rush was back asking if they'd like another glass of wine before the bar closed. Ellen quickly agreed. Sydney had dropped her off to go shopping. She wasn't driving. Before turning towards the bar she asked Marielle but she declined with a "No thanks."

Then she and Rush were alone. "So you're back to school?"

"Yes, as an overage student. I'll be pressed to keep pace."

Marielle thought the same. At night school, working towards her degree, there were many her own age or even older but at Law School she might feel matronly. "So I can now throw away your Police Department business card?"

Rush sensed a final separation and was quick to respond. "No. You might need another escort to some fancy event. I've only worn that tie once." He noticed her smile at his small joke, "Here. I'll give you my cell number just in case you get desperate." He pulled out another card to jot down his number and passed it to her.

"Rush I'm sorry about your father. He sounded like a fine man...but I should be going."

Ellen, overhearing, was back with her drink. "You're leaving?" As Marielle said her goodbyes Ellen was disappointed. She hoped to ask more questions, delve into what might be going on between Rush and this mysterious woman. She'd certainly tell Sydney all about it although, admittedly, Marielle's attendance might have only been out of polite respect. Still, she had her suspicions.

Marielle drove from the Hall, intending to pick up groceries and a bottle of wine before reaching home, and was thinking about Rush, his friends she'd briefly met, and particularly bothered by that name that she should know. Stopping for a light, it came to her. One of her first year texts was written by Morris Newman. He was a professor at Law School. She'd be in his class this September. At least there'd be one face she'd know.

***

The final day of the working month was to be David's final day of working on Isla. His last patient was to be Madeleine Thornhill, age sixty-eight, no children, divorced, disabled with chronic back pain. In her interview with David she admitted it wasn't her back that had now led her to use Isla's services. The constant back pain wouldn't kill her, percocet and oxycontin might, but her continued usage of fentanyl would. The only way to beat her addiction or another overdose was with the help of David and Heidi.

Tomorrow morning the Twin Otter would rumble in to pick up and carry its passengers back to Porto del Norte. David wasn't to be one of them. He already told the staff that Dr. Manuel would be back on a permanent basis and that he would be leaving but the clinic could continue to operate with all of their valuable assistance. The men stood awkwardly not sure of what to do or say; Evalina, Carmenia and Estella all cried but within minutes decided that they would have a final dinner, el banquete, in honour of David. He would have to do the fishing but they would prepare the catch along with other dishes. David had anticipated there might be a special farewell dinner and, before leaving Bonojara International, had bought six bottles of wine. At this last dinner on the island the 'No Alcohol' rule could be overlooked.

He had already prepared envelopes to give to the staff. He would do that at dinner. Inside were equal amounts of US dollars but on the outside, in Spanish, were his instructions that these were not to be opened until they were off Isla. He would have to speak to Gustavo, to make it clear, to have him promise to be reasonably sober on his return to the island. David emphasized that the new apprentice for the crematorium would be coming back with him and would need immediate instructions so as to assist in its continued operation.

At dinner he could also expect, particularly from the ladies, to ask why he would want to spend his last few days on Isla all alone. He had already explained that he had things to do, to clean up, ensure that everything was left 'en buen orden' for Dr. Ernesto's arrival and takeover. In fact he had little left to do. Most items had already been taken care of but he'd have to review that all his instructions were complete and thorough. More important were the two letters he had yet to write. The one to Jose Fuentes should not be too difficult. The other would be. It might take a few drafts before he would find the right words to say exactly what he meant.

***

t was Friday, the end of the week since Marielle had been to Madison Hall. Over this time Marjorie's interests and efforts to have her friend do something, anything, to keep a connection to Rushton Sterne had lessened, but had not disappeared. Today as they sat together at lunchtime Marjorie was describing the meal she prepared for dinner tonight with the 'newest' man in her life. The recipe was for four and she was hesitant to halve the ingredients as "that never seems to work". That was why she had frozen half and now it was in the freezer of the cafeteria's fridge a few feet away from Marielle. Marjorie was insistent that it would make a perfectly romantic meal for two, whoever Marielle might invite for dinner this weekend. Clearly her preference was that it should be Rushton as she pointed out that this 'poor man' was in need of sympathy over the loss of his father. This potential 'tete a tete' with Rushton seemed to interest her as much as talking about her own dinner date.

"You know he's nice enough, polite, a gentleman. Still...even though he's been a widower for three years his wife...or her ghost...still bosses him around, or if she doesn't, his daughter does. He really hummed and hawed when I invited him to dinner at my place. I think he suspects I'll come out of the kitchen in my negligee. I mean fidelity is fine if you're still married but if you're not and still have some life left in you, it's time to use it while you can."

Marielle half expected her last comment would segue into yet another segment of 'Advice to the Lovelorn' but instead Marjorie picked up a carrot stick and began, noisily, to chew on it. Marielle's mind was also doing the same, digesting the message on her voicemail this morning from Lenore. She had emphasized her words as if they were of great importance and that Marielle would be more than happy to hear that Luis was now back in the City. Lenore suggested that he undoubtedly would be "muy feliz" to hear from her. Marielle's immediate thought was to simply erase the message. She then did, but not before jotting down Luis' phone number and, not entirely understanding why, slipping into her wallet. It fitted in between two business cards. One was Rush's with his cell written on the reverse. The other she'd been given after a meeting with lawyers on Wednesday. Luc Julian was young, bright and had a gallic mop of hair over a handsome face. As the meeting concluded he had zeroed in on Marielle sensing from her name she was also bilingual. She fluently replied automatically to his

French but begged off his suggestion of 'un dejeuner rapide' before they returned to their respective offices. However, as he gave her his business card he emphasized that his cell number was on 'vingt quatre heures', an obvious invitation to call him anytime.

As Marielle slotted the numbers of Luis, Rush and Luc side by side she thought of their backgrounds, a Latino hombre, an Anglo gentleman and a French homme, all attractive in differing ways. A nursery rhyme jumped out from her childhood memory and she smiled at the thought of these three men being in a tub, possibly a hot tub, together. If she, possibly naked, jumped in with them she could envision two of them enjoying it, one squirming with embarrassment.

***

It was only six blocks from the neighbourhood offices of Stanton & Stanton to the Sterne residence. As he drove towards his own driveway Rush was thinking about Ted Stanton's suggestion. Rush had stopped to see Ted to sign a few more necessary documents concerning his father's estate and the taxes that would be assessed against it. "Death and Taxes", as Ted intoned, went hand in hand. Asking about Rush's plans once he had his Law degree Ted seemed pleased to hear that Rush's intentions were not to bury himself in the lower rungs of a large downtown firm, specializing in some eventual lucrative aspect of Law. No offer or commitment was made but Ted made it clear that there'd be an opening right here at Stanton & Stanton. He pointed out that even with Irene's valuable assistance running a one man law office was not for a man now about to be sixty-three.

Now after parking his car in the garage, right beside his father's Buick, Rush walked around to the front walk and door. In the past he would have walked down beside the garage to the rear entrance of his lower level apartment but now with his father gone he would go directly to the front door. There to pick up the usual advertising flyers, the evening paper, to check the mailbox before unlocking the front door to enter inside the hollow sounding house. More out of habit than necessity he checked each room all seemingly calling out for need of human occupancy. As he expected everything was in order and he was about to head to the stairs when he heard the sound of a door slamming and within seconds a knock on the door.

A uniformed man, about his age but broader and bulkier, had a smiling face under a cap signed with a badge: XpreXserX.

"Mr. Rushton Sterne? Yes? Good. I have a package for you. Please sign here, on this line. Thank you. Have a nice evening."

After locking the front door Rush carried the small package downstairs. He still felt more comfortable here; upstairs he felt he was intruding. Taking a paring knife from the drawer in his kitchenette he sliced open the package. A CD sleeve fell onto the counter and he then pulled out a sealed letter simply addressed 'Rush'. He was still standing at the counter as he began to read it but, without being conscious of doing so, he sank into a chair.

I was sorry to receive your note about your father's death. Coincidentally my father died a few weeks ago and I had a rushed trip to Trinidad to arrange matters. Wouldn't it have been strange if their deaths had been on the same day.

I'm now back on Isla Cresciente and, as I write this, totally alone here. I gave my resignation to Jose and fortunately Dr. Manuel, who I succeeded, will return to take my place, a situation that will ensure that the Hospice will continue to function, as well as making our nurse Heidi very happy. When the plane returns they will find my instructions. The first will be to take my body from the clinic to the crematorium. The other instructions concern the disposal of my few possessions here plus ensuring that this letter is taken back to Bonojara to have it expressed to you. I also hope that they include Sibelius Fifth Symphony that they will find playing in the clinic. As I self administer the dosage, I will be listening to it perhaps hoping my last conscious moment will coincide with its last chord.

So, why am I doing this? I assume as you read this you'll be saying 'No'. Sorry but that will be too late but I will tell you this is not a last minute decision. It has been building, brewing for some time within the last decade. I have been searching for something that has been elusive. A few times I thought I might have found it but it quick-silvered away.

Granted I did find solace in my many excesses but never satisfaction.

I do accept some recognition as a physician, caring and curing, saving or prolonging lives. In turn I have hurt and damaged other lives especially those who offered their love. If I remember my fourth year English - wasn't it Wilde who said 'cowards killed with a kiss'? Perhaps my only constant has been our friendship. For that I truly thank you.

So Rush I just feel that the world doesn't need me nor I it. The patients I assisted here on Isla felt the same. I accepted their reasoning, hopefully you'll accept mine.

I do have a (deathbed?) confession to make.

This is to apologize to you, my friend. When I asked you to Isla to help determine what had happened to Vuk I already knew. I suspect your policeman's mind might have conflicted with your friendship for me. You probably knew there were gaps that Isla was keeping from you.

On that confusing morning when the Hurricane was threatening Isla, the first plane load had flown off leaving three of us to await the plane's return. I went down the path towards the clinic fighting the rain pelting my face and saw Edo standing in the doorway of the men's quarters. I saw his face and his body frozen, a hammer in his hand. On the deck was Vuk, with rain washing blood away from his head. I checked. He was still alive but with a severe head wound. As I was doing this Edo came back to life, blubbering out his story that Vuk had been a commanding part in the atrocity that took the lives of his father, brother and uncle. Some of the Medecins I'd worked with in Africa had told me of the cruelty and slaughter when they'd been in the Balkans. I had seen enough of the victims of barbarism in Africa. I cannot say that Vuk would have lived if I had done my best then to save him, get him back to a Hospital, but right then and there I knew he should die, possibly a kinder death than he deserved.

So I killed him. Edo and I carried him to the clinic where I gave him an injection to guarantee his death. We only had time to get him into the crematorium before the plane came back. That is why Edo and I had to be the first to come back, fire up the crematorium and cast his still warm ashes and bones into the sea.

So I did kill. Others died by my hand but with their prior consent. Vuk did not, but I have no regrets. Now, ironically, my ashes will be spread into the same sea as his.

I did feel justified in misusing you. I wanted to protect Jose's island, to keep it out of any investigation and intrusion from the Republica. I admit I also didn't want to see Edo in any legal difficulties.

However I did lie to you. I do not ask your forgiveness, only your understanding of why I did.

So Rush, all the best to you. Go on, enjoy life and, should you be fortunate enough, find someone to share it with.

David

Rush sat, the letter in his hands, the silence of the house enveloping his body and mind inanimate. He didn't need to read the letter again. It had immediately embedded itself in his mind as if David had been there to voice each word, face to face, directly to Rush except that Rush was unable to reply, argue, countermand, reverse this final step that David had already taken.

Finally he stood up and moved slowly around his small room in a type of trance, still holding the letter, but not knowing what to do, what his next step would be. Finally the fog parted as he saw the small winking light on his laptop indicating there were messages. The simple mechanics of using his fingers, focusing his eyes on the computer rebooted him back into the rest of the world. The only important email was from Jose Fuentes, a simple 'please call me asap', then leaving a phone number. Rush would call later knowing what Jose would want to tell him.

Still aimless but needing some type of distraction Rush went outside to stand on his small patio overlooking the lawn and the garden. His mother had been the gardener with Russell and Rush needing direction in helping her. After her death the two men had tried to keep it alive and colourful but each year the flower beds shrank in size and the lawn became larger. Grass was easier to grow and needed no special talent to be cut. Rush saw that this was now needed. He went back inside to change into old clothes, pants ripped at the knee out of usage not fashion, a faded top from past badminton matches. Mechanically he started up the mower and began, with geometric but not conscious precision, to delaminate the lawn. After completing the back lawn he did the same for the front. The early evening June sun still had heat and Rush was sweating on finishing. As he went back into the house he wondered what he could do next as a distraction to the continuing video running through his mind, picturing David alone on Isla planning his own death, with Rush unable to rewind, stop, or change the script.

Inside he stripped and then showered and was towelling off when his cell phone rang. Still dripping he reached for it expecting that it was Robin's normal Friday night notification of the upcoming schedule for badminton.

"Hello."

***

Marielle found her mailbox empty as well as the entry hall. The Bentley sisters were not gatekeepers this Friday night. Inside her apartment she found room in the freezer section to wedge in Marjorie's dinner offering. Checking her phone she had two messages. The first was from her sister excited that she had a date tonight. Marielle was happy that Sylvie was forgetting Remi but could only hope she would be more selective before falling in love again.

The second was from Marjorie: "Can you believe it...I get home and there's a message from Numbnuts. He's sorry but his daughter has an emergency and he has to go to her house. It's probably only a leaking faucet. Damn. After all the time I spent preparing dinner. Well from now on he can have his daughter prepare his dinners. I've had it with him...but listen dear lady...just because I've come up empty tonight is no reason for you to be alone. Remember my advice. Call someone...lure him over to taste the treat I've made and the added lusty treats you can serve. Break out the candles and chill the wine. Time to have some fun...I'll expect to hear all the dirty details on Monday. Go for it."

Well she did have the dinner, the candles and the wine. What she needed was a little courage to pick up the phone. Was she afraid of rejection or of success and, if so, what kind? Luc would be guaranteed to provide excitement but only for the night. Luis was perhaps a changed man but there was still a lot of baggage between them. Rush was a proven dinner companion but did she want to encourage such a nice guy? Her wallet held all their phone numbers.Should she put them in a hat and pick one? Did she need to? She looked at the table set for two.She reached to open her wallet. Taking out a card she picked up her phone.

Her mind was still wondering but her finger firm as she pushed in the numbers.

***

EPILOGUE ONE

Three Weeks Later

Michael was glad to be back, his exams now completed. He felt comfortable, but not totally confident, that he'd passed all of them. Growing up on the family farm he had worked hard, never capable of matching his father's energy, strength, or stubbornness with the aim of leaving, to use his brain more than brawn. Now walking through the fields, towards the woods and the creek, he still felt the tug of the land within him. Ahead of him, chasing either real or imaginary rabbits, Found was zig-zagging in pursuit. He'd been found, as a pup, the only survivor of the litter in a bag left at the end of their driveway three years ago. Found was certainly of mixed heritage but his keen nose and want to dig strongly showed a terrier background.

The family always had at least one dog, often two. Michael's favorite, who slept either at the foot or on his bed if allowed, was Sport. He was very protective of Michael and had attacked Lennie and Walter when they, behind the barn out of view of any adult, had been cuffing seven year old Michael's head and shoulders. In turn Sport attacked them and was kicked by both of his cousins but this did allow Michael to run to safety. Sport had remembered, snarling whenever he saw or smelt either brother. Now Walter was dead, stabbed, murdered. Michael had, in silent protest, driven his aunt to pick up Lennie on his release from penitentiary. They had sat, mother and son, in the back seat, whispering together. He was glad to leave them at their home.

Found was now into the woods charging towards the creek that had overflowed with the heavy spring rains, rising to flush the underbrush, capturing much of the soil and conveying it downstream. Found was now barking, signalling a find. As Michael neared he could see Found's paws burrowing into the soft soil until his jaw was pulling at a root. As he came closer he saw it wasn't a root. It was a brown leathered forearm, its bony fingers reaching out as if asking to be released, to be pulled up from its grave.

EPILOGUE TWO

Three Years Later

In her forty-five years at Stanton & Stanton, Irene had kept pace with technological advances. As a teenager she had nervously started on an IBM Selectric typewriter and a new, at the time, push-button phone. Now she had a computer pad connected to a high speed printer and a telephone screen that immediately identified who was calling the law firm. She could see it was the live-in nanny on the line.

"Good Afternoon. Stanton and Stanton. How may I help you?"

This was her customary greeting to whoever called, whether stranger, family or friend. She was always formally polite to everyone, controlling any tonal inflection.

"He is on the phone right now. Would you care to wait?"

On receiving the affirmative Irene answered "Thank you. Please hold" before pushing that button. She had never warmed to this woman. Irene thought that she was at least seventy but acted and dressed much younger. However the main reason for Irene's coolness was the nanny's possessiveness over her charge. Both were often to the office but Irene rarely, very rarely, had been allowed the opportunity to hold the little girl, to cushion her against her own breast, to inhale the sweet smell of a child, murmur maternal affection. Furthermore the nanny insisted on calling the little girl 'Marjie', a selfish contraction of her own name. Irene always made sure to call her by her proper name 'Margo', although her parents spelled it the French way, with an 'x' on the end.

"Thank you for waiting. I'll put you through to Mr Sterne."

***

Printed in the United States
by Baker & Taylor Publisher Services